PICKLEBALLERS

PICKLEBALLERS

ILANA LONG

BERKLEY ROMANCE
NEW YORK

BERKLEY ROMANCE
Published by Berkley
An imprint of Penguin Random House LLC
penguinrandomhouse.com

Book design by Kristin del Rosario

Library of Congress Cataloging-in-Publication Data

Names: Long, Ilana, author.
Title: Pickleballers / Ilana Long.
Description: First edition. | New York: Berkley Romance, 2024.
Identifiers: LCCN 2024004988 (print) | LCCN 2024004989 (ebook) |
ISBN 9780593642238 (trade paperback) | ISBN 9780593642245 (ebook)
Subjects: LCGFT: Romance fiction. | Novels.
Classification: LCC PS3612.O495 P53 2024 (print) |
LCC PS3612.O495 (ebook) | DDC 813/.6—dc23/eng/20240212
LC record available at https://lccn.loc.gov/2024004988
LC ebook record available at https://lccn.loc.gov/2024004989

First Edition: November 2024

Printed in the United States of America
1st Printing

For Steve, my partner:
sometimes in pickleball,
always in adventure.

THE SERVE

ONE

Plink.

"Not enjoying this."

Plink. "This does not feel cathartic." Plink. "At all."

Plink ... Plink ... Plink.

"I was fine at home, you know," Meg said, swiping at a blonde flyaway that had escaped her hair tie.

"You were absolutely *not* fine. You were feeding a necktie into the garbage disposal," Annie countered, even as she kept her eyes pegged on the bounce. "Come on. Give this a chance. You've been playing pickleball for all of thirty minutes."

Plink. Meg knocked it over the net. Plink. Annie tapped. Plink. Meg popped it up. Annie leapt, fielding the shot from three feet over her head. She flicked the ball back into range.

"Ooh! Good try," Annie cheered in her cartoon-bunny voice. Also known as her regular voice. "Just . . . try to keep it a little lower. And watch that you don't step into the kitchen."

"The kitchen?" Meg Bloomberg eyed the court, half expecting a microwave to jump out in front of her. Nothing made sense anymore. Not her husband Vance's unexplained departure. And not her best friend's insistence on dragging her here to play pickleball.

"The kitchen. That's the line you're stepping on." Annie pointed to the ground. "But you're doing great." As if calculating how much was too much information, she hesitated before adding, "But you might want to relax your arm a little. And loosen up your wrist. Scoop. Yeah. Like that. But . . . not quite. Don't forget to reset every . . ."

"Argh!" Meg groaned, throwing her hands up in despair. "Why are you torturing me with this stupid game? The only thing I want to do is crawl into a cave and hibernate until summer."

"You're upset. Understandably. Also, bears only hibernate until springtime. Just . . . FYI," Annie hastened to clarify, blinking beneath the bangs of her short hair. She adjusted the seam of her fitted tennis skirt. "Maybe we should start slower. Some short drops. How 'bout that?"

"Or maybe," Meg suggested, "I need to hit it harder. Just whack the fucker. Really, really hard. Pretend it's Vance's head . . ."

"All right. Take it easy. Deep breaths." Annie mimed. "Pickleball is about control. Let's keep practicing our close shots at the net. Okay?"

Growling low in her throat, Meg stonewalled. She narrowed her lids and pouted, a manipulation she had been successfully practicing on Annie Yoon for the better part of twelve years—since their houseshare days back at the University of Washington.

Annie gave it a good five seconds before caving. "Fine. Go to the baseline. I'll serve it to you, and you can hit some long, hard shots. Will that make Meg happy?"

"Yippee," Meg deadpanned.

Annie laughed. "I promise you. You are gonna fall in love with pickleball." But even as she was saying it, her voice dropped off when Meg's expression crumpled at the word "love." Despite Annie's efforts to distract Meg, this morning's shock was still too raw.

It was hard to believe that only a few hours ago, her life had been completely upended. If Annie hadn't shown up . . . She shuddered. But of course, when Annie had heard about Vance's note, she had rushed to Meg's apartment, still in her sensible shoes and scrubs. She'd snatched the note from Meg's shaky fingers and read it to herself. Disbelieving, she'd read it again. Out loud.

Sorry, babe. I just can't do this anymore. V.

"Can't do this anymore?" Annie had spat, her friend-protecting hackles rising. She smoothed the wrinkled scrap of paper, then flipped it over. "A Home Depot receipt!" Annie's nostrils flared, and she brandished the receipt as if holding up evidence for a jury. "For a caulking gun? Are you shitting me?" This last part of her tirade was lost in a mumble when Annie's inner swear-censor from her job at Seattle Children's Hospital kicked in.

Nevertheless, the intensity of Annie's indignation felt validating. So, although she was loath to leave her apartment with eyes puffy and red from crying, when Meg's bestie suggested they go to the courts to hit out her frustrations with a game that she had never played before, Meg agreed.

It had seemed like a reasonable idea, at the time.

But now, standing on a frigid Seattle pickleball court in January, Meg shivered, gobsmacked by this unexpected twist of fortune. She took a steadying breath. How had this happened? Her husband of two years had up and walked out. And for the life of her, she hadn't a clue what he'd needed to caulk.

The injustice! A seething fury built in her, from the soles of her neon high-tops to the tips of her wavy golden ponytail. Tugging a pickleball from her pocket, Meg rolled it between her fingers.

She reared back with her paddle arm. Letting out a guttural grunt, she whacked the plastic ball. It soared through the air, trailing the smoke of a thousand fires, and slammed into the net.

When she yanked another ball from her pocket, she paused to consider the fluorescent green surface, the Wiffle holes dotting the plastic—before letting it feel the full force of her fury. With a war cry, she punched the ball with the paddle and admired the trajectory as it flew over the net and hit the chain-link fence with a satisfying ring.

Wrenching the last ball from her shorts pocket, Meg grimaced. This one was stuck, trapped by her fingers inside the tight pocket. "Rrrg," she groaned, twisting it free. She held the ball to the sky and a fresh flash of anger filled her when she noticed her wedding ring glinting on her finger. With every ounce of strength in her petite frame, she shouted with such force that her throat hurt as she thwacked the ball hard, sending it rocketing over the fence and into the parking lot, where it rolled lazily under somebody's car.

With the balls gone, Meg crossed her arms over her chest and panted from the exertion.

Annie blinked. She tilted her head. "Feeling better?"

"A little." Meg opened her mouth. Closed it again. Sighed. It was the truth. She now had several ideas of where Vance could stuff his caulking gun.

Annie Yoon pressed her lips into an encouraging smile. "Meg?"

"Yep."

"I told you pickleball would be cathartic."

Meg sniffled, blinked a tear from the corner of her eye, and mustered up a weak smile. Resigned, she stood on the baseline, paddle in hand. "Fine," Meg said. "Let's play your damn game."

TWO

The walkway leading to the passenger drop-off lot was a trudge from the pebbly beach. Meg picked up the pace, enjoying the stretch in her legs and breathing in the familiar tar-and-sea scent of the Bainbridge Island ferry docks. Even as she marveled at the evergreen-blanketed landscape, she hoped this would be the last—the very last, she promised—Crafty Cat Collar transaction.

Squinting into the thin June sunshine, Meg waited at the appointed spot and watched for the green station wagon. The box of six custom-designed cat collars wasn't heavy per se, but to her, they may as well have been a box of bricks. Or albatrosses. Leaden albatrosses the size of semitrucks. With this last commission, she would reach her goal in filling the backlog of orders. Meg clung to the hope that maybe soon, with the cushion of the small inheritance she had received from her dad's trust, she could find more satisfying, or at least more lucrative, ways to waste her college degree.

For the whole of her brief marriage, she had ached to give up the kitschy crafts—a side gig she developed to help bring in some cash while Vance got his dental practice up and going—and return to her artistic calling. And while Vance had wasted no time in filing for divorce, dismantling their marriage as easily as upending a board game, she knew that getting back to painting would take time and patience. Her heart yearned for the smell of oils squeezed onto a palette. How freeing it would feel to unload this final box.

She waited for her customer, alternately watching sailboats bob and rock in the Sound, and peering down the road toward Winslow, where she had ventured earlier this morning for her soy mocha and to take advantage of the island's peaceful vibe. Cradled by mountains, the seaside island was the opposite of Seattle's bustle and crowds, although the thirty-five-minute crossing meant the city was only a stone's throw away. Well . . . if the thrower had a bionic arm. Or a hydraulic catapult.

Meg glanced at her phone. The buyer was late, but Meg didn't mind. The ferry waiting area, like the boat ride, was rife with little pleasures—like taking in the vistas over the water and breathing in the cool tang of the salt air. With her painter's eye, Meg framed her surroundings. In the distance, the green pines formed arrows pointing toward the white sky. In the foreground, the choppy gray water lapped against the ferry pylons. She could shake something creative out of that view, couldn't she? A throb of doubt answered her and sent her mind sailing back to her latest artistic attempt.

This morning, she had left the canvas, still tacky with fresh paint, leaning against the wall like a discarded flat tire. Gloomy clouds gathering, rain blurring into an undefined splash against the horizon. Uninspired, basic stuff. As soon as it dried, the painting would join its abandoned brethren in the closet. Of course, hiding the canvas would not put an end to Meg's unspoken fear, the one that had been nagging at her for some time now. What if she couldn't paint anymore? After such a long break from producing anything meaningful, would she be forever relegated to the land of tacky glue and stud guns? Sure, Annie's pickleball initiative was a great body-and-mind distractor, but at her core she still craved the sense of accomplishment that came with imagining something bold and authentic: real art.

Beside her, a mammoth station wagon slowed to a stop. Meg straightened and put on her Crafty Cats face. After all, this was a special commission and the buyer had paid extra for personal delivery. But Meg's view of the driver was impaired by the commotion brewing inside the car.

The glass lowered an inch. Startled, Meg took a reflexive step back. Six piglet snouts poked through the window crack.

So . . . not cats.

The doors clicked and a woman's voice rose above the squeals. "It's open, dear. C'mon in."

She weighed her options. Skip this, hang on to her dignity, and go home and eat some ramen. Or . . . just do this.

Bracing herself, she inhaled and slid into the backseat, yanking the door shut before any porky friends could make their escape. Instantly, she was beset.

Yes. This would be it for the pet collars.

"Here you go," Meg offered, trying to squeeze the box between the headrests. "You can adjust the sizes pretty easily—"

"Oh, no, dear. You go ahead. They've been so excited all day!" the driver exclaimed. One piggy's excitement was so great it stabbed its hoof into Meg's forearm. "You do the honors," the woman added, "and decide which one suits which."

One last time, Meg reminded herself as she made a mental note to stop for wine on her way home. Grabbing a handful of rubbery pinkness, Meg tried to fit a cat collar on a piglet, but, using Meg's thighs as a springboard, the piggy bolted away. Next, Meg attempted flailing toward a skinny, spotted squeaker, but it, too, ejected from her grasp. By her fourth essay, Meg got the picture.

"So exciting," her round-faced patron whispered, and clapped her hands in glee.

Enough, Meg decided. There were limits. Even for Meg. Stretching for the door, she tossed the box onto the backseat and flung herself from the vehicle, shivering with the heebie-jeebies.

The woman's enthusiasm remained undeterred. "Terrific!" she cried. "Look at them! We're all so excited." Her head turned toward the writhing mass of piglets at the window. They squealed and grunted and surged at Meg as if she were a fresh bucket of slop. "I'll Venmo you," the woman called as the car rolled away.

Meg blinked, shell-shocked. With a brisk shake of her head, she cleared her thoughts and checked the time. Forty minutes until the next ferry departure back to Seattle. She could wait out the two hours until the next one and relax in one of the quaint cafés, but waiting often entailed a wandering mind. And when her mind meandered, it trundled around Lonely Land and Self-Pitytown, visiting famous tourist spots like the Pit of Forever Single and the Valley of the Creatively Mediocre. She had to stay busy to keep her mind off Vance. But the dreadful paintings and attempts at pickleball were like sticking duct tape over the holes in an old garden hose—temporary patches before new leaks sprang up elsewhere.

Pickleball! That was what she'd meant to remember. Meg picked up her pace toward the walkway. She needed to leave Bainbridge on that next ferry, or she'd be late for her pickleball meetup with Annie. When Annie got mad, she turned into an enraged pixie armed with toxic fairy dust. Best to stay on her good side.

But in truth, Meg did not want to miss this afternoon's games. Each time she stepped on the courts, the adrenaline bump lifted her mood, and the unexpected camaraderie of the sport warmed her spirit. As Annie had promised, pickleball was rapidly becoming an addiction, and she had zero desire to crimp her cravings. The thrill of flinging herself into fresh pursuits felt as central to her core as her zest for her tried-and-true passions—like painting and hiking and her deep-rooted friendship with Annie. Since Vance's departure five months ago, buds of true Meg-ness had begun to reemerge, unfurling like time-lapse blossoms.

To Meg's relief, when she rolled onto the pier in her hatchback, a dockhand wearing a wizard hat for no apparent reason waved her onto the ferry. *Yay!* she rejoiced as she pulled into the final slot in the car line. Every time Meg did not have to bear watching the ferry's huge form getting tinier and tinier as it chugged away, she felt like she had won the lottery. And even though the ferries ran every hour or two, by nature, Meg was not a waiter. Well, she had been a *waiter*, a waitress actually, but an artist must make ends meet somehow.

She ambled up the stairs and through the heavy metal door to the interior of *Wenatchee*. Meg had ridden *Walla Walla* and *Tacoma* as well as this ferry, but on each voyage the majesty of the ship made her feel like a tourist. Bright lighting, cavernous seating areas, and comfy chairs gave the open room the feel of a cruise ship. Along the bulkheads, seating booths looked out over enormous, double-paned windows with views to Puget Sound.

As she searched for a seat, she paused to view the old photographs and the artwork exhibited along the ferry walls. Meg lingered, marveling at a series of intricately carved cedar panels and at a lithograph image of a Native American Haida Raven. There were newer works, also, and Meg halted at the perfection of a small painting, a savage scape of a ferry careening across Puget Sound, hounded by the off-kilter form of Mount Rainier. It was the kind of art that delivered emotionally, the kind of art she wanted to produce.

A rush of hope lifted her mood. With the Vance debacle behind her and the last of the Crafty Cat Collar deliveries completed, she could rediscover herself. Meg counted this sighting as a sign. Or at least a push in the right direction. The world wanted her to return to her passion for painting.

When she felt the ferry shift, Meg speed-walked to the rear of the ship so as not to miss the spectacle. The view from a departing ferry never grew old. She pushed the door hard against the outside wind and tugged her hood over her flying hair. Even on this sunny June day, although it was technically almost summer, a chilly bite of wind whipped around the railings. She was glad for her puffy coat.

Seagulls swooped and cawed and the ferry captain expertly avoided bouncing against the pylons as the ship left the dock. For an instant, she thought the pier itself was gliding away, so smooth was their departure; only the bracing wind on her cheeks and the visual cues told her the ship was in motion. She grasped the green metal railing and took in the shrinking Olympic Peninsula—rolling hills and rocky beaches in the foreground; the craggy, snow-topped peaks in the distance. On crisp, clear days like today, the scenery looked like a movie set—too beautiful to be real. Overhead, blue skies prevailed, while the white fog of a marine layer clung to the horizon. She breathed in the wind, the salt, the sound of the gulls, and the gentle rocking of the ferry.

A blast of wind sent her rushing inside to the narrow entry alcove, where Meg came face-to-face with a display rack packed tight with flashy flyers for the Seattle Ferris wheel, whale-watching tours, and 3-D film offerings at Pacific Science Center. She lifted a glossy trifold from the wall mount.

Bainbridge Island, the brochure proclaimed. Destination for Vacation and Industry. And piglet collar delivery, Meg inserted.

In the photos, well-dressed Gen Xers sipped cabernet at a winery. Gen Zers hauled backpacks topped with camping gear up a snowy incline on the nearby Olympic Peninsula. An older couple walked along the rocky shoreline holding hands. When she spotted the image of her millennial cohorts, Meg was surprised to find that the photo boasted a smiling, athletic throng of pickleballers.

Did you know, read the caption, that Bainbridge Island is the birthplace of America's fastest growing sport? Pickleball!

Right here in her home state? Meg's interest was piqued. Standing there in the little alcove, she scanned *The History of Pickleball* with interest.

In 1965, three dads, Joel Pritchard, Bill Bell, and Barney McCallum, repurposed their old backyard badminton court, inventing a sport using wooden paddles and plastic balls. Initially, pickleball was meant to entertain the kids over the summer, but the adults had such fun that they took over the backyard court. Meg could understand the draw. The sport had an addictive allure. She continued reading. Although the game involves no pickles, some suggest pickleball was named after the Pritchard family's dog, Pickles, who loved to lick stray balls. Forcefully, Meg steered her mind away from the obvious imagery.

Amazing, Meg mused, that so many years later pickleball had at last become such a sensation. And she could see why. Not only was pickleball a great mental distraction from her loneliness, but she felt healthier and stronger physically. Her calves and arms showed the contours of new muscle tone. Each day she played, she improved. If she continued to challenge herself, one day she might even gather the nerve to sign up for a tournament.

She stuffed the brochure in her bag to remember to return to Bainbridge. It would be fun to pickle at the source of it all. Maybe she'd drag Annie along, too, if she could convince her friend to take a day off, Meg thought. And as she wandered past booths and benches teeming with families and snuggling couples, she longed for her friend's good company. Five months since her ex had up and left, and still, moments like this socked her with loneliness. Not for Vance and his brassy charisma, but for the companionship of being around someone who knew her ups and downs yet still agreed to get on the roller coaster.

Catching a whiff of coffee, Meg followed her nose through the wide doorway where the *Wenatchee*'s café gleamed with the stainless steel fittings of a 1950s cafeteria. She hadn't had anything to eat since this morning's scone at the ferry landing, and by now she had passed beyond peckish. Joining the end of the line that snaked into the service area, Meg spotted a metal cauldron puffing steam and her spirits flipped like a switch. The contents of that soup pot were a magical mood elixir.

Oh, how Meg adored clam chowder. The rich cream base seasoned with savory herbs, the cooked-just-right cubed potatoes, the chewy, perfect clams. How could such a little crustacean pack such a flavorful punch? Meg wondered as she slid her plastic tray along the counter. Three people waited in front of her while she salivated. Two. Then it was her turn.

"Medium clam chowder, please."

To Meg's surprise, her request echoed in stereo, overlapping with a velvety bass.

She smelled him before she turned her head—the man beside her who had ordered the same chowder at the same time. Pine-covered mountain trails blew off him like a sexy breeze that mingled with the clam chowder's aroma. The scent of heaven.

"You go ahead."

"Sorry. I didn't see you there," she mumbled. "You're ahead of me. You go first."

"Go ahead. Please." Beneath unjustly thick lashes, a pair of golden brown eyes took her in. He grinned a charming, uneven smile.

From behind them, a balding man with a foaming latte on his

tray growled, "Get the lady a clam chowder, will ya, and we can all keep moving."

"I love clam chowder," Dreamy Eyes said. "Those chewy clam bites and the little potato cubes . . ." Meg Bloomberg stared at the curve of his shoulders beneath the lightweight T-shirt. Why was she still wearing her puffy coat? And the hood was up! She yanked it down and smoothed her hair.

"I think we're holding up the line . . ." He gestured for her to slide forward, but to her mortification, she could not budge, could not speak a word.

"Or," he said, "I'll scoot forward." Nodding his chin, he indicated the buildup behind them. "We don't want to incur the wrath of the masses."

"Okay." After that scintillating bit of genius, her tongue went on strike. *Come on. Say something, Meg.* She searched her brain for anything besides song lyrics. "I hope it's hot," she managed.

"I hope so, too. Enjoy your chowder," he said, and carried his tray through the doorway.

I hope it's hot? Ugh! If she weren't so concerned about hurting herself, she would bang her forehead against the cash register.

Still. He was supercute, and for a split second, she cheered herself. Yay. She had spoken to a cute guy. And granted, her participation in the conversation fell short of stellar. Four words. And one of them was a contraction. But a gal's gotta start somewhere.

She wandered the tiled floor, tray in hand, and found a miraculously vacant spot at a booth with a table. Meg took off her bulky jacket and settled herself by the big picture window. She stirred the good stuff from the bottom and blew on the spoonful before sipping. The chowder was, in fact, hot.

Outside, sunlight glinted off the choppy waters of the Sound. The points of whitecaps splashed against the giant ship, but only the sliding scenery and the lightly vibrating bench beneath her thighs reminded her that she was on a boat.

It felt good, that vibration. Soothing. And stimulating, Meg had to admit. She sipped her chowder and let her mind go blank, dimly recalling the beauty of Bainbridge; the lush, green mounds of the peninsula; the long, sturdy pines that drove their thick trunks toward the sky. That man in the café was very good-looking. And it had been a while. How would it feel to run her hands over those pecs? Draw her fingertips down his contoured shoulders? When he pulled out his wallet, her eyes had lingered on his back pockets. His hands were nice, too, especially his neatly trimmed fingernails. Meg loved short, sharp nails that scraped along her back. Her eyelids slipped closed.

Yes. Just like that. Dreamy Eyes moaned in her ear, her reaction to his hot breath traveling along her body right down to the bowl of her hips. His tongue traced the hollow of her neck. With a feathery touch, his fingers slid along her back and skimmed her skin. It felt nice. Really nice. The vibration between her thighs sent a shiver through her, and without warning, an "Ah!" escaped her lips.

Suddenly, Meg became aware of her lapse in decorum. She opened her eyes and pretended to study the empty chowder carton as she burrowed deeper into the cushioned comfort of the booth.

"Did you enjoy it?"

Mortified, Meg startled. Her head snapped up and her cheeks flooded with warmth.

Holy hand grenades, it was him. Mr. Sexy Manicure. For real this time. He leaned over the table, so close that the scent of his skin dizzied her. His shirt fell open over his metal belt buckle.

"Did I enjoy . . . ?"

"The chowder. Delicious, right?"

"I . . . Yes. Very good."

"I like the T-shirt."

What shirt was she wearing? Ah. Sasquatch with a speech bubble that said, *I think, therefore I am.* His eyes twinkling with mischief, Hot Guy nodded at the caption. "I hear Bigfoot's got a lawsuit going. Everyone's using his image, and he's not making a dime." Reacting to her grin, he added, "And of course Descartes gets royalties every time someone uses his catchphrase."

She glanced back down at her shirt. "I had no idea. This shirt's a marketing nightmare." His lips pricked up with that lopsided smile.

"*Now arriving, downtown Seattle,*" announced the voice from the loudspeakers. "*Drivers and passengers, please return to your vehicles.*"

"Well. That's me," he said. "Take care."

"I'm Meg," she said much louder than she intended. "Hi." She stood and held a hand to him. "Meg."

"Nice to meet you, Meg." His handshake was gentle and firm at the same time. The perfect combination. Nothing sexual about a handshake, Meg told herself, but all the while she was noting the smooth-rough combination of their touching skin. "Ethan Fine," he said.

She remembered herself. "Nice to meet you, too."

He shoved those hands into his jeans pockets and bent forward in a half bow. She watched his backside for an inappropriately long time before she shook off her daydreaming and collected herself.

Ethan Fine. Meg slipped on her puffy coat. *I will never see you again, but thank you for a lovely four minutes.*

Her brain hummed, still fizzing with the buzz of awakened desire.

THREE

With the polite social awareness of a long-trained northwesterner, Meg waited until the last second before turning over her engine in the ferry's hold. The hatchback purred to a start, and she rolled forward, following the line of cars. But before she had moved half a car's length, the toot of a horn grabbed her attention. *Honking on the ferry! Party foul.*

Meg glanced, irritated, at the honker. The pickup truck in the line beside her had not rolled forward with the rest of the cars.

"Hold up!" the driver shouted, jumping from his truck. He raced to Meg's window and gave a gentle knock with his knuckle. "Would you mind? My battery's dead."

Rolling down her window, his head came into view and every vestige of annoyance vanished when she spotted the casually tousled hair crowning the face of her clam chowder dreamboat.

"My truck's dead," Ethan Fine repeated. "Oh. Hi!" His smile opened at the sight of her. "It's you! That's lucky. Listen. I've got cables. Could you . . . ?"

"Jump you?" she offered, her voice pitched way too high. "I could jump you." Holy crud. Did she actually just say that out loud? "I mean. I can jump your car." The tips of Meg's ears burned as his lips tugged upward.

"Ah," he said. "That would be great." He smiled with his mouth open enough for her to see him run the tip of his tongue beneath his teeth. It was as if he had yelled *Sex!* at the top of his lungs. Her brain paused for a commercial break as it replayed a frame out of her ferry booth fantasy. What was going on with her?

Recovering from her steamy time out, she hurried to connect the cables. The two of them worked quickly, rushing to beat the clock before the ferry loaded again for Bainbridge. Revving the engine, she nodded for him to turn his key. With a vroom, his truck roared to life, and he leaned out to give her a thumbs-up. Instead of feeling relief, Meg tamped down the twinge in her chest. The truck had started, true. But that small success meant Clam Chowder would be driving out of her life forever.

Leaping from his truck, Ethan disconnected the cables. "Meg . . . Listen. I really appreciate the jump. Could I, say, take you out for a drink or a bite to eat? To thank you."

Selling off the last of the cat collars *and* a spontaneous date with a cute guy? Maybe she ought to pat herself down to make sure she wasn't dreaming. Annie wouldn't mind if they pushed their game a little later. Well, she would. But it would be worth it.

• • • • •

They lingered over lemonade and duck fat fries at Damn the Weather, a trendy-casual gastropub just a few blocks over from the ferry terminal, and all the while Meg imagined smothering him in the ketchup and licking it off. Who *was* this Meg Bloomberg? Until an hour ago, this guy had been a stranger. Pretty much was *still* a stranger. Meg prided herself on treading carefully when it came to risk factors. In social situations, proceeding with caution and developing trust were her modi operandi. But now that Ethan Fine was gazing at her while overdousing his fries in malt vinegar, could she allow herself to go with the flow and permit herself this fantasy of wanting and feeling wanted? In the months since Vance's departure, her ex had been stepping out all over social media with his dates du jour. Why not permit herself to sit here and dream a little?

Afterward, standing on the sidewalk, he fished for his keys. "Let me make sure I can get my truck started again." She smiled, still dazed with duck fat and desire. "And I'd love to get your number."

The ignition clicked, and then nothing. He tried again. Nothing.

"Dang," he said. "I guess I should have driven around on the highway for a while to recharge it before stopping so soon. I don't think it's got enough juice." He gave the ignition another fruitless try. "Nope. Nothing." Drumming his fingers on the steering wheel, he said, "Yeah. This keeps happening. It's a hybrid, but even those batteries don't last forever."

"Want me to try the cables again?"

"Nah. It's Sunday. I'm gonna leave it here and get a new battery in the morning. I live on Bainbridge, but when I work in Seattle, I stay pretty close to here. Right in Queen Anne."

"Can I give you a ride?"

"Are you sure?" He looked at her with those hopeful eyes. "If it's not too much trouble."

"No problem," she said. *Be cool. Be cool, Meg.* "It's really close. And I have nothing to do today," she lied. Yanking her phone from her back pocket, she shot Annie a quick text. Canceling. Sorry. Met a hottie. More soon. It was seconds before the reply came back. WHAT?!! TELL ME NOW.

Meg enabled Do Not Disturb and tossed her phone into the hatchback. She brushed the baguette crumbs off the passenger seat and plucked three apple cores off the floorboard before tossing them into the back. Really, she could start a compost back there. "Sorry it's a mess. And that seat belt kind of sticks."

Grinning, he folded himself into her passenger seat. "I really appreciate this."

She plugged in his address and tried not to be obvious about sneaking glances at him during the quiet car ride. As they pulled up to a quaint cottage on a leafy side street, Meg tilted her head out the window. "Cute place."

"Bed-and-breakfast. Gotta love breakfast." He reached for his seat belt. "Thanks so much for the lift." He tugged at the buckle. "This thing is really stuck," he said, yanking at the shoulder strap.

"Let me help you." Meg jiggled the buckle. "Dang it. Sorry about that. Hold on. It gets jammed."

And with that, she hopped out of the car and swung open the passenger door. She reached across him with both arms, tugging. "Nope. Dang. It's never gotten this stuck before." She put her body into it, wiggling with each pull, but the angle was all wrong. "Maybe if I . . ."

Without a second thought, she vaulted into the car and straddled him. "Damn thing won't move." Her legs clamped on to him for leverage as she pulled and tugged, her thighs bouncing on his hips.

"Whoa."

Meg glanced up. Oh god. What was she doing? His mouth hung open in astonishment, his eyebrows frozen in cartoon arches. In for a penny, in for a pound, she figured. She went back to yanking at the obstinate buckle.

"As much as I am enjoying this," he whispered, "I don't think it's working."

"No. You're right. I need to—" She twisted her torso and snapped open the glove compartment. When she swung back around, she had flipped open the pocketknife and wielded it toward his waist.

"What?! No!" he cried. "No. No. No. No!" He pressed his back into the seat, his expression morphing into panic. "Take whatever you want. My wallet's in my back pocket. Just don't—"

Suddenly aware that she was holding a sharp blade and waving it near a man's crotch, Meg reared back. "Oh. No!" She lifted both hands in surrender, holding the knife aloft. "I was just going to try to cut off the seat belt. To get you out."

"Oh." He relaxed minutely. "Oh god. Thank god." The blood began to drain back to his cheeks. "Put the knife away. Please."

"Yeah. Sorry," she said, tossing it back into the glove compartment. "That's for apples," she added pointlessly. "That was a bad idea. I'm sure I can—" She went back to the process of tugging and bouncing, bouncing and tugging. Despite their joint jiggling, the buckle held tight. "It's persnickety."

"Persnickety?" he asked, a disbelieving lilt in his tone.

Maybe this was the new Meg Bloomberg. Bouncing on a strange man's lap, wielding a knife, and talking like a crustacean in a Disney movie. When she clocked his worried expression, she burst into giggles. "I'm sorry. You must think I'm . . ." She yanked again. Hard. "Whoopsie!" Her hand slipped off the buckle and into the dash. "Ow." She pouted. "That hurt."

Catching his eye, she couldn't help herself. She burst out laughing. "Oh my god. What am I doing?"

His stunned expression made her laugh harder, and at last, he broke, too, exploding with hilarity.

And suddenly, they were both rolling. In swelling and falling waves, they howled together. They would cool down for a moment, but each time their eyes met, they roared again. The momentum propelled them until they were laughing so hard they convulsed with the giggles. Her stomach hurt. His eyes streamed. It felt cathartic to crumble onto him, heaving with the unstoppable fits of laughter.

They wound down like slowing clocks, and she lay there, panting against his chest. "Sorry about this," she mumbled into his shirt. Then they were silent, her face resting on his chest. Meg felt his heartbeat against her cheek and realized her own pulse was racing.

Tentatively, his hand reached up the nape of her neck, his fingers curling along her scalp. "I don't mind it so much." His voice rumbled against her ear.

"Me, neither," she whispered, and lifted her face to his. When he gripped her waist and pulled her tight against him, there was no hesitancy to his touch.

And before her brain connected with what her hands were doing, she was snaking her fingers below his T-shirt, up his smooth skin to his marble chest, pressing against him with the kind of unthinking need she hadn't felt in years. When he reached down to the side of the chair and released the seat latch, they dropped back together, and she thrilled at her own, unexpected desire. The illicit naughtiness of it. How un-Meg could she get? A stranger! Tied up! In her car!

Then his hands were in her hair, desperate and greedy. When he moaned into her mouth she succumbed to the exquisite sensations, the sound of his unrestrained hunger melting her to putty.

And then . . .

Then there was no more room for talking.

FOUR

"Shut the front door. Shut up!" Annie announced, shoving Meg playfully. "What were you thinking? A stranger? Tied up? In your car? I am so jealous, I hate you!" Annie said, shoving Meg once more for good measure. "Not really. You know I love you." She squinted, grabbing Meg by the collar and clamping her into a bear hug. "I am so proud of you. Look at you. Stepping out of your comfort zone and snogging some stranger in your wittle bwue hatchback!"

"Ew. You make it sound so creepy. Can you keep your voice down, please?"

Across the parking lot, the click-clack of pickleballs on paddles echoed across the courts.

In an exaggerated whisper, Annie dropped her voice from dentist's drill to squeaky toy. "I'm so excited for you. You deserve a little happiness. Tell me everything. Did you . . . you know?"

"Screw some random ferry guy in my car on a side street in Queen Anne? Do you think I've lost my mind?"

"Oh. Okay. Good. I mean. Save a little mystery for the next time. When are you going to see him again?"

"About that . . ." Meg hedged. "It all kind of happened so fast. And his phone died and mine fell under the seat when he tilted it back. And then I guess we . . . forgot."

"Forgot?" Annie's expression indicated that this was the part of the story that was unacceptable. "You got his name, right?"

"Yes, I got his name," she conceded. "It's Ethan. Fine. But he doesn't do social media, so don't bother stalking him."

Annie pursed her lips. Certainly, if Annie had been in Meg's place, she would have memorized Ethan's number and Googled his full life history by now. But actually, Annie would never have been in her place. For that matter, Meg couldn't believe that assertive woman in the hatchback had been the same Meg that Vance had pegged as a pushover. Even though her actions had been wildly out of character, Sucker Meg had to hand it to Seat Belt Meg. Despite her embarrassment immediately afterward, and her relief this morning knowing she would never have to face Ethan again, in her heart of hearts, the tingly memory of her actions made her feel downright liberated.

Annie adjusted her visor carefully over her cute cut. "I don't know what to do with you sometimes," she sighed.

"Play pickleball?"

"Excellent suggestion." Armed with their paddles, they marched through the gate to the high school's courts.

Compared to Meg's days as a pickleball virgin back in January, the courts were thick with players. Once school let out in June and as the days neared the summer solstice, the sky stayed bright until ten at night, allowing anyone with an itch to play time in the day to squeeze in a little pickleball. By four in the afternoon, all six courts were crowded with players—from fast-as-lightning teens to athletic senior citizens. The sport connected the physics professor and the dog walker, the available singles and the married couples, the professional baseball player and the amateur Ping-Pong enthusiast; all ethnicities, ages, faiths, and classes were blurred to oblivion by the addictive game. Some of the players were picklechasers—ballers who spent too much time in their cars racing from court to court trying to find the perfect game, beleaguered by FOMOOP—fear of missing out on pickleball. But most, like Meg, were regulars. As she glanced toward the sidelines, Meg noticed the soccer mom whose tennis skirt matched her tween daughter's; an eighty-two-year-old who had once arrived with a pillowcase filled with zucchini from her garden to share around; the ex–Olympic rower who rode his bike to the courts, played hours of pickleball, and then rode home; and five of the six Daves. Groups of four paddles lined the pavement, evidence of the spare players jockeying for an open court.

By the time their own waiting paddles hit the front of the line, Annie had wrangled one of the Daves and Rooster to play opposite her and Meg.

Rooster, too, was newish to pickleball, having learned to play little more than a year ago, but if he hadn't told her, she wouldn't have guessed. As a former tennis player, he had taken to pickleball like butter to bread. Although Rooster would play against her for this game, she and Rooster often partnered as teammates, and they balanced each other well. They were an unlikely combination: Meg, with her energy and speed in a pint-sized container, alongside Rooster's smooth and accurate play. He was a youthful seventy— still strong and good-looking in a rugged, Mr. Clean kind of way. Like an aging rock star. Without the drugs and the long hair. So not at all like a rock star, actually.

Annie took a ready stance beside Meg. Lifting her chipper voice over the bounce of the plastic balls on the surrounding courts, Annie reminded her friend, "Point your foot where you want the ball to go. And say the complete score before you move to serve." Annie could have been one of the professionals in her neon green hoodie, which matched the piping on her black tennis skirt, which matched the logo on her visor and her ankle socks. Beside her, Meg had thrown on a Kraken ice hockey sweatshirt. After a couple of jogging bounces to warm her shorts-clad legs, she steadied herself and checked her stance.

"That's it," Annie cheered. "Look at my partner go!" For a couple of months, they had practiced playing half-court "skinny" singles or just-for-fun matches with other beginners in the early mornings, but in recent weeks Meg had begun playing with Annie's community of players—the Lakeview league—who took over the crumbling high school tennis courts after school and over the breaks. Nets sagged over chalky asphalt. Toward the corners of the six courts, cracks stretched in slender lines toward the center of the playing area. Annie had warned her: the courts were crap, but the community was quality. Meg had been welcomed by the easygoing and friendly group.

A shrill shout startled Meg. "Just serve the damn ball!"

There were exceptions, of course.

From the sidelines, Jeannie, a sportsmanship-challenged regular with a killer backhand, jeered, "Are you playing, or should we all take a break and get a friggin' latte?"

"Cool it," Meg's opponent Rooster warned. On the other side of the net, the older man held steady in his ready position, unruffled. A model of fairness and patience, Rooster threw a restraining glare at the clump of waiting players. "She'll serve when she's ready. And watch your language, Jeannie. There are kids here."

"Yeah," remarked Andrés, who was all of thirteen, from the next court over. "Watch your damn language."

Thank heavens for Rooster. Other than Annie, he was one of the few people willing to play with or against a beginner. But not everyone on the courts was as patient. Rooster's partner gave an angry huff. "Enough talk. Let's play," Buff Dave complained. With six Daves on the courts, each one needed a nickname.

"What's the hurry? It's pickleball! Everybody take it easy," Rooster soothed.

At the end of her short rope, Jeannie threw up her hands. She used her paddle to direct traffic and guide her three gal pals to vulture themselves behind Meg. They set up camp, angling to commandeer the court. Meg gulped and held her ground.

"Screw you, Rooster," Jeannie griped. "There are people waiting."

By now, volleys had ceased on the neighboring courts, the players' attentions captured by the impending picklebrawl.

The only other sound came from the farthest court. "Michael Edmonds!" Michael Edmonds yelled, shouting his own name as he proclaimed a victory shot for the umpteenth time.

There was no need to turn in Michael Edmonds's direction. Meg did not need to look; she could picture him: a goofy, off-kilter smile on his face, his long arms raised to the sky like goalposts as he announced his own win. Annie, however, swiveled at the sound of Michael's voice, and for a long moment, she stared wistfully in his direction.

Her friend's distraction sparked the memory of yesterday's encounter, and before she knew it, Meg, too, had wandered off to visit the mayor of Daydreamland, where Sexy Seat Belt Guy waited with his cheeky banter, his manicured nails, his accidental deployment of the airbag—

"Earth to Meg . . ." Annie whispered, and Meg's head shot up, caught. Annie gasped with mock shock. "You were thinking about that hot ferry guy. I knew it!"

Jeannie mumbled, "This ain't the nail salon, ladies. Play!"

"Oh my god. You were, weren't you? You got all googly-eyed . . ."

"That's it. Get off the court."

As he stepped out of the portable toilet, Dress Shirt Dave tucked in his shirttails and checked his collar. "What is going on out here? I can hear you all bickering from inside."

Jeannie widened her stance. "They won't play, and they won't get off the courts."

Meg's shoulders curled inward. Maybe they should just give up the court. She didn't want to cause a scene. Already, Dress Shirt Dave's presence meant the argument had gone too far. His cool head held a lot of sway on these courts.

Dress Shirt Dave wiped his hands with antibacterial gel and shook his head with paternal disappointment. "Listen, Jeannie. We're on school grounds. If we want to be allowed to keep using these courts before the remodel, we have to act like adults. Play nice, all right? We want to do everything we can to make sure they go ahead with the new pickleball courts."

Meg nodded her support. Along with the plan for the new building, the school district was thinking of tearing down the decrepit courts and replacing them with state-of-the-art, dedicated pickleball courts. This afternoon, a construction crew had been milling about and meeting with school administrators. Among the players and in her own heart, optimism was building. New courts would be a boon to the whole community.

"And anyhow," Dress Shirt Dave pressed, keeping his tone agreeable, "you of all people ought to know better. Aren't you a teacher?"

"I'm a friggin' school counselor. And so what?" Jeannie puffed out her chest. "Not at *this* school."

"I'm ready." Meg waved her paddle for attention. "I'm serving. I'm gonna serve now." She took a powerful breath. In through the nose, out through the mouth. She arranged her left foot to point where she wanted the ball to go and checked her posture.

"Serve!" Jeannie called from six inches behind her ear.

Everything in Meg's petite frame clenched, from her gold-streaked waves to her pink toenails. "What was the score?"

Across the net, Rooster gave a shrugging shake of his head. "Hell if I remember." His eyes darted toward the sidelines, a sudden sheepishness overtaking him. "Sorry, Laverne. I mean, *heck* if I remember."

"No sweat, sugar pie." Rooster's wife, Laverne, did not glance up from her cell phone. Stationed in a folding lounge chair, she waved away the interruption to her texting. "No problemo."

"Zero-zero," Annie reminded Meg helpfully.

Annie kept her voice light. "We've got this. Paddle up," she cheered. The phrase was as much of a reminder as it was a greeting, a motto, and a way of life among pickleballers.

From the opposing side, Rooster threw both hands in the air to stop the action. "Time out," he called. He approached the net.

"Now what?!" Jeannie cried, apoplectic.

Rooster leaned over the net and met Meg's eyes. "You're doin' fine, kid. You just keep doing you and don't let the prattle rattle ya." Rooster and Annie shared a quick glance, like they were in on this pep talk together. "Remember. There are only two things out here that matter. You and the ball. And the ball doesn't really matter." He marched back to his baseline. "Okay. We can play now."

"Sorry," Meg whispered.

"No sorrys in pickleball," Rooster shot back.

Meg collected herself. She shut out the static and grounded herself in the here and now, absorbing the familiar landscape of the high school pickleball court. She filled her lungs with the picklebally air and concentrated on finding the confidence to play her best.

Meg cradled the plastic ball against her paddle. Pressing her fingers into the pea-sized holes of the 2Win tournament-quality ball, she prepared for the solid thwack and quick action of a professional pickleball.

"4–10," Meg called, mustering her confidence. "Second serve."

She dropped the ball and swung the paddle. Smack! Meg's serve flew over the net. Not as deep as she hoped, but passable.

Zoom. The plastic sphere hurtled back to her, much faster than she anticipated. It was all she could do to run forward and hold her paddle out in front of her to block her face. She swung hard.

Smack! It always felt good, hitting the ball with all her might.

"Hit softer!" Annie whispered. "Remember. It's about control."

The clever part of her brain agreed with Annie. Change the tempo of the hit, and the bangers won't be able to slam it back. "Soft!" the little angel on Meg's right shoulder urged.

"Ugh!" Meg hit the ball as hard as she could while the tiny devil on her left shoulder laughed and laughed.

Up the ball flew. Up to the candy spot, the one that nobody in their right mind could resist. Meg's ball soared and soared, straight up toward Buff Dave's right hand: his forehand slam hand. Her blunder was too tempting to ignore.

Bam! Buff Dave's wrist snapped forward, aiming the ball nearly straight down.

Quick as a flash, Meg dug her paddle beneath the hurtling sphere. It landed hard and boomeranged off her paddle. The ball soared back over the net.

When he saw it coming, Rooster tried to block the incoming missile. But his reaction was too late. The ball smacked against the edge of his paddle and ricocheted into his eye. Rooster crumpled. "Aw, fuuuuu—!" spewed from his lips as he went down. A collective gasp passed over the courts.

On the far court, unaware of Rooster's injury, a shout of "Michael

Edmonds!" sounded as the man congratulated himself on a well-placed shot.

"Rooster!" Meg cried. She moved to leap over the net, but she changed her mind at the last second, when she envisioned landing in a heap beside him. Instead, she raced around the post to where Rooster sat on the cracked asphalt, his hand cupping his eye.

"Oh. Shit. Shit that hurts. Mother-fightin' son of a shoemaker—"

"Let me see it," Meg encouraged. "Take your hand away."

Fingers trembling, Rooster pulled his hand from his eye. Meg sucked in air through her teeth.

"Ooh," Meg said, tamping down the wince and forcing a nonchalant shrug. A redness was spidering itself through the whites of Rooster's eyeball. The brow and the socket were an angry shade of pink, save for the peach-toned negative space mark that remained where one of the holes in the pickleball had hit. "I'm so sorry."

"No sorrys in pickleball," Rooster responded automatically, his voice barely a groan. "I'm okay. I'm okay."

"Rooster. Can I take a look?" Annie appeared by his side, her playfully competitive demeanor gone, replaced by her serious doctor mode. She gently probed the eye, causing Rooster to let out a pained moan. "You're lucky it missed your eyeball, but you're going to bruise around the socket. Will you please invest in some good sports glasses? In the meantime, how 'bout you lie down awhile on Laverne's lounger?"

"I'm fine. I'm fine. Come on. This'll heal right up. We gotta be prepared for all kinds of blips out here on the courts." He rocked himself back to standing. "See?"

Laverne perked up from her lounge chair. "Darlin'? You all right?"

Rooster waved off her concern, limping toward her. As he hobbled, Meg took note of an O-shaped welt on his arm; Rooster earned his pickleball badges and wore them with pride. "Stop all your fussing," he said. "It's a scratch."

But Laverne was already digging into her commodious purse. "I gotcha." She pulled an ice pack from a Mylar freezer bag.

Meg couldn't help but smile. The woman thought of everything and looked out for everyone. When Annie had introduced Meg to the Lakeview league, Laverne was one of the first to welcome her. Laverne's support, Meg noticed, extended beyond ice packs and sideline advice. Rooster's wife kept up the group's spirit as the unofficial league cheerleader, even though she herself was an NPC, a member of the Non-Pickleballing Crew ("Why would I wanna play that game? It's like Ping-Pong but standing on the table. I don't understand why everyone feels the need to shrink everything. Miniskirts, minigolf, minicars. And now we got mini tennis! What's next? Mini margaritas? No thank you.") Nevertheless, from her lounge chair, she rooted for Rooster, surfed social media, and sipped something from her Hydro Flask that kept her in good cheer for hours at a time. Now Laverne tut-tutted and pressed the ice pack to her hubby's swelling eye.

Rooster resigned himself to receiving her ministering. "Put my paddle in line, will ya?" he asked Meg. "We can play together. I'll be good by the time it gets around to us again."

On the far court, a group of advanced players waved Annie over to join them. "You played well," she assured Meg before heading toward the big-kids' court. "I'll be right over there if you need me. Playing with . . ." She pointed a thumb at Michael Edmonds, then gave a lewd wiggle of her eyebrows before busting into giggles. Meg rolled her eyes good-naturedly.

Annie was at the top of her field for pediatric medicine, but when it came to Michael Edmonds, she turned into a middle schooler at a slumber party. Unfortunately, while she and Michael made for a solid pickleball partnership, what Annie believed was successful flirting, Michael perceived as Annie blinking a bug out of her eye.

While Meg waited, she watched Annie play with a combination of awe and envy. A year ago, Annie Yoon had been a beginner, too. But in typical Annie fashion, she did not wait for the pickleball skills to come to her; instead, she practiced mornings and evenings, took lessons, listened to critique without taking it personally, and managed to absorb and apply new techniques. That was Annie, all around. She applied herself with singularity toward any challenge.

Meg's skill building moved at a slower pace. Before pickleball, Meg's hand-eye coordination consisted solely of activities related to her Crafty Cat Collar business—like loading the hot glue gun and bedazzling cat tags. Neither of which required much reaction time. Training her hands to work in sync with her brain while still paying attention to her legs made for glacial progress, but little by little, she was improving. She hoped.

So, Meg set her and Rooster's paddles at the end of the waiting stacks, unashamed to point the handles down to indicate their beginner's status. But while the other teams moved forward in groups of four, it grew more and more apparent that nobody wanted to join Rooster and Meg's beginner's match.

From his spot next to Laverne, Rooster nodded his chin toward their progressing paddles on the ground. "Looks like we're up next. If anyone will play with us."

"I don't mind if you have to wait a bit longer," Laverne said.

Peering down at her hand, Meg scanned the open expanse of her ring finger. How did Rooster and Laverne do it? How did they make their love last? Meg still could not understand where she'd gone wrong. She had bent backward to support Vance: had fallen into the habit of sacrificing her desires—selling crafts instead of dedicating her energies to her painting, canceling plans whenever he had time rather than hanging out with her girlfriends—in order to devote herself more completely to their relationship. She made the shifts willingly, but there was also some shame, trailing her like a shadow, in putting aside her own happiness for his. He once observed that she would cheerfully take on the most odious of tasks rather than say no to a request. "Always a people pleaser," he'd said. In her heart, she knew he meant pushover, and the memory of the label prickled across her neck.

And what had her desire to please cost her? Their last night out had been a double date with Vance's potential business partner and his wife. Beforehand, they passed the full-length mirror by the front door. He wore a smart suit coat and tie—which she had bought him—and not a hair was out of place. She sported a vintage boho skirt with strappy sandals. Vance had shaken his head. "Would it be so hard," he said, "to dress it up with some heels and makeup? I'm trying to make an impression here." In minutes, she had thrown on some lipstick and changed her shoes. Sometimes, it was easier that way.

Marriage was complicated. Like one of those brainteasers where you have to look in the back of the book to find the answer, and then you kick yourself 'cause it seems so simple and everybody else you ask figures it out right away.

"Open court," Jeannie shouted as she and her posse trotted toward the fence. Meg's head jerked from her reverie, and she frowned. Meg's and Rooster's two lonesome paddles had reached the front of the line, but pickleball doubles required four players.

It was late by now, and the clouds had resettled higher in the sky. On the courts, the remaining players shaded their eyes from the blinding laser beam of the descending sun. Any pickleballer facing west swatted at the air and whiffed the shot, calling, "I can't even see the ball!" and "We're switching sides at six points."

Meg squinted at the open court. She wondered if it was worth it, waiting to play now when she wouldn't be able to see anyway.

"Don't worry," Laverne said helpfully. "Someone at the end of the line is bound to jump in with you, because everyone just wants to play." But on the sidelines, the crowd avoided eye contact with the beginners. "I just need a water break" and "We already have our four" and "I think I forgot something in my car" and eight less believable justifications bounced around over the sounds of a jackhammer and the crack of pavement.

Beside the courts, preparations for the school remodel were well under way with the destruction of the nearby parking lot, and the construction workers were taking advantage of the extra daylight to finish up for the day. To Meg's surprise, she noticed Jeannie striding toward the site, chatting with an older woman, and then leading her toward the courts.

Jeannie cupped her hands around her mouth and bellowed, "Yo! People." She indicated the visitor in slacks and a flower-print blouse. And pumps. Clearly an NPC. "This lady is Grace Helms, with the school board."

Grace looked agog at the fifty-odd players on the courts, amazed at the sport's popularity. "Yes. Well. Hello, everyone. Looks like fun!"

On the courts, play resumed. The school board woman pressed on, louder this time. "It's that we'd love to have a representative from your pickleball community join in on the conversation about the direction of the courts. We're meeting now—" Grace pointed toward the rubble of the parking lot, where, beside the bulldozer, a group of construction workers were meeting with the foreman. "Could you send someone? Just a few minutes. To have a word."

"I'd meet with y'all," Jeannie said, "but I'm wiped. I've been playing"—she checked her phone—"for four and a half hours," she added, loudly broadcasting this badge of honor. "And I still have an hour or so in me."

"I could meet with them," Meg offered, shaking Grace's hand. "Meg. Bloomberg. I'll be happy to do it." She would enjoy it. Pitch in a bit. Help her community.

Jeannie tagged her on the elbow. "Yeah. You do that," she said, knowing Meg's absence would free up some court space. "And listen. Tell 'em that when they rebuild, we want them to install lights for nighttime play."

Buff Dave sidled up beside her. "A cover would be good, too," he suggested. "Like a roof, so we can play in winter." A throng of players who minutes earlier had made themselves scarce when Meg was looking for a game suddenly reappeared. "And a bathroom," Ginny said. "Yeah," Mustache Steve concurred. "Something that actually flushes."

With each new idea, Grace Helms's mouth took a downward turn, and at last, her voice rose above the overlapping proposals. "I'm afraid the construction crew won't be taking suggestions. They would like a representative just to keep the pickleball players in the loop."

Mustache Steve's brow dipped in concern. "What kind of loop is that?"

"The school board is exploring some different plans for this space."

The tone turned, and the tangible presence of confrontation swooped in like a cloud. On the far courts, balls clattered to the pavement and, sensing the arrival of a storm, the players began to close in on the cornered visitor.

"Different plans?" Jeannie's tongue chopped the words. "What kind of different plans?"

By now, even Dress Shirt Dave, always cool under pressure, squinted at Grace Helms. "They're not thinking about removing these courts, are they?"

For a moment, the district rep's mouth froze, stuck in an O. "There is a plan in the works to . . . take out the courts and restore the wetlands here."

"Wetlands!" Jeannie exploded. "Wetlands are for the birds."

Ms. Helms had only time enough to take in a choked breath of air before she was beset by irate cries. "What?" "Are you kidding me?" "No!" "How could you?!" "You can't take away our courts from us. It's not fair!" A string of expletives spewed from Jeannie's mouth, so foul that the school board rep's cheeks sprouted pink splotches.

Poor Grace Helms glanced at Jeannie and, finding no sympathy there, shifted her appeal to Meg. "Why don't *you* come with me, and the project leader can explain better than I can."

Meg jumped to the rescue. "Sure. That's fine. I'll talk with them." To the group, she gave her assurances. "I got this. I'll just explain how important these courts are to us, and I'm sure we can get them to reconsider." A brief back-and-forth ensued, with Jeannie offering to head over there and "kick some ass," but it was agreed that Meg's tactics might be more efficacious. Visibly relieved, Grace hustled away with Meg in tow.

As she followed Grace Helms toward the construction zone, Meg's confidence grew. She strode, guns blazing. How dare they threaten her pickleball haven? On the outside she remained composed, sensible. With a bit of sweet-talking, she could change their minds about removing the courts. Heck, she could probably get them to build a roof and a bathroom. Jeannie's approach would never have worked. Meg was much more suited for the role of negotiator because she was a . . . Her brain tripped over the phrase "people pleaser." That was the old Meg. She was diplomatic. Persuasive. Yes. That was it.

They approached the group discreetly so as not to disrupt the conversation in progress. A yellow-hatted construction worker gestured over toward the pickleball courts.

"Over on the left-hand side we're taking out this parking lot. And those courts as well, but we won't get started on them until the end of summer. I understand the school and a lot of players in the Lakeview community make active use of these courts. Oh, good," he added as he noticed the school board rep approaching. "A big thanks to Ms. Helms here and the whole school board for throwing their support behind this new proposal for the space that is currently being used as courts."

Currently used as courts! By the time Meg was through with this meeting, not only would they keep their courts, but they would be upgraded to pickleball heaven. She would wait until the contractor finished his spiel, she decided, and then she would approach him one-on-one. Diplomatically.

Meg lifted her hand to shield her eyes from the glare of the descending sun, but still she squinted. The speaker was standing due west of her. He was, undeniably, hunky. Maybe it was an effect of the sun on her shoulders or the residue of yesterday's sexy encounter, but a flutter of libido tingled her fingertips at the sight of this guy's cargo pants–clad stance.

Mr. Stance-tastic said, "We've consulted with the school district and with the city, so everyone is on board. The neighboring city park will prioritize student use of their fields, so there won't be big losses to the school's athletic department. And then the real work comes in," he added. "After the destruction, restoration."

Bathrooms first, Meg decided. That would be her absolute first request. The needs of too many pickleballers sometimes left the portable toilets in such a state that players had to race to the nearby park out of a sense of human decency.

Cargo Pants was on a roll now. It was pleasant to let his words wash over her, listening without really having to pay attention. He described the details of the construction plan in a textured voice, so rich and rugged and . . . familiar. "After surveying the landscape, and with the gracious support of the district . . ."

A roof. Right. A roof should be next. The courts didn't have to be enclosed. Just something to keep the rain off in winter. Like the covers over the school's basketball courts. That would work great. And lights on timers. That would be energy-saving. That idea would appeal to a guy with a T-shirt that read *Plan It Earth*. Her eye skated along his T-shirt sleeve and traveled along his arms—strong arms that could carry her away in his manly pants.

She blinked hard. *Gee whiz, Meg. Get a grip.*

"I would like to say again how much we appreciate the sacrifice this community is making in supporting this initiative to allow nature to reclaim her territory. If any of you have any questions at all, please, don't hesitate to—"

Where had she heard that "please" before? The word skipped around the edges of her memory, but no, she couldn't place it. And what had she been about to ask? Something about bathroom rooves. Was "rooves" even a word? It sounded weird. What a nice, strong chin he had. A chin that could slice bread. This man was *fine*.

Just then, the bright sun dropped behind the trees. At last, Meg got a good look at him.

Wait a sec. He really *was* fine. As in Ethan Fine. From the ferry.

And the seat belt.

She stood there, mute with surprise and wondering if she had fallen into another vivid fantasy. But as she gaped in stunned silence, that dreamy, clam-chowder-lovin' man finished with "and that's why we will be permanently closing down the pickleball courts."

Ethan Fine. Mr. Stance-tastic.

Destroyer of Courts.

At the instant of her realization, his gaze passed over the listening board members and landed on her. His expression hovered; he appeared confused at seeing her out of context. He blinked with surprise. "Meg?"

He was looking right at her! She thought she would never see him again, and there he was staring at her with those same soft lips and marbled shoulders and a small nick in his cargo pants where she had finally managed to cut him out of the seat belt. Her brain melted to fuzzy mush. Her tongue felt too big for her mouth. She had to get out of there. She had to go. Her mouth said, "Cargo!"

"What?"

"Gotta go," she amended.

Still he stared, boring a hole through her with his sexy, court-killing gaze. She opened her lips, but no more words were forthcoming. So Meg bolted, equally disappointed with her lack of diplomacy and her terrible sentence-building skills.

FIVE

Daylight spooled out before Meg like a sixteen-hour-long punishment. It seemed a fitting coincidence that the worst day of Meg's year would also be the longest. Today, on June 20, Meg's divorce became final. Bracing herself for this eventuality, last night Meg had hit a new low that involved canned spritzers and an ill-conceived painting project that she'd mentally titled *Too Much Brown*.

"Forget about Vance," Annie had insisted last night when she'd called smack-dab in the middle of Meg's self-pity party. "You have me. What more do you need? And don't forget: you still have pickleball!"

"Ugh. And I screwed that up, too," Meg moaned. Jeannie and the other players had laid into her when she returned to deliver the news about their doomed courts: Why hadn't she spoken out for the pickleball community? She was supposed to persuade them to build a state-of-the-art replacement, not let them destroy their only playing space. Was she going to let "those people" walk all over her?

"Don't worry about Lakeview," Annie said. "Something will work out."

Meg's chest tightened with the weight of her secret. She hadn't told anyone, not even Annie, about how she had been mortified into muteness by the very same Ethan Fine who found innovative uses for a rearview mirror.

"You should get in touch with that project manager," Annie urged. "Talk to him. Negotiate. You're good at that kind of thing. Well. At least, you're better than the alternative. Did you hear about what Jeannie did?"

Meg had not.

"Oh, this is good. Jeannie marched into the school district office and demanded that the taxpayers' objections be heard. And after that, she showed up on the courts going on and on about it—until Dress Shirt Dave pointed out that the taxpayers were the ones who voted for the wetland restoration. Not to mention that Jeannie lives, like, ten miles south of our district." Annie prodded, "Come on. I need you back on the courts."

"I don't know." It had been three days since Meg had fled the construction meeting, too stricken by his presence to say a single word to Ethan Fine. After announcing the court closure to the disappointed players, Meg didn't have the guts to face the whole crew again.

"Nobody is mad at you. They're mad at the situation. You better be back on the courts. I don't have to go in tomorrow till the afternoon, so I can play in the morning. Meet me there. I mean it. Don't stand me up."

It was Annie's conviction that the pickleball paddle was the ideal weapon against life's bad bounces. Meg hoped she was right.

· · · · ·

So too early that morning, after a coffee injection, Meg forced herself off the couch and into her workout clothes—bike shorts and a retro, disco-era T-shirt from the Seattle Folklife Festival. Some fresh air and exercise would do her good, she told herself as she grabbed her paddle and slipped behind the wheel. Pickleball was a spirit lifter. And truly, she missed hitting the ball around until her wrist ached.

"That's how you know you're making progress," Annie had assured her. "By the amount of swelling. If you don't need an ice pack and four ibuprofens, then you haven't worked hard enough."

Meg gave a cursory glance around the parking area and was relieved to find that neither Ethan nor his crew were on-site yet. She did not want to face him after absconding in embarrassment.

The gate clanged shut with her arrival, and she felt further reassured when the Lakeview crew greeted her warmly. Even Jeannie approached her, smiling. "Well, look who's back. Our official pickleball representative." The welcome was delivered with such a Cheshire cat grin that Meg wondered what Jeannie could be up to.

She was scoping out the courts, searching for Annie, when her phone dinged. Sorry. Got called in for a couple hours. Will be there ASAP.

Meg slogged past the players, carabinered her backpack to the chain link, and laid her paddle in line on the pavement with a thunk. She had been counting on Annie's no-nonsense support to get her through her marriage's final curtain on this excruciatingly long day.

"How goes it, kiddo?" Rooster flagged her over to where he squatted alongside the court in the shade by the school building's brick wall. How great to see a genuinely friendly soul. Rooster reminded Meg of her dad, the way she liked to remember him, before those painful final months. It wasn't that he looked like Meg's father—but he was patient in the way that he listened more than he talked.

Meg tried to smile, but she was nowhere near being able to pull it off. Between the dissolution of her marriage and the dissolution of the courts, she felt hopeless. Her shoulders slumped. "I don't know why you partner with me, Rooster. Everything sucks. I suck at life. I suck at this game. I'm never gonna get any better."

"That's horseshit and you know it. You're getting better all the time."

"Great. The Good Try award."

"Mm-hm. Why don't ya take a load off?" He patted the pavement beside him. "I'm wondering if you've met my friend Meg Bloomberg. You might know her. Blonde. Artsy. Lots of energy. She's the one with the positive outlook."

Meg felt tears prick her eyes. "She's not here today."

"I know you're going through a rough patch." Meg had spent more than one pickle practice bemoaning Vance and his abrupt departure. She wasn't surprised Rooster remembered that today her divorce became official. "You wanna talk?"

Meg shook her head. "Nah. I think I'm just gonna power through. Thanks, though."

"Yeah. Way to bottle up the misery." He thrust his hand at her and wiggled his fingers. "Hand over your phone."

She regarded him skeptically but dug her cell from her back pocket. "Call whoever you want. It's not gonna make me feel any better."

"Listen." He dropped his voice. "Try something for me. Whatever this situation is that you're in, I want you to think about the absolute worst-case scenario. I mean, really, the worst thing it could lead to. Think about how you're feeling now and just expand the hell out of it."

Meg glanced at him sidelong. She wasn't crazy about this kind of touchy-feely stuff, but she didn't want to hurt Rooster's feelings. Rolling her eyes, she conceded.

Staring into the white sky beyond the chain-link fence, Meg

pictured the worst-case scenario: Alone forever, lonely and without direction. Beleaguered by guilt over passively allowing the court's destruction. A loser at pickleball and a failure of a painter. Yeah. That would be about as bad as it could get. Meg felt the frown form on her lips.

Click. Rooster snapped a shot and beamed at her from behind her phone.

"Hey! What?"

"Now, don't get mad," he said when she snatched the phone from him. "And don't you dare delete that, darlin'. You keep that there, and when you want to see your worst self, and I don't mean that in any unkind way, but when you want to see yourself at your lowest, you take a peek at that photo. It won't be fun, but then you'll remember: this, too, shall pass."

"You mean it'll remind me about how sucky I can feel."

"Nope. This picture is evidence. When you see it, you'll remember the pain—as sharp and defeating as it feels today. But you know that feeling won't last. Once you recognize how you beat those challenges in here . . ." He pointed at his chest. "You can start to grow here," he said, tapping a finger to his temple.

Groaning, she acquiesced and shoved her phone deep into her back pocket. "How does Laverne put up with you? And where *is* Laverne? And anyway, why aren't you playing?"

"Laverne is on her way. And I am taking a fiver."

The chance of Rooster taking a break without ample reason was slimmer than the possibility of the Seahawks living down the game-losing final play of the 2015 Super Bowl. Impossible. "Come on. Really. Why are you sitting out?"

Rooster lifted his baseball cap. A welt the size of an organically farmed egg rose from his bald head.

"What happened?"

"Hit myself. With my own paddle. Damn near knocked me out. I thought I had this idea on how to execute the Golden Pickledrop!"

"Rooster," she scoffed. "The Golden Pickledrop? Really?"

One evening, after a sweaty, three-hour practice, Annie had reverently described the fabled swing. Rumor had it that the secret could be discovered on Bainbridge Island, where pickleball originated. There, according to legend, expert pickleballers practiced a stroke that would send the ball spinning toward the net—where it would pause midair before making contact. The ball would slide horizontally, dancing along the tape, and then, magically, drop straight down.

She gave Rooster the side-eye. "You don't really think it exists, do you?"

"The Golden Pickledrop? It's a real thing. I'm telling you. If we could manage a stroke like that on purpose, we'd have a win every time." He waved her away. "Go put our paddles in, kiddo. I'm just waiting here for Laverne and then I'll hit with you. You can do some stretches before go time. Showtime. Go-with-the-flow time." He flashed a smile. "I'm thinking of a new career in rap music."

"I think retirement suits you better."

A clatter sounded from the construction area. Even though another encounter with Ethan might send her anxiety over the edge, a part of her hoped to turn and find that Fine specimen, looking like a manly action figure. Only actual size. Alas, it was just Laverne, struggling through the gate pulling a loaded red wagon behind her. "Yoo-hoo, the party has arrived!" she called. "Snacks, treats, drinks, and a live DJ: yours truly!"

Laverne pecked Rooster on the lips and snapped into action, directing traffic as players on the sidelines rushed to help unload the bounty. A gigantic speaker was lifted to a spot near the gate. "If you all are going to be competitive, we need to pump up the volume. I brought the party. You bring the pickleball."

Laverne set up a card table and topped it with bowls of chips and kettle corn, and then she set about programing her playlist with '80s hits, disco-pop, and hip-hop. Rooster winked at her, and the couple's positive energy felt contagious. Meg set her paddle in the line.

Just then, the gate clanged, and Annie huffed onto the court. Her body was a whirlwind of motion and her squeaky voice raced. "You wouldn't believe the traffic on I-5 . . ." She did not finish the sentence.

Spotting Meg, she dropped her backpack, her paddle, and her windbreaker onto the pavement like a trail of breadcrumbs. The instant she reached Meg, she opened her arms. "Come here."

Meg moved into her embrace, oblivious to the stares of the other players. Wordlessly, Annie held her, unmoving, until at last Meg patted her shoulder.

"I'm okay. Gee," Meg said, breaking away self-consciously.

From the lounge chair, Rooster feigned disinterest in the scene. He gestured at the waiting paddles. "Well, look at that. We're up next," he said. "Wanna play, Dave?"

In unison, five guys said, "No thanks."

Meg bristled at the circular frustration of being a beginner. If people would play with her, she could get more practice. With more play time, she would improve, and she would no longer be a beginner. As she listened to the ticktack of balls against paddles, the nerves on her skin threw Meg back to her schoolyard pick days. Now, waiting players avoided eye contact and rummaged in their backpacks. The cornucopia of stall tactics was broken only when a strangled cry rent the air.

All heads snapped toward the bang of the portable toilet, where Dress Shirt Dave was struggling out the door. From the expression on his face, he might have just swallowed motor oil. He gulped some air. "Good god! That's disgusting! What happened to our toilet?!"

Jeannie appeared, a smug grin plastered on her face. "I don't know. What happened to our toilet?" she asked, her voice thick with sarcasm. "Anybody besides me tired of waiting around for Little Miss Ponytail to take a stand? You know what they say. Action speaks more often than words." Sure, Meg took umbrage at the ponytail reference, but the botched proverb bothered her even more.

"Jeannie . . ." Dress Shirt Dave glowered. "What did you do?"

A flash of movement caught Meg's attention, and she turned her head to find none other than Ethan Fine striding across the parking lot. His face was awash with contained fury. Something was up, something that thrilled Jeannie and infuriated Ethan.

If there was one thing Meg hated, it was conflict. Maybe "hate" was too strong a word. Disliked. Hate would cause conflict within herself. As Ethan marched closer, her insides rolled up like a potato bug.

She barely had an instant, but she bolted. Fast as she could, Meg ducked into the nearest hiding spot. Her heart pounded in her ears as she locked herself inside the plastic box and willed herself to avoid looking at the urinal cake.

Although she could no longer see him, his voice reached her clearly. "Excuse me." He sounded calm, collected. "Hi. I'm with Plan It Earth. The team doing the wetland restoration. Is your court rep around?"

A silence ensued, followed by a spray of comments like "She was right here." And "That's her paddle, I think." Annie added, "I just saw her a minute ago."

Meg cringed as she listened. And she couldn't help but glance at the urinal cake. Who in their right mind would give something like that a food name?

"Hello, *sir*." It was Jeannie's voice. Was she doing a Cockney accent? "Jeannie Delaney. You can consider me the community lesion."

"Liaison?"

The gravel in her voice returned. "That's what I said."

"Listen." It was Ethan's voice again. "I don't want to point fingers, but we do have cameras on our worksite, and it looks like *one of your pickleballers*"—he emphasized—"lifted our on-site plans for the project and carried them this way."

"That's right."

"What's right?"

"It was me. I took 'em," Jeannie said. "Your plans were crap, so I put them in the crapper."

"You what?!" Dress Shirt cried.

"I stuffed 'em down the crapper."

Meg stiffened, deeply regretting her choice of hiding place.

"Look," Ethan explained, his voice never rising. "First off, do you know how difficult it is to remove garbage from those things?"

"*I do*," said Dress Shirt. "I read that sign six times a day."

Ethan continued. "You know we're trying to do something good for the environment. It would be great to have you all on board. We could partner with your community. Maybe help you find a different space where you can build state-of-the-art courts. Somewhere that doesn't endanger the wildlife."

"Where are we supposed to find the money for new courts?" Jeannie challenged. "Start a GoFundMe? *Weekend warriors need your help.* That'll go over well."

Meg's eyes were beginning to water. And what was the soft thing under her shoe?

"I'm gonna let this go," Ethan allowed, "but if you all want to keep playing, you're going to have to find a working solution. One more stunt like this and the district is going to lock up the courts."

A moment passed, then Jeannie shouted, "Are you threatening us?"

"No. I'm just— Look. Let's agree to disagree. For now, I don't think we're going to get anywhere in this conversation."

Meg closed her eyes, hoping to dull her sense of smell, but now she was even more aware that her tongue tasted like the space smelled. Hopefully, Ethan would leave soon, and Meg could get out of there.

For a moment, there wasn't a sound. Placing a tentative hand on the door handle, she heard him add, "And if Meg Bloomberg shows up, let her know Ethan Fine would love to talk to her."

Meg's breathing halted. She listened at the door as Ethan's footsteps crunched away on the gravel and heard Jeannie in the distance snarking, "That jerk is doing everything he can to make our lives miserable."

Meg counted another thirty excruciating seconds, then cracked the door open a sliver. The coast looked clear. Swinging the door ajar, she all but tumbled from the portable toilet.

Cycling some unsullied air through her nose, Meg got her bearings. The picklers had moved off and regrouped on the courts, but she could still make out the continued grumblings. Scanning the area, Meg was considering sneaking to her car before anyone noticed when Annie's voice jolted her to attention.

"Meg Bloomberg!" her friend exclaimed with sarcastic surprise. "Someone was just looking for you." Annie measured the air with her hand. "About this tall. Hunky dreamboat. Evil incarnate. Oh! Ethan Fine. That was his name. Perhaps you've heard of him."

Caught, Meg grimaced. "About that . . ." She took in her friend's narrowed eyes. "I'm sorry I didn't tell you before. It's just that . . . it's complicated."

"I bet." Annie shook her head, more amused than mad. "I mean, look on the bright side. Maybe you can buckle him into your hatchback and get him to change his mind about closing down the courts. Offer him a lube and tune or something."

"Har de har. Not funny."

"It's a little funny."

"I'd need a magnifying glass to find the funny." Then, without warning, Meg found herself tearing up.

"Oh, honey," Annie cried. "What's wrong? Come here." She beckoned Meg into an embrace that lasted all of three seconds. "Nope. Okay. Get off me." Gently, Annie pushed her away. "You smell like the elephant house at the zoo."

Meg's eyes stung, and she shook her head briskly to ward off the waterworks. "I'm so embarrassed. Everything I touch just crumbles. I finally start to enjoy pickleball and then the one guy who seems into me is the same guy shutting down the courts. And I don't even have the guts to speak up for Lakeview and stand up to him. And even if we could keep our courts, we could never afford to fix them without the school's funding. And anyway, nobody ever wants to play with me because I'm a beginner."

"You better stop that crap right now. You *know* none of that is true." Annie hesitated. "Except maybe the last part." She shrugged. "But you won't always be a beginner."

"I wish I had a magic wand"—Meg tapped at the air—"and I could just ping, and make everything better—"

Just then, a ping chimed from the courts. Another ping echoed from the phone inside somebody's gym bag. *Ping. Buzz-buzz-buzz. Ping. Na-na-hey-hey-hey*, a chorus of phones rang out.

Laverne sat upright and pointed at her screen. "Son of a sailor and all the saints! Did y'all just see this post?!" Meg and Annie moved toward the commotion as Laverne rose from her lounger. She held her phone aloft and announced to no one in particular, "Check out the grand prize being offered at the Pacific Northwest Picklesmash Leagues Tournament!"

The words "grand prize" reverberated off the chain-link fence and swooped over the flimsy nets, the portable toilet drama forgotten. With a flurry of activity, thirty adults and two teenagers all jumped on their cells and the news hopscotched from one player to the next. "What?!" "Is this for real?" and "Did you see the prize . . . ?"

Laverne's voice cut through the commotion.

"Attention. Attention, everyone." Laverne called on her long career as a stage actress. "Coming this August: For the first time in the Northwest, all levels can compete in the Picklesmash Tournament. And, to sweeten the deal, an anonymous donor has contributed"—Laverne's voice ticked up a notch—"a cash prize worth fighting for!"

Mumbles of excitement and surprise echoed around the court. This group would have battled it out for a nice trophy. From the parking lot, a car door slammed, and Mustache Steve held his phone toward the crowd. "Hey! Did you guys see this?" he called through the gate.

Jeannie gestured at the group of players, phones in hand. "We're on it, Mustache. Read the room." Mustache Steve lifted his palms in surrender and Meg said a silent prayer for the students who were assigned Jeannie as their school counselor.

Laverne returned her attention to the screen. "Twelve doubles teams will represent each Pacific Northwest club. The grand prize will be awarded to a club or league of players that demonstrates not only skill and athleticism, but unity of community and the spirit of positive pickle-energy." At this, Laverne cast a meaningful glare at

Jeannie. "And because this tournament aims to encourage new learners and support beginners, at least one team from each club must be a beginner partnership."

Beginners? Meg was a beginner.

Around her, brows were raised and eager glances exchanged among the players. Jeannie smirked and poked an elbow into Kiki's ribs, and Meg could guess what she was plotting. With real money at stake, Lakeview wouldn't waste their chances on a win by including true beginners. They would choose their strongest players, pose them as beginners, and easily pull in the win.

Meg shrugged to herself, accepting defeat early so it wouldn't be so painful when it smacked her in the face. It was, after all, the longest day of the year. She was officially divorced, the man she had dry-humped in her hatchback was loathed by her pickleball community, and there was something squishy stuck to her shoe. Did she honestly expect any kind of win today?

In a fair world, this would be a great chance to try out a tournament. But if pickleball players had one thing in common, it was their competitive nature, and she doubted anyone would offer her and Rooster one of the coveted twelve spots if some big money was on the line.

Laverne continued, "Tournament sponsors will strictly monitor beginners' statuses. Players may only compete as beginners if this is their first pickleball tournament."

Suddenly aware of the quiet gathering around her, Meg lifted her gaze from the green asphalt. Glance after glance flicked her way. Her pulse skipped. She and Rooster were the only players on the courts who met such requirements. Everybody knew it.

"Worth fighting for? You betcha. The winning club will receive"—Laverne, practiced at the art of the dramatic pause, did just that—"funding from our donor. Ten thousand dollars for the winning league."

A hush descended over the doomed schoolyard courts as the news sank in. One by one, the crowd absorbed the potential for their courts, for the Lakeview league, for the future of their game. Peering at their faces, Meg observed a palpable shift as the dreamy vision took hold.

"New courts." Annie's voice lilted with the possibility. "If we could find a space, we could fund new courts."

Quick as a blink, the players leapt into action. Hands reached for Meg's and Rooster's paddles and one of the Daves hooked Meg by the elbow and dragged her toward the courts. Another Dave pulled Rooster from his lounger.

"Neither of you has ever played in a tournament, right?" Meg shook her head and Buff Dave adjusted his service stance. "All righty." He knocked the ball twice against his paddle. "Let's get you two trained up!"

SIX

Slowing her blue hatchback, Meg peered through the pinhead dots of rain on the windshield and wound her way to the courts at the back of the school building. Her eyes searched the construction area at the other end of the cordoned-off soccer fields, looking-not-looking for the figure of the man causing so much strife to the Lakeview players. A shadow passed overhead and, looking up, she spotted a hawk swooping away from the commotion. Her heart twinged. Seattle was blessed with public parks and walking paths, thick with emerald pines. Creeks jumped with salmon, and deer and bobcats made their way through backyard trails. While one version of Meg wanted to confront Ethan and let him know where he and his crew could shove their wetland restoration project, another Meg hoped to see the plan come to fruition. And a third Meg wished she could rip his shirt off and pinch him to make sure he was real. But today, she capitulated to version number four, Passive Avoidance Meg, and parked her car beside the courts, as far from the construction zone as possible.

When she opened the car door, a light mist sprinkled onto her skin and she looked to the sky. Like most Seattleites, she read rain clouds as easily as billboards. These were no threat: a high, thin layer of grayish white enveloped the sky. Small potatoes.

Now that June had tipped into July, Seattle's summer was firmly established. Nothing, certainly not a weak mist, could keep these players from their passion, especially now that the league was prepping for a tournament. Through the chain link, Meg spotted four courts already going. On the remaining two courts, Jeannie and her groupies attacked the wet surface with industrial brooms and squeegees. The uneven slope of the land made them susceptible to heavy puddling.

When she sloshed through the gate, most of the players shouted out friendly hellos and encouragement—except for Jeannie, who lived by a different set of civilized norms. Now that Meg and Rooster were Lakeview's hope for a tournament win, the community was invested in Meg's improvement. She would feel insulted by the circumstantial shift in her picklestatus, but she was too busy feeling flattered.

"Oh! Good," Annie said to Meg and Rooster. "Let's see if we can find a fourth. We can play together while I wait for Michael Edmonds."

Annie's cheery attitude surrounding all things pickleball had intensified lately, and with reason. By popular consensus, Lakeview's players had decided that Annie would partner with none other than her crush, Michael Edmonds. For the upcoming tournament, their advanced partnership would require countless hours of practice time. If Annie's enthusiasm for the tournament had percolated before, now it exploded in seismic geysers.

Rooster's gaze swept the courts, seeking the lanky player known for shouting his own name in victory. "Where *is* Michael Edmonds?"

"I don't see him," Meg said.

Annie frowned. Her head swiveled to and fro as she hoped Michael might emerge from beneath the back stairwell to the school. "He mentioned we would practice together."

"Now?"

"We didn't set a time," she hedged. "I just figured . . ." Shrugging off her disappointment, Annie added, "He's so private, you know."

Rooster and Meg shared an empathetic glance. Michael Edmonds *was* a man of mystery. The only tidbit people knew about him was that he used to play over on Bainbridge Island, Lakeview's rival league, and he took a lot of ribbing for it. The other thing most everyone knew was that Annie was smitten with him. Everyone except Michael Edmonds, apparently.

"Such a private person," Annie repeated. "Michael. Edmonds," she said reverently, and let her focus wander to the parking lot, still searching. Meg's heart tightened for her friend. She knew Annie had switched around her work schedule to make way for more weekday practices.

Jeannie, who was stuck waiting for a court behind Meg's and Rooster's paddles, rolled her eyes as two more players sporting identical fluorescent T-shirts strode through the chain-link gate at the already crowded courts. "Great," she complained. "Now we got Team Peter and Portia." Leave it to Jeannie to find fault in two of the nicest people ever to play pickleball.

But then Meg's pulse tripped. Behind the neon-dressed figures of Peter and Portia, Ethan Fine, sporting his hard hat and hard body, marched toward the parking lot. For exactly a week since the portable toilet fiasco, surreptitiously, she had watched him direct the crew at the worksite. And more than once, she'd spotted him loitering near the pickleball fence. Even now as he passed, Ethan slowed long enough that she was sure he was scanning the courts for her. From beneath her lashes, she studied him. On his shoulder, he hauled a metal pipe. The image added a page to Meg's long-nurtured Men in Hard Hats calendar fantasy. In fact, that might be the centerfold.

She pirouetted back toward the nets before he could spot her.

Near the gate, in all their hot pink and green glory, Team Peter and Portia smiled their matching smiles. "A beautiful day for pickleball," Portia said.

"Always a good day when it's a pickleball day. Especially with an upcoming tournament!" Peter concurred.

Meg risked a glance back toward the construction site. Alas, Ethan had disappeared among the construction crew, indiscernible from the candidates for February, March, and April.

Jeannie squinted accusatorily between Peter and Portia. "Wait just a second. How did you two get spots to play at Picklesmash?"

"We're refereeing!" Peter clarified. "And we need some practice. Is it okay if we ref your game?"

Meg shrugged. "Sure. If I can get four people together. We only have three players so far."

Portia pointed to a stray paddle that lay on the asphalt behind Annie's, Rooster's, and Meg's. "Well, how about that person? Whose paddle is that?"

"That's Dave's," Annie said.

"Buff Dave or Regular Dave? Or Finance Guy Dave. Oh. Or Reflux Dave."

"No," Annie hedged. "The other one."

"Dress Shirt Dave?"

"Nope." Annie shook her head. "Dave," she emphasized, with portent.

Ah. Boring Dave. There was nothing distinctive about him, and all the other Dave names had been taken. Nobody actually called him Boring Dave, but everybody thought it. He stood on the sidelines, spreading cream cheese on a plain bagel.

"Dave," Annie called. "Wanna partner with me? Michael's not here yet, so it's you and me against Rooster and Meg."

Dave assessed the situation. Partnering with Annie was a sure win, especially against a pair of beginners like Rooster and Meg, but it meant he would have to play nice against the newbies. Pickling beginners 11–0 was a sportsmanship no-no. He would have to allow them a couple of points, at least. Dave shrugged. "I guess."

It wasn't a whopping vote of confidence, but it was a match.

A gust blew a whorl of leaves across the courts as the players moved into position. At Laverne's snack table, paper cups fell like bowling pins.

"Zero–zero," Meg called, and hit a deep, powerful serve. A great serve. One of her best ever.

"Wait." Peter held a hand up. "I'm sorry to have to stop you, Meg, but your foot crossed the baseline before your paddle connected with the ball. That's an automatic foul. Side out. Right, honey?" he asked.

Portia nodded sympathetically, but the point was lost. As play resumed, the referees continued to interrupt for rule clarifications, including but not limited to illegal serves, volleying while inside the kitchen without letting the ball bounce first, inappropriate language, and delay of game, and once to call a time out because Boring Dave's shoe was untied.

Meg practiced patience. Generally, only the bigger tournaments used certified referees. But local tournaments often had volunteer refs for the final matchups, and there were plenty of pickleballers, like Peter and Portia, who just loved to referee. Not only did they get to attend the tournaments for free, but they scored prime viewing spots for the exciting higher-level games.

However, for Meg, here on their community court, the referee calls added an element of distraction. Between all the stopping and starting, the unpredictable gusts of wind, and Annie's killer backhand, Meg and Rooster found themselves facing game point and looking down the barrel of a bleak eight-point gap. 10–2.

Just then, the growl of a muffler drew Meg's attention. Beyond the tall fencing, a yellow sports car sped into the parking lot and screeched to a stop. The noise was loud enough that play ceased, and necks strained to see who had disrupted the calm rhythm of the pickleballing.

The car door opened. A pair of long, toned legs exited the car first, translucent white socks up to the thighs. A gap of bronzed skin remained tantalizingly visible below the plaid schoolgirl skirt. Meg glanced across the net at Boring Dave, who stared unabashedly.

"2–10. Second serve," Rooster called, and served to Annie's mesmerized partner. The ball bounced and whizzed past Dave. He did not move a muscle. Like every man on the courts and two of the women, he was transfixed by the voluptuous vision moseying through the gate.

Wiggling her paddle in greeting, Jeannie sported an uncharacteristic smile. "You made it!" With a downright chipper bounce to her step, Jeannie linked arms with the newcomer and ushered her onto the courts. "Hey, everybody. I want you to meet the newest member of our league. Édith LeBeouf."

"*Bonjour*, pickleball people. I am very glad to be here!"

Jeannie handed Édith a paddle. "Here. Try this one. It's mine, but you can borrow it. It's got great action." Meg narrowed her eyes, highly suspicious of Jeannie's generosity. With a lift of her chin, Jeannie explained, "I poached Édith from the Shoreline league. Wait'll you see her play."

"Oh, *non*," Édith said, brushing away the compliment. "I am learning every day. It is all for fun." Meg could not begin to imagine what Jeannie was up to, but it couldn't be good.

By now, a crowd had gathered to investigate the newcomer. The predators of the pickleball savanna began circling the buxom brunette as if she were a weak antelope with a leg injury.

"Put your paddle down, Édith. Come play," one of the hyenas offered.

"Oh. I must not cut the line . . ." she said, placing her paddle at the end.

The three alphas of the pack moved fastest, snatching up their paddles from their spots and launching them onto Édith's pile. Following the food chain pecking order, the players yanked their paddles from waiting piles and shifted them into the vacated matches.

Édith's lips parted with surprise. "Actually, I am waiting. For my boyfriend."

And on cue, all heads swiveled to the sound of the silver Mercedes convertible that zoomed around the construction site and swerved into the parking spot beside Édith's car. The driver tucked his artfully stubbled chin and emerged from his seat, paddle in hand.

No. No. Not possible.

Meg squinted. That swagger! That casual carelessness that said, *I think I'll write my farewell on the back of this Home Depot receipt.*

The player strutted toward the courts, paddle in hand. There was no mistaking that air of confident machismo.

Vance!

SEVEN

Meg's pulse did a plunge off the high board into a tiny bucket of water. The workings of her mind pedaled overtime to catch up. Her pickleball haven was under attack. She ticked off the complications on her mental tally chart. 1. Her ex-husband 2. was playing pickleball 3. with her foxy replacement. At least there were only three annoying things. Could be worse.

Édith's chestnut waves swayed effortlessly across her shoulders as she sashayed over toward Vance and kissed him. Meg could not believe it. Who shows up to play pickleball without a hair tie? Make that four annoying things.

Oblivious to Meg's presence, Vance patted Édith on the butt. And then he spotted Meg. She wished in that very moment that she could be anywhere else. Even back in the porta-potty.

"Meg!" He had the grace to release his hold on her replacement. "Hello," he said in a tone one might use with a great-aunt who had overapplied her rouge. "Good to see you. Have you met . . . Édith? Édith, this is Meg. *You* know"—he insinuated, with portent—"*Meg*." The air quotes were implied.

"Ah! It is you, the cat crafty person." Édith gave a girlish, rapid wave and her breasts moved in sync. "Your crafts, they are so cute!"

Meg looked down quickly before anyone spotted her mortification. Tugging at her nylon bike shorts, she cursed herself. Why couldn't this have been a cute tennis skirt kind of day?

Turning, she sought out her friend for support, and when their eyes met, Annie took a protective step toward Meg. Hackles raised, she crossed her arms and manifested a glare that came off like Tinker Bell with menstrual cramps. Meg would have laughed if the whole situation weren't so painful. And Rooster, who had a corner on the empathy market, uttered, "Mm-hmm." Meg looked up to match eyes with him, and he nodded slowly. "Mm-hmm," he said again. Sometimes she had the sense that Rooster could reach into her skull and understand what she was thinking. Right now, she didn't mind it so much.

Vance laid his paddle on the pile on top of Édith's, and a game of chicken ensued. One of the three alphas was going to have to leave the pile. Five players simply could not play pickleball. The men glowered, locked horns, and took virtual claw swipes at each other's athletic shorts until the wiriest among them, Phil from Oregon, cracked.

Phil withdrew his paddle. "Fine. I guess I'll just leave," he said, sulking. "Who's got my balls?" he called to the crowd. "Somebody's got my balls. They have my name on them." Jeannie snickered, and her girls followed suit.

"Yeah. C'mon, you guys," Jeannie guffawed. "Who has Phil's balls?"

"They're yellow with holes and one of you has them." Phil rummaged through his gym duffel. "I brought two 2Win tournament-quality balls, and now they're both gone!" He reached into his shorts pockets. "Oh. Forget it. I have my balls."

A chorus of chuckles followed Phil from Oregon as he took his balls and went home.

Vance, unaffected, shrugged. "C'mon, babe. Let's play." Meg al-most joined him, until she realized she was no longer the babe he meant.

Annie shifted to block Meg's view of the courts—and of Vance. "How 'bout we get out of here?"

Meg shook her head. "I can't believe this."

"Come on. I'll get you a soy mocha. We should go."

"Pickleball is *my* thing. Since when is it *his* thing?"

By now, Annie was tugging at her elbow.

"No. You know what? I was here first," Meg said stubbornly. "This is my group now." Besides, part of her wanted to wait and watch the train wreck. Annie had introduced her to pickleball gen-tly; it was weeks before she played with anyone else, much less in front of a crowd of spectators. Vance was a pickleball newbie. This could be good.

The throng parted to make way for the striking pair. Édith's stretching regimen captivated an audience. Vance jogged in place, cracking his neck and swinging his paddle at the air.

"Zero–zero. Start," Vance called.

Then he served a rocket, low and deep.

Meg's eyebrows leapt. Vance had always been athletic, sure. He played tennis, which was certainly an advantage, and he kept fit with weight training and running. But clearly, this was not his first pickle-rodeo. He swung with finesse, dropping to the corners and racing to the baseline to return a lob. It didn't make sense. Where did he learn to play like that? *When* did he learn to play like that? What had Jeannie said? That she'd poached them from the Shore-line league? Had he been playing when they were still married? How many more betrayals was he going to serve up?

And Édith, for cricket's sake. She was a pickleball savant: swoop-ing, pirouetting, stalling just long enough before a shot that Meg thought she'd never get to the ball, then lunging at the last moment to deliver a perfect lob. Car-stopping gorgeous, and now this. Meg felt her pickleconfidence slipping away.

By the time Édith bounced off the court, she glowed with a light sheen of perspiration. Her cheeks flushed pink, and her lips parted. "Pickleball is so fun, *non*?"

There was nothing to say, really. After all, pickleball *was* fun. That was the point.

"It is so new and so fresh, this pickleball. What a beautiful sport." Édith lifted her shoulders as if to say she couldn't help it if she was so damned talented.

Jeannie smirked, nodding at the throng of spectators. "That's why I went nosing around the Shoreline courts. I was scouting for newbies," she said proudly, gesturing to the marble-muscled Édith and the sporty Vance as if she had personally sculpted them from clay.

Silence descended on the spectators as the ramifications of Jeannie's comment settled on the crowd. Meg prickled. A whorl of leaves picked up off the pavement and Meg looked up at the sky. Overhead, a pregnant gray cloud gestated, waiting to dump its rain baby all over the courts.

Buff Dave spoke up. "So. Wait. Neither of you have ever played in a tournament before?"

"A tournament! We're hardly at that stage," Vance laughed, placing a humble hand to his chest.

Meg bit back a scream as she realized Jeannie's intentions. She should have left when Annie suggested it. Then she wouldn't have been party to her own doom. It was one thing for her ex and his new girlfriend to show up at the courts and outshine her, but threatening her shot at Picklesmash was quite another. She sensed the inevitable plunge, like being suspended at the top of the roller coaster.

"The thing is"—Jeannie piped in as if the thought had just occurred to her—"we do need a beginner team for the Picklesmash Tournament. To represent us."

Rooster raised a finger in the air. "Now, hold on a minute. That's me and Meg. *We're* the beginner team. We've been prepping."

"Uh-oh," Vance warned, grinning with his whole face. "We don't want to start a war here. You folks work this out and we'll be over here playing full-court singles. You all are welcome to watch. I mean, *I* would."

As the striking pair jogged off to the far court, the crowd stared after them. Meg wanted to say something commanding, something that would reassure her league that she and Rooster were the better choice. Meg searched her mental hard drive and came up with *No results found.* The confrontation sent pangs into Meg's chest; she felt like she was having a lactic acid attack without even enjoying the Brie.

The dull thunk-thunk of raindrops began to drum on the pavement. Annie piped up. "Hey. Come on, you guys. This is a community," she said. "We support each other. Meg and Rooster are working hard, and the point of the tournament is to support beginners, right?"

"No," Jeannie said. "The point of the tournament is to win some money and put it toward new courts somewhere so we can keep playing." She jerked her head toward Meg. "And thanks to Puppy the Pickleballer here, who rolled over for a belly scratch instead of showing some teeth, our courts are on the line. We need a win."

Now the rain hitched up a notch. The pavement darkened quickly and began puddling. Some folks scooted away for cover, but most were too enthralled with the impending picklebrawl.

"Sure," Annie countered diplomatically. "And we're going to keep working hard. It's the only way to get results. We all want the best for our club, right?"

"If that's the case, Annie . . ." Jeannie got right up in her face. "Where's Michael Edmonds? If you two are hogging up one of the advanced team spots, shouldn't he be here working, too? Like me and my partner Kiki here. We're busting our butts to make sure we win this thing. If you and Michael don't want it badly enough, pass it along to a couple of my girls who don't get the chance." She stuck her thumb behind her, indicating her posse of minions.

Annie stuttered, "Michael Edmonds will be here. He's just . . ."

Jeannie widened her stance. "Michael Edmonds *should* be here. Practicing. Or did he change his mind and go back to playing with his old Bainbridge pals?"

More droplets bounced off the pavement. Another, then another fell, pinging Meg on the top of her staticky head. A gust of wind whipped the courts. The nets snapped and flapped like rogue sails.

Jeannie seemed oblivious to the foul weather—in addition to her foul nature. She was still holding court with the remaining looky-loos. "Look. We don't have time to mess around. We have a common goal, and a common enemy—that numbnuts who is shutting down our courts. So frankly, I don't know why we're even talking about who gets the beginners' slot." She gestured with rhetorical obviousness at Vance and his superstar girlfriend. As an afterthought, she turned to Meg. "No offense."

Meg flushed. She had come to understand that people who said *no offense* were the same people who said phrases like *I don't mean this in a bad way, but . . .* right before uttering a self-esteem-squashing zinger.

She opened her lips to defend herself, but suddenly the rain called for attention. Over the course of a minute, the drops changed from a pitter-patter, to a drumroll, to a downpour that turned the court into a pond.

Players exploded into motion. Laverne and Reflux Dave went for the speaker and slid it under the slim protection of the school's brick facade. Dress Shirt Dave reached into his pack and pulled out an expertly folded poncho.

The rain powered up to deluge. "See ya," "Later," "That's my cue," came the parting calls from Kiki and Knee-Brace Joe and Samantha and Shanthi and fourteen-year-old Wylie and that guy with the sports glasses with the lenses popped out, to protect his eyes without all the bothersome fogging.

Reflux Dave broke into a tentative jog, then slowed to a walk. "Forget it. I shouldn't run. I hafta take it easy," he yelled over the rain. "Wish me luck. I'm having my gastrointestinal surgery tomorrow."

Meg hoped it would work out. Even if it meant they would have to come up with another name.

Vance's voice cut through the downpour. "Bloody hell! The car!" He was already running toward the open-topped convertible and covering his head with his backpack.

"Watch it," Jeannie muttered. She jostled into Meg, shoving her aside in pursuit of her gym bag. "I don't want my paddle to get soaked."

If Meg did not speak up right this moment, there would be no regaining her footing, no opportunity to fight for her place in the tournament. Pulse pounding, Meg tapped Jeannie on the shoulder. Jeannie whirled on her.

Meg kept her nerves in check, and the words shot out of her.

"We'll play for it. Me and Rooster. Give us a couple of weeks to prac-tice together. We'll play a determining match. And whoever de-serves the spot gets it."

Jeannie smirked. "Okay." Her tone was overbright. "That sounds fair."

When she turned to Rooster, she found he was not beaming with his usual supportive grin. In fact, he was frowning. "Can I talk to you a sec?"

Now the rain puddled as it spat down and splashed off the pave-ment. Rooster directed Meg away from Jeannie, toward the narrow awning against the school building. "I know it's bad timing, but . . ." His fingers probed at the goose egg bump on his forehead. "Laverne and I are headed to Bainbridge Island. We have a family situation. You know that I wouldn't go if it wasn't necessary." He waited for her to arrive at the unfortunate conclusion. "You're welcome to come out once in a while over the next few weeks. But I can't guar-antee I can get back to Seattle to practice too much. I want to. I just don't want to make you a promise I can't keep."

"Oh," she processed, trying to shield him from her disappoint-ment. If he was on Bainbridge, they wouldn't be able to practice, and she wouldn't be able to get better, and there would be no ques-tion that the spot would go to Vance. "Of course. No. Of course." Meg glanced at Jeannie, snuck a look toward Vance, and pressed her lips together. "You do what you have to do."

By now, a few of the Daves, Annie, Jeannie, and Laverne had all squeezed into the narrow space beside Rooster. The eight of them huddled against the school building in the shelter of the slim aw-ning. The pounding rain and the roaring wind formed a wild cur-tain beyond the overhang. Meg unballed the yellow plastic poncho she kept in her bag and struggled to stick her head through the hooded hole. It was uncomfortably steamy inside. She looked like a badly designed pup tent.

From the other end of the rain shelter, Laverne let out a low whistle. "Oh boy. You'll never guess who just posted." She held her phone aloft. "This is from an hour ago."

Finance Guy Dave peered at the screen. "Is that . . ." He blinked rain from his eyelids. "Is that Michael Edmonds?"

"That's him, all right," Jeannie scoffed, and took a closer look at Laverne's phone. "Where the hell is he?"

Laverne passed the phone along the line. To Rooster, to Jeannie, to the Daves, and at last to Annie and Meg, who huddled and gazed at the phone, disbelieving.

"Is that," Meg asked, *"Walla-Walla?"*

In the photo, Michael Edmonds leaned casually against a green handrail. Behind him, the Space Needle, Smith Tower, and the Seahawks' stadium stood out from the downtown skyline. The dark rain clouds that were now taking their toll on Lakeview formed a backdrop to the Emerald City, so named for its preponderance of pine trees. Michael Edmonds's face was lit with sunlight as he posed on the deck of the ferryboat.

The ferry to Bainbridge Island.

Buff Dave zoomed in on the photo and pointed at the item protruding from his backpack. "Well, look at that."

Meg peered at the screen and gulped. Definitely the handle of a pickleball paddle. Everybody knew that Lakeview's rival, Bainbridge Island, was Michael's hometown, and most suspected he still had allegiances to his native league. Shooting an uneasy glance at Annie, Meg said, "He probably brought it with him so he could practice over there."

"Practice! With the competition?" Buff Dave grunted. "Not likely."

Warily, the sopping crew eyed one another, weighing their suspicions. Boring Dave spoke. "You don't think he's really— Do you?"

Jeannie snapped, "Say it, Boring Dave. You know it. I know it. We all know it." Venom flared in Jeannie's eyes. "It's like I said. He's whoring himself out to that Bainbridge league!"

Dress Shirt Dave blew a gasket. "Jeannie. Watch your language. This is a school!"

"How much do you think Bainbridge is paying him to shill for them?" Jeannie goaded. "They want that win, too. Everybody wants a prize like that. They're probably using him to puff up their advanced standings. He's two-timing us. Michael Edmonds has switched teams and left us high and dry."

"Can't a guy just go to Bainbridge?" Dress Shirt Dave asked.

"Oh, stuff it, Dress Shirt," Jeannie countered. "We all know that jerk is trying to beat us the sneaky way. He's headed out there to practice with the enemy and learn the secret to that trick shot. I hear those Islanders know the key to the Golden Pickledrop."

Dress Shirt Dave pursed his lips. "First of all, the Golden Pickledrop. There's no such thing. Hard work, practice, and patience. Those are the only secrets to a good shot. And second, I know Michael Edmonds." He backtracked. "As well as any of us do. And I don't think he's the kind of guy to switch teams."

"I'm sure he's just helping them," Annie insisted. "Coaching. To be nice." Meg worried at her friend's hopeful tone. Annie's personal investment in their pickleball partnership was obvious. "He'd never skip out on me."

"If that's what you wanna tell yourself," Jeannie muttered under her breath but over the rain.

Meg didn't want to believe the image on Laverne's screen or Jeannie's dreaded predictions. Michael wouldn't do that to Annie. Or the team. He wouldn't betray them. Would he? Meg slipped her arm around her friend's shoulder. Frustration percolated beneath the split ends of Meg's blonde ponytail.

Just then, Jeannie's expression shifted to pure glee. "Oh! Look!" She snickered and poked a finger toward the parking lot. "This is gonna be good."

As Meg peeked from beneath the hood of her yellow poncho, her body tensed. On the other side of the lot, Ethan Fine shielded his eyes from the rain and jogged from the construction site toward his truck.

Jeannie was shaking her head in anticipation. "You gotta watch this guy get into his truck!"

In one swift motion, Ethan gripped the door handle and pulled, ready to dive inside and escape the downpour. Meg's heart stuttered a full measure of sixteenth notes, when, with a thundering crack, the door powered open from the built-up pressure.

A torrent of pickleballs poured from Ethan's vehicle.

Ethan jumped back in surprise. The flood cascaded from the driver's seat and tumbled onto the pavement. Jeannie clutched her belly and laughed as the truck continued to vomit fluorescent green pickleballs of an obscene magnitude until, at last, all that was left were the dry heaves. For an encore, four final balls took the opportunity, with a syncopated tick-tack-tickity-tock, to plop from the open car door onto the puddled asphalt below.

"Oh man!" Jeannie whispered. "Look at his face."

Ethan's face was, in fact, stunned by the heaps of pickleballs stuffed into the cab of his truck. From beneath the lip of her yellow slicker, Meg watched as he ducked for a moment into the passenger side and emerged with an empty duffel.

Suddenly, Ethan's head swiveled and, like a searchlight, he scanned the courts. When his gaze hit on the sopping bunch of pickleballers huddled beneath the minuscule overhang, without hesitation, he broke into a vigorous jog.

"Aw, crap," Jeannie said. "This guy has no sense of humor."

Each puddly step resounded with a splash alongside Meg's heartbeat. He was headed straight for them. There was nowhere to hide and nothing to do besides bury her head right here in the sand. But to her dismay, there was no sand beneath, only pavement. She could try it, but she might crack her skull in the effort.

Before long, Ethan Fine's soaked work boots splashed into her line of view. He was standing five feet from her! She dipped her chin toward her neck, causing her yellow poncho to cling to her cheeks.

"Is this your doing?" he asked.

"Do you mean," asked Jeannie, "did a group of unjustly evicted pickleballers shove a shit ton of plastic balls in your car? Or was it, say, the Easter Bunny? Survey says . . ."

Annie's chirpy voice jumped into the fray, doing its best to smooth over the rough edges of Jeannie's sandpaper tongue. "Sorry. It was us. It was us. Well," she clarified, "actually. It wasn't me. I would never. I mean, if you're going to punish someone, please don't take it out on our whole group. Keep in mind that this"—she indicated the steady stream of pickleballs floating their way—"this was an individual act of vigilante rebellion and in no way represents the official sentiment of Lakeview Pickleball."

Before she was premed, Annie was prelaw. Annie was nothing if not extra. Meg loved that about her.

"So let me get this straight," Ethan said. "You are neither taking nor denying responsibility for stuffing a bunch of brand-new pickleballs into my truck."

"Ha!" Jeannie countered before she could stop herself. "You think I'd waste my good balls on you! I stuffed it with my busted balls."

Ethan sighed and stepped out of the wetness into the slim

alcove beneath the overhang. His body was so near to Meg that even with her poncho hood pulled low, she could smell the delicious change in her surroundings.

Just then, Meg caught sight of a lone pickleball rolling toward her feet, pushed like an autumn leaf in the flow of the rainstorm. Bending, she grabbed for the renegade ball, but her fingers made electric contact with another set of fingertips. Their eyes connected.

"Hello, Meg," Ethan said.

"Hi," she squeaked. In her sticky, yellow poncho, it was mortifying to see him.

Ethan's gaze looked from Meg to the faces of the hostile throng, and concern wrinkled his forehead. "Are you with these people?" he asked, as though he were trying to connect the seat belt sexpot to the shrinking woman in the yellow slicker. Seriously, this day really couldn't get any worse.

Her tongue felt fuzzy. She could admit she was one of these pickleballers and be on the receiving end of the blame for Jeannie's pranks. Or, she could pretend she had been kidnapped by a band of pickleball addicts in desperate need of a fourth.

But her efforts to deny any connection to these picklers were in vain. Jeannie, of all people, linked her arm through Meg's. "She's with us. Like it or leave it. Or better yet, just leave."

"And what am I supposed to do with all these pickleballs?"

"Good question. And *good* luck," Jeannie said, sarcasm lengthening her words.

"Where did you get so many, anyway?"

Jeannie shrugged. "Every week, we fill a garbage bag with the balls that bust on the courts. So I was like, well, that sucks. So I started, you know, taking 'em home and making earrings and Christmas ornaments. I stick a pencil through 'em and, you know"—she mimed a spray can—"paint them silver or gold. I do decoupage, snow globes, multimedia collage, the works. You can find them online; look up Deck the Balls. But mostly I just make 'em and give them to friends."

Meg gaped at Jeannie, stunned by this revelation. Jeannie had friends?!

"I mean," Jeannie continued, "otherwise, what happens to the broken balls? Once they're cracked, they just go in the trash. So, I got this idea. *Your* plan to screw up our courts is cracked, too . . ." She gestured rhetorically at his truck. "It's poetic justice, butthead."

"Yes. I see. This has been enlightening," Ethan said, and scooped up the armload of pickleballs that had been swirling in a puddle. He tossed them into his duffel. "I guess the ball is in my court now," Ethan said, pinning Meg with a look that set her off-balance. Then he took off into the downpour, hightailing it to the truck.

Rooster, perceptive as ever, caught Meg's reaction. Reading her crush beneath the awkwardness, he gave her a knowing look. He shifted his gaze to the distance and said to no one in particular, "Whoo-wee. Looks like somebody just got a tug on their fishhook." Darn that Rooster! Was he reading her mind?

Still glaring at Ethan's departing form, Jeannie muttered, "Sheesh. I'd flip that guy the bird, but he'd probably just try to protect it."

Dress Shirt Dave, who had been wordlessly watching the proceedings, now shook his head in disappointment. "I wish you hadn't done that. There are kinder ways to make a point."

"Aw, puh-lease," Jeannie crabbed. "What are you, the polite police?"

"If such a thing existed, I would gladly join them," Dress Shirt retorted.

Noticing Meg's expression, Annie touched the crinkly plastic of Meg's poncho. "You okay? You seem shaken up."

Meg nodded absentmindedly, but her brain was stuck on a treadmill with no emergency stop: *I have a crush on the enemy of my people.* And while the rain poured down like a curtain, she strained to hear what the storm was telling her. The solution came to her, loud and clear.

Escape.

With one brief ferry ride, she could spend a week on Bainbridge, and if she dipped into her savings, maybe two. She could practice with Rooster. She could track down Michael Edmonds. She could escape Vance's encroachment on her territory and still fight for her place on the team. And she could cut off this complicated, cargo-panted fantasy at the root. Because she felt way too vulnerable to be infatuated with public enemy numero uno.

Bainbridge Island. Birthplace of pickleball. A painter's dream. Already, she could picture the blanket of pine trees, the crisp salt air, the majestic backdrop of the Olympic Mountains. Besides, she deserved a vacation.

"I need to get out of here," Meg said. Her eyes slid to Annie—"I mean *really* get out of here"—and they shared an instant understanding that only best friends are capable of.

"Good idea," Annie agreed. "I'll check the ferry schedule."

THE DINK

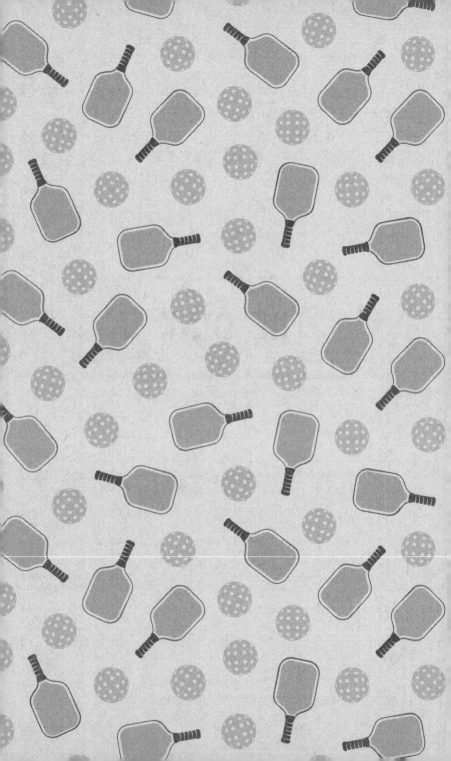

EIGHT

Meg counted cars. Seven cars in front of hers. Now six. Five. Almost on. Four cars ahead of her. Two. A woman in an orange vest squeezed on a single car, then waved one more forward. She felt that familiar clench in her nerves. Meg rolled her window down, brimming with cautious optimism. She smiled with what she hoped was polite but not too kiss-assy good cheer, but it made no difference, because the no-nonsense ferry worker placed her palm in the air to stop Meg's approach.

"Full," she explained when Meg opened her mouth to protest. "You'll be the first on the next one."

Meg huffed, impatient in her desire to get the heck out of Seattle. Sure, she was running away, but as she saw it, an adventure on Bainbridge could be just the jump start she needed to move forward. So, ninety minutes later, when she was finally waved onto the ferry, she pressed on the gas a little too hard, garnering a steely glare from the dock lady.

Rolling onto the metal ramp, Meg drove to the front position on the open car deck. She stepped out of the car and took a deep, fulfilling lungful of the diesel-infused salt air. Despite the wait, it was always a victory to make it onto a ferry on a summer weekend morning, especially considering so many folks took advantage of the Fourth of July to take a couple of extra days off. This was Bainbridge's prime time.

Being the first driver on had its perks. She pulled right to the front of the boat. Framed like a movie screen by the ferry's walls, Puget Sound's open water spread out before her like a perfect picture. She was on the ferry, on the way to a fresh start, and she could not help but feel that she had escaped Seattle just in time.

Of course, fleeing was in both Meg's nature and nurture. The Bloomberg family were experts at bailing out when turbulence overtook the plane. Ned Bloomberg, Meg's father, did not plan his escape. Nevertheless, when the irony of living the life of a non-smoking health nut who developed lung cancer got to be too much for him, his brain called it quits and his body followed. After he deserted this world, Meg's mom, Dina, departed. Not to Resting Hills, but far away from the daily reminders of his missing presence. Dina quit her molecular research job and disappeared to Bribri, Costa Rica, on the pretense of learning about medicinal plants from the indigenous villagers.

It had been three years since Ned's death and Dina's spontaneous departure. Mrs. Bloomberg did not return, and when Meg called her to commiserate about the end of the Vance era, her mother, as expected, was not in range to receive her call. Dina only rode her motorcycle into the nearest town with service to call Meg on her birthday or when she had a hankering for pizza.

Fleeing Seattle and its downpour of awkward situations seemed like the logical, self-care choice. The only thing missing from Meg's perfect escape plan was her best friend.

"I'll keep trying," Annie had promised on the phone last night. "But it's so last-minute with the holiday weekend. And nobody wants the night shift."

Meg wished Annie weren't so darned responsible.

"Just don't show up."

"Uh-huh. Maybe I can leave the kids a note. 'Take your meds, and if anything goes wrong, here's a scalpel.'"

"Sarcasm corrodes relationships."

"I was the one who told you that and now you're using it against me." Meg could hear a muffled page in the background. "*Dr. Yoon. Dr. Yoon to 204 . . .*"

"You should go," Annie urged. "Take a week for yourself. Think of all the weeks and months you spent putting your energies into supporting Vance's practice. You get to do something for *you* now. Get yourself over there. And remember, don't worry about the money." Meg's heart squeezed with relief. The inheritance Meg had received from her dad had given her enough buffer to kick the cat collars to the curb, at least for a little while. And last night, as a gift to celebrate Meg's new beginnings, Annie had offered to pitch in generously for Meg's hotel room on the island so she wouldn't have to dip into her savings. She could take time out for herself. She'd feel guilty if she didn't feel so grateful.

"Besides," Annie continued, "Bainbridge is full of trees and beaches and mountains and nature, and you love nature. Get yourself some space away from your ex and from that Ethan jerk. Those assholes." Meg could picture Annie shielding her mouth to whisper the last word.

"I just wish you could come with me."

"Text me when you get there," Annie insisted. "And I want to see pictures of you playing on those courts where pickleball started. And if you see Michael Edmonds, tell him . . ." Her sigh was so profound the phone vibrated. "Tell him to call me. I'll join you as soon as I can—if I can."

Brushing off her disappointment, Meg looked for the positives. She had made it onto the ferry, her room was paid for, she had found a way to continue practicing with Rooster, and she was taking an active step away from the court-closing tension and the confusing mixed feelings she harbored for Ethan. Annie was right. It was time to put herself first.

As cars continued to fill in the parking lanes, pulling bumper to bumper with scant space for her to walk between, Meg squeezed along the narrow walkways, spying through the windshields and imagining the purpose of each traveler's journey. A man and woman drinking Starbucks and dressed in "Northwest casual" could be returning home to Bainbridge. The pair, she was certain, would remain unspeaking in their car for the length of the thirty-five-minute crossing. Not so for the load of college students who poured out of a Volvo, their hiking gear and bikes piled on top and behind the car like a parade float.

She snapped a classic selfie in front of the shrinking Seattle skyline—the same one Michael Edmonds must have shot on his way to coach his old friends or switch allegiances. Meg meandered to the railing on the side of the boat. Overhead, blue skies prevailed, but the white fog of a marine layer clung to the horizon. By and by, she could make out Mount Rainier, poking its still-snowy crown above the clouds.

This time when she pushed her way inside the main cabin, she found a spot near the rear where the space felt quieter; families engaged in conversations, and passengers reading, or scrolling on their phones. She settled herself in a booth across from a sleeping tourist, jacket pulled over her head. Meg took off her bulky windbreaker and suppressed a shiver. The air felt too chilly for her T-shirt and jean shorts. Reason and good sense had no place when packing in last-minute-vacation mode.

Her gaze drifted toward the café, where the scent of chowder and coffee wafted lazily into the main cabin. She caught herself looking for Ethan there, with his manicured fingernails and worn T-shirt. Blinking the image away, she combed her fingers through her hair and chastised herself, embarrassed by her desire to glimpse one of the very reasons she was fleeing.

She felt a sting of loneliness. Without Annie here, this trip wouldn't be the same. She tried to mollify herself with a reminder of what awaited her: the fresh air, Puget Sound, and pickleball. And painting; with high hopes for inspiration, she had packed her travel oils in her backpack. Where better to be creatively motivated if not by the natural wonders of the Olympic Peninsula?

"*Now arriving, Bainbridge Island,*" announced the voice from the loudspeakers. "*Drivers, please return to your vehicles.*"

Collecting herself, Meg slipped on her coat. Before departing the table, she took another glance at the sleeping figure across the booth. The nice thing to do would be to wake her now that the boat was arriving.

"Excuse me. Miss?" Meg said. "We're here."

The jacket slipped from the woman's head as she sat up. "God, I needed that nap," she said.

"Annie!" Meg stuttered, her hand lifting to her mouth. "You're here!" she exclaimed.

"I found coverage, baby. My first vacation in a year."

Meg flung herself at her friend and crushed her into a bear hug. She marveled at how put-together Annie remained for someone who had been sleeping on a ferry. Her capri pants and white cotton blouse might have been recently ironed. Meg wouldn't put it past her.

She tugged her by the elbow and, together, they skipped down the stairwell. All the while, Meg laughed, disbelieving. Annie's sudden appearance had kick-started Meg's energy.

They ducked into the little blue hatchback that waited like a good dog at the front of the deck. When the dock assistant removed the block that prevented the car from rolling right off the ferry into the Sound, Meg's jaw twitched. Did that ever happen? Meg released the parking brake while her brain tried to tamp down a daydream featuring her car, with her and Annie in it, taking a flying plunge.

"You doing okay?" Annie asked. "You look a little pale."

"I'm fine." Meg smiled weakly. Her past had crumbled, and the only certainty in her future was an island hotel reservation. And who knew with reservations?

But here was Annie. She turned to her friend. "I'm really glad you came."

"You didn't think I'd let you go through this all by yourself, did you?"

Meg nodded her gratitude, a swell of emotion lodging in her throat. She blinked to cover the sting in her eyes. As Annie settled into the passenger seat, Meg joked, "Don't worry. I had that seat belt fixed."

And Meg drove off the ferry, no longer alone.

NINE

"Is it okay if I unpack into the top drawers of the dresser?" Annie asked, although she was already refolding her vacuum-packed underwear. "I like to settle in, even if it's only a few days."

Meg eyed her, amused as Annie hung up her T-shirts and clipped her shorts to the pants hangers. Even when they were in college, when they were bumbling from hostel to hostel on road trips, they had traveled this way: Meg's backpack bursting with un-folded, flowing pants printed with elephants or sea turtles; Annie's socks and underwear partitioned into separate Ziploc bags. Now, bundling the contents of her backpack into her arms, Meg dumped them into the bottom drawer.

"I can't wait to lie down." Annie flounced onto one of the downy mattresses. "Oh. This is heaven. Let's hold off on playing pickleball till tomorrow. I think I'll go to bed early." Her eyes flagged, then snapped open. "Or maybe I better get a bite to eat. Or sleep. No. Eat first. Very conflicted."

Meg laughed. On the drive from the ferry, Annie had talked wistfully about sleep, as if it were as elusive as the Golden Pickle-drop.

Food first, they decided, and trudged down the narrow stairwell into the quaint café on the bottom floor of the Outlook Inn.

Perched on a low hill overlooking the sunset on Pleasant Beach, the inn held a privileged seat. As she sank into the cushy chair, Meg felt her shoulders drop and her city-tension melt. Now, this was relaxing.

"Wow," Annie said. She wasn't looking at the view. She was gazing at the newspaper articles and documents pressed below the dining table glass.

They were historical artifacts, articles and photos dated from the 1940s. *Roosevelt to Announce Executive Order to Remove Japanese Americans from Pacific Coast.* A notice stated *Instructions to All Persons of Japanese Ancestry,* while another headline declared *Sad Farewell While Troops Stand By.* In a photo beside one of the articles, a mother and her teenage daughter clutched each other. To Meg, they looked like any mother-daughter pair, set off on a shopping expedition or headed to school. Except that identification tags hung from these women's coat collars, as if they were the items at a shop to be cataloged.

Annie tapped on the table glass and pointed out a photo of a woman dressed in several layers of coats and carrying a toddler. "I've seen this picture before. It's from the time of the Japanese exclusion order during World War Two. They evacuated the residents here and sent them to concentration camps. Even though my family is Korean, my grandma talked about how tough it was to be Asian here during the war. The Japanese and anyone with Asian features, really—everyone was perceived as the enemy. But the community on Bainbridge—they were the first to get sent to the internment camps." Annie traced the line of the toddler's cheek. "She's so cute. That must have been scary. If I were that mom I'd be freaking out."

"Can I get you ladies a coffee or a glass of wine?" Jolting at the voice, Meg looked up to see a straight-postured, slender Asian woman in her sixties peering at them over her reading glasses.

"Water, thanks. A pitcher, please," Meg said. "And a club sandwich."

Annie perused the specials chalkboard. "I'll take a lemonade. With mint if you have it. And the onion rings. And the burger. No. Wings. Actually, the burger would be great. Mustard on the side, please. And instead of fries could I have a . . . No, forget it. Fries are fine."

The woman smiled, wrote down the order, and tucked the pad into her crisp apron before marching back to the kitchen. Her confident bearing gave Meg the impression that she owned the inn.

While they waited, Annie and Meg continued to peruse the photos beneath the table glass, both absorbed in their own thoughts. But their food arrived quickly, and Annie dove in. Meg observed with wonder as Annie ate twice her body mass in onion batter.

Sensing Meg's eyes on her, Annie smiled between bites. "I miss hanging out with you like this," she said.

It hit Meg then. How much she missed grabbing a quick bite or being each other's Saturday night. The years with Vance had eclipsed her other relationships, and it occurred to her that she liked who she was when she was around Annie. More relaxed. More fun. More . . . herself. She missed that girl: the old Meg.

"I miss you, too. It's good to sit and talk," Meg said.

Annie squeezed the ketchup bottle with two hands. "And eat."

"You deserve a break, that's for sure. How's work been going?"

Annie groaned. "This week was crazy. I had a kid who put a magnet up his nostril, and then put a second one up the other nostril to see if he could drag it down. Not a bad idea, actually. Good problem-solving instincts."

She downed an enormous bite of the burger, a feat that might have choked a less determined person. "So good!" she said. "Help me eat these onion rings, will you? What else? Oh! I can't believe I forgot to tell you about this. This woman came in with her kid; she didn't want me to treat him. She only wanted to show me that his diaper rash looked exactly like Bob Ross." She swirled her fry around in the ketchup. "She wasn't wrong."

Meg laughed. It felt so good. She couldn't think of the last time she had laughed aloud—at least outside the pickleball court. Annie let out a giggle of her own and then it slipped into a frown. "I gotta say, though. All this trying to find balance is exhausting. I work my ass off so I can be the best at my job, and then I work my ass off on the courts so I can beat everybody. Pretty soon I'll be left with no ass at all, and my pants will slide right off."

Meg's lips lifted and she nodded, but truthfully, it was hard to relate. Meg had not thrown herself into a pursuit for . . . she didn't know how long. After months of moderate effort, she was still a beginning pickleball player. After two years, her tepid marriage had failed. If she had to level with herself right here, right now, she worried she might always linger in the levels of domestic and athletic mediocrity.

"What about you?" Annie asked. "What's making Meg happy these days?"

"What makes Meg happy?" she repeated slowly, buying time. Unbidden, an image of Ethan popped into her head. Now, what was she supposed to do about that? "I guess I'm just trying to get through this, one day at a time." She scrunched her face into a facsimile of not caring and picked at the label on the ketchup bottle.

Sliding the collection of condiments out of the way, Annie reached across the table to squeeze her friend's arm. "Maybe it's time to get onto one of those dating sites and put yourself into the mix again."

"Says the woman who hasn't dated since prom." Meg dipped an onion ring into the lake of ketchup on Annie's plate.

"Touché," she countered, but her wistful expression reminded Meg that Annie had come all the way to Bainbridge not only to help Meg through a tough time, but also in pursuit of the mysterious Michael Edmonds.

Annie added, "At least you sidestepped falling into another rough relationship. I can't believe that ferry guy turned out to be the one closing down the courts."

Meg sighed into her lap. "Why do I always pick the wrong guy?"

"You just need to learn to not not pick the right guy."

"You lost me at the second 'not.'"

Yet her friend's mention of Ethan wormed its way into Meg's thoughts. Although she knew he was staying in Seattle to oversee his court-wrecking initiative, he had told her that his home was on Bainbridge. Could he be here now? Discreetly, Meg scanned the beach out the picture window. What did she expect? For him to appear like an apparition on the pebbly shoreline? And why was she so drawn to flirting with the enemy? She'd come here to get away from that confusion.

No. She could only control what she could control, and right now, Meg wanted to focus on Meg Bloomberg. If only she could take this mini vacay as an opportunity to spark her own passions, then maybe she would be in a place where she could consider dating again.

But first, she needed to break out of her habit of lukewarm ef-forts. The one thing she was good at, the one area in which she excelled, was painting, but to date, all that her art background had gotten her was a stack of canvases in her closet and a small follow-ing of people who were a little over-the-top about their cats. To-morrow, she decided, she would toss herself into her painting and pickleball with passion. Tomorrow, she intended to step it up.

• • • • •

Meg muffled a yelp of pain as her toe drove into the bedstead. The digital clock read 5:40 but the blackout curtains blocked the break-ing daylight. She trapped the cell phone flashlight between her chin and her chest while her hands riffled through her drawer for her painting kit. Lifting it into the dim light, she unrolled the travel bundle. Her fingertips skimmed one of her paintbrushes and she held it aloft. She weighed the perfect balance of the stem and flicked the soft horsehair bristles along the inside of her palm. It was the journey, not the product that drove Meg's passion for painting; the tactile act of creating something from nothing. The fresh opportu-nity of dipping into a spot of paint, blending it on her palette, and watching something unique appear. She dug out the travel kit of oil paints, the wooden palette, her dab rag, and . . .

Wait a sec. Canvas. Did she forget the canvases?

Another minute of sifting followed, but no luck. There was an art store in Winslow, but that wouldn't be open for hours. Stumped, she shone her flashlight around the room, as if stretched canvases might be included in the room rate along with the fresh towels.

But no. She would have to punt. There was probably some sur-face she could paint on, down in the reception area: the back of a place mat, a cardboard drink coaster. The world, as Meg saw it, was full of empty canvases. Packing her brushes back into the travel kit, she hustled down to the hotel café.

As expected, Meg found the room deserted of people at this early hour. A weak glow of dust-filled morning light filtered through the broad window. She seated herself at a booth, the same one with the photos beneath the glass, and stared out the window at the bay. The shape of the landscape was barely visible beneath the breaking dawn, but Meg could make out the thin layer of fog that floated over the still water and crept up the legs of the pier and toward the pebbled beach.

There were napkins on the sidebar, and she spread one beneath a cardboard coaster. The front of the coaster was decorated with a stylized art deco image of the Outlook Inn. The backside was conveniently blank. Squeezing shades of greens, browns, and blues onto her color-spattered travel palette, Meg set up a Northwest landscape assortment of hues. Painting in miniature was a challenge to begin with, and the dim lighting didn't help, either.

As if she had conjured them, the lights blinked on in the room. Her head spun to find the same stately woman who had served their lunchtime feast. Meg squinted in the fresh light. "I hope it's okay if I'm down here."

"Make yourself at home. We don't serve breakfast until eight. Vacation hours. But you're welcome to sit." The woman disappeared into the kitchen.

Meg's fingers dabbed the brush into the light green and blended it with a smidge of brown. She laid down a light background coat, right down to her horizon line. She blended the paint below the line, adding cobalt and coal gray to darken the shade as she moved toward the foreground, where her details grew darker and more refined. The porous cardboard coaster absorbed more of the oils than her canvases, but it was an interesting effect, one that gave some texture to her background.

Without much mental input, Meg's hand began to fill the stippled shoreline, the flat strokes that made up Pleasant Beach, blocky gray rocks, and swipe-stroked evergreens. Even her thinnest brush made painting the pier pylons tricky on her tiny canvas. The result was pretty, although tame. Realistic landscapes were a staple of her early work, and although it was technically a strong piece, Meg scolded herself. The view from the window. That was comfort-zone stuff. A warm-up. Her better self would create from the heart. Stretch. Embrace the challenge.

Clanging sounds poured from the hotel kitchen. An unmistakable, earthy scent tingled her nose. Coffee. That was usually a good first step to stimulating the creative process. Meg treaded to the kitchen and rapped gently on the doorframe. "Sorry. I know you're not open yet, but would it be possible to grab a cup of coffee?"

"Of course. Come on in. I'm Mayumi." The woman stretched out a hand. "Are you enjoying your stay?" she asked with the comfortable air of ownership.

"It's beautiful here," Meg said, reaching out for the handshake and introducing herself. "Look, I don't want to be a pain," she added, "but could I order a pastry or something?"

"Actually." Mayumi waved Meg toward an industrial-sized stainless steel fridge. "Our cook doesn't get here for another hour. But I was just thinking I was getting hungry, too." Yanking the door open, Mayumi perused the offerings. Over the proprietor's shoulder, Meg noticed several plastic containers labeled with the same Japanese characters.

Mayumi jiggled one of the containers and said, "We can eat this."

"That writing. What does it say?" Meg asked, pointing to the taped label.

"Everything on this shelf is labeled *Mom. Me!*" Mayumi confided. "I have two teenage sons. It's like living with grazing locusts. If I didn't save something for myself, I'd never eat."

She pulled two small plates and a couple of souvenir Bainbridge mugs from a cabinet and set them up on the counter. "Peanut butter and jelly," Mayumi said, placing a sandwich on each plate. "The world's most perfect snack, in my opinion. But not something I've ever had the guts to put on our tourist menu."

When they carried their food into the dining room, Mayumi caught sight of the painted coaster. She said nothing, and for a moment, Meg worried that the hotel owner was upset that she had used the table as an art workspace, but Mayumi sat at the next table and waved Meg into the seat across from her. They munched on the sandwiches, and all the while Mayumi stole glances at Meg's coaster landscape. When her self-consciousness finally got to her, Meg said, "I forgot to bring my canvases. I hope you don't mind; I was super careful about protecting the tables . . ."

"Not at all."

"This sandwich is delicious."

"Glad you like it. The jam is from last year, but it's nearly blackberry season and I have my jars ready."

Meg smirked. Blackberries. Loved the taste, hated the prickers. The invasive spread of Himalayan blackberries in the Northwest had become a much-debated local blessing/curse. The loathers vehemently argued the need to poison them into extinction, and the lovers treasured the tasty opportunities. It was clear which side Mayumi fell on.

"I like the stylized quality of your painting." Setting her coffee on the glass surface, Mayumi tapped at a newspaper article beneath. "If you're looking for surface area, you could paint these tables. I'd pay you, of course."

Meg glimpsed the images and articles beneath the glass. "I wouldn't want you to have to move these photos."

"Yes. They are important reminders," Mayumi sighed. "But it's not easy to see them every day."

"You could make an album . . ."

"I suppose." Suddenly, Mayumi straightened. "Listen. I've got a better idea than painting these tables." Her eyes twinkled. "What would you think about painting a fence?"

A fence? Was this a joke?

"You'll know what I mean when you see it," Mayumi pressed. "Coasters are small. Your work needs a broad platform."

Meg's lips began the slow climb. She recognized the gimmick from *The Adventures of Tom Sawyer*: the part where Tom managed to get another kid to do his chores for him. Whitewashing a fence was not an obligation, Tom explained, but a privilege.

On the other hand, Meg *had* left her canvases at home. Was she really planning on dabbling in coasters for the duration of the vacation? Besides, painting was like pizza or sex. A painting project of any sort was better than no painting project at all.

"Just take a look," Mayumi suggested, waving Meg toward the door. "I'll make you a trade. Free room and board. As long as you need to finish it."

Now *that* intrigued her. She wouldn't have to rely on Annie's generosity. Meg would love to be the one to cover their hotel bill. And she could earn a swankier, longer vacation. Besides, a fence did create opportunities for incorporating the outdoors into her vision. In fact, she reasoned, this could be her shot to imagine something unique. Something notable. Shouldering her tote, Meg followed Mayumi outside.

The fence divided the property between the inn and the beach, a classic picket with a swinging gate at the center of the pathway. From inside the enclosure, Meg squinted at it. Through the slats, she glimpsed a family with small children. The kids tossed rocks into the water until their mother pulled them back from the quiet shoreline. In a few hours, the beach would be busy with strolling tourists and picnicking families.

Tilting her head, she checked out the fence at an angle. A hint of an idea formed. The interesting thing about a fence was this: Some were designed to keep people out. Others to keep people in. Maybe she should take away the gate so that the enclosure would lose its function. She could concentrate on the slats as a canvas. That was the beauty of art. Removing the element of practicality was part of the challenge.

The other interesting thing about a picket fence—now Meg's mind was really rolling—was that it alternated between positive and negative space. Meg could take advantage of the missing pieces by implying something that was lost, or incomplete. On the other hand, she could focus on the positives, and let the viewer fill in the gaps.

Meg trailed a finger along the point of a picket. When she lifted her eyes, Mayumi was smiling at her. The more Meg thought about this unlikely canvas, the more intrigued she grew. Her mind made up, she gave a sharp, decisive nod.

"Excellent," Mayumi said. "Paint is in the shed, and you can have an open budget if you need more. I know how to snatch up talent when I see it. Take all the time you need."

Traipsing over to the shed, Meg slid open the door and found a large can of light blue exterior paint. She picked out a thick, nylon-haired brush, ideal for laying down a base coat. The paints were crusty, but once she figured out where she would go with this project, she could pick up more suitable supplies in Winslow.

By the time she lugged the supplies to the fence, the bay reflected a hazy pink in the brightening morning light. Stirring the paint with a stick, she whisked the separated liquids and wiped the excess from the side of the can. Without thinking, she put brush to wood and dragged it up along the grain. She pulled the paint down and then did it again. And again, on another picket. Three pickets. A sudden tightening in her throat gave her pause.

What was she doing? Improvising was one thing when painting for pleasure, but for this project, she needed a plan.

She plunked down on the grass, right where she was, stared at the three grayish-blue slats, and channeled the painter Salvador Dalí. The surrealist claimed that he would stare sometimes for hours or days at a canvas until a painting appeared to him. That, and ask his wife to stand bare-buttocked before him until he had an epiphany. Meg surveyed the beach and turned her head back toward the inn. There were no buttocks to be found, so alas, no inspiration.

She painted a fourth and a fifth board. No. It was no use. She should have a plan. Painting without an endgame was irresponsible and reckless. Cats marrying dogs. Balloons and barbed wire. Meg stared some more at the fence.

"Meg?"

Meg started. For an instant, she thought she had imagined that voice. Her parents, her old friends, and of course Annie had said her name with that same lilting clarity that indicated they were authentically happy to see her. Her name sounded just like that, but better. Like honey on the tongue.

From her patch of the grass, she did not have a clear view through the slats, so she rose onto her knees and peered over the top of the fence. Her heartbeat did a double cartwheel back handspring.

Ethan!

Bolting to her feet, Meg rose. Blood rushed from her head, and she threw her arms to the sides to steady her stance. "Whoa!"

"Didn't mean to startle you," he said, laying his hand on his salmon-toned cotton dress shirt.

His relaxed manner contrasted her inner freak-out. He looked different from the last time she'd seen him, no longer the rugged, hard-hatted Stud-in-Boots from the construction site. Now, with his quirky grin and that fresh color against his sandalwood skin, he gave off an effortless air of sexy-hip-sophisticated-casual. "We ought to stop running into each other like this," he said.

What in the world was going on with her tongue? It had transformed into a sea sponge and swollen to twice its usual size. And what was with her eyeballs? They widened, performing a perfect impression of a surprised goldfish.

"I didn't know you worked with Mayumi," he continued, with what Meg noted was valiant effort. Of its own volition, Meg's head bobbed up and down. He said, "We go way back. We worked together on shoreline preservation when she expanded the inn."

She clipped the jumper cables to her mental battery and opened her mouth. She really needed to participate if it was to be a dialogue. Right now.

"I'm painting the fence." What was up with her sparkling conversation starters?

"I see that. Excellent coverage. Just the right size brush. Good decisions on the coat thickness," he said, standing there in his dapper duds and backed by the wild Sound. What a contrast to the Ethan of a few days ago—the man who had stood in the pouring down rain, threatening the very life of their courts. This upmarket Ethan was so out of context. And why was he staring at her? Ah. Because this was a dialogue. It was her turn now.

"You . . . live on the island, right?" Good job. It may have been stating the obvious, but at least she'd managed to ask a sensible question. She'd even remembered that she was surrounded by water. Baby steps.

"Part of the time. I'm usually working on more than one project at a time. So, if I've got a job on the mainland, once I get it going, my crew can get a lot done without me." At the mention of his mainland job, they pitched into an abyss of awkwardness. Meg, finding no portable toilet or other suitable hiding space, dropped her gaze to the ground. The silence between them began to stretch like a rubber band wearing thin. At last, the elastic snapped, and their words tumbled out on top of one another.

"I'm sorry about your courts—"

"I'm sorry about the balls—"

"What?" they both asked.

He jumped in quicker. "I'm really sorry that the restoration is affecting your courts. I wanted to say something the other day, but I didn't get the chance. I know how important the courts are to your group."

"No. It was wrong, what happened . . . with your construction plans and the . . . toilet," she said. "And with Jeannie's balls. That was low."

One of his brows dipped. "Low-hanging balls?"

She couldn't help the laugh that came out as a snort. The left side of his lip hitched upward, like he thought her snort was cute and not disgusting. Which further pushed her toward the conclusion that, despite garnering her entire team's loathing, *he* was cute and not disgusting. She was relieved, at least, to run into him again in neutral territory. Here, the war over the courts was a distant skirmish on somebody else's land.

"No apology necessary," he said. "That truck prank—that was funny. Driving home was like being in one of those ball pits they used to have at the fast-food places before they realized kids were pooping in them."

Meg grimaced. "Kids were pooping in them?!"

"Well, maybe. Or that might have been an urban legend." How could a person be talking about poo and still be so attractive?

"I don't know if you've noticed," he continued, "but those school courts sit up against the marshland. I've seen all kinds of wildlife nearby. Northern shovelers, pied-billed grebes. I once saw a green heron right near there."

"For a guy in construction, you know a lot about the wetlands." It occurred to her that she knew nearly nothing about him. On the afternoon of their seat belt snafu, the "getting to know you" portion of the day had quickly turned into "getting to grope you."

"I'm not in construction," he said. "I'm an environmental consultant. I partner with companies to negotiate broad-range solutions on environmental concerns. My work usually involves helping businesses ascertain the impact of development and construction. But right now, the school district hired me to—"

He stopped suddenly. "God, I sound like an asshole. I help people make their businesses more environmentally friendly. That's what I do."

Meg smiled at his self-effacing honesty. The idea that he felt nervous talking to her, too, put her more at ease.

He continued, "I don't know if you could tell, but that answer was rehearsed. My elevator pitch. You know. Something brief you could say in an elevator between floors if someone asked you what you do for a living. It sounded pretty good at the time. But I think it works best if you're in an actual elevator. Captive audience," he said, shrugging.

She considered him. Maybe it was the thrill of being the central focus of a nice-looking guy, or perhaps it was the paint fumes, but his side of the story was making more and more sense. It *would* be cool to see eagles and herons so near to the city. Being surrounded by nature was like being around a beautiful work of art. It awoke something central to her spirit, Meg thought as she ogled the bronze skin of his collarbone. But before her lust had the chance to entirely take over the controls, thankfully, he pointed at the paint can and said, "So. You're a handy person?"

She had forgotten she was still holding the brush. A glob of sky blue paint pooled between the brush handle and her clutching fingers.

"Handy? Definitely not. I am actually kind of unhandy. I am"— she hesitated—"an artist." For years, a part of her had felt like a fraud, claiming to be an artist when she made her living crafting. But now that it was out of her mouth, now that she had put the descriptor into the universe, she felt committed. After all, the fence was a real art project. She was an artist. It felt good to say so.

"Cool," he said, nodding at her from the other side of the fence. "So, is this going to be a mural? What will you paint?"

Now, that was a good question. "TBD," she said. "I'm planning to stare at the fence until an idea pops into my head."

"The Dalí technique, huh?" Her heart might have leapt right at him then if not for her rib cage.

Ethan's phone dinged. He pulled it from his pocket and checked a text. "Hmm. My meeting just got postponed till this afternoon. Feel free to say no, but do you want some help painting?"

Meg tamped down the urge to spring up and down with glee. "Sure. I think there's another brush in the shed, but"—she ran her eyes over that swanky shirt—"I don't know if you're really dressed for—" She gestured, feigning noncommittal. *Take off the shirt. Take off the shirt. Take off the shirt*, her brain pled while her face worked overtime to remain neutrally uninvested.

"It's a warm day. I can take my shirt off."

That steamy afternoon in her hatchback, Meg's fingers had explored the sculpted angles of his chest, but to see Ethan unshirted in the golden sunlight, now, that would be a salivating-worthy treat. He undid the top button and bunched the hem. Meg's inner soundtrack played a synthesized backbeat when first, his taut, tanned abdomen appeared. His khaki pants hung low on his pelvis. Above his belt buckle, Meg caught a glimpse of the curve of his hip bone and noted the sexy trail of dark hair beneath his belly button. She let her eyes linger on his chiseled torso while she had the advantage; he was momentarily blindfolded by his own shirt as he slid it over his head.

"I'll get a brush." He jogged toward the shed. Meg gaped after him with a new appreciation of Dalí's buttocks-inspiration method.

She poured out a splash of the paint into a pan for him, and when he returned, he sat cross-legged near the gate.

"Go with the grain," she offered, which was obvious, but gave her something to say. She was much more nervous with him seated shirtless, paces away, than she had been making out with him in her hatchback. Her mind was spinning now, and she worried—what would Annie say if she saw Meg playing arts and crafts with Lakeview's tormentor?

Meg painted in silence for several minutes, but the movement of the brush in her hand and the easy mindlessness of the task made Ethan's nearness all the more apparent. One picket at a time, each on their own side of the fence, they moved closer and closer to each other.

She could do this. She could even make conversation. Like a grown-up. "So, did you grow up on Bainbridge?"

"Yep. Bainbridge born and bred."

"Do your parents live nearby, then?"

Ethan's breath hitched. "Yes"—and he tipped his head to qualify his answer—"and no. My mom still lives here. My dad's . . . out of the picture."

Dammit. She had stepped in it. Not even ten paces into the pasture. "Sorry. I . . ."

"No. Don't be." Shifting the focus off himself, he asked, "Do your folks live near you in Seattle?"

Meg wished she had never started this line of questioning. "I lost my dad a couple of years ago. Cancer. It was terrible. But . . ." Steamrolling past that oversharing moment, she continued before she could get tangled up in a condolence-o-rama. "My mom is still around." She paused. "Well. Sort of. She moved to live in a village near Bribri, Costa Rica. I don't talk to her much." This was going horribly. "We're not fighting or anything like that. It's the cell coverage. It's like miles outside of the nearest . . . This is too much information. I am going to stop now."

Holding his paintbrush in his lap, he turned toward her. His gaze rested on her face, calm and unflinching, as he absorbed her words without judgment. Instantly, her skin warmed under his full attentions. Her eyes flicked to the ground.

After a moment, he said, "Looks like we got a base coat on a good part of this fence." His voice was light, and she was grateful for the change of subject. When she looked up, he was still watching her. "How long will you be staying on Bainbridge?"

"I guess I plan to stay until I finish this commission," she said, only now realizing that completing the fence would take some time. That meant more opportunities to take advantage of Bainbridge's state-of-the-art pickleball courts. And, a hopeful tingle in the back of her brain suggested, maybe time away from the scrutiny of the Lakeview league to get to know the real Ethan. It was a serendipitous trifecta. A win-win-win.

By now, Ethan, that inner-conflict-inducing dreamboat, had maneuvered tantalizingly close. He was so near that she could make out the shape of his lips. They looked soft, like plump slugs, only much nicer.

Meg swept her brush up the rough exterior. Ethan's brush descended, tracing the grain. Their brushes moved in tandem, grazing up and down the pickets, matching each other's pace. She could feel, with the slightest nudge of her imagination, the sensation of his fingers dancing up her body. Up. And down. Her breathing matched his; they responded to each other instinctively as their brushes dripped with paint. Meg sighed, feeling quite physically the effect of his nimble fingers applying the perfect pressure. Their eyes met.

"Meg!" Her head whipped around to find Annie standing on the elevated porch. Her friend's expression was glazed with confusion. "Is that . . . Are you painting the hotel fence?"

Meg leapt to her feet, blocking Ethan from view, and looked at the fence as though it had manifested itself from thin air. "Yes. Yes, I am."

Squinting her suspicion at Meg's awkwardness, Annie muttered, "We're still playing later, right?" Annie shifted to get a better peek at the figure sitting beside the fence.

"Yes." Meg moved a foot to the left for better blockage. "That's right. Playing later."

"Who is that?"

Meg shrugged and wiggled her hands, going for confusion. "I'm painting this fence right now. So . . ." Annie did not budge. "I'll see you inside. Later."

"'Kay . . ." Annie replied, drawing the letter out. "See you later, then." She shook her head, bewildered, and disappeared back inside the hotel.

Phew! Annie was none the wiser about the unpopular target of Meg's infatuation. When she turned back around, she noticed Ethan observing her expectantly. "My friend is here with me," Meg explained. "Not *with* me. Just *with* me." She hoped the emphasis was clear. She didn't want him to think she was unavailable. She was wide-open. That was the message she intended to send.

The spell broken, Ethan wiped the brush dry on a picket. He stood, stretched, and tugged on his shirt. The sight was not nearly as appealing as the reverse process. "I'll leave you to it."

And because she wanted to detain him a moment longer, she blurted, "Come back anytime."

A second passed in which Meg waited for an hour. "I'd enjoy that," he said at last. Ethan made to leave, but then turned his beautiful head back to her. "I just had this thought—there's this place near here that I think you'd like. Can I take you on a drive? If you're not too busy."

With an air of calm, she shrugged and said, "Yeah. Why not?" but her insides were throwing an unsupervised house party.

"I'd say let's take your car"—he grinned—"but you know where that would lead." Was it possible to be embarrassed and thrilled at the same time? It was.

Popping open the door of his truck, he gestured for her to hop in. A little volcano of giddiness burbled inside her as they pulled out of the hotel drive. Checking over her shoulder for Annie, she figured she would come clean later.

But first, she hoped to get a little dirty.

TEN

Ethan shifted his truck into reverse and pulled onto the country road. A dark curtain of trees arched over the right side of the road and balanced the bright morning sun, which twinkled on the bay. Wind in her hair and sun on her face, Meg hung her head out the open window. It felt amazing to be riding along a deserted road and she smiled to herself, remembering the last time she was in a car with Ethan. Every nerve ending stirred with anticipation. His fingers, and those nails, were only inches away from her thigh. When Vance left, she had worried she would never feel the pleasant tingle of infatuation again. But here she was, tingling.

She gaped at the sea of pines. Along the winding shoreline, western hemlock and Douglas firs towered overhead and she stretched her neck to peer at the top of a particular Goliath. "Do you see that one? Gosh. It's huge."

"That's what she said," they said in unison. He turned to give her a wry grin.

Ethan spoke over the sound of the wind. "Did you know you can do a Bainbridge tree tour?"

"I did not know that."

"If you look to the left once we go past this turn"—he pointed toward Eagle Harbor—"you'll see a seven-stemmed red cedar. It's a historic tree. It's right by the dock where Bainbridge's Japanese Americans were forced off the island to detention camps during the war. That's where we're headed."

Meg recalled the photos of the evacuation under the table glass at the Outlook Inn. The island was such a place of beauty, but even a paradise like Bainbridge could have a painful past. It seemed a curious place for a first real date, but Meg was willing to roll with it.

"This is it." Ethan pulled onto a side road and turned into a parking lot. "I like to come here when I want to do some thinking. Might be good for you to look around. For your painting." Meg smiled into her lap while Ethan dashed around to her side and popped open her door. It wasn't like she was incapable of opening a door for herself, but on him, the gesture was sweet.

Meg took in the forested landscape that bordered the waterfront. A shaded wooden boardwalk threaded a path through the trees. She followed him, curious, down the slope. To her right, a hillside covered in mossy rocks dropped off toward the marina. On the other side, the woods were thick with pine trees. Meg savored the vista and took in the layered aroma of the evergreens.

Ahead, a curved wooden wall, more art than structure, bordered the walkway. When she caught up to Ethan, she noticed a jigsaw of plaques fixed to the wall. Rows of tiles etched with names and ages. *Isosaboru Katayama, 61. Keiko Kino, 6.* Tile after tile.

Meg read the display description about the 1942 Civilian Exclusion Order, created, ostensibly, to prevent US residents of Japanese descent from spying for the enemy. From this departure point, 227 Bainbridge men, women, and children became the first group of Japanese Americans in the nation to be evicted from their homes and sent to prison camps in Idaho. Meg's gaze traveled along the nameplates. Someone had strung rainbows of paper cranes along the walls in tribute to those innocents. Glancing down at her arm, Meg noticed goose bumps pocking her skin.

She and Ethan continued to the next section, pausing to study a wood carving of a teenage girl peeking from behind real barbed wire. Beside Meg, Ethan asked, "So, how are you going to decide what to paint on that fence?" He wasn't just making conversation. His question was sincere.

Turning her attention back to the memorial, she studied the carved image before her. The young woman clutched her schoolbooks to her chest. A prison watchtower loomed behind her. If only she could create something of value: a work that would leave people wondering, questioning. Something like the effect she felt standing here, staring into the wooden woman's eyes.

Meg pressed her lips together. She inhaled and lifted her shoulders. She let them drop.

"It'll come," he assured her. "Inspiration. She's an elusive muse, right?" Pretty poetic for an environmental consultant. And the way the sunlight landed on his profile . . . Gee whiz, he was something else.

They meandered along the nature trail section of the commemorative park and stopped at the viewpoint overlooking the ferry landing. Her gaze traveled back toward the exhibit, noting how unobtrusively the designer blended the art with the landscape. Taking a walk had given her some insight into her art after all.

Ethan rested his elbows on the railing and clasped his hands together. Before them, the trees in Pritchard Park leaned over the gray, flat water in Eagle Harbor.

"Did you grow up here?" she asked.

"Not too far. On the peninsula." He waved toward the mountain range, bumping her with his forearm. Reacting instinctively, his fingertips touched her back as if to steady her. She felt the heat of his fingers through her T-shirt, spreading from the dot on her spine where he made contact. Too quickly, he took his hand away when a flash of movement came to life in the flats below, and Meg gasped at the awesome sight of a great blue heron taking flight. Her heart clenched with the tight reminiscence she always felt when she spotted a heron. They had been her father's favorite.

"Whoa!" she exclaimed. "Do you see that?" With a wingspan wider than she was tall, the stately bird swooped low over the water, flying with the aerodynamics of a perfect paper airplane.

"Wow!" Ethan laughed. "That was something." He showed her the shot he'd captured on his phone. "I'm in a birding chat." His embarrassed grin was adorable. "We've had a lot of herons, but that one was a beaut."

As they strolled on the boardwalk back to the parking lot, she kept sneaking peeks at him, this grown man full of childlike wonder. Still, somewhere in the back of her head, a warning pinged. *Beware, Meg. This is a man whom your pickleballing community would gladly toss into the bay. Proceed with caution.* And yet—wasn't restoring the wetlands a cause she would normally get behind without a blink? And here was a guy who had made a career out of standing up for his beliefs. That was a good thing, right? And his arms were so tan and fit. Okay, that was superficial, but she had to be honest with herself.

On the drive back to the Outlook Inn, she watched his face as he concentrated on the road. There was something sexy about the set of his jawline, the stillness of his focus. She couldn't stop her mind from drifting. Meg pictured that same look of concentration on his face, imagining her body moving beneath his. The pleasure of the image seeped down her chest, and into the curve of her hips. Ethan's hand was on the gearshift. She stared at his long fingers, those short, manicured nails, and daydreamed about his touch, about how those fingers would feel, trembling against her thigh, scraping her ribs, grazing her throat.

"Can you pass me my sunglasses?" He nodded at the console. Caught in her steamy reverie, she startled. Only half-recovered, she dug them out of the cup holder and, butterfingers, dumped them in his lap.

"Oh!" Without thinking, she groped for the lenses, rescuing them from his crotch before handing them to him. She grimaced. "Sorry."

"Don't be," he said while his eyes remained focused through the windshield. "Other than a brief fling with some wanton woman I met on the ferry, that was more action than I've had in a long time."

She felt the blush build from behind her ears. He focused on the road, but she watched the slow lift of his lip.

Whatever this might turn into, it felt too soon to bring up Vance, but she wondered if his action-less comment had something to do with his own complications. It comforted her to think that maybe he, too, knew what it felt like to try to move past the exes to get to the wise.

At the Outlook, he leapt from the driver's seat. "I'll walk you in," he said, and Meg's pulse quickened with anticipation. He followed her up the path and through the gate of the unpainted fence.

Halfway up the porch stairs, he paused. "You know, I really enjoyed this," he said. "The painting. Visiting the memorial. It was nice hanging out with you."

"Yeah. Me, too. Oh, hey." She managed to come across as fittingly casual. "Would you want to . . . I don't know. Get a cup of coffee or something later today? Or tomorrow?"

"Sure." When he grinned, a tangible force passed between them like a current. "Oh, no. Wait. Actually—" Make that an electric shock. "I can't. Maybe this weekend. If you're around."

Her cheeks hurt. Her smile dimmed with the recognition of the brush-off. "Okay. Well. You know where I'm staying," Meg said as brightly as she could.

What a fool she was. She had let her imagination run away with the circus. Another ten minutes, and her imagination would be dressed in spangles and swinging from the high trapeze. Anyhow, she reasoned, it was best this way. How would she ever have explained to her team that she was cavorting with the enemy? Or was it consorting? Certainly, the former would be more fun.

And his features had taken a turn toward the serious. "Listen. About your courts. I know it's not ideal for the pickleball players, but I am hoping I can get the Lakeview league on board with us." Her brain twinged in warning. "This wetland restoration . . . it has the potential to positively impact the whole region."

Ah. The wildlife project. All day, she had been falling for him, while he had been working an angle. A lump of embarrassment clogged her throat.

"Imagine going to a school where blue herons swoop past your lunch table. And just think of the message you'll be sending the students. That you value the future of the planet. Their future."

"Sure. The students," she parroted lamely.

"If you can talk with your community, things will go a lot more smoothly. Know what I mean?"

She nodded, masking her hurt. So this was what his attentions today had been about. Not because he was attracted to her, but that he saw her as the key to placating the Lakeview league. Meg nodded, her neck going about the mechanics of agreeing while her mind knew she would do nothing. First, Annie had asked her to intervene with Ethan on the players' behalf, and now Ethan was coaxing her to act as go-between. Why did people keep asking her to get mixed up in this conflict? Would they ask a jellyfish to do a handstand? No! That would be illogical. Didn't these people realize she was equally invertebrate?

"Really glad to see you again," he said, leaning toward her. Could she have been wrong again? Had he, too, felt the undeniability of their attraction? Reacting to his nearness, her lips parted without asking her brain's permission.

Then he squeezed her shoulder.

Not that. The shoulder squeeze was five fingers into the friend zone. Worse. His shoulder squeeze meant *Thanks for agreeing to do an unpleasant favor, and have a nice life.*

Meg blinked. Forcing a smile to hide her disappointment, she said, "Glad to see you, too. And good luck with everything." She clenched her teeth to keep the smile in place until he descended the stairs, and then, willing herself to keep the self-berating at a minimum until she hit the room, she turned toward the Outlook's front door.

"Oh! Wait," she heard him say. She spun to find him holding his car keys in his hand. Perplexed, he searched his jeans pockets.

"Did you forget something?"

"Yeah. Yeah, I did."

Ethan marched up the steps and stopped very, very near to her. In her chest, her heartbeat shuddered like a snare drum. He had that same look on his face as when he concentrated on the winding road. That intensity. He swallowed and steadied himself.

When his face bent to hers, her face mirrored his movement. His fingers skimmed the back of her neck before raking gently into her hair. And then his lips grazed hers in a whisper of a kiss.

If it was a delusion, she hoped she would not come to her senses. She sank into the sensation. For an infinite instant they remained, her heels lifting off the landing, the gentle press of his hand on the back of her scalp. His hand and his lips. His lips and his hand. His touch flooded her until, with slow regret, he pulled away. She remained planted, frozen in the sensation of his smooth lips on hers.

"Yep. That was it." He tossed his keys in the air, caught them, and skipped down the stairs. "See ya soon, Meg Bloomberg."

ELEVEN

Annie, dressed in her pickleball skirt, was ready to go, but there was no leaving the hotel room until she got Meg to unload the details. With her fine-tuned lie detector on high, Annie said, "So, let me get this straight. You're saying that guy this morning, the gardener . . . Let's call him Shirtless Wonder. Sits down next to you and helps you get started on painting a mural on the fence. And then you get in his car with him and go to Winslow to buy, what was it, a weed whacker?" The last part, Meg realized too late, was clearly pushing it, and Annie wasn't even half buying the tall tale.

Annie sighed. "All right. Let's go with that and say that happened even though you're doing that thing where you bite the side of your tongue and your eyes are all shifty. Say it is the landscape guy. I guess a shirtless gardener is a step up from caulking gun Vance. Or court-killing Ethan."

"You know. Maybe Lakeview is being too hard on Ethan. And the wetland project. There are benefits. I mean, the birds were there first, right? And can you imagine how cool it would be for the high school science program to have an active research site right at their front doorstep?"

For a moment, Annie simply stared. "No." Annie shook her head. The wheels turned and the cogs clicked into place. "Nuh-uh.

Oh. My god. There is no gardener. Shirtless Wonder . . . is Ethan Fine!"

Meg threw her hands to her face and groaned.

"Aha!" Annie cried. "I was right. I knew it!" With all her prelaw and medical school training, Annie had missed her calling as a detective. Or a mom of a teenager. She was way too good at bullshit detecting. "What is up with that guy's chest? Does he bench-press pianos?"

"Oh, Annie." It was a relief to be found out. "You're not mad?"

"Mad?" She sighed. "I want you to be happy. It's just . . ." She scrunched her lips to the side. "Be careful, okay?"

"Okay, Mom." Smiling, Meg threw her pickleball gear into the hatchback. Just loud enough for Annie to hear, Meg added, "Did I mention we kissed?"

"Come on, now." Annie punched her shoulder. "Spill it. We're not leaving for the courts until I get all the tea. Was it as steamy as the tied-up-with-a-seat-belt snog?"

Reliving it, Meg enjoyed the retelling. "It was different than the kiss in my car. That was all handsy and hungry." Meg turned to her friend and let out a dreamy sigh. "Annie. I had no idea a kiss could be like that. It was . . . a lava kiss."

"Ooh. A lava kiss. Do tell."

"Yeah. Like when our lips met, it felt like magma. Like my body was made of liquid fire, just ready to explode."

"You mean like an orgasm?"

"Oh my god. Enough. You took it one step too far. Just stop now." She smiled as she spoke, not at all offended. It had been a fantastic kiss.

"Me, stop? You're the one who's all moony-eyed and can't stop talking about Ethan Fine. *Blah, blah, Shirtless Wonder. Blah, blah, lifting a piano. Blah, blah, orgasm.*"

"I'm pretty sure you were the one who said all those things."

"I think we should move on to what brought us here." Annie fished in the glove compartment and yanked out the shiny trifold brochure that Meg had picked up on the ferry. "Let's see what we've got in our Bainbridge bag of tricks."

Pointing, she exclaimed, "Aha! The commemorative Founders Courts at Battle Point Park. Where pickleball went public! I'm so excited! Rooster's gonna join us so you two can get some practice in. I bet I can find a practice partner out there, too, until I locate Michael Edmonds. Whaddya say we go vay-cay cray-cray?"

"I don't know," Meg said, suddenly daunted by the prospect of playing on the famous courts. She tried to refold the brochure, but managed only to crumple rather than crease it. "I mean, what am I practicing for? Vance and Édith are going to end up getting—"

"Hey." Annie snatched the glossy flyer and whipped it into submission with a couple of deft movements. "Listen to me. Stop that. Here we are in one of the most beautiful places in the world, with nothing to do but enjoy the fresh air and do the things we love to do. Right? Come on. What do I always say?"

"Vinegar makes an excellent surface cleaner."

Annie glowered.

"Put lemon juice on apple slices to keep them from browning? Wait. Use soda or beer when trying to kill garden slugs because they can't fart out the carbonation and their stomachs explode."

"You've learned so much from me, but no." She gave Meg her sternest glare. "You've picked up a new sport. You've kissed a hottie. You are on the right path, my friend. But now you need to get out of your own way."

Meg's nostrils flared, but then she shook off her negativity like a wet dog. It was true. How long had she put her life on hold? It was time for Meg to do something for Meg for once. "You're right," she agreed. "You are right."

"What did you say?"

"You're right."

Annie bathed herself in Meg's words. "I don't think I can ever hear that enough."

As Meg steered the blue hatchback onto the quiet road toward Battle Point Park, she glanced at her copilot and smiled. Get out of her own way. How hard could that be?

· · · · ·

"Whoa. Holy Swiss cheese in a gift basket!" Annie uttered as they drove into the lot. They slammed the car doors and rushed to admire the sight. Tilting their heads toward the metal arch, they gaped, wide-eyed, at the entrance to the sport courts. At the top of the archway, a metal banner sparkled in the sunlight, emblazoned with the words FOUNDERS COURTS. A pair of pickleball paddles added to the elegant design, splashed against the backdrop of a gleaming net.

Annie shook her head in wonder. "This is where it all started. Right here on Bainbridge. We're standing on the steps of history."

The courts sprawled before them in all their splendor: newly painted, navy blue courts delineated by crisp, white lines. The playing surfaces beckoned, blue islands in a sea of green asphalt. Six dedicated courts. Beyond them, four converted tennis courts. This was pickleball Valhalla. As Meg neared, the ticktack noise of the bouncing plastic filled her with anticipation.

On the closest court, players warmed up by tapping the ball lightly, sending it over the net in low, arcing dinks. At the far courts, a ripped pickleball coach in a muscle-revealing tank engaged a group of white-haired players in a third-shot drop drill. The notice posted on the fence claimed, BEGINNERS' LESSONS. COME JOIN THE FUN. ALL ARE WELCOME. —COACH CHAD. Deep in her brain, a long-unused competitive spirit lifted its head from its hibernation. Lessons could be fun, and if she upped her skills, she'd have a better chance of winning the beginners' spot.

Annie had moved on from gawking to stretching. "Come on," she said, her body bent into downward dog. "I'll hit with you till Rooster shows up."

They set up on opposite sides of the well-maintained court and warmed up, dinking crosscourt. Annie's shots skipped over the net in perfect, low arcs, while Meg practiced her backhand dinks. Every second or third shot, Meg smacked the ball into the net, but at least she was keeping them low. It was an improvement over her "towering inferno" shots, as Rooster liked to call them.

"Enough stalling," Meg joked. "You ready to get whupped?"

Annie laughed good-naturedly before serving with little mercy. Playing skinny singles taught Meg aim—the ball could only bounce in half the court. Although she stretched herself and concentrated on returning Annie's wicked drops, as expected, Meg got pickled. The game ended at 11 to donut.

"Well, that was fast," Meg mourned. "You couldn't let me win? Just once."

Annie shrugged. "It's not in my nature. You know how competitive I am. Luckily I won't hold you to the tradition: when you get pickled, you have to walk home naked. Fortunately for you, you can't walk across the Sound."

"Not without a really long snorkel."

"Hey! Meg made a funny. That's the spirit. Come on. We'll go again. Maybe I'll let you have a chance." She wound up a serve but stopped short before the paddle made contact.

"Hold up." Annie pointed with her paddle. "Do you see that guy in the parking lot? Is that . . . Michael Edmonds?"

Narrowing her gaze, Meg spotted the man. It was true, there

was a strong resemblance. At least from a distance. The guy had the bearing of Michael Edmonds, but doubt built when he climbed into a white SUV. Everyone knew Michael Edmonds drove a silver sports car.

"Never mind," Annie said. "Looks like him though, doesn't it? Weird. Did you know that in earth's entire population, there's only a one in one hundred thirty-four chance that a pair of exact doppelgängers exists?"

"I did not know that."

"That's a pretty low percentage compared to the birthday paradox percentage. Did you know that in any group of twenty-three people, there is a fifty-fifty chance that two of them will have the same birthday?"

"Did *you* know," Meg countered, "that seventy-six percent of people who quote statistics still have a stash of Pokémon cards stored in a closet at their parents' house?"

"Now that you mention it, I bet I could get good money for those." Annie deflated. "I really thought it was him."

Meg tucked her paddle under her arm and marched to the net. "I think it's time you and I had a little talk about the Michael Edmonds in the room," she said. "Admit it. You are obsessed. You need to do something about it."

Annie sighed. "I shouldn't have said anything. Anyhow, the whole point is moot. I can't even think about having a relationship. I can't even believe I took time off to go on this vacation."

Meg glared at her friend. "Weren't you the one who just told me to get out of my own way?"

"Yeah. And you should. But I prefer to set up a friggin' obstacle course in my own path."

"Nope. Not happening. If you want me to move on, you need to do the same." Meg shook her head. "'Cause I have to say, Banannie, I don't really get it. What do you see in him? You hardly know him. You said so yourself. No one really does."

Everyone on the Lakeview courts had their guesses, but the real Michael was a man of mystery. Rumors circulated: That he was married. That he spoke fluent Thai, Russian, and Arabic. That he could look at a jar of marbles and tell exactly how many there were. That he was helicopter rich off an app he'd developed that let you swipe right to find pickleball partners. That he had won a chimpanzee in a poker bet. Meg believed all of it, and Annie, none. Or so she always said.

"I'm gonna tell you something super embarrassing. I can't explain it, but you're totally right. I am . . . fixated. I have this recurring fantasy about him."

"Really . . ." Meg asked, waggling an eyebrow.

Annie swung her paddle, smacking Meg on the back of her arm. "Ow!"

"Not that kind of fantasy." Annie shook her head in mock disgust. "We go on dates and eat fancy dinners together in nice restaurants and we both love opera, and we get married and have three dogs and two very good-looking and clever children. Serena and Gabriel."

"So . . . you've thought this through."

Annie's expression was guilty with the confession. "I know he's just my partner on the courts. But he's always so helpful, and he gives me tips about my swing, and he's so handsome. All right. I think about him all the time. I guess I've pretended that we were this couple." She sighed. "I don't know if he likes me, too, or if he's just being . . ." She searched for the word. "Cordial."

"Annie." Meg's tone was kind. "You have to talk to him. How will you ever know if he feels the same?" In all the time she had known her, Annie had always kept her heart in check. Meg honestly couldn't remember the last time she had even gone on a date.

"I know. I should ask him, right? But I want *him* to say something. I want it so much," Annie said, pouting. "I keep thinking he's going to give me some kind of sign that he's interested in me. The real me. Not just my awesome backhand."

"Why don't you ask him out? See if he's interested?"

"And ruin our perfect fantasy relationship?" Annie's lips quirked up. "Besides, who am I kidding? I don't have time for a social life. I'm at the hospital all the time. And when I'm not, I'm playing pickleball. Otherwise, I'd never leave the hospital or my bed. Every day, when I'm not working, I go through the same decision angst. Which do I need more—sleep or pickleball? Pickleball usually wins." She grinned. "There's not much room for anything else, ya know?"

"No rest for the pickleballers." With a friendly bump to the shoulder, Meg jostled Annie, who listed sideways into the net.

When Annie righted herself, she shook off the fantasy and morphed back into her no-nonsense norm. She waved Meg off, pointing her back to her corner. "Okay. Enough talking. Zero–zero, start," Annie called, and hit the ball crosscourt to Meg.

"Oh. Are we starting?" Meg swung her paddle and returned with force.

The ball traveled back and forth, an easy volley. "Tell you what. Let's make a pact." Annie whacked the ball, keeping up her patter as she hit. "No more talk about Ethan. No more Michael. Today, it's Meg-and-Annie time. Pure vacation."

Annie must have been taking it easy on Meg, letting her return the ball time after time. "Sounds good to me," Meg agreed. "So what does pure Annie-time look like? Say you could do anything. Anything at all. What would you want to do?"

"I wanna pickle. And I wanna sleep." Annie smacked the ball

with fervor to punctuate her passion for her two favorite verbs. "What do you want?"

Meg thought. Something about the rhythmic plick-plack of the bouncing ball steadied her thinking. "I wanna paint. And I wanna pickle." The ball came faster now, speeding up with their growing energies.

"We have overlap," Annie noted. "We could make a Venn diagram. Call it pickle in the middle," she said, striking the ball with a power punch. It zipped past Meg and skidded behind her, right to the baseline. Annie punched the air. "Yes! Man, that felt good."

"Nice shot." Both women turned at the sound of Rooster's familiar voice. "Sorry I'm late. I made some new friends my own age," he said, waving his paddle toward the repurposed tennis courts, where the raucous shouts and laughter of septuagenarian athletes echoed across the pavement. "How 'bout you let the old folks challenge you to a few games . . . if you're not scared of getting your heads handed to you by people twice your age."

During the two hours that followed, they joined in with the friendly members of the Bainbridge crew, and the hours slipped by like minutes. Pickleball had a way of cranking up the bass on Meg's energy until there was nothing left to do but dance.

"You played well," Rooster said when they finally stopped. "But remember. Paddle up," he demonstrated. "And keep the ball lower. If you move your feet and bend your knees, you'll have better aim and leverage so you don't pop it up."

Annie nodded. "Yeah. Get to the net faster. And in between each shot, reset."

"Get your feet under you," Rooster advised.

"And then slide right back into position after you hit."

"Should I be writing this down?" Meg asked, a twinkle of snark in her voice.

Rooster shrugged. "You're a smart cookie. You can remember it." Rooster tapped a finger against his temple. "The noggin and the body work together. Use 'em while you still got 'em."

It was good advice, all of it. But nothing she hadn't heard before. The problem wasn't knowing what she was supposed to do. It was managing to actually do it at the same time as a plastic sphere was hurtling at her paddle. All in all, though, she and Rooster had built their teamwork skills today, and she was beginning to think they really did have a shot at Lakeview's beginners' spot.

Too pooped to pickle any longer, Meg plopped down on the bench beside a well-put-together lady in her fifties. White stripes traveled down the seams of her lavender tracksuit. The sun glinted off the gemstones on her beringed fingers as she reached out to shake Meg's hand.

"Marilyn," the woman said by way of introduction. "You're joining us from Seattle, is that right?"

Meg nodded. "Are you looking for a game?" She could muster the juice to squeeze in one more. Maybe.

"Oh, no. I'm done for the day." She leaned toward Meg in a way that gave Meg the impression she was inspecting her. "You and your friend Annie look like you know your way around the courts. Are you here on vacation? Or are you Picklesmash players, spying on the competition?" she asked, joking but not joking.

"Annie plays in tournaments, but I haven't before. This will be my first—" Meg's voice stopped hard on the last word. If they thought Annie and Meg were there on a mission to check out their Picklesmash competition, they would be iced out in no time and wouldn't get the court time. Why did she have to be so transparent?

"I mean. We're on a pickle-cation."

"Mm-hm," Marilyn hummed, her tone thick with suspicion. Luckily, Meg was saved from further scrutiny by the pinging of

Marilyn's phone. The older woman glanced at the screen and then raised a neatly manicured finger. "Excuse me a sec."

Marilyn turned her back. "Michael, darling!"

Michael? Meg's ears pricked up. There were lots of Michaels out there, she reasoned. But still . . . "At Winslow Vineyards? Tonight?" Marilyn asked. "I'll try. You guys get started without me. I'm not sure I can make it in time." Meg twisted her neck to peek over Marilyn's shoulder at the image on Marilyn's phone.

Pipin' potatoes with all the fixin's! There he was peering out from the screen: none other than Michael Edmonds! If Meg didn't bruise like ripe fruit in the tropics, she'd pinch herself to make sure she wasn't dreaming.

"All right then, dear. If I don't see you, we'll catch up soon." Meg bent to tie her shoelace just as Marilyn turned back in her direction.

"My word!" Marilyn declared. "Is it five o'clock already? Sorry to jet, but we have some rec club business here on the courts. If you'll excuse me . . ." Cupping her hands over her mouth, Marilyn shouted. "Yoo-hoo. Everybody. It's five o'clock," she called, and offered Meg a sphinxlike smile. "So nice to meet you and your friends."

She watched as Marilyn marched off to conspire with her pickle peeps. As they huddled together, Meg had the distinct feeling they were plotting something. But what? Pickleballers were generally welcoming to newcomers, but Meg suspected that joining in with Bainbridge's crew required a secret handshake and a six-digit passcode.

With no one left on the court, Annie waved Meg toward the hatchback. Meg puzzled over Marilyn's phone conversation, wondering where Michael Edmonds fit into this curious jigsaw. Maybe she should mention her suspicions about Michael and Marilyn's connection to Annie. Or better yet, she should try and get more intel before crushing Annie's dreams. Was Marilyn and Michael's connection a pickleball threat, or a romantic one as well? Marilyn might have a few years on Michael, but it wasn't out of the question that their relationship might extend beyond dinks and drinks.

Lost in her own thoughts, Meg almost ran into Annie. Her friend had stopped in her tracks, one hand holding her phone and her other arm shooting out and blocking Meg's path.

"No. Way," Annie fumed. "That . . . jerk!" she exploded, shaking her head. "This goes beyond acceptable. I knew we couldn't trust him. I could just—" She finished off the threat with a sound like a squirrel choking on a nut, while shaking her fist at her invisible foe. Annie's eyes blazed as she scrolled up her phone screen.

"What happened?"

"What happened?" Annie spit out the words. "Your cutthroat Romeo, Ethan Fine, happened. That's what happened."

The blood in Meg's hands drained toward her fingernails. "Ethan?"

Annie pointed at her screen. There, in a post from Jeannie, captioned with enough expletives to kill a nun, Meg saw the photo of the court's front gate. It was secured with a padlock. A placard with the Plan It Earth logo was clipped to the chain-link fence beside it.

Meg's blood simmered when she read the sign. COURTS CLOSED UNTIL FURTHER NOTICE.

THE VOLLEY

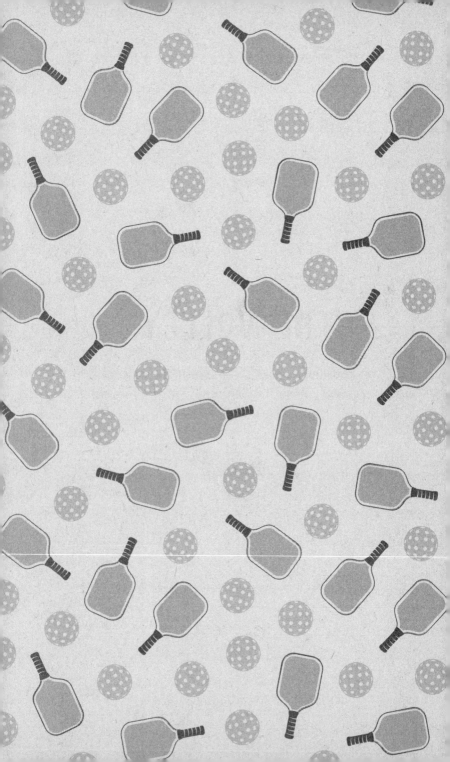

TWELVE

The betrayal threatened to knock Meg's knees out from under her. A padlock! "What the—" Her voice stuck like a fishbone in her throat. Locking lips with Ethan had blinded her to his real M.O.—locking their pickleball courts!

Poor Lakeview! Her league was supposed to have the whole summer together to play and practice—preparation that was imperative to the league's success if they hoped to win the money for new courts. Ethan must have locked them up earlier than promised and then escaped the fray to Bainbridge. The nerve. How could she have been so easily taken in by that infuriating Adonis?

It was the boots. She'd always had a soft spot for work boots. Blowing out a shaky breath, she vowed to stand up against this latest affront to her league. When and if she ran into him again.

But for now, there was a more immediate entanglement to tackle. She glanced at Annie in the hotel bed beside her. By seven o'clock, Annie had turned herself off like a light switch and now her bangs hung over her face and her mouth drooped toward the pillow. Sneaking a furtive glance at her sleeping friend, Meg hesitated, one hand on the door. She hadn't told Annie what she had overheard about Marilyn's plans to meet up with Michael Edmonds tonight at the winery, but she was determined to follow up.

As she slipped out of the room, she texted Rooster. OMW. Then, remembering it was Rooster, she followed up with Heading to the winery now. Operation Michael Edmonds, Rooster had called it after she filled him in on what she'd overheard. He had leapt at the chance to be her wingman this evening for her intel-gathering mission.

She found the winery in the heart of Winslow's quaint downtown. Cute café tables dotted the sidewalk in front of a weathered brick building with shuttered windows. Meg wouldn't have been surprised to see swinging saloon doors or a horse clopping down the street, the scene so resembled the set of an old-fashioned western.

Sweeping into the winery in stealth mode, Meg kept her eyes peeled for any signs of Michael Edmonds. A first glance around the space did not reveal Michael, but her gaze lingered on the atmospheric decor. Overhead, wrought iron candelabra chandeliers hung from the raftered ceiling, while repurposed wooden barrels bound with steel hoops supported the glass dining tables. Meg felt a small pang as she took in the cozy winery. The scene took her back to the pre-Vance days, when she and Annie would hang out in places like this—making up preposterous life stories about the other couples at the tables and laughing until their sides hurt.

She smiled when she spotted Rooster waiting for her. "M'lady." He pulled out a stool at the bar for her. "You hear about that lock they put on the courts?" Meg nodded her head in dismay, but Rooster lifted a palm to continue. "I'm sure the guy had a good reason."

Leave it to Rooster to suspect the best in everyone. He'd been a fan of Ethan's from the moment he guessed at Meg's affection for him under the rain-soaked school awning. But now Meg pressed her lips into a tight line, berating herself. Couldn't she, just once, be attracted to a nice guy who wasn't dead set on crushing her every new hope and dream?

A coaster appeared on the bar and Meg looked up to see a pretty, raven-haired bartender with a sophisticated updo. "Will you be tasting today?"

"Sure." When on Bainbridge, do as the Islanders do.

Rooster put a hand over the wineglass that she slid in front of him. "None for me, thanks. A sparkling water would be great."

She poured a thimbleful of white wine in Meg's glass. "This is our Riesling. Light and crisp. My name's Lynette and I'll be happy to answer any questions you have about our pours."

Meg sipped. It was quite nice. But she wasn't there to just drink. Quickly, she recapped the phone call she'd overheard about Marilyn's meetup with Michael.

"I suspect you're right about our elusive Mr. Edmonds hiding a secret up his sleeve," Rooster said, pulling out his phone. "Check out what Laverne shared with me. Here's his post, just half an hour ago." Meg studied the image. Michael Edmonds seated among the wrought iron and repurposed barrels. Yep. This was the place. He could be tucked into any of the dimly lit alcoves.

"Don't see him here, though," Rooster said. "He might already have come and gone."

"I hope not." Indicating Rooster's cell, Meg said, "What's with you and social media all of a sudden? I thought you and Laverne were technology averse. The two of you share a phone!"

"Yes. We did. But things have changed. This is my new phone." He showed it to her proudly, like a game show host presenting a prize. "Never really needed one; never been away from her before," he said, a rare blush capping his bald head. "But now I need my own . . . I'm expecting news." He let the statement dangle, daring Meg to ask. She bit.

"News?"

"I wasn't gonna say anything to anyone. Things are still touch and go, but . . ." He leaned in for the boo-yah. "We're having a baby."

Okay. This was news. Rooster was seventy. Not unheard of, but late to be starting out. But Laverne? Either a world record or science gone awry.

"Aren't you a little . . ."

"Excited? Of course we are. But nervous, too. My goddaughter Lulu is on bed rest, and we've been on pins and—"

"Oh! Your goddaughter. I thought . . ."

Rooster laughed. "Laverne? That *would* be miraculous. No. Laverne and I—by the time we found each other, we were a little long in the tooth for childbearing. But bless Lulu's heart; she's like a daughter to us. That's why we came here to Bainbridge. She lives here. This little one'll be the same as if she were our grandbaby." His expression clouded momentarily. He recovered, shaking off his daydream. He lifted his fizzy water in a toast. "And damned if I'm not gonna be the best pop-pop around."

They clinked glasses, and Rooster mentioned, "You played well today."

"Yeah. Did you see me beat up on those old people?"

"You must be very proud."

Meg grinned and sipped at her drink. Again, she scanned the crowd at the tables. Where was Michael?

Rooster said, "You keep playing as well as you did this afternoon and pretty soon we'll kick Vance right off the courts."

Her jaw tightened.

"You're making that face again," Rooster noted.

"What face? This is just my face. It's what it looks like."

"No. The face from the pickleball court the morning I took that snapshot of you. That 'I'm already defeated before I've even begun' face. You make that face sometimes when we're losing a game."

Did she? Once, she'd overheard Jeannie call her "the Choker." Rooster's words drove it home. The moment she lost a couple of points in succession, it felt impossible to reset, too difficult to wipe away the residue of a badly placed shot. And with that mindset, there was no coming back for the win.

Rooster met her eye. "You deserve someone who treats you with trust. With genuine affection. That ex of yours was an eggshell in the omelet."

"I'm fine. Really."

"If you say so," Rooster commented. "But ya know, I used to make a living reading people, and you, Meg Bloomberg, are an open book."

"You were a psychic?"

"A poker player. And an airport cargo manager. And a Zamboni driver. I worked in the fisheries department for a while, too. And a long time ago, I got myself thrown around on the rodeo circuit. Those were some days I don't care to remember. But sometimes, I force myself to do so. Just like you should take a good, long look at that photo I took of you."

The memory pinched at her. "Not something I'm generally in the mood for."

Rooster considered her. "It's no fun. But you have to study your mistakes before you can move on. Don't beat yourself up. Just think about it. Why didn't you get out of that marriage earlier? What signs did you miss? And once that acceptance seeps in, you can go forward. And next time, use that to set yourself up for the win."

Yes—that was what she had tried to do. With Ethan's kiss, she had dipped her foot back into the tidal pool. But the moment she let herself feel invested, she had been knocked over by a rogue wave. The image of Ethan's padlock clipped to Lakeview's gate flashed in her thoughts, and Meg groaned. She sank her head toward the bar.

"Was it something I said?" Rooster asked.

Meg was itching to unload her frustrations. Annie would go off the rails if Meg confessed her confused feelings for that pickle-locker. But here was Rooster, who had a way of putting things in perspective. She could come clean to him, couldn't she?

"Can I tell you something? It's about Ethan Fine." Rooster lifted a brow and said nothing. Already she felt like she had said too much. "I . . . like him."

"Is that so," Rooster said without an ounce of surprise.

Meg shook her head, disheartened. "Everybody hates him. He locked our courts. He's destroying our only place to play—"

"That may be so," he conceded, "but you never know another person's story until you know that person's story. And you have to let go of the idea that anybody else's opinion should alter your faith in your own good choices."

Rooster swiveled toward her on his barstool and fixed her in his sights.

"Life's like pickleball," he said. "You gotta release the bad patterns and habits that are dragging you down before you can make any progress. Remember how last month you thought you'd try going back to that sideways service stance? How'd that work out for you?"

Meg smiled despite herself. She had gone kicking and screaming from that old, useless serve. The new, forward-facing serve turned her game around. Even crabby Jeannie was taken by surprise when Meg's serve whizzed past her. Then, for no good reason, her stubborn feet and body spent a whole game trying that terrible sideways serve again. Over and over, she hit the ball out-of-bounds or into the net or wide. At the time, Rooster had stared patiently forward.

She supposed it wouldn't hurt to learn from her mistakes and move on. She would have to tread carefully with Ethan, but Rooster was spot-on when he said she couldn't control her feelings. If only she could decide what to do with them.

Lynette swooped in with a fresh pour: a finger of red wine. Without fully processing its arrival, Meg downed it in one swallow.

"It's one of our best sellers," the bartender said. "The Shiraz is a bold, full-bodied blend with smoky undertones—"

"That's fine. Could you?" Meg pointed near the lip of her glass. "Thanks, by the way," she said to Rooster. "For being the designated driver. I don't think I even offered."

"No problem. I don't drink anyway. Eighteen years sober. And counting."

He flagged Lynette for another sparkling water. His gravelly voice highlighted the confidential quality of his words. "I confront my screwups most every day. They hang around like the smell of old fish, but I keep rolling forward, dragging that part of me. I acknowledge that. The rodeo? Hell. I was so busy drowning myself in alcohol, I was barely living."

Half consciously, Meg slid the wineglass away with her fingers. She was feeling . . . What was she feeling? Ungenerous. Incomplete.

"You okay?" Rooster asked. "Don't know about you, but I'm famished. Let's get some grub in the belly. Give us some fuel to keep on the Michael hunt."

Her gaze swept the tables again, looking for the lanky pickleballer with a goofy grin. At Rooster's questioning look, she shook her head. "Still no Michael. But the mussels look good."

There was no way to be dainty about eating Penn Cove mussels. Rooster, too, made quick work of digging into his shepherd's pie. As they devoured the delicious meal, she pictured Rooster, night after night, sitting at the dinner table in comfortable conversation with Laverne. Two halves of the same whole. How was it that so many couples balanced each other, while her marriage had felt so lop-sided? "Did Laverne stick with you then?" she asked. "Through all of your tough times?"

"Lucky for me, Laverne met me after I turned myself around. Met her at an AA meeting. She'd come every year on her sister's birthday to talk to us, and after three years of hemming and haw-ing I asked her out. By then, Laverne's niece, Lulu, was a university student, but Laverne had cared for her since she was eighteen, when her parents were killed by a drunk driver."

"Ugh. How awful."

"You're tellin' me. But you can see why backsliding was never an option. In my head, I still look back at that vision of myself, dead drunk and cussin' up a storm at the bull that threw me. So wasted I nearly got myself trampled to death. And that would have been all on me."

She dunked some crusty bread in the buttery mussel sauce. Rooster's comments loitered in her thoughts. "Doesn't it make you sad? Or mad at yourself, when you think about the crappy stuff in your past?"

"Absolutely. That's the point." He nodded. "Feel it. And then put it aside. The bad choices—those were my mistakes. I can sulk and whine, or I can make a better place for myself: marry an amazing woman and be Pop-Pop to a grandchild I never imagined I'd have. Twenty years ago, I wouldn't have had the nerve to imagine such a future for myself, but here I am, living my best life, right?"

Meg licked melted butter off her fingers and nodded her agree-ment. Rooster had opened his heart to her. She could let her guard down a little, couldn't she?

"You know that photo you took of me? I can't even look at it. It's so . . ." She rolled her eyes at her own folly. The wine and Rooster's trust had loosened her tongue. "You know what I pictured when you told me to think of the worst-case scenario?"

He tilted his head. She braved forward. "I pictured a future me: alone, and jealous, and unfulfilled," she said, shaking her head at the table. "And it wasn't a future without Vance that I worried about. It was— Well. I worry I won't get back to the me I was before him. How can I ever open myself up to anyone new if I'm scared that the same thing will happen again?"

Seltzer glass in hand, he pointed his index finger and met her eye. "Nobody can take you away from you." As his words settled, she managed a small smile, grateful to be chastised with such good advice. She planned to stick with herself for the long haul.

"Hey." Rooster pointed his chin toward the tables. "Isn't that the woman from the courts? The one who you said was meeting Michael?"

Meg swiveled to see the back of a straight-postured woman with neatly coiffed hair. She was seated alone, a laptop open in front of her. As she peered at the screen, she scrolled with her mouse. Her other hand rolled her nearly empty wineglass between her long fingers, occasionally clinking one of her massive rings against the crystal stem.

Marilyn.

THIRTEEN

"That's her. That's Marilyn," Meg said, nodding. "If she's here, Michael Edmonds can't be far off. Come on. Let's ply her for the goods."

"What are you, a mobster?" Rooster chuckled. "Why don't you go on over there on your own. I want to give Laverne a call and see how Lulu is doing on bed rest. Besides, you'd probably have better luck. You know how perps clam up around me."

Giving him a smile, Meg put on the air of someone taking a trip to the bathroom and moseyed toward the table. She casually skidded to a halt beside her mark. "Marilyn?"

The stylish hairdo spun toward Meg. In a swift motion, Marilyn snapped the laptop shut. Had she been playing online poker? Surfing porn? Or maybe something seedier, like shopping for multiple pairs of bedazzled flip-flops on Amazon, planning to try on each one with different toenail polish. Not that Meg had ever done that herself.

"Margaret, is it?" Marilyn asked.

"Meg. From Lakeview. What a surprise. Are you waiting for someone, or can I join you?" Meg tried to sound casual.

"Please." Marilyn gestured at the chair and Meg began to sit. "But weren't you heading to the restroom?"

Meg shook her head, then nodded. "No. Yes. I was. But. I don't have to go anymore." *Smooth*, Meg thought.

In the awkward moment that followed, Meg reviewed her options: 1. Ask Marilyn point-blank if she knew what Michael Edmonds was plotting on Bainbridge. Or 2. Go back to the inn, take a bubble bath, and eat a pint of salted caramel swirl ice cream. Rationally, she knew the lactose would upset her system, but it would be worth it.

"I'm glad, actually, to run into you here," Marilyn said. "I'm afraid I might have been a bit short with you at the courts. Forgive me, won't you? Because I was thinking about you after we met. Your league's playing at Northwest Picklesmash, isn't that right?"

Taken aback, Meg nodded. How had *that* happened? Marilyn had circumnavigated Meg's investigation with an inquiry of her own. Rings clinking against her empty wineglass, Marilyn said, "I was wondering. And certainly, I would understand if this crosses over rivalry lines, but would your Seattle league want to float us one of your beginners so we can fill our tournament slot for Bainbridge?"

The request was so out of the blue that Meg almost laughed. Why on earth would Lakeview lend their players to the competition when such high stakes were on the line?

Reading Meg's surprise, Marilyn added, "Of course, only if you have extra newbie players. You could hang on to your A-team beginners. Maybe just help us out with a spare player or two who want a chance to participate, for the sake of sportsmanship."

Meg felt a need to defend herself. "Rooster and I may not be advanced players, but we are not 'spares.' Sure, there's another team that's pretty good, but we fully intend to earn Lakeview's beginners' slot—" Meg stopped herself before she gave away too much. Which was already.

"The thing is," Marilyn pressed, "right now we just have one solid player for that beginners' slot. He's quite competent really, and he's never played a tournament." Benevolently, Marilyn added, "I watched you play. You do all right. If you have another team in line for your home team's spot, maybe you would consider playing with our beginner. Play for Bainbridge. Your friend Rooster wouldn't mind, I bet."

A current of disbelief rippled through her. What nerve! How could Marilyn suggest that she dump her league and toss Rooster to the henhouse? No. That wasn't the right metaphor. Maybe cast him chicken feed. Nope. Surely there was a fitting metaphor with roosters. The situation was screaming for it. Aha! Throw Rooster to the chopping block. That was that metaphor.

"Rooster and I stick together," Meg said. "We're a team."

"Fair enough," Marilyn conceded. She slipped her laptop into her roomy purse. "Listen. I'm heading home for an early night. I'm expecting a call from pickleball early tomorrow." Marilyn winked and leaned toward Meg as if they shared an old friendship. "But I like you, Meg from Lakeview. So how 'bout you pop by my house tomorrow morning and I can show you a bit of pickleball history you won't get at the Founders Courts. We can hit a bit on my private court."

Meg opened her mouth to reiterate that she was not interested in switching sides.

"Just for fun," Marilyn clarified. "That's the point, right?" And before Meg could begin to ask about Michael Edmonds, Marilyn pressed an art deco business card into Meg's palm. "Come by around eight. You won't be disappointed." And with that, Marilyn swooped out of the winery.

Before Meg could register her own defeat, Rooster slid into her vacated seat. "How did it go? Did you find out about Michael?"

Meg was still shaking her head, bewildered at her poor grilling skills. "She sidetracked me. But I'm meeting up with her tomorrow," she said, rallying. "And I'll squeeze her till she squeals."

"Okay, Al Capone," he teased as they headed toward the door. "What went wrong? Did she threaten to put your feet in concrete and dump you in the river?"

"I think she's too subtle for that," Meg said, and tossed Rooster the car keys. "She strikes me as a poisoned chalice sort of gal."

"Mm." He smirked. "Yet another reason I stopped drinking."

• • • • •

The next morning, leaving Annie to relish a late lie-in, Meg ambled toward the address Marilyn had given her. As the soft waves of Puget Sound rolled in along the shoreline and dragged the rocks back to the water with a musical jangling, she strolled past cute, cozy cottages with views of the pebbled shoreline. Stands of old-growth pines lined the road and formed forests behind pastel-painted gingerbread homes. Meg slowed when she heard an arhythmic tock-tocking, and she followed the sound until she halted in front of a ranch home sporting a low, flat roof that looked unlike the modern cottages beside it. She knew that sound. It was the dulcet tones of pickleball.

On three sides of the house, stretches of evergreens guarded the property. This must have been one of the earlier-built homes in the area, before Bainbridge became a summer haven for Seattle software mavens and sultans of coffee. The house number matched the address on Marilyn's card. Incredible. Marilyn really did have a pickleball court behind her house!

Striding around the western hemlocks, Meg found herself looking at a simple asphalt court set up on an old sport court. The poles that supported the net bore signs of rust, but the net was new, and the pavement had been swept. A lone player stood at the back of the court, practicing her aim against a blue line that was taped to the garage. Meg called, "Marilyn?"

The middle-aged woman turned her expertly coiffed head, and her cosmetically stabilized brow almost lifted in a hello. "Meg." There was a smile making a valiant effort at the corners of her lips. "I'm glad you came."

Meg glanced around the backyard court and wondered what surprises Marilyn had in store. Marilyn, catching Meg's curiosity, said, "So what do you think? It took all my savings, you know, but when this particular place came on the market, there was no way I could pass it up."

Meg wondered aloud, "This house?"

"Well. This court."

Meg wrinkled her nose. How could this blacktop rival the Founders Courts? Moss grew around the corners of the court boundaries. The surrounding pines dropped their needles on the surface. Encroaching trees closed in the space behind the baseline. It was convenient to have a court in the backyard, sure. But a blacktop court cracked easily, and the surface paled in comparison to the upscale Founders Courts nearby.

"This, right here"—Marilyn paused, smiling her sphinxlike grin—"is the original pickleball court. *The* court. The very one where, in 1965, four friends joined together to save their children's summer . . ."

". . . and discovered they loved it more than their kids did," Meg recited. "This is *that* court?" Meg clutched the paddle and took in the view anew. "I can't believe it!"

"It's true. You're standing on the source. Shall we have a match?"

Well, duh. Meg nodded her enthusiastic assent. Wait till she told Annie and Rooster she had played on the original courts. Later in the afternoon, they had practice time reserved on the Founders Courts, but this warm-up was a pickleballer's dream. Marilyn seemed pleased for the company and down to earth in a way Meg had not noticed at the winery. It was true what they said about pickleball: it was like a fairy dust that coated everyone with happiness and good cheer.

Steering Meg to a bench beside the court, Marilyn offered Meg a paddle. "That's the service side." Marilyn waved Meg to the other side of the net. "Here and at the Founders Courts, first server faces the Sound." In Seattle at the Lakeview club, the starting server faced west toward Bainbridge to honor the original pickleballers. And here she was, standing on hallowed ground!

But Marilyn's comment about the Founders Courts had jogged a reminder loose. Michael Edmonds! Meg was not going to let the opportunity slip away again.

With a casual air, Meg mentioned, "Speaking of the Founders Courts . . ." Excellent segue, Meg congratulated herself. "When we were on the courts yesterday, did I hear you on the phone with Michael Edmonds?" Marilyn cocked her head and her eyes narrowed with penetrating interest. Undeterred, Meg stuck with it. "I thought I heard his name. I know him from Lakeview."

"Do you, now?" Marilyn's eyelid twitched with the hint of a smile.

So Marilyn all but confirmed there was something shifty going on. Before she lost her nerve, Meg laid it on the table. "Do you know what he's doing on Bainbridge?"

For a long moment, Marilyn glowered, assessing her. Maybe a subtle approach would have worked better. But before Meg could backpedal, a decision flashed across Marilyn's features.

"Listen, Meg." Marilyn pressed her cool fingers against Meg's forearm, disarming her. In her clipped, no-nonsense manner, she said, "You seem like a sensible person. And ultimately, I'm hoping you'll reconsider playing for Bainbridge in the Picklesmash Tournament. So, in the spirit of pickleball camaraderie, I will let you in on a secret. But you mustn't breathe a word to anyone."

Marilyn leaned forward. "Michael Edmonds," she whispered, "is our secret weapon."

Meg felt the thrum of her pulse. So, Michael Edmonds was training the enemy. That weasel! But just to be sure she understood, Meg asked, "Secret weapon? What does that mean?"

Marilyn mimed locking her neatly lined lips. Then she opened her mouth, threw the invisible key inside, chewed, and swallowed.

Forcing her composure, Meg shook her head in disbelief. Poor Annie. What a piece of work, that Michael Edmonds! Just wait till she laid eyes on that backstabbing pickleswapper.

A breeze laced with the scent of burnt sugar blew past. Marilyn startled. "Oh! I have a pie going!" She bolted toward the back door, calling, "Hope you like blackberry for breakfast."

But as Meg stood center court stewing over that traitor Michael Edmonds, the pie's rich aroma softened her fury. She ran a hand along the net, caressing the tape, and her gaze traveled up and up to the dark green canopy of the evergreens.

It *was* peaceful here on Bainbridge. There was no doubt she loved the vibrant culture across the water in Seattle: the seafood restaurants, cute coffee shops, the theaters and nightclubs, the vitality and ubiquity of the arts communities. Like in Seattle, the island teemed with authors, painters, and musicians. But here the pace of life was more relaxed, more in tune with nature. She could totally understand why Marilyn, or in fact anyone, would choose to live here. Yes. Hints of a future life sparkled around the corners of her consciousness. Meg breathed in a deep lungful of berry-and-pine-scented air.

The sound of footsteps on the blacktop cut through her daydream, and she pivoted toward the noise.

"Well," Ethan Fine said, oblivious to her shock. "If it isn't Clam Chowder."

FOURTEEN

Meg gaped, her confusion giving way to surprise when her brain confirmed what her vision suggested. It was him, that dastardly, dashing Ethan Fine, sauntering onto the court.

Her lips stuttered before the words tripped out. "What are you doing here?" Meg asked, trying and failing to keep her voice cool as she wrapped her head around this turn of events.

"I was wondering the same thing about you," he commented.

They blinked at each other and at the same time said, "Marilyn invited me."

Still adjusting to the shock, she took in his full appearance. He wore a sports tee, the kind made from a material that clings to the pecs and accentuates the abs. When her eyes traveled down his torso, they halted. His right hand loosely gripped . . . a pickleball paddle?!

"Is that a . . . pickleball paddle?" The question, in light of the circumstances, was idiotic.

Ethan's gaze flicked to his hand. "Sure looks like one."

Of course he played pickleball. He looked like an *ad* for pickleball. Meg thought, *I would buy a lot of pickleball*. A reactive grin angled up Meg's cheek, but she stopped it in its tracks.

Wait a sec. She was furious with him.

The chill Bainbridge aura that had soothed her moments earlier drained away and her mind recalibrated. Michael Edmonds, pie, the original courts, all of it vanished as she set about facing the enemy before her.

She narrowed her eyes at him. Ethan Fine, master of pickle sabotage, was a pickleballer?! Yet he had padlocked Lakeview's courts! The truth of his manipulations sank in: he had understood the impact of closing their courts on their preparations for the tournament, yet he had done it anyway! And then, to add insult to injury, he'd had the nerve to kiss her and make her feel all moony over him. That infuriating, wetland-preserving Adonis! What a weasel.

The porch door smacked shut. Meg forced herself to stop staring and turned to see Marilyn hefting a fat blackberry pie. "Ethan. Glad you could make it. This is Meg. I invited her today because I thought you two should meet each other." She looked from one to the other. "Or have you already met?"

"Yes. Actually, Meg and I have met on a couple of occasions," Ethan said, gazing at Meg with his sultry, hooded eyes. Dammit! Why wasn't he acting all sorry and drenched in guilt for putting the kibosh on her league's dreams? And why did his stare make her feel like combusting into flames? She felt the reaction in her belly, her barbecue burners heating up. She could have grilled a T-bone, easy.

Ethan was still chatting, oblivious to Meg's inner incinerator. "My mom and Marilyn have known each other for years."

Marilyn's eyes twinkled with laughter. "Oh yes. She used to bring Ethan here all the time. He would run around like crazy through these woods. We had to watch him like a hawk to keep him from putting pine cones in his mouth."

"And that was just last week," Ethan deadpanned. The mischief in his eyes was so appealing. Dagnabbit! A pickleballer! The nerve. For the better half of June, he had worked beside their courts, hefting pipes and posing for her imaginary calendar, and never once did he give any indication that he was a player. Even times when they clearly needed a fourth.

She would bring it up. The locked courts. The destruction of Lakeview's dreams. She would lay into him right now and give him a piece of her mind.

Marilyn set the cast-iron skillet on the wooden bench. The bubbling blackberries dripped from the crumble crust.

Maybe a piece of pie first; piece of her mind later.

"How 'bout you two hit a bit while it cools," Marilyn suggested. To Meg she said, "Ethan's a natural. He played badminton on the US national team."

A professional net athlete? She would not play with him. Not in a million years, she thought as her gaze skated along the tendons powering his calves. Those were picklecalves, all right. Go figure. Not just a pickleballer, but a champion athlete. Somehow this made things worse. If he had been just an average, run-of-the mill jock, it would have been easier to stomach his vendetta against Lakeview's courts. But a guy like that? He should know better than to take away the training ground for the up-and-coming players.

"That's all right. I have plans to play later today with my *friend*," Meg said, emphasizing the last word to clarify where her allegiances lay. "Anyhow, you're probably out of my league." She narrowed her eyes at him coolly.

"I was just thinking the same thing about you," he said. "But I hope not."

Meg gulped. How infuriating it was, the way his voice instigated a melty feeling in her belly. And when he extended a pickleball—never looking at it but only at her—she took it, promising herself to chew him out after the game. And after the pie.

Fine. She would play, albeit recognizing that she had held off just shy of a millisecond. And anyhow, she couldn't lay into him with Marilyn standing right there. That would be rude! But she would show him—she would refuse to enjoy it.

And then they were warming up. While they dinked, somehow she managed to get the ball back to him. His stylish shots appeared effortless while hitting their mark consistently. She had played with and against plenty of people who boasted that they were life-long racket sport enthusiasts and retired tennis pros, but badminton's technique transferred perfectly to pickleball. Ethan's hits were accurate and relaxed. She watched him command the court, admiring-not-admiring his athleticism and grace.

Marilyn waved from the sidelines. "All righty. Now, who wants pie?" These Bainbridge folks were so darn likable, it was hard to be mad. Perhaps, she began to think, Ethan was right to padlock the Lakeview courts. Who knew what crazy stunt Jeannie might pull next; something to jeopardize the rest of the school's expensive re-model? Obviously, his consulting company couldn't take that risk.

Besides, Meg's fortuitous discoveries were beginning to blur the edges of her ire. Look at where she was! Playing on the original courts. Ethan in shorts. Blackberry pie for breakfast. It was barely nine in the morning, she realized as they broke for pie, and there was already cause to celebrate.

The blackberries tasted divine—the ideal blend of citrus and sweetness with a kick of vitamin C that tingled Meg's cheeks and set her salivary glands humming. She scraped her fork along the plate, capturing the last slivers of berry juice, and stopped short of licking the plate only after a cautionary glance from Marilyn when she lifted it to do so.

"Delicious," Meg declared, and leapt up to help clear.

"Leave it," Marilyn commanded. "I'll get it later." She was already sorting through her bag of pickleballs and choosing the greenest, bounciest one. Marilyn marched to the service side of the court and assumed a ready stance. "Let's try something. The two of you against me. I'll play this side. Cutthroat style."

"Marilyn . . ." Ethan started. "The two of us against one of you? No offense, but . . ."

"Tch." Marilyn's fingers snapped together. "Zip it."

Meg joined Ethan on the opposite side of the court. "Do you want me to . . ."

"Zero–zero," Marilyn said, announcing the score and closing any arguments. Immediately, she served a zinger that whipped right past Ethan.

"Oh. It's on." Ethan nodded, accepting the challenge.

"1–zero." Marilyn pulled a new ball from the hip of her stretchy leggings and powered off another serve. This one, Meg returned to corner court.

Marilyn was spry and had no difficulty covering the full court. And while Meg played with enthusiasm, Ethan's talent was his patience and technique. In between points, he shared strategies, using his paddle as a screen to hide his lips.

"She's a power player," he whispered. "Let her beat herself. All we have to do is hit soft. Dink. Place our shots and let her whale on it right into the net."

And it worked. As a team, they complemented each other. Where Meg had speed and strength, Ethan had finesse. Marilyn, however, continued to pepper Meg with rocket shots.

"Slow it down," Ethan encouraged. And the next time Marilyn sent a bullet across the net, Meg dampened it and dropped it into the kitchen. Marilyn was still at the baseline, and although she ran toward the net, by the time she got there, she popped the ball and it flew right into the woods.

"I got it," Marilyn said, and slipped between the bordering trees to scrounge around in the underbrush.

When she was out of earshot, Ethan commented, "See? If you return force with force, the bangers will beat you every time. But if you take off the power, they can't get to it."

"I'll have to remember that."

"I knew you two would play well together." Marilyn returned, waving the plastic ball overhead like a prize. Handing the ball to Meg, she said, "Ethan is playing in the tournament, but we are working on finding a solid partner for him. Ethan, dear, I'm trying to get Meg to jump ship from Lakeview. You ought to convince her to play in Picklesmash on our beginner team with you."

Hold on. What? "*You're* playing in the beginner slot for Bainbridge?"

"Oh yes." Marilyn nodded. "He's never played in a pickleball tournament before. You two would make a good pairing. Mind you, he already has a partner, but I think you might be a better fit. And you said yourself last night at the winery: your Seattle team may be going with a different beginners' matchup. Seems like when opportunity knocks," she said, rapping on an invisible door, "you should answer the doorbell."

Meg could hardly believe what she was hearing.

A surge of indignation built from her nylon laces to her elastic hair tie. Now it made sense. This must have been his sadistic plan all along. Close their courts. Lock up the gate. Pit the players against one another. Then crush them in Picklesmash and take the spoils for Bainbridge. Now, wasn't that a bag of pickles!

And how dare Marilyn suggest that Meg consider dumping Lakeview to throw herself in with their chief competition. Besides, playing for her Seattle team wasn't only about proving that she could succeed, or that she could take down Vance in a pickle-off. She wanted to contribute to Lakeview's opportunity to earn the funds to build new courts. And even though Jeannie had treated her like doggy doody and threatened to replace her with her nemesis, Lakeview was still her community. They were like family. And didn't all families have a dysfunctional relative like Jeannie, anyway? Someone who would get super wasted at Cousin Caroline's wedding and loudly proclaim that the groom looked like Mr. Potato Head? She was losing the thread, but the point was that even though she was clearly attracted to Ethan—because he was undeniably the hottest thing since the surface of the sun—he had methodically machinated a malicious scheme against her peeps, and she was not about to let him get away with it for one second longer.

Her rib cage heaved and she glared at him. Meg was a teakettle on the verge of a boil. A lit firecracker. "Can I speak with you for a second?" she asked, sounding more together than she felt.

Ethan exchanged a wary glance with Marilyn.

"I'll just"—Marilyn looked around for a prop—"take this spoon inside," and she ambled through the screen door.

Alone with Ethan now, Meg glowered. Dammit, she had really liked kissing him, and now it was her job, nay, her duty, to tear him a new one.

"What the hell, Ethan?" She felt her nostrils expand with her ire, and even though she knew it was not a good look on her, she flared away. "You act like you're all sympathetic about us losing our courts because your company is shutting them down, but really, you can't wait to slap a Plan It Earth padlock on them and keep us from practicing so that your Bainbridge buddies can leap up and take Picklesmash from us. And what's with the save-our-wetlands crap, huh? Was that just some cover story so you could take down our league? I mean, do you even *like* birds?"

"Whoa. Whoa. Whoa. Slow down. I—"

"Don't 'whoa' me. You play pickleball and you never mentioned it? And then you lock up our courts so Lakeview can't practice? You've been plotting this all along, haven't you? You and your . . . pie-baking, pickleball-starting, planet-saving, jerky Bainbridge friends." That had not come out as venomously as she had intended.

"Hold on." Ethan's tone was calmer than she wanted it to be. *Go ahead*, she thought, *just try and defend yourself*. She was itching to do a dramatic stalk-away. "You're talking about the padlock I put on the Lakeview gate?" he asked.

"Yes. That's the one. Why? Are you padlocking multiple courts?" She did not hide the snark.

"Okay. Yeah. That was me. I put the lock on 'cause the courts were soaked from all the rain, and they were in such bad condition that you had moss growing. The surface was so slick I was worried you guys would get hurt. I just locked them up for a few days so my crew could pressure-wash the surface. It was kind of a peace offering. I left a note, but it must have blown off. Anyhow, they're open again, and not so slippery . . ."

Her mouth worked pointlessly. "Oh."

So he'd locked the courts out of kindness. That put a damper on her indignation.

"And I'm sorry I didn't let you know that I played pickleball. I wanted to, but then that Jeannie woman . . ." He grimaced. "I hate to think what she's like when she's really angry."

It was true: Jeannie's methods of showing her loyalty to her league were unconventional. Meg could hardly blame Ethan for withholding when the alternative was to face Jeannie's wrath.

"But, as for Marilyn's suggestion that you consider playing on Bainbridge's beginner team—I mean, I already do have a beginner partner. But he's on the fence about playing in a tournament. And you just seem like a solid player. So if Lakeview is already set on their roster for the tournament—"

"Lakeview is *not* yet set on their roster."

The screen door creaked. Then stilled. Then squeaked again. Then Marilyn swung it fully open, no longer hiding behind any pretense that she hadn't been eavesdropping the whole time. "Meg, dear." She gave Meg a mollifying, close-lipped smile. "Give it a try. How 'bout you come out and practice with him a few times? See where it goes."

Ethan tilted his head and gave her a baleful, puppy-dog plea. It was annoyingly persuasive.

Meg's throat let out a frustrated growl. She wanted so badly to beat the pants off Vance for that spot. She wanted to crush him beneath her pickleball shoes with her treads, which were especially conducive to lateral movements. And here she was, standing not two feet away from the one guy who could bring up her game.

"Fine. I'll practice with you," she said. A grin split his cheeks. "But only so that I can earn my spot on Lakeview's roster. You're going to have to keep looking for a partner of your own, and then you better be ready, 'cause my partner Rooster and I are gonna bring it!"

"Deal." They shook on it, and the heat in his eye contact scorched her eyelashes. She let down her guard and allowed her lip to creep up her cheek. He'd padlocked the courts so he could clean the moss! What a relief to know that he was not a total asshole. And that was a good thing, because with the way he looked in those shorts, it would be a shame to hate him.

From the doorway, Marilyn feigned disinterest in their private conversation. "Anyone up for another piece?"

"More pie, Meg?" Ethan asked, his voice low. "I know I would like another piece. Once I had a taste, I knew I wanted more."

And both of them knew they were not talking about the pie.

FIFTEEN

Meg bent to stretch her knees and shoulders. She was glad for the additional practice with Annie. It would hone her skills for her upcoming practice with Ethan. The anticipation excited her, as did the tension of wanting to impress him. All the court time in the three days since their arrival on Bainbridge burned her shoulders and glutes. But her body felt strong and well tuned.

It had been a long time since she had felt desire, and been desired in turn, and this made her world sparkle. Here at the Founders Courts, the landscape shimmered brighter than the other day, the grass lusher and the players more jubilant.

While she and Annie dinked in the kitchen, the familiar pick-pock of their bouncing pickleball reverberated on the pavement and fanned out into the open spaces by the soccer and ball fields. An older man walking his dog paused to watch them and asked, "What's that game called?" He hmphed at the name and said, "Looks like fun. Maybe I'll give it a try sometime."

Annie smiled when he left. "If I had a dollar for every time someone said exactly that . . ."

"You'd have two dollars?"

"At least."

Nearby, on the repurposed tennis courts, Coach Chad dinked

over the net while a bevy of white-haired friends gossiped and laughed as they waited to rotate into the lesson. Because of the afternoon heat, other than the Island Haven retirement community van, the lot was nearly empty of cars. Meg guessed it wouldn't remain so long. As the day wore on and the weather cooled down, Islanders of all ages would arrive to de-stress after work.

They moved to either side of the court and Annie knocked it over the net with a diagonal dink. "You know, you've inspired me," Annie reflected. She kept a steady patter going to the rhythm of the bouncing ball. "I'm going to try to make myself . . . more open to new opportunities. Like you did with Ethan."

Over lunch, Annie had lapped up every detail of Meg's description of her encounter with Ethan on the original courts. By then, the Lakeview courts had reopened, and their group chat confirmed that another note, the one about cleaning the moss off the asphalt, had been recovered from the trash. Both Annie and Meg suspected Jeannie, Lakeview's official pot-stirrer, of tossing the evidence.

Annie pressed on. "No, really. I'm impressed. You are putting yourself out there. I don't think I'd have the nerve to, you know, unbutton enough to kiss a guy I'd just met. I guess what I'm saying is," Annie chatted on, "I'd like to be more available. Put myself out there."

"Like *risk it for the biscuit*," Meg teased. "What does that mean, anyhow? Is there some biscuit that everyone wants?"

"Is it a dog biscuit?" Annie opined. "Or is it a cookie biscuit? And what's the trade-off? I mean, biscuits are pretty low value in my opinion."

"There are things in this world we may never fully understand." Just then, Annie lobbed the ball. Leaping to reach it, Meg swung at the air, missing the ball by a good foot.

"Woo-hoo. Point!" Annie called. "No falling asleep at the wheel.

You should have seen that coming." She coached, "When I scoop my paddle low, you should turn and start running right away so you're at the baseline in time for the return. I love me a good lob. Did you know a lob follows a perfect parabolic curve?"

Leave it to Annie to love pickleball because of the math involved. "That is *fascinating*."

"Did you know that the diameter of a parabola is called the latus rectum?"

"*You're* a latus rectum." Meg's shot dropped right at the baseline.

"Your momma is a latus rectum—" Annie called, racing for the return. When she came up short, she gaped at Meg. "Wow. Great shot!"

Meg panted as she reveled in her victory, a genuine smile blooming on her face.

Strolling to the net, Annie gave her a congratulatory paddle tap. "A few months ago, you'd never picked up a paddle. Now look at you! When you and Rooster get to play in the tournament, you two will smoke the competition."

The ache in Meg's triceps called out to her, and both ladies concurred that it was time to pause for a fiver. "So . . ." Meg started, "I heard Bainbridge is playing in Picklesmash. With Ethan in their beginners' slot." She might as well spill the whole story. "And they want me to play with him."

Annie's eyes grew to the size of coffee saucers. "What?! The nerve!"

"I'm not going to. But I told Ethan I'd practice with him. Just because Rooster doesn't have a lot of availability." Flustered, she explained, "I just don't want you to think I'm going behind Lakeview's back. And . . . I really want you to like him."

Annie's expression shifted, and her eyes brimmed with empathy. "Meg." She shook her head like she was about to explain what should have been a given. "You don't have to justify it to me. You *like* him. And I like *you*. So according to the transitive property of equality, I *already do* like him."

The logic was lost on her, but Meg felt a weight being lifted. Annie opened her arms.

"Come here," Annie said, gesturing. "You know you can tell me anything and I will never not love you." She crushed Meg into a bear hug and rocked her friend back and forth for a reassuring minute.

Finally, Meg muttered, "Okay. But I'm telling everybody you used a double negative."

Giving Meg a decisive squeeze, Annie's chipmunk voice whispered into Meg's hair, "When a double negative conveys a positive, it's grammatically correct."

Meg's laugh came out as part snort, part cry. She was just so grateful for Annie's all-forgiving friendship.

"Hi-de-ho, ladies." Rooster appeared, toting his paddle. Spotting the fresh emotion on Meg's face, he asked, "I'm not interrupting anything, am I?"

Annie tapped her paddle against his. "You're just in time. Meg, you ready?"

She sniffled, smiling with the relief of the recently unburdened. "I could go for another game or two."

Rooster gave her a smug grin, accepting the challenge. "A game or two? Oh, you better paddle up. 'Cause we're playin' till the wheels come off."

· · · · ·

A new stream of picklers trickled onto the courts, having come straight from work. Meg noticed one guy slip off his tie and change into pickleball shoes, while two cars over, a woman bent over in her passenger seat used her car as a phone booth and emerged as a pickle-ball superhero. Meg buzzed like she always did when the pickleball forces gathered—feeling that anticipation that she might win a game. Or lose a game. Or simply play a game.

For the next two hours, Meg played so hard that her sports bra could be wrung out into a shot glass. Even so, every few moments, her hits suffered from distraction when a reminder of Ethan's existence would ping her brain. They had planned to meet up the next evening when he finished working, and the thought of hitting with the hottie popped up as often as pickleballs on a learner's court.

At last, Rooster and Meg hobbled off the courts, spent. Annie, who had joined them for a water break, offered Meg a wry smile. "You should rest up. You'll wanna be fresh for your game tomorrow."

"Game?" Rooster asked.

"Meg has a play date."

"Glad to hear it. I'm rootin' for ya, kiddo." And it was clear that she and Ethan had Rooster in their court.

Behind Annie, movement caught Meg's attention when a sleek sedan glided into a parking spot. Marilyn stepped out of the car, but before Meg could call out a greeting, her words halted in her throat. A second car had arrived in the lot a few spaces beyond Marilyn, and a tall figure stepped out. Her brain took a moment to make sense of the familiar vision: the anchorman hair, the broad shoulders, and the goofy smile. Meg gasped. After all her searching: Michael Edmonds!

Rooster must have caught a glimpse of him, too. His shoulders jumped and he squinted across the parking lot. "What the . . . ?!"

"What is it?" Annie asked, turning her head over her shoulder, searching, just as Michael strode behind a red cedar.

"Michael Edmonds!" Rooster mouthed to Meg while Annie's head was still turned.

"I know!" Meg repeated soundlessly, her face equally distorted with disbelief. Meg had given Rooster the rundown about Marilyn's claim, that he was "Bainbridge's secret weapon." And both hoped that Michael's coaching would not give Bainbridge too much of a leg up. Still, Meg hadn't yet told Annie what she had learned. She needed to be certain her intel was founded on fact before she told Annie anything. But here he was, impossible to miss. Michael Edmonds at a Bainbridge Island pickleball court.

Confused, Annie swiveled back. "What are we looking at?"

"Nothing . . ." Even to her own ears, it didn't pass for believable.

Rooster came to the rescue. "Birds," he said. "Bainbridge is famous for . . . strange birds. Important ones. Look!" He pointed into the cedar branches. "A . . . a . . ."

Annie wasn't buying it. "A. What."

"A tufted . . . red-beaked . . . downy . . . thing."

Slowly, Annie turned back and studied the tree suspiciously.

"Help! Somebody, help!" came a woman's voice from the court holding the seniors' lessons.

Alerted, Rooster's attentions leapt to the courts. "Somebody's down!" he cried. "It's Chad. Coach Chad's in trouble!"

"Get a doctor," came a cry from the courts.

The birds forgotten, Annie perked up. "I'm a doctor!" Her spine straightened with readiness. "I'm coming!" she shouted before taking off at a sprint.

Meg followed with Rooster loping behind. By the time they caught up, Annie was in full-tilt doctor mode. Although Chad stood on his feet, his face was tomato red. He listed sideways and had thrown his arms out to steady himself.

Annie asked, "Are you okay? What's going on?" Chad's face swelled. He gesticulated wildly.

The eight older ladies—all wearing sporty leggings, turtleneck shirts, and recently styled hairdos—shrugged their bewilderment. A squat woman in shatterproof goggles explained with maddening patience, "We were in between drills, and . . . Coach Chad—" Her hands fluttered at Chad, whose eyes flamed with panic. "Coach Chad was looking parched. And then Pearl here"—she gestured to her friend—"offered him some grapes from her garden, and then suddenly . . ."

Eyes bulging, Chad clutched at his throat.

Annie engaged. She gripped Chad's shoulder and spun the muscly man with a fountain of force. Positioning herself, Annie clasped her hands beneath his diaphragm and thrust upward. Bullet-like, a large, green grape flew from Chad's mouth and soared across the courts.

Chad sucked in a lungful of air. He sank to the asphalt, supporting himself with a hand on the hot pavement while he caught his breath. Annie knelt beside him and checked his pulse.

Panting for air, Marilyn raced onto the scene. "Chad!"

"I called the paramedics," Pearl told the group.

"Will he be okay?" asked an elderly woman with circus-orange hair.

"Yes," Annie assured her. "He'll be fine. But that ambulance is a good idea—just to have him checked out."

Other bystanders streamed onto the scene. "That was amazing!" one newcomer effused. "You saved him!" another said.

Then a new voice spoke up. "You jumped right in there with such . . . passionate abandon."

Annie turned her head, and her face blanched as she spotted none other than Michael Edmonds. There he stood, steps behind the gawking bystanders, smiling at Annie as if she were half the saints and all the unicorns rolled into one.

Annie blinked. Her gaze told a thousand tales. She spoke

wordlessly of an ocean's worth of hours spent pining for his love, of how their time together racing to the net, matching strides, side by side was more than a simple partnership. How when he dashed to retrieve a well-angled cross shot, she, as if on a pulley or attached by a rubber band, moved in tandem. Not everybody had what they had. In Annie's fantasy-ridden mind, this was more than simply a pickleball connection. This was love. And now the tenderness in his words confirmed that he felt the same way.

At least that's what Meg read in Annie's gaze.

"Passionate. Abandon," Annie repeated slowly, turning the phrase over in her mouth. Her thin voice warbled. "Oh, Michael Edmonds."

Michael tilted his head in what appeared to be confusion. Maybe he was having an out-of-context moment, but it looked to Meg like he had forgotten Annie's name.

"Annie," Meg offered quietly.

His lips lifted, captivated by her achievement. "Annie," he said. "You are an angel."

Annie stood. The concentration in her expression shifted from lifesaving mode to a more intense sort of determination. She stepped over Chad's prone figure, taking care not to step on his fingers. She cut through the circle of bystanders and beelined it to Michael Edmonds.

Annie Yoon hesitated only a moment, her petite frame tensed with decisiveness. Then, she rose onto her tiptoes, threw her arms around his shoulders, and planted one smack-dab on Michael Edmonds's lips.

If Michael was surprised, he did not show it. He kissed Annie back, more profoundly than might have been appropriate with all the octogenarians around. If there had been any question of whether Michael Edmonds's interest in Annie extended beyond pickleball, that sizzling kiss was the answer. When at last he broke away, he shook his head to clear the fog. "Well," he said. "That was . . . unexpected."

Sirens blaring, an ambulance arrived, and the paramedics cleared a path through the throng. One of the seniors gestured to Annie, and an EMT tapped her on the shoulder. "You the doctor?" he asked. Annie smiled into the distance, her face fixed on the tree branches, her body detached from the chaos around her. "Excuse me. You the doctor?" he repeated.

She blinked away her dreaminess and shifted back to attention. "Yes. I'm Dr. Yoon."

Meg glanced between Annie and Michael and back again. This must be what Annie meant when she'd said Meg had inspired her to take bold chances. Annie hadn't just opened the door to new possibilities, she had taken it square off its hinges.

SIXTEEN

The early-evening sunlight cast net-shadows of elongated criss-crosses onto the blue pavement. From the silver arch that marked the Founders Courts' entrance, Meg's pulse bumped up a notch when she spotted Ethan stretching his leg over the bench of the picnic table. The way his smile sprang up when he noticed her sprinkled her with flattering confetti. He straightened and bowed theatrically. "Welcome, Lady of the Pickleball. We have-eth reserve-ed this spot-eth for the full hour."

"Whatever you do," she quipped, and tipped her cap, "don't quit your consulting job for a Shakespearean acting career." But truth be told, she was charmed to be the target of his flirtation.

They set up on the neatly painted courts, and Ethan suggested she retreat to the baseline and practice her drops into the no-volley zone. Ah, she thought, so he really *did* intend to practice pickleball, and today's plan was not some elaborate ruse to sneak off with her and have sex behind the courts—as she had hoped.

With Ethan's attentions pegged on her, she flubbed her first shot and sent the second bouncing onto a picnic table. The third-shot drop was a tricky move that required unyielding attention, and since she was distracted by Ethan's presence, her success rate was about one in four. Once in a while, she managed to hit a searing drop. Alternatively, she whacked the ball with too much force, and it went flying into the net.

To Meg's dismay, Ethan's focus was all business. "You have the skill, but you're inconsistent. You can't let the game get in your head. Let your limbs move freely. Don't overthink it," he observed after they had been playing for a bit. "Give your body the chance to do what it wants. The body knows best, better than your brain."

Easy for him to say when he is standing there looking all edible and talking about moving bodies. She swatted at the ball, all the while watching him on the other side of the net. His taut calves compressed with his steps. His shirt lifted to reveal a thin arrow of hair on his muscled abdomen. An arrow that pointed directly to . . . Now *that* was what her body wanted. Maybe her brain, too. Either way, it became more and more difficult to keep her eye, both literally and figuratively, on the ball.

"Let's take a break." His words sounded muffled to her daydream-riddled brain. He strode to the picnic table to grab his water bottle, and she watched his Adam's apple bob when he took a deep drink. He said something more, but she was mesmerized by the sexy sheen of sweat beading on his collarbone . . .

"Right?" he asked. She had missed the question.

"Sorry. You were saying?"

"Just that you have the skills, but you have to put the confidence behind your swing."

"I know. I know," she said, forcing away her lusty thoughts. She knew Ethan was right. Here was an opportunity to improve; she must not waste it. If she and Rooster managed to secure Lakeview's beginners' slot, she didn't want to be a lead pipe attached to Rooster's helium balloon. Practicing with one's top competitor may have been unwise, but if it gave her an advantage, it would be worth it.

With her attention back on her pickleskills, the next hour flew by, and when they realized that nobody else had reserved the courts, they decided to play on. Forty minutes into their bonus time, Meg pushed through the mental and physical fatigue and landed in that rhythmic, hypnotic state of pure adrenaline. Cushioned by the addictive embrace of pickleball, all other distractions vanished. She thrilled when she put a slice to the back corner right past him and won the point.

"Woo-hoo," she cheered. "That might have been the greatest sports highlight of my life."

Laughing, he added, "With the way you've been improving, I bet you've got a lot more where that came from."

It was a magnetic trait, his habit of being generous with his faith in her. Meg beamed at the compliment, especially coming from a real athlete. "Were you always a jock?" she asked.

Ethan scoffed. "Not at all. You should have seen me in middle school. But . . . No. Forget it."

"Come on," she urged. "I won a point off you. I should get something. Truth or dare. Tell me your most embarrassing middle school sports moment."

"Don't *I* get to choose truth or dare?"

"Not this time. Most embarrassing moment. Spill it."

"Okay." He winced at the memory and prepped himself with a shake of his head. "In middle school, I was on the small side and kind of a pudgy guy. And the gym uniforms didn't fit right. So my mom found a substitute shirt with a picture of the school mascot, a tiger, on the front. I didn't pay much attention to the back, but apparently it said *Tiger Cub*." Ethan paused, drawing out the punch. "After that, the kids all called me Chubby Cubby." Meg put a hand to her mouth, imagining his mortification. "Yeah. Exactly. Made it hard to get a date in high school," he joked.

It was hard to picture a younger, awkward Ethan, when this

grown-up version was so athletic and confident. Before long, though, he got his retribution when he aced her on a serve.

"First kiss?" he asked, and she told him about the homecoming dance with sponge-tongued Jeff Belger. Fortunately, kisses since then had been on the up and up. Thinking back to her make-out session in the car and the romantic smooch with Ethan on the porch, she grinned. "But I've had better since then."

Back and forth they went, sharing the truth about first loves. Him: Maureen Chen. Fourth grade. They traded Halloween candy, and he let her have all his chocolate. Her: a summer camp fling with Howie Leventhal that ended when the song he "wrote for her" turned out to be by some guy named Keith Urban. The evening light grew golden as they revealed their favorite foods and films and books and worst work experiences. Him: mussel debearder for a local shellfish company. Her: costumed mailbox mascot for a trade show. Meg's wins were so disproportionately rare that she resorted to cheating to get him to answer some questions, blatantly serving the ball to him when he wasn't even standing on the court.

"Fine," he said. "Even though you're a cheater, I'll let you have the point. And I'm gonna take a risk here. Let's see what you come up with. Dare."

Meg's eyes slid to the side in thought. Deciding, she said, "I would like to see you perform an interpretive pickleball dance."

Ethan smirked. "Oh. You want to see the pickledance," he taunted. "Many, many people have requested the pickledance. And I have not danced." He hid his face behind the paddle and lowered it dramatically as he revealed his eyes. "But for you, Meg Bloomberg, I will dance."

Flinging his hand with the pickleball overhead, he struck a powerful pose, somewhere between a bullfighter and a ballerina. To her delight, Ethan issued a series of flamenco steps across the blue pavement, making up a tune to his steps. Then, stopping short with his back to Meg, he froze again, and switched his accompaniment to a raunchy backbeat. Swinging his paddle, he segued into slow and tempting swivels of his hips. Into it now, Ethan dug into the role. He swished and twerked while she cheered her approval. As she applauded, he bumped up the silliness factor on his risqué moves.

Turning his head her way, he announced, "And now, the grand finale."

Stalking languidly over to the pole supporting the net, he grabbed on with both hands and began to pole dance. She squealed with laughter. Pleased with the effect, he hammed it up, spanking his butt with the paddle and singing, "*Ooo. Pickle-ball. Ooo! Pickle—*Oh. Hello."

Ethan stopped spanking himself and waved cheerily to the old man and woman who stood at the entrance to the court, open-mouthed.

Meg shrugged a hand toward Ethan by way of explanation. "Pickle-ball," she said, pretty much ensuring that they would never play.

In the wake of the couple's wordless departure, Meg and Ethan busted out in giggles. Once they cooled down, Ethan said, "Okay. It's my turn again. Because you cheated to get that dare, you owe me a truth." He squinted at the sky. "Lemme think of a good one. Ah." He decided. "Who was the last person you were in love with?"

Meg let out an uncomfortable laugh. For nearly a week now, thankfully, Vance had been the last person on her mind, and she really did not want to get into the whole saga yet. Certainly not when things were going so well with Ethan. She tried to throw him off task.

"You have to play fair," she teased. "You didn't win a point, so you don't get to ask me that. And anyway," she said, "this truth or dare is distracting me from my pickleball growth trajectory. I have a lot of learning to get in before dark."

Acquiescing, Ethan gave her arm a tender squeeze before moving back to his side of the net. The sun would set soon, and they put the silliness aside, agreeing to focus on drills while they still had daylight.

The rhythm of play took over. As they hit, her brain and body absorbed Ethan's graceful, assertive play, learning by his example. She fixed her attention on the bend in his knees when he scooped the ball for a dink shot, and on the flick of his wrist in his slice. She copied his movements, feeling the change in her body as she relaxed into the drills.

Even so, she had miles to go. Arching her back, Meg reached for an overhead slam and whiffed the ball.

"Let me help you with that shot." And in a blink, Ethan had sailed gracefully over the net and slipped beside her. "Watch," he said. Ethan tossed a ball into the air. As it reached its zenith, he pointed with his left hand. "Spot the ball with your finger," he said, snapping the paddle down and sending the ball sailing to the opposite baseline.

"Not only will that help you track the ball, but pointing distracts and intimidates your opponent. They know a slam is coming. And a well-aimed one at that. You gotta get in their heads," he said, tossing one ball then another and smacking them to the opposite side.

"Pickleball is like any small-team competitive sport. It's just you against one or two people, so skill is only part of the battle." Meg watched in amazement as he produced a seemingly endless string of balls from his ample pockets. "You've got to psych them out. Show them you came to play. It can be as obvious as your swagger when you walk onto the court, or as subtle as calling out 'Got it!' as you point at your intended slam. Grunt or yell as you hit. It freaks out the competition." Ethan stood behind her, and the warmth coming off his body sent a chill up her neck. "You try it now."

He placed his fingers on her hip and handed her a ball. Her skin, exposed right at that spot, burned with the heat of his touch. "Throw, point with your left, then bam!"

She tossed the ball. "Now!" he commanded. She lunged forward, so flustered by his nearness that her paddle whiffed the ball. Again.

He shrugged. "Let me take you through it in slow motion." There was that hand on her hip again, steadying her. He traced his fingers along her forearm, and as they leaned back in unison, he clasped his hand over hers and tipped the paddle down onto the imaginary ball. She'd never imagined practicing pickleball could be so damn sexy.

"That's it," he said. "You got it."

She did have it, and for once she planned to do something about it. She spun toward him in his light hold. "Dare," she whispered, tilting her face to his.

"I thought you didn't want to play anymore," he teased. But his smiling eyes accepted the challenge. His fingers gripped the hem of her crop top and tugged downward, pulling her closer. For an endless second, she absorbed his nearness, the waves of heat between their bodies.

His mouth swept against her neck and he breathed her in. "You smell so good."

Embarrassed, she giggled. "I'm a little sweaty."

"I like it."

Then his lips were on hers. Everything was sensation, rocket lift-offs in every centimeter of her body. His hands traveled along her vertebrae, tracing down her spine and squeezing her hips to his. Her body reacted. Under his touch, she sizzled. *This is happening,* she thought. A smoking-hot guy was making out with her on a pickleball court. It was like eating chocolate truffles while getting a massage. Could this much pleasure be legal? She dug her hands beneath the hem of his T-shirt and raked the tips of her fingers up toward his ribs.

He laughed suddenly. "All right. All right." Running a hand through his hair, he stepped back and put his hands on his hips. He shook his head at the pavement. "You're getting me all . . ." Forcefully, he blew out the air from his lungs.

Despite herself, Meg grinned, happy to have been the cause of his reaction.

"It's the pickleball," she kidded. "It has that effect on a lot of people."

"If it did, more people would play pickleball." He collected himself and loped back around to the opposite side of the net. "All right. Give it a try now."

Meg shook off her distraction and readied herself. She really wanted to impress him. Wanted him to jump back over the net and congratulate her. Mainly, she wanted to kiss him again.

But she wanted to earn it. Concentrating, she tossed the ball overhead, pointed, and swung her paddle arm into the air. She lined up the shot, holding the parabolic trajectory in her sights. Then, targeting his feet, she snapped down hard with her wrist. She struck the ball with force and watched it rocket over the net.

Meg had seen horror movies where the filmmaker slowed the action, underlaid suspenseful music, and zoomed in to focus on the doomed victim's expression. She just never thought she would see the same moment unfold in real life.

Until now.

The ball powered forward like a slo-mo missile, flying over the net, zipping through the air, picking up speed, and slamming home—directly in the center of Ethan's shorts. She heard him gasp, watched his features cramp, stared helplessly as his body crumpled into a heap on the court's hard surface.

Mortified, Meg dropped her paddle and raced to the other side of the net. "Oh my god! Oh my god! Ethan!"

On the asphalt, Ethan writhed. He rocked from side to side but uttered nothing save a high-pitched keening. The sound bounced off the courts and echoed off the distant, snow-capped Olympic Mountains. Far away, from the national forest, Meg thought she heard a moose answer what he must have believed was a mating call.

Throwing herself to her knees beside Ethan, she said, "I'm so, so sorry. Are you okay?" Instinctively, she reached toward the wounded area.

Ethan threw his arm up in a defensive block. "No! No!" He twisted his body like a roly-poly. "Let me just"—his face contorted—"lie here a minute."

With great effort, Ethan rolled onto his side and then lay still as stone, his hands clasped between his thighs.

"What should I do?" Meg fluttered about him, helpless. "I don't think there's any ice around here." She took his unresponsiveness as encouragement for better ideas. "Can I take you to the hospital?"

"I got it under control." He sucked in his breath.

"Let me give my friend Annie a call. She could come take a look."

Ethan dipped his brow, hovering between bewilderment and incredulity.

"She's seen more penises than anyone I know. She's kind of an expert. Granted, they were little penises." Meg clarified, "Kids' penises."

At that, Ethan's reaction shifted to horror. "Not like that!" She waved her hands, erasing her previous statements. "She's a doctor. At Seattle Children's."

Shaking his head, Ethan struggled to sit. "Nope. No thanks. I think I'm okay."

She helped him stand. "I'm so sorry," she repeated. Not only for injuring him, but for breaking the romantic mood. She berated herself immediately for her selfish thoughts, but dang it, things had been going so well and now . . .

"I'm gonna hop into the bathroom a sec and . . . check things out. I might be a minute."

He hobbled into the nearby brick building. For a full minute, Meg waited, her body tense and her heartbeat pounding in her ears. Being a woman had its ups and downs, but at least she could never be hit in the penis with a pickleball.

Without warning, the air was rent with a curdled scream.

The hairs on the back of Meg's neck jumped to attention. "Everything okay in there?"

For a moment, she heard no response. At last, hoarse and cracked, Ethan's voice answered, "Yep. Just . . . peeing."

• • • • •

A pink and orange glow of evening provided an ironic romanticism to their walk home. They ambled along the shore toward the inn. Ethan set the pace; he still lumbered awkwardly, his movements cautious.

"Before the"—Ethan gestured vaguely at his shorts—"incident. Well, before that, I was thinking. We play well together."

"You think?"

"Definitely. We have a rhythm. It feels natural. You know what I mean?"

She nodded. It was an easy chemistry they shared—not only on the court, but even here as they meandered along the rocky shoreline. The waves of Puget Sound came in low and deep, and when the water receded, it pulled along the myriad pebbles with a noise like coffee percolating. When he slipped his smooth fingers through hers it felt nice. As comfortable as breathing.

Silently agreeing that the walk to the end of the beach would be challenging, they stopped, taking a seat on a broad driftwood log that formed an ideal bench above the tide line. High on the shoreline, the sand was dry and soft beneath her feet. The smell of seaweed, the cool evening air, and the tinkling of the pebbles pulled by the waves intoxicated Meg, and she made sure to file this moment away to revisit over and over again.

Turning, she found Ethan's eyes on her. She smiled as he dipped his fingers through her hair and held her with his eyes, steady with focus. Her mind floated, a heady elation that intensified when he closed his eyes and tipped his head to hers. A curling sensation like a perfect wave traveled from her mouth to her belly and down to her toes. The tip of her tongue tasted his warm mouth, and the contrast thrilled her.

"When can I see you again?" he asked into her mouth.

"When you open your eyes," she answered archly.

Ethan slid off the driftwood log onto the sand and pulled her on top. "How 'bout tomorrow?" he asked. "Or late, late tonight?" Hungrily, she kissed him, allowing her hands to roam to the curve of his shoulders, along his chest, and down to his navel. She gripped his belt buckle and tugged.

"Ah! Ow!" he cried suddenly.

She jumped off him. He crab-scooted backward along the sand, dragging his legs. "Okay. Ow. Ow. Okay."

Ethan squeezed his eyes shut while Meg looked on, concerned. "Argh!" he groaned, flopping onto his back in the sand. He cursed at the sky. "Well, that sucks."

"I'm really sorry," she said again, and helped him to his feet.

"It was an accident." He tugged her close and gave her a peck on her lips. She leaned into him and deepened the kiss.

"Okay." Ethan backed up suddenly. "We gotta stop." He shook his head in dismay. "Or I'm not going to be able to get in the car."

He pulled her to her feet. As they meandered, Ethan's arhythmic footsteps crunched against the pebbly beach. Squeezing her hand, he blew out a frustrated breath. "It could be a while," he said, "before I can . . . till I can handle it."

"Or till I can handle it."

Ethan chuckled seductively. "You know what they say. Absence makes the fond grow harder."

"I don't think that's what they say."

"Okay. That's what *I* say."

The sunset had melted into dusk with little fanfare, but in the gathering darkness, she felt a palpable dissolving of her past relationship. Closure, and something new, too. On Puget Sound, the base of the marine layer glowed a dull orange and a concurrent heat grew in her chest. When they reached his car, they held hands beside the passenger door, unwilling to let go of each other. Ethan lifted her hand to his lips. Playfully, he kissed the back of her hand, then her thumb, and each of her knuckles, one by one.

Then suddenly, he stiffened.

An odd expression crossed his features. Folding his hand over hers, he gave her fingers a pat, the sort of pat one would give a toothless grandpa who ordered popcorn at the movies. His voice dropped to a businesslike monotone. "I better get you back to the Outlook."

Meg studied his changed expression, confused. She felt a slow numbing fizzle through her. "Is everything okay?" she asked.

"Fine."

But she could tell. It was not fine. His brow hooded his eyes. "Everything's fine."

"Are you sure?"

"Um." The pause was excruciating. "I was just remembering. I don't think tomorrow's gonna work out. And I have some other stuff coming up over the next few weeks, so . . ."

They both knew how lame it sounded. She stared at him, perplexed. Her belly felt hollow, and her legs threatened to give way. What was going on?

He opened the door for her. The small act of chivalry made his sudden detachment all the more painful. Her chest tight, she swallowed hard when she got into the car. He slumped into the driver's seat and sat there, his attention on a distant thought. She heard him sigh.

"Ethan? Did I say something wrong?"

"No. No." He opened his mouth to explain. "Nope." If he had to say it three times, it was obviously a yes. "It has nothing to do with you." *Please don't say it*, she thought. "It's me," he muttered.

Dang. He said it.

Ethan pulled the car onto the road, and for the blessedly brief drive, neither one said a word. Her head reeled. Over the past weeks, she had fought off her misguided fury against his well-meaning intentions for Lakeview's courts. She had allowed him in and reveled in the pleasure of his attentions. Now, for reasons she could not comprehend, he had gone from hot to ice-cold. What the hell had just happened?

· · · · ·

The darkness had descended in earnest by the time she trudged up the pebbled path, through the gate of the blank fence, toward the

Outlook Inn. The cool night breeze skipped across her skin. Confusion rattled around in her head; Ethan's sudden shift had thrown her emotions off-kilter, and now she felt sad and mad and confused all at once. Meg's mind rolled back the tape. What had gone wrong? True, she had smacked him in the crotch with a pickleball. But other than that . . .

She could make out the lights in their upstairs room at the inn. Thank goodness Annie was here with her on the island. Annie was a constant—solid, sensible, and even-keeled. She would make sense of the situation. Meg was nearly at the steps to the entrance when she halted in place. An odd sound emanated from the hotel's porch.

What on earth? It sounded like a dog whining, but stranger. Had one of the island's wild coyotes breached the porch? In the darkness, she could make out a hunched form, the source of the noise. She approached cautiously, her heart in her throat.

"Annie?" All at once she recognized her friend, crunched into the porch's dark corner. Curled against the wooden floor, Annie leaned on the inn. She was weeping, cradling her phone in her palms.

"Annie! What happened?"

"Mich-uh-uh-l," she managed. Anguish dampened Annie's ever-optimistic voice. "Mich-ael Edmonds," she clarified between her tears.

Meg's fingernails pressed into her palms. Had Annie discovered Michael's pickleball betrayal? What a terrible friend Meg was. Once again, she had been so wrapped up in her own story that she'd neglected to help Annie avoid making a crushing mistake. Before Annie went and put herself out there, before she invested herself with that brave kiss, Meg should have been the one to tell her that Michael Edmonds had taken his considerable pickleskills and snuck back to his old Bainbridge pals.

She plopped onto the creaking wood and squeezed in beside her friend. The evening was rapidly becoming an emotional pit of doom, but Meg tried to push her own misery aside. She enveloped her friend in her arms, but Annie continued to sob and shudder until, gradually, her gasps grew farther apart.

With effort, Annie breathed until she calmed. She brushed her bangs off her eyelashes, swallowed hard, and swiped at the tears that left mascara trails on her cheeks.

Steeling herself, Annie held her phone aloft for Meg to see.

SEVENTEEN

@Edmonds2.0
Checking in on my old Bainbridge crew.
Also, Bella found this rock on the beach.

The selfie showed a beaming Michael Edmonds, locked in a kiss with an exuberant brunette. The woman held her hand close to the camera to display the meteor-of-a-diamond glittering on her finger. The stone shimmered like a billion suns.

Meg stared, slack-jawed, at the phone. For a split second she hoped that this was one of those AI images that jumbled reality. But no. It looked too human, too authentic with emotion.

Annie shook her head, disbelieving. "How?" she asked. "How did this happen?"

Meg's brain was still connecting the inconceivable dots. "Wait. Michael Edmonds is . . . engaged?"

"I kissed him." She dissolved again. "I just kissed him, and he didn't say anything!" she cried. "What about *passionate abandon*?" she said, imitating his awed tone, but her raw hurt turned it into a mockery. "I thought . . . I thought he liked me. Why didn't he tell me? Oh! I am so stupid! For as long as I live, I am never kissing anyone again."

"First of all, you are by far the smartest person I know, and second, I really doubt you're never going to kiss anyone again."

"How do you know?" She sobbed, releasing a trail of phlegm from her nostrils and forming a spit bubble between her lips. It was not a good look. Meg, as only a best friend would, held out her arms for another hug and accepted the fact that her shirt would need to be washed immediately.

"All this time. All this time I wished and wished. Yeah, I know. He was my pickleball partner, and in my mind, I made it into this big thing. This thing that was apparently all one-sided," Annie admitted, her muffled voice buried somewhere near Meg's armpit. "But then . . ." She gasped for air. "But then—I took a chance. I did it and . . . he kissed me back. Right? He did, didn't he?" Meg nodded. "And I thought: At last! Finally! It's going to be easy now that it's out in the open. It's not just in my head. But I didn't know anything about him. I'm so embarrassed. Can you imagine what he must think about me? How can I partner with him now? How humiliating. Ugh! I'm so dumb."

Meg did not say what she suspected—that Michael wouldn't be partnering with her anyway. That all signs indicated he planned to skip out on Annie to bring in a win for Bainbridge. Instead, she said, "You are not dumb. Just a hopeful romantic."

Annie brooded, glaring tragically into the darkness toward the sound of the lapping waves. "You remember when you asked me what I saw in Michael?" she asked. "I just realized, that guy I'd been crushing on all this time? He was just some fantasy I invented. How could I be such a fool? Seeing that—that picture of him with another woman . . . engaged! I didn't know anything about him, did I? We never really talked. He doesn't talk much."

"Except to yell 'Michael Edmonds!'" Meg raised her arms in victory.

With effort, Annie raised a small smile. "He has such a nice face. So warm and open. And he spent time with me. On the courts, of course. Which, I realize now, was like, normal practice time. But then—after I got Coach Chad to cough up that grape—he said I had passionate abandon. Me! Passionate abandon. I really thought that was a sign."

Her gaze wandered sideways. "All this time I sat around and pined for him without telling him how I felt, and I wasn't sure if he even, you know, saw me. And all of a sudden, yesterday, he did. Nobody's . . . I guess nobody's ever recognized me like that. Seen how much I care. That's important to me. To be noticed."

"I notice you. I appreciate you."

"Yeah. But no offense, you're not my type." Stretching her neck, Annie stood and groaned from stiffness.

Meg slung her arm around her friend and squeezed. "C'mon. Let's get you upstairs."

In the room's entryway, they paused in front of the full-length mirror. "Ugh, I'm a mess," Annie said, wiping at her face. Then, catching Meg's eye in the reflection, she narrowed her gaze. "Um. And you don't look so hot yourself. How did it go with Ethan?"

Meg did not know how to answer. She shook her head. The best she could come up with to explain his spontaneous detachment was, "Weird."

"Weird like Fifty Shades of Weird, or weird like uh-oh weird?"

"Uh-oh weird. Like, suddenly-gave-me-the-cold-shoulder-for-no-reason weird."

"Uh-oh. What happened?"

Meg shrugged. Maybe he'd arrived at the same conclusion that Vance had come to—that she was not a worthy match. That her game was not at his level.

Annie shook her head. "Nuh-uh. Whatever bullshit you are telling yourself right now, cut it." Annie's face was firm with her rebuke. "I mean it. These boys do not know who we are. They have no idea what we are capable of. We are awesome, self-aware women, and they are missing out." Meg's eyes widened. The self-pity and help-lessness her friend had expressed moments earlier had left the building, replaced by righteous indignation. Meg's hurt had eclipsed it all.

Holding up her hand for a high five, Annie insisted, "Give it to me."

Meg groaned, wary. She was not in the mood to play along. Besides, she did not feel self-aware right now. And far from awesome.

"Don't leave me hanging."

Grudgingly, Meg conceded with a weak slap on the hand.

"Not like that. Give it to me."

"Fine." Meg smacked Annie's hand.

"Ow." Annie wiggled some sensation back into her fingers. "That's more like it."

They lay on their beds, and despite the high fives, Meg retreated to ceiling-staring. The air cooled and, through the open window, Meg listened to the coins-in-a-pocket jingle of the water pulling against the rocky shoreline.

When the idea came to her, Meg popped up onto her elbows. "Let's do something different. Get out of here for a bit."

"What did you have in mind?"

"We're not far from the Olympic Mountains. There are tons of trails."

Annie's eyebrows climbed up her forehead and threatened to leap off the ledge, but Meg pressed on. "Just a little hike. A day trip. I promise it won't be Everest."

Meg could already picture the rocky crags and dense pines that rose to form the Olympic Mountains. Who wouldn't find inspiration amid the trees and open skies? Getting out into nature would spark her creative juices, not to mention the hike was bound to distract her from her Ethan woes.

But for Annie, she used a different tack. "Think of it as cross-training for pickleball." Mentioning pickleball was usually the ticket to convincing Annie of anything.

A wince passed over Annie's face. "Ugh. Pickleball." Her gaze fled to the downy comforter, and she talked to the stitching. "What am I gonna do now? Picklesmash is three weeks away. How can I practice with Michael Edmonds if I can't look him in the eye?"

"You're not supposed to look him in the eye. You're supposed to keep your eye on the ball." Meg mimed an exaggerated rim shot.

Annie snorted. "You are so annoying. That's not even a little funny."

"It's a little funny."

"A very little. Like, I'd need a microscope to find the funny. That funny is so distant I'd have to rent the Hubble telescope for a whole month to find the funny." Annie sighed through her nose. "Fine. Let's go on your stupid hike."

THE LOB

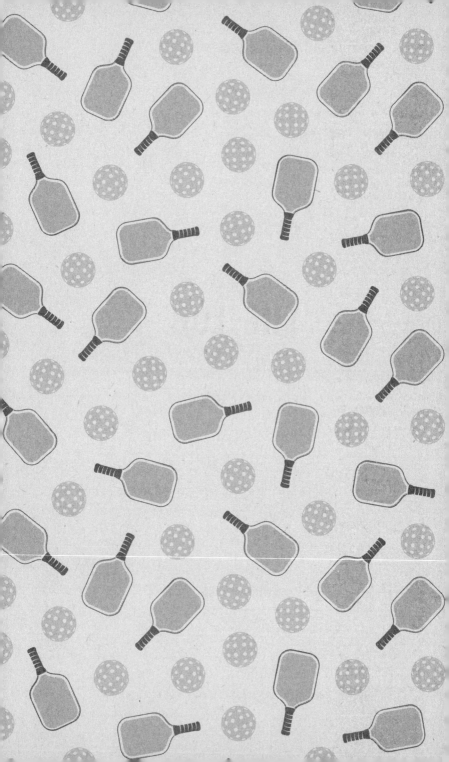

EIGHTEEN

Washington State teemed with world-class hiking trails, but when it came down to breadth and majesty, the Olympic Mountains could not be rivaled. Annie popped out of Meg's car and stood stock-still, gaping. "Whoa," she whispered. Even from the parking lot, the view was impressive. Before them, the mountains loomed like stone giants, dignified and powerful. In mid-July, snow lingered like pointy hats on the peaks. As she and Annie wrangled their packs from the hatchback, Meg drew in the earthy scents particular to the Pacific Northwest: pine mingled with the dense smell of wet dirt and decomposing wood.

Meg's fingers landed on her phone in her back pocket. She hesitated, resisting only an instant before checking for a text from Ethan. But no. There was nothing. There hadn't been anything for a full day. Burying her disappointment, she pocketed her phone, displacing her car keys, which tumbled onto the asphalt.

Annie rolled her eyes. "Gimme those keys. They're gonna end up in a stream somewhere." She zipped them into her pack's waterproof storage pocket. "Oh, good," she exclaimed. "Here's Rooster."

Rooster's vintage Buick chugged into the lot, bumping over the gravel and sending up pebbles as he peeled into a spot. Rolling out of his car, he stretched his arms into the sky and gave a low whistle at the view. "Beautiful." He asked, "Did I tell you Laverne gave me a hall pass so I could hook up with you two out here?" before he was disabused of ever using such terminology again.

"I may not know the hip lingo, but I know a great idea when I think of one. Get a load of this." Rooster paused for suspense. "I rang up a friend of yours. I thought I'd surprise you both and invite him along for the hike."

Rooster's passenger door banged and rattled a couple times before it jerked open and out tumbled Ethan Fine. Well, wasn't that a kick in the pants, Meg thought, her fingers gripping the straps of her pack. Thanks to Rooster's good-intentioned cupid act, the guy who'd just rejected her would be her companion for the next god-knew-how-many hours. So much for a stress-free hike in a magical setting. Instead, she'd be breaking a sweat while her heart was breaking. Perfect.

Meg and Ethan blinked at each other, both trying to get a handle on how to approach this unexpected turn of events. Annie's gaze shifted nervously between them.

"Hi." His tone was cool. But polite.

"Hi." She tried not to let her voice waver.

Rooster tilted his head. "Well. Not the warm reunion I imagined." He shrugged. "But hi-de-ho, let's hike."

Ethan tossed a glance over his shoulder at Meg and, with a noncommittal shrug, followed behind Rooster. Annie beckoned to Meg, hoisted her overstuffed backpack, and took to the trail. Meg was left with little choice. Here she was at the entrance to a beautiful hike, her plans for escape foiled. She could stand here all day looking like she'd raided an REI store for no reason, or she could go along. Letting out a frustrated grunt, she trudged after them.

At the wooden trailhead sign, they tied permits to their packs, snapped photos of the trail map, and reviewed the notices and sighting announcements. In his loud, gravelly voice, Rooster read, "'In the case of wildlife sightings, take precautions. Make noises to alert animals of your presence. If you spot an aggressive animal, back away from the area and alert a ranger when able.'" He narrowed his eyes. "What kind of animals do they have in the Olympics?" Rooster wondered.

Meg got nose to nose with the fine print. "Cougars, and mountain goats, and bears."

"Oh my!" Annie tried.

"Yep. Okay," Meg said, and marched forward on the trail.

"Cougars, and mountain goats, and bears," Rooster chanted in a growly singsong.

"I can still hear you," Meg said, fighting a smile.

"*Oh my!*" Annie whispered.

Catching Ethan's lips twitching with a grin, Meg scowled and bounded forward.

The group made their way into the woods. Scooting ahead, Rooster led Ethan up the gradual rise. The guys' easy conversation floated down to where she and Annie followed. "It's fine. This'll be fine," Annie said, giving her friend a sidelong glance. Meg was pretty sure that was what the captain had said right before the *Titanic* hit the iceberg.

Distracting herself, Meg put her focus on the narrow trail that snaked through the towering old-growth trees. Pace after pace, her anxiety began to thaw, and soon, the splendor of her surroundings dimmed her inner monologue. And although her antsy fingers still drummed against the straps of her pack, one thing was certain. It wasn't so easy to be blue when surrounded by the green majesty of the Pacific Northwest.

This was what Meg loved most about living in the PNW. Around her, ancient trees bent at odd angles, their boughs dressed in mossy shag carpets. Sprouting from those spongy blankets, fern fronds uncurled their fiddle tips. The heavy scent tickled her nostrils. Beneath her feet, the earth was as dark and wet as Seattle's famous coffee grounds, and above, the sky was a creamy shade of gray. Those born or bred in the Northwest felt as at home in the woods as the moss. Their rain-swept surroundings nourished them. Meg paused a moment to appreciate the small glints of sun that flashed on the bright treetops, setting them afire in contrast to the dull matte of the sky.

Even the boulders were magnificent: great Ice Age relics that could tell the history of this area, but instead chose to maintain their stoic and watchful silence. Those sturdy sentinels weighed down the forest floor and kept it from soaring away like some fairy-tale setting. With respect and awe, the four of them strolled wordlessly, allowing the power of the place to seep into them.

The tinkling sounds of a stream grew louder, and when they rounded a bend, they saw a brook trickling below a wood-planked bridge. The scene looked as pastoral and perfect as a movie set.

"Like heaven on earth," Rooster crooned. "Come on. Let's snap a picture."

For the first time since leaving the parking lot, Meg and Ethan caught each other's eye, and neither of them knew what to do with that. The discomfort stretched as Rooster directed them to stand in front of the bridge, nudging them to get closer. They adjusted stiffly while Meg's insides squirmed. The space between them might as well have been a wall.

For a long moment, Ethan and Meg posed like a miserable pair of air-bookends until Annie came to the rescue and squeezed in the middle, flinging her arms around them.

Rooster aimed his phone. "Here. I'll take a selfie of the three of you." When Annie clarified that a selfie could be taken only by oneself with oneself in the picture, Rooster balked. He insisted that a selfie meant the photo was "a picture you took yourself." The matter was debated in good cheer, which may have been Rooster's intention all along. At length, Rooster acquiesced and decided that all four of them should stand near the bridge and capture a group selfie.

The photo shoot complete, Annie settled herself on a fallen log. "You guys go ahead. I am going to rest here for a few minutes. I'll catch up."

Ethan leveled his gaze with Annie's. "You all right?" he asked, his brows dipping with concern. "Can I help?"

Annie shook her head. "It's a bridge."

Plunking down beside her friend, Meg put a gentle hand on Annie's shoulder. Of course. How could she have forgotten? For as long as she had known Annie, her friend had nursed a fear of crossing bridges. Yet Annie's apartment was on the Eastside and the hospital was in Seattle. The only way to cross Lake Washington was via I-90 or the 520 bridge. "I thought you worked it out. I mean, how are you getting to work every day?"

Annie hung her head. "Here's the thing. I don't drive. I've been carpooling with one of the nurses. I close my eyes and hold my breath until I'm over the bridges." It was a surprising revelation. Not to mention amazing breath control. "Actually, that's not completely true," Annie amended. "I take a breath in between the bridges. When I'm in the tunnel."

"This is a little bridge," Rooster said. "It's really low. You'd only fall like two feet, even if the boards all rotted and we came crashing through—"

Annie threw her hands over her ears and squeezed her eyes shut. "La-la-la," she sang.

"I have an idea," Ethan said. "Here." He reached out a hand and pulled Annie to her feet. "Come on. We'll carpool." Annie looked to Meg to check her reaction, but before she could utter a peep of resistance, Meg and Ethan had swooped to either side of her and linked arms.

Eyes squeezed tight and her fingers stuffed into her ears, Annie allowed herself to be tugged along. The bridge, which was strongly built and wide enough for the three abreast, accommodated them easily. One step at a time, they supported her across the bridge while Rooster followed. At last, they shook her gently, to alert her to the presence of solid earth.

Annie turned her head back to look at the bridge. She tugged down her Columbia fleece and pulled up her Gore-Tex hiking pants. "What are we standing around for? Let's go, people!"

Bounding forward, she turned toward Ethan and squinted at him in mock fury. "Thank you," she mouthed.

He gave a single nod and clapped her on the shoulder.

How could he be so sweet, and yet so misery-inducing? It was infuriating. While the rest of the crew traipsed forward, Meg hung back on her own. Her mind poked through the bin of their brief fling, trying to figure out where it had gone awry. But before long, the drop-off grew sheer enough that she needed to pay closer attention. Meg shook herself out of the gloom and concentrated on her footing. The terrain had shifted, and now the path sloped upward, and the soft dirt gave way to a steep incline of rocks and stones. Beside the path, the mountainside dropped down sharply.

Ahead of her, Annie slogged forward, hugging the rising mountain wall. With each step, her body slowed and stiffened. They continued this way for several tense minutes. At a spot wide enough to stand two abreast, Meg caught up to Annie. "How 'bout we check the trail app," Meg said. "Make sure we're going the right way."

"I used to hike around this area a lot," Ethan said, and Meg remembered that he had grown up on the peninsula. This mountain might have been his playground. "There's pretty much just the one way up."

But Annie's face was fraught with nerves. "Is it the drop-off?" Meg asked. Her friend did not respond, but her eyes darted toward the precipice.

"Let's take a look at the route," Meg insisted, pressing on her phone. Ethan may know the way, but she could take care of herself. "Looks like we keep going forward. It splits off later, but here it's one trail. It's practically a straight line. With curves . . ."

Rooster peered over Meg's shoulder. "Isn't that another bridge? That looks like a doozy."

Meg shot him a glare that could have stopped a hostile takeover.

"I should have stayed at the inn," Annie moaned.

"And miss all the dramatic tension?" Rooster commented wryly. "Lighten up, kids. Look where we are!"

Meg's head tipped up. Beside her, old-growth hemlocks and cedars grew as wide as Volkswagens and as tall as halfway up the Space Needle. She drew in the earthy scent, taking it all in. After getting the nod from Annie—hesitant as it was—Meg led the way.

Heeding Rooster's suggestion, she focused on the present, observing each detail as she strode between the evergreens. Meg's steps sprang on the thick and spongy earth, over remnants of fallen trunks that had decomposed years before. The air brushed her cheek, cool and crisp. In patches, snow lingered, and in the distance, frozen peaks gleamed like jagged, white teeth. Ahead, Ethan's boots left sexy indents in the dirt and his lightweight pants cradled his perfect ass. How was that for focusing on the present?

"Hold on." Rooster halted midpace. "What's this?" He pointed to where the path diverged. The main trail moved into the shelter of the woods, but a sliver of a trail shot off to the side and clung precariously to the ridge.

"That's the old game trail," Ethan offered. "I haven't been on it since I was a kid. It's like a shortcut, but I don't think it's used anymore since the park service revamped the main trail."

Meg trotted a few paces down the slender offshoot. There, nailed to the jigsaw bark of a ponderosa, she spotted a paper shoved inside a plastic sleeve. Someone had written *Experienced Hikers Only*, and then a contradictory dare: *There is no success without challenge*.

Meg stared down the wisp of trail that clung to the side of the mountain. "We have to go this way."

A disbelieving cough escaped from Rooster's throat. "Like hell we do."

Not unkindly, Ethan said, "I don't think it's such a good idea."

Annie surveyed the path dubiously. "Wouldn't it make more sense to travel on the main path?"

Meg glanced at the light gray sky. Ahead, she heard the melodic tinkle of a stream. She recited, "Two roads diverged in a wood, and I took the one less traveled by."

"Yeah, yeah," Rooster interrupted. "And that made a big frickin' difference."

"I don't think that's the exact quote," Annie quipped.

Meg's gaze took in the two paths. How many times had she taken the easy route, too complacent to shake things up? Crafting collars instead of creating art. Escaping to Bainbridge instead of staying to battle it out for the beginners' spot. And even with Ethan, she had managed to circumvent any conflict. Rather than demand that he explain his sudden change of heart, she had slunk away—only to end up hiking up a mountain with him and *still* not having the guts to find out why he was acting like they were water cooler acquaintances on a cubicle break.

She had made one non-choice after another. When was the last time she had pushed herself to try something *because* it was hard?

She squared her shoulders. "As I see it, we have two choices," Meg told them. "We can climb this mountain the easy way, the way everybody and his grandma does it; or we can accept the challenge and try something new."

Annie raised a hand. "I vote the easy way."

Rooster lifted his hand and grimaced. "Easy way."

"I mean . . ." Ethan shrugged to indicate his agreement with Annie and Rooster.

That was it! The three of them, joining forces! Ethan had drawn a line in the sand. And heck if Meg was going to take one more moment of his controlling attitude.

"Forget it," she insisted. "You're all coming with me. This whole hike was my idea, so I get to pick." She stopped short of stomping her foot. She knew she was losing her cool, but she was six feet deep into this temper tantrum, and she wasn't about to back out.

Without another word, Meg bushwhacked down the path and disappeared into the thick of the woods.

NINETEEN

Annie's fingers dug into Meg's upper arm. Although there wasn't a chance she would admit it, Meg was beginning to agree with Ethan's initial assessment—the side trail was downright dodgy. They clung to a path that hung along the cliffside like a rickety gutter. Instinct shouted at her to turn around. After several tense minutes, the trail—if the indentation in the foliage could be called a trail—moved inland.

"Look." Meg made her voice light and reassuring. "No more cliffside. This is better, isn't it?" she said, taking the opportunity to unpeel Annie's fingernails from her skin. While Annie's feet dragged, Meg continued her assault. She barged forward, kicking aside gigantic ferns and stubbing toes on poorly placed rocks that were small enough to hide beneath the ground cover, but big enough to be a nuisance.

The back of her neck prickled where she felt Ethan's eyes on her. If he wanted, he could convince the group to turn back. And they would listen, because these Olympic Mountains were his childhood backyard. But he stayed quiet and let Meg lead the way. Because even if this trail was a dud, all of them had the sense to recognize that hiking in the old-growth forest was a journey through wonderland. Nature here had an explosive quality, as if the massive trees and boulders were the debris left over from some ancient cosmic fireworks display.

They picked their way like this for half an hour until Meg paused, uncertain. Either they had lost the trail or reached the end. The mountain walls met at a small, stony patch of land. To one side, the earth dipped down into a bottomless chasm. Across the gap, Meg could see rock face on the other side—several feet away.

"There used to be a suspension bridge that crossed to the other side," Ethan said. "When they widened the main trail, the Park Service took it out."

"Oh well." Annie's theatrical sigh tried in vain to convey disappointment. "Looks like the end of the line."

"Too bad," Rooster concurred with unmasked sarcasm. "Give me a sec before we head back, will ya?" Rooster ducked into the woods. "I gotta see a man about a horse."

As they waited, Annie plastered herself against the wall and Meg peered out over the drop-off. Heights never bothered her. In fact, she found the combination of the wind, the view, and the circling of gray jays overhead stimulating. It was a shame they were forced to turn around. Once she started on a project, her every pore pushed her to complete it. This mountain? She really, really wanted to make it to the top.

Maybe after they backtracked, if they still had gas in the tank, she could convince them to continue up the main trail. But she knew Annie and guessed that Rooster, too, would be done. And Ethan? He was here only because Rooster had dragged him along. She would be on her own if she wanted to make it up the mountain.

"Holy shit!" Rooster called. "You gotta see this!"

Ethan tromped through the thick greenery, moving with care toward Rooster's voice. Meg followed, and Annie, faced with the choice of seeing what the fuss was about or being left alone on the ledge, trailed behind. Twenty paces past the landing, Meg's legs halted.

"That," Ethan said, "is *not* the Park Service bridge."

From one side of the mountain to the opposing cliff four feet away, someone had laid a plank bridge, the width of a pair of tree trunks. How its creator had managed to set it across the divide was a mystery. On the opposite side, a queen bed–sized patch of earth hugged the other side of the gap.

Mouth drying to sand, Meg gaped. If she could caption the view, it would read *The World's Worst Obstacle Course*. The danger did not end on the bridge landing. Behind the slim spot, a knotted rope climbed up fifteen more feet of cliff face. Meg's gaze surveyed the rising rope to where it was secured in a thick knot around a tree trunk at the top.

What kind of sadist had built this terror trap? And what kind of idiot would opt to take on the challenge? She turned to the metaphoric mirror and was surprised to discover her own reflection. *This* kind of idiot.

Sure, she recognized the sheer stupidity of considering the dare, but at the same time, she was dead done with taking the easy way out. This was her chance to step out of her comfort zone. Risky? Sure. Life-endangering? Definitely. But maybe upping the stakes was exactly what Meg needed to give her life a serious shove (once her brain used that word, she retracted it immediately). A nudge in the right direction. This was her chance to turn over a new Meg.

"I'm gonna do it."

Annie made a tiny choking noise. "What? You can't."

"Meg." Ethan's voice had a strained quality. "Look. I'm going to backtrack and head up the main trail. If you want"—he hesitated—"you can come with me."

She wished his invitation hadn't sounded so stilted. She didn't need his obligatory compassion. "I'm going to cross here," she repeated. "Look. You guys don't have to come along, but I really need to do this."

"Oh, no," Rooster said. "Not by yourself, you don't. Can't say I'm happy about it, but if you're going, I'm going."

"You two are being idiots," Annie said. "I'm going down the mountain." She looked pointedly at Ethan for backup. "We *all* should go down the mountain."

Measuring the progress of the debate like a spectator at a friendly pickleball match, Ethan lifted his brow placidly, but he said nothing.

"Annie," Meg pushed, testing. "I'm telling you we can do this. Together."

"Peer pressure is the tool of the intellectually stunted."

Rooster tested a foot on the plank bridge. "More solid than it looks."

Annie scoffed. "Now you're on the crazy train, too? Tell you what. I'll wait here and watch you two lunatics. Ethan and I, the sensible humans, are going to stay on solid ground to administer medical care and make the 911 call." She tugged her cell phone from her pocket. "Yep. I have a signal. You're good to go."

Ethan inched toward the edge to inspect. A rock, dislodged by his shoe, bounced once and disappeared over the precipice. There was no sound of it landing. Coolly, he assessed Rooster, then shifted to Meg. Her blood fizzed under the intensity of his stare.

"Okay. I'll do it," he said, still staring at her, calm as tea with crumpets.

"*Et tu, Brute!*" Annie groaned.

Terrified as she was, Meg felt her shoulders relax minutely. "Great." Her eyes swept the cliffside, planning her traverse. "This would be a piece of cake if we had some rope."

Annie brightened. "Oh! I have a rope." She slipped her pack from her shoulders and dumped the contents of her bag. Out tumbled a hefty rope. Heavy-weight carabiners jangled from the coil. "I told Mayumi we were climbing a mountain and she lent me this stuff."

"No wonder your bag was so heavy."

Without missing a beat, Rooster looped the end of the rope around a sturdy pine and threaded it through. He tugged on the rope to tighten the grip. Using the carabiners as guide loops, he threaded a harness around his pelvis and legs.

"Wow." Ethan said. "Where did you learn how to do that?"

Rooster shrugged. "Cowboy trick," he said as he designed a similar harness for Meg. From the impressed look on his face, Ethan's esteem for Rooster had just jumped off the top of the graph.

Meanwhile, Meg's brain was doing an excellent job of obfuscating the danger. A rope tied around the waist made crossing an abyss on a double-wide log bridge safe. That made sense, right? In fact, this was going to be a cakewalk. Too bad there wasn't cake at the end. Meg loved cake. Especially chocolate cookie crunch cake. Or mint-chip ice cream cake. Yes. That was the one she preferred.

Near to her, Ethan's voice was quiet. "Hey . . ." Meg glanced up from her cake reverie. His lips parted, like he was about to say something.

"You ready?" Rooster called, cutting off the moment.

"As I'll ever be." Still locking eyes with Ethan, she waited, hoping that in the intensity of the moment, he would say something. *Don't do it* might be preferable. *Stay here with me.* If only it were that easy. If only they could go back to playing truth or dare on the pickleball courts.

But although Ethan continued to hold her in his sights, he said nothing.

Meg gave her waist strap a decisive tug and scooted toward the makeshift bridge. If she didn't go now, she might not go at all.

With her fist, she gripped the end of the rope that she would secure on the other ledge. The near end was fastened around the pine, and Rooster grabbed on, leaning his weight back for added safety.

Meg exhaled her anxiety. This was about conquering obstacles. She would not be forever known as a kitschy crafter, a people pleaser, or the sucker who'd kissed the Destroyer of Courts and then caved under his stare. She would become the hero of her own story.

Her second boot was on the plank now, and she inched along, committed. Squinting through her eyelashes, she watched her footing. Four feet of DIY bridgework was a hell of a lot longer and scarier than it seemed from the ledge. She inhaled in staccato puffs and held the air inside her lungs, too tense to release it. Just four steps. Three. Two . . .

At last, her foot made purchase on the opposing ledge. Exhilarated, she raised her hands above her head. "Woo-hoo!"

Above their applause, Rooster's voice reached her. "How was it?"

"Great. Easy," she lied.

Her hands shook but she managed to get the trembling under control, and she tied the end soundly around the thigh-thick trunk of an established ponderosa. When she looked back across, Ethan was already harnessed up.

As he stepped onto the planks and began inching across, Ethan's jaw set, and only the tremor in his fingers gave away his nerves. Two steps in, his body swayed unpredictably, and for an infinite instant, Meg's terror turned her veins to ice. Then, recovering quickly, he straightened. Still, Meg did not exhale. It was so much worse watching someone else traverse the gap than crossing that death-maw herself. Especially when that someone happened to be a man she apparently still cared about with infuriating persistence, if the thunderous thudding of her heart was any indication. At last, Ethan launched himself onto solid ground. Before either of them had their senses back, he had enveloped her into the circle of his arms.

Ethan's body was trembling. "That was terrifying," he whispered into her hair. Every centimeter of her skin reacted. She wanted to hold him and keep him safe and stay like that until the sun went down for the last time in human history.

But then Ethan pulled away. He put his hands on his knees and collected himself. As he lifted his face, his gaze hooked hers. What were they? What was this?

Oblivious to the drama playing out on the other side of the chasm, Rooster posed on the ledge beside Annie. He stared into the middle distance, arms outstretched and one knee bent. Blowing powerfully through his mouth, he bent at the waist and pressed his palms flat to the gravelly ground.

"What's he doing?" Meg called across. Annie shrugged.

Rooster rolled, one vertebra at a time, to a standing position. He pressed his palms together at chest level. "Sun salutations."

He held completely still, a picture of calm. Then, in six quick, balanced strides, he joined Meg on her side of the ledge. He shrugged off Meg's astonished expression. "I visualized success," Rooster explained.

"Annie?"

"Still a no. A no-way-in-hell." Her perky good cheer returned. "Thanks, though. Now that you've crossed the Bridge of Death, I'll just watch you guys struggle up the side of the cliff on that knotted rope that looks like it has the weight-bearing capacity of dental floss. I can call the emergency chopper. And if by some miracle you make it to the top, I'll take your car to Port Angeles and wait for you there. Or better yet, I can flag down some lunatic stranger out looking for hitchhikers. That would be a safer choice than you all are making. But you guys go on ahead. I'm staying on this side."

The three of them unharnessed and left the cable tied across the plank bridge. Truth was, Meg hoped that for the way back, Ethan could show them a saner way down the mountain. Could she come back this way if she had to? People were capable of all kinds of things when under duress or sufficiently incentivized. Weren't there videos online of mothers lifting minivans off toddlers and cheerleading teams scaring away bull elephants? If there were not, there ought to be.

Now that they had made it across the chasm on the plank bridge, there was the cliff wall to contend with. A splintery climbing rope hung down its sheer face. She scanned the platform ledge hoping to miraculously find another option. Other than the straight-up ascent, there was a narrow path along the ridge that might have once worked as a switchback before erosion chewed gaping chunks out of the trail. Now only a mountain goat or Super Mario would entertain that climb. So, if they wanted to reach the top, the rope was the only option. Meg channeled the epic motivation of a panicky cheerleader facing off against a water buffalo and jumped to grab the lowest knot on the rope.

She hooked it. For a moment, she hung there. Her feet swung three feet off the ground. She pivoted and threw an arm to reach the knot above her while heaving her body upward. Her fingers gripped the knot but slid off the splintery twine. Although she adjusted in time to remain clinging to the lower knot, her body banged against the cliff wall.

"Careful!" Annie yelled, her voice falling at the end with recognized pointlessness.

Meg mustered her strength and gripped the rope. With all her might, she pulled. One hand over the other, using her legs to stabilize and lift, Meg raised her body up, up, up the rope. She dragged herself to the top with every stitch of her strength. Finally, when her shoulders leveled with the ledge, she hesitated only a moment before sacrificing grace for efficacy. Thrusting with her last ounce of force, she threw her torso onto the rock platform. This time, she did not have the energy to shout "Woo-hoo!" so she just thought it really hard.

She rolled onto her back and breathed through her mouth until she recovered enough to scoot to the edge. Already, Ethan was midway up the rope, climbing with the ease of a natural athlete. Lifting himself onto the top of the climb, he gave her what might pass for a congratulatory nod. Then he dipped his head over the edge and reached down for Rooster. "Just get to here. I'll help pull you up."

"I got this." Rooster waved Ethan off. "You're lookin' at Spider-Man." Rooster leapt for the rope and power-armed up the first five knots. "I got monkey-grip. Skills like an orangutan!" Stretching and contracting, his legs worked the rope like an inchworm, while his strong hands—

Rooster gasped. "Oh shit!" And they watched in horror as Rooster lost his grip and began to tumble, flailing in helpless slow motion. As he fell, his eyes connected with Meg's, and she threw her arm in his direction on instinct, but she was way above him. His body thudded down to the ledge, landing on the ground with a reverberating shudder. The awful sound sent an electric shock down Meg's spine.

"Oh my god, Rooster!" she cried.

"Rooster!" Ethan shouted. On the hard dirt, Rooster lay on his back, his arm slung beneath him at an awkward angle. Unblinking, his eyes reflected the open sky. He did not move.

"Oh no. Oh no! Rooster!" Meg's heart pounded in her throat. Why wasn't he moving?

Ethan called across the gap. "Annie! Can you see him? Is he okay?"

In a millisecond, Annie was crouching beside Rooster on the ledge, two fingers against his throat.

Meg's voice trembled. "Is he . . . ?"

"Rooster." Annie took control. "Can you hear me?"

"Oof. Ow. I think I hurt myself."

His face contracted in a mask of pain. Meg's momentary relief that he was alive was replaced by worry. "Should we—" she started.

"Stay where you are," Annie commanded, and Meg wasn't sure if she meant it for her and Ethan or for Rooster. There was very little space on the ledge, so the two of them stayed put, hovering over the worrisome scene below. Not that she could have gotten down easily if she had wanted to. Annie placed a cautionary hand on Rooster's chest to keep him lying down. "Where does it hurt?"

Rooster's forehead wrinkled. "Annie? You . . . you crossed the bridge. All by yourself."

Annie's head jerked up. Her neck swiveled back to the rickety planks that spanned the yawning abyss, and her eyes went wide. Her body teetered. For a frightening instant, Meg feared Annie would faint, and then what would she do with two incapacitated hikers, knocked out on a cliff's ledge on an uncharted trail in the Olympic Mountains?

Ethan shouted down, "What's happening?"

Rooster moaned. "My hand." His face scrunched up with a rush of pain. "I think I landed on it." He rocked a shoulder forward, trying to dislodge the hand beneath him.

Shaking herself, Annie came to her senses. "Hold still. Let's check the rest of you first, before we get that hand out."

Meg turned to Ethan, her face wreathed with concern. He

shook his head helplessly; there was nothing they could do. Below, Annie instructed Rooster to wiggle his toes. She checked out his legs, his back, and his skull, until Rooster lost patience and waved her off. Rolling toward his good arm, he struggled to sit up. His other arm dragged along, and when Meg got a look, she sucked in her breath. His right thumb and pointer finger dangled beside his palm like limp hot dogs.

"Oh no. No. No. No-no-no." Meg shook her head, refusing to accept what her vision proved.

"No, what? What's no? Why does she keep saying no?" Rooster pointed his face down toward his hand. "Ah! My hand! Holy shit! Look at my hand!"

It was impossible *not* to look at his hand.

"It's okay. You're okay," Annie soothed. "Let's see if I can stabilize this until we can get you to a hospital." While she unzipped her pack, Rooster winced, cradling his hand in front of him like a grenade. Annie produced a roll of medical tape and a wrap and created a thumb brace using a piece of a plastic spoon she found at the bottom of her pack. "You can never be too prepared."

She dug out an orange pill container and he held up his good hand in protest. "Whoa. Nothing stronger than aspirin, okay?" Nodding, Annie found some aspirin and he gulped them down gratefully. With his thumb and finger secured, Rooster got to his feet.

Rooster's and Meg's eyes met, each person concluding silently what they all knew. Their hike was over, that was clear. But what was more, her tournament partnership with Rooster was done for. Meg's chest clenched with compassion for Rooster's pain, and disappointment for her own. There was nothing to do but head down and get him to a hospital.

"Dammit." Rooster bowed his head. "I screwed everything up."

Rooster's features were racked with regret. With one fall, they had lost their shot at winning the Lakeview beginners' spot. It wasn't Rooster's fault. If anything, Meg was the one who had insisted they do this. Still, it crushed her to have to release that final hope of teaming up to contribute to winning those new courts, not to mention beating out Vance and Édith for the Lakeview slot.

And that wasn't the only bump in the road. She had made it over that ridiculous bridge and up that damn rope. Now they would have to do the whole miserable obstacle course in reverse. She scooted to the edge to peer over the lip of the cliffside. It hadn't seemed so high on the way up.

Below her, Annie fidgeted as she surveyed the rickety bridge. Her Adam's apple bobbed. In Rooster's moment of need, she had skittered across the planks without hesitation. Crossing back would be another story.

Not one of the hiking crew moved, miserable with inertia. Rooster injured, Annie terrified, Meg worried. And there was Ethan. On a ledge above a cliff, stuck. Unable to do anything, alongside a woman he wanted nothing to do with.

The plink-plink sound of a rock bouncing down into the canyon jostled them from their individual pity parties. Awake now, with her danger radar on high alert, Meg turned toward the eroded switchback that snaked its way toward the crowded ledge. She gasped when she spotted the sound's source.

Head tipped forward, horns pointed, legs splayed, the intruder let out an angry bleat. No doubt about it. That mountain goat was pissed.

TWENTY

Beneath a shaggy coat of white fur, the goat's coal black eyes bore down on the hiking crew. Ethan and Meg's narrow perch at the top of the knotted rope kept them above the danger, but Rooster and Annie still crouched on the tiny ledge below. They froze in surprise, their bodies mere feet away from the goat's pointy horns and powerful hooves. Behind the pair, the chasm of the valley yawned, crossable only by that rickety bridge. In front of them, the stupid rope climbed the sheer rock face. The goat lowered her head, a low growl rumbling from her throat.

But the trouble did not end there. From her vantage above the scene, Meg spotted the source of a deeper threat. Behind the menacing creature, a kid on unsteady legs wobbled, wide-eyed, toward his mother. Great, Meg thought. Rooster and Annie were in goat territory, and now that momma goat was fixin' to lift a minivan off her baby. Substitute "hikers" for "minivan," and some crazy shit was about to go down.

And holy crap, who knew mountain goats were so big? The beast was the size of two Megs, at least. Maybe two and a half, if it was the upper half.

A billion thoughts streamed through her head in a matter of seconds. That stupid sign in the parking lot—what had it suggested in the wildlife warning? Yell? Walk slowly backward? Make yourself big? Offer dog treats? Hold on. Did those instructions apply to cougars, or mountain goats, or bears? Oh my!

She could distract the creature, make some noise. She should stomp her feet. If only she could unbind her muscles, she would rise up and stomp. Maybe two times. Come on, right foot. Stomp. Stomp. Left foot, let's stomp. Everybody clap your hands. She turned to Ethan, eyes blazing with panic, and whispered, louder than intended, "What do we do?"

Momma goat lifted her head, searching for the sound. She looked up to the clifftop, her gaze passing indifferently over Meg's tense body.

Ethan shouted, "Hey! Goat! Hey. Over here." He waved his hands in the air, drawing her attention.

The goat inspected Ethan and Meg from beneath her hooded lids. Momma goat's glare sent an alarm through Meg's body, but it was enough to shock her out of her frozen posture and get to her feet. She followed Ethan's lead. "Yoo-hoo. Up here, goat. Goaty. Goat-goat." Meg flapped her arms like a flailing Icarus, and that shaggy head cocked to the side. "Yodel-lay-hee-hoo."

The goat budged, inching toward the base of the rock wall, where the bottom of the rope dangled. Beside her, the kid tromped up to the twined rope and began chewing on the lowest knot.

Between her teeth, Meg used her ventriloquist skills to warn her friends. "Hurry! Go back." But Annie and Rooster still crouched, poised like wax figures in a horror display. "You have to go back across that bridge!" Was she worried that the goat might read her lips? Logic wasn't playing a large role in Meg's actions.

Finally, Rooster's eyes widened with understanding. He stood and made a move toward the plank bridge, but Annie grabbed him by his elbow and shook her head violently. Her expression read two ways: desperately, she knew she should back away from the angry goat, but her terror of the bridge glued her feet to the spot.

From their perch, Ethan jumped to action. Barking and clapping, he performed a goat-distracting clog dance, which, if nothing else, confused the creature momentarily. Meg nodded her chin at Annie. "Now!" Meg urged in her weird ventriloquist voice.

Rooster tugged at Annie and pulled her toward the gap. Her eyes bulged, wild with fear, and a high-pitched whine came from between her clenched teeth. Annie gripped his shoulder and allowed herself to be budged, an inch at a time, along those death trap planks. With his bad hand clutched to his stomach and his good hand loose on the rope, Rooster edged his way backward across the rickety bridge.

Below the pair's shuffling feet, splintered shreds of rotting wood puffed off the boards and fell to their doom. The goat, attracted by the sound of movement, shifted. Meg needed to do something, quick, to regain the goat's attention. "Yoo-hoo," Meg sang out, and joined Ethan in an ill-conceived tap dance.

But Annie had halted, planted in panic on the bridge.

"Come on, Annie," Rooster coaxed. "One more step."

"I . . . can't."

At the sound of Annie's trembling voice, momma goat turned, dipped her head, and bared her horns, prepping to bounce a minivan, an SUV, or a tricked-out eighteen-wheeler. She bleated an angry, I'm-gonna-mess-you-up kind of bleat. She dragged her hoof along the chalky ground and snorted. Then, coiling her stocky body, she readied herself. The goat sprang forward and rushed the bridge.

"Come on!" Rooster tugged. At last, jolting with urgency, Annie leapt to safety across the last inches of plank.

The goat came to a scrambling halt, skidding sideways before the precipice and using her considerable bulk as a roadblock. Her kid, who had skittered after her, slid into her body, narrowly avoiding a plunge over the edge.

Rooster took advantage of the commotion. He gripped Annie and yanked her down the path, backing away with a keen eye on the enraged beast. Before they disappeared behind the trees, Rooster yelled out, "Try to find the main trail. And call us as soon as you can!" Meg could hear their footsteps thundering down the path. And then they were gone.

Still, momma goat peered hungrily toward the woods, and Meg feared she would spring across the chasm after them. But instead, the goat turned and scanned the shallow ledge before lifting her head and drilling her gaze into Meg.

Really, she had nothing to be afraid of anymore. Right? Rooster and Annie were safe. So were she and Ethan. The climb was a sheer wall, straight up. Unless goats could climb ropes. Wait. Could goats climb ropes? No. Definitely not.

However, the goats must have appeared from somewhere.

"Come on. We can get a signal to reach them when we're at the top. Let's get outta here, quick." Ethan pointed his chin off to the right.

Meg followed his gaze and eyed the slender trickle track that hugged the cliff. That game trail might switch back and climb the mountainside. Was it only a matter of moments before that mad mommy made her move and maneuvered up the mountain? Meg shook her head briskly. Occasionally, her mind alliterated when she felt apprehensive, and alas, her anxiety was approaching its apex. She took a deep breath. It helped.

"We'll head uphill," Ethan said. "Eventually, we'll end up back on the main trail."

Still shaking even as they quickstepped out of there, Meg said,

"Ethan—" Her voice dropped off. "I'm sorry. I'm sorry I got us into this mess. We should have stayed on the main trail and we never would have—"

"Let's just keep moving," he said, his long strides pushing her to keep up. "We have to put some distance between us and those goats."

The ascent was brutal. The afternoon sun burned, and when she wiped the sweat from her brow, sunscreen leaked into her eye. She blinked away the pain, but the heat of the day and the rigor of the climb weighted her spirits. Ten minutes in, her thighs trembled, and by thirty minutes, they threatened to give way. How long would they be climbing, and when or if they reached the top, then what? Would they be able to find the main trail?

And to make matters worse, Ethan seemed intent on scaling the slope in silence. Guilt brewed. After all, it was she who had pressured him into trading in his lovely day hike for a goat-infested odyssey.

And she had other concerns, too. Not just about feeling responsible for Ethan's situation, but for Annie's and Rooster's as well. She should text them, let them know she and Ethan had made it away from the vicious goat, and try to form a plan to reconnect.

Pulling her cell phone from her pocket as she tried to climb without tripping, she checked for a signal, but the cold must have knocked out the phone battery. So she picked up the pace and caught up to Ethan, following the steep incline on a trail that sometimes thinned or disappeared entirely.

Between bouts of worry and woe, she revisited self-doubt. Rooster's pained expression mirrored her disappointment. With a fistful of crushed fingers on his racket hand, there was no way they could partner together in the tournament. Meg still wanted to be the heroine who helped bring in the win for her community. And she also wanted her shot at playing in a tournament and kicking Vance's picklebutt. She thought about what Marilyn had suggested: that she and Ethan partner up.

But Ethan was currently double-timing it up a mountain so he wouldn't have to spend an extra minute alone with her. Meg wanted to yell at him, to stop and ask him what the hell was the big problem, but her fear of his disinterest stopped her. She was not the master of her own ship. She was not even sure if she could swab the decks and pump out the head. Truth be told, she felt a little seasick just thinking about it.

What was it Rooster had said that night at the winery? *Feel it. And then put it aside.* There was nothing to do but concentrate on getting up the current hill. One foot in front of the other, she pressed herself to continue. Despite the cooling air, sweat trickled down the nape of her neck. Up the boulder field she went. Brambles bit her legs and spiderwebbed ferns swept her arms, but at last she could see where Ethan was headed.

Ahead, the tops of the trees gave way to the late-afternoon open sky. Even the air smelled different near the peak: cool air so fresh that it smelled like nothing at all. Snowy patches as large as footprints dotted the earth. In front of her, a glow between the trees brightened. Beyond the silhouetted trunks, the brilliant, cloudless sky looked white. When Meg peered past the woods, she exhaled with relief.

The summit.

Meg stepped out from the canopy onto the top of the world.

Beneath her feet, the pristine snow glittered. In the distance, the peaks of the majestic Olympics still wore their snowy crowns. The valley spread below her, a blue-green quilt, patched with evergreen trees.

Hearing her footsteps, Ethan turned to her. His face had

changed. Gone was the casual coolness. Instead, something about his expression looked tender, and a bit broken. "Meg," he said, and on his tongue her name sounded so vulnerable that a knot leapt to her throat. He began, "I think we should talk . . ."

Here it comes. Meg shivered with the icicles of imminent rejection. Was he planning to double-dump her, just to be certain: to leave her here on top of the mountain where she would freeze to death and eventually be discovered among the remnants of her last granola bar and a few stale gummy worms? She braced herself for the ax as she clutched the icy husk of her dead cell phone . . .

Which had begun to ring.

TWENTY-ONE

The ringtone knocked her back to her senses and, frenetically, she tried to get her frigid fingers to cooperate. Whoever it was, they could help get her off this godforsaken mountain before nightfall. By the sixth ring, she managed to swipe open the call.

"Meg?"

Meg let out a cry of relief. It could have been Santa or the secretary of state or both, and she would not have been more stunned.

"I got a vibe," Dina Bloomberg said. The line cut in and out, rendering her mom's voice a distant, staticky lifeline. "Is everything okay?"

"Oh, Mom." Meg released a sigh that emptied her lungs.

"Uh-oh. That doesn't sound so good. What's going on?"

"It's . . . it's . . . Oh, Mom." Her gaze landed on Ethan's. "I can't really talk right now. I'm on top of a mountain."

"A mountain—"

Tears stung Meg's eyes, and a droplet cooled quickly on her eyelash. Where to start? There was nothing Dina Bloomberg could do from Bribri, Costa Rica, to help Meg right now. But it had been months since she had been able to reach her mother. And now, when she was at the top of a mountain in the valley of her life, she wanted to unload. About everything. About Vance and his stupid

Home Depot receipt, about her pickleball plight and Rooster's busted hand, about the damn blasted goat on the fricking freezing mountaintop, and about the annoyingly unattainable man standing not ten feet but a million miles away from her.

She turned away from Ethan and dropped her voice to a whisper. "It's that everything kinda sucks right now."

"Oh, sweetheart," Dina Bloomberg sighed. "Aw. I am so sorry, honey. My poor, sweet darling. What can I do?"

Come home, Meg thought. *Come back to the Northwest and be here to kiss my metaphoric bruises.* Meg pouted, knowing how selfish it was to ask her mom to put her life on hold to give her daughter a hug. But it had been almost three years since she had seen her in the flesh, and was it asking so much? Stepping toward the vista, Meg faced the expanse of space and whispered, "I miss you, Mom." She angled her mouth close to the receiver. "I don't know. I wish you were here. Not here, here. Because I'm on a mountaintop. But when I get down, if I get down, and back to Seattle . . . I just miss you."

There was silence. The buzzing background noise on the other end of the line had stopped. "Mom?" Meg peered at her phone.

The call had dropped. As fast as her stiff fingers could manage, she dialed the fourteen digits and waited. One ring. Two rings. Then, nothing. Her phone's black screen blinked up at her, mocking.

Meg glared at it in disbelief. "Stupid . . . phone!" she grunted, resisting the urge to throw it down the mountain. She cradled the useless thing like a frozen candy bar that was too cold to eat without breaking a tooth. What was the point of frozen chocolate, anyway? It ruined the taste. Maybe she could warm it under her armpit. Not the chocolate, but the phone. But that would only make *her* colder. Damn phone. Damn escape plan. She should have stayed put in Seattle and fought for her place on Lakeview's team. Or kept her two feet on the non-mountainous ground back on Bainbridge.

When would she learn that running away was just another way to run smack into something worse?

Like freezing to death.

"Meg." Ethan stood at a distance, his eyes scanning the dimming sky. "We oughta get a move on. Take advantage of the daylight. Look." He pointed into the distance. Whatever uncomfortable issue he had been about to broach had been replaced by pragmatism.

Her relief at dodging the conversation shifted to concern once Meg's gaze followed Ethan's finger. A curtain of shade was creeping across the wide landscape. How late in the day was it?

Using a trick her dad taught her when she was little, she held her fingers at arm's length along the horizon to calculate the time until sunset. Ten minutes per finger. Squinting between her hands and the sun, she counted three fingers' worth. Half an hour!

"We only have thirty minutes till the sun goes down!" A fresh panic set in. What would happen if she survived and he didn't? Would she eat him? She considered the dilemma for longer than she was proud of. No. Never. Instead, she was going to freeze to death as the sun went down, with the oat and honey bar, six gummy worms, the sweaty thermal, the dead phone, and the man who despised her and who wouldn't be good eating anyway because he didn't have a lot of fat on him. She tried to keep the freak-out in her voice to a minimum. "We're gonna die if we have to sleep up here in the cold. How are we going to get down before nightfall?"

"Meg." Ethan's calm repetition of her name was beginning to irk her. "First of all, those finger measurements work best at sea level. The sun won't set for another hour. At least. And we're not going to freeze to death up here. It's kinda warm today. Look."

He gestured toward a snowdrift. At the edge of one glistening patch, a yellow crocus poked through the ice. Its delicate petals, no bigger than Meg's pinkie nail, trembled in the light breeze. It stretched—unhindered by the unforgiving elements—and reached for the sun.

A flower. Huh. She guessed it was not *that* cold. In fact, the weather was kinda balmy. So she was not going to freeze to death with only the remnants of a breakfast bar. And she should not forget the gummy worms, which may have been left over from Halloween. But the point was she had resources, and if that fragile flower could brave the elements and come out smiling, so could she. She had crossed a plank bridge, faced off against a goat, and summited the toughest climb of her lifetime. Damn straight she was not going to die here.

Ethan said, "I know this peak. It's about an hour's hike from where I was planning to camp tonight anyway. We'll make it, no problem." It was then she noticed Ethan wasn't sporting a daypack like hers, but a full backpacker's overnight pack. How could she have missed that? "And it's lower in elevation, so it'll be fine for sleeping if you don't mind roughing it."

For the time being, thanks to Ethan's preparation, at least they would last through the night. And with her layers and boots, she was warm enough. But still, as Ethan began bouldering down the incline, she swallowed her hopes to melt the frost that glazed their every interaction and wondered if she should press him on the conversation he had started before her mom's call. Instead, she followed silently, picking her slow steps, loping over the slick rocks, and wishing her mind would stop stress-alliterating like a sappy inkslinger in a sonnet slapdown. Sigh.

As she stepped deeper into the gathering evening, Meg's senses went on high alert. She listened to the crunch of their shoes along the stony path and noted the change in the forest. The pines here were interspersed with alder, cottonwood, and maples. By the time they approached the forest, the sun had disappeared behind the trees, and Meg's pulse whirred at the thought of being outside in the dark. The sensation was amplified when, within the blanketing canopy of the woods, the terrain changed to softer dirt and the sound of their footsteps was eaten right up by the earth. As she marched, her gaze traveled up the rugged trunks toward the sky, searching for the last patches of twilight. Pace by pace, for what had to be way more than an hour, she treaded the monotonous trail, wishing she didn't feel like a wound coil begging to be sprung.

"Here we are." Ethan's words woke her from her thoughts. They had meandered into a clearing backed by a grove of enormous trees. By now, night had fallen in earnest. Her eyes strained to get a better view of the campsite, but beyond the small space, the trees grew together so thickly that they formed a coal black wall.

"I'll build up a fire," he said, gesturing to a circle of stones set on the dirt. The remains of a few charred logs lay in a shallow pit, the blackened scraps of an old campfire. "And then we can eat. I brought plenty of food for both of us."

"So, you've camped here before?"

"This is where I planned to come when Rooster said he was hiking in this area. Though it's usually not so hard to get here," he said, and she could sense both the effort and the strain in his joke.

Ethan knelt low to the fire pit, scraped magnesium into a nest of dried leaves, and struck a spark off his flint. Meg wanted to sit beside him, wanted to help build the fire, but she sensed him maintaining a circle of space around himself. So instead, she found a suitable log across the fire pit. As she watched him work, she waited, biding her time. When a flame appeared, he nursed it—wordlessly placing small sticks, cradling the fire, blowing on the flames. Her thoughts vacillated. Instinct told her to break through the discomfort and just go for it: leap over the fire, jump into his lap, run her tongue up the length of his neck, and bite his earlobe. But reason pinned her in place.

By the time the flickers grew into a bona fide campfire, a fresh awkwardness had settled over them like a scratchy wool blanket. Ethan, too, seemed to be twisting through an emotional wash cycle. Whatever had caused his cool detachment back on Bainbridge Island, whatever he had been struggling to say at the summit, weighed heavily on him again.

She dug out the smushed gummy worms from her pack and stuck a piece in her mouth. It was a mistake because a chewy bit stuck in her back molar. She tried to pry it off with her tongue, but when she noticed his eyes on her, she let it dissolve naturally.

"Did you want one?" She proffered the unappealing goo.

He shook his head, nodding toward the pouches of dehydrated food. "This should be ready in a few minutes," he said, and returned his attention to the water pot he had set to boil. His eyes flashed with firelight. He seemed to be avoiding looking at her. Meg wished she could come up with something to say that would break the stiff mood between them.

Ethan poked the fire with a stick. He poured the boiling water into the pouches of food and set them aside. He adjusted the fire logs and stared at the coals. And when the food had steeped enough, he reached beside the fire and handed her a foil bag, open at the top and steaming. She still felt the tension coming off him in waves, but for the moment, the food took precedence.

"Whoa." She peered inside the pouch at a heaping portion of spaghetti and meat sauce. When the scent of the Bolognese sauce and rosemary hit, she swooned. "I can't think of anything better right now. Thank you."

She dug in. The sauce was thick and piping hot. The pasta was perfectly al dente. No matter that the spaghetti was chopped into rice-sized pieces. It was campfire food, and after a long hike, nothing could taste better.

And as the warmth of the food traveled through her system, Meg felt strengthened. From beneath her lashes, she studied the cool expression on Ethan's handsome face. She couldn't stand it one moment longer. It was time to get to the bottom of the issue. An image of that brave little crocus at the snowy summit flashed through her mind. She, too, would use all the force of her will to crack through the ice.

"Ethan?"

He glanced up, and she had half an urge to drop it, but now that she had done the hard work of starting, she might as well get to the point. "You . . . you wanted to talk about something?" She pushed the words out before she lost her nerve. "Back on Bainbridge, on the courts, we were getting along so well, or at least I thought we were, and then suddenly— Did I say something wrong? Or was it the . . ."

"Are you married?" His question was so direct, she wasn't sure she had heard him right.

"Am I *married*?"

He stared at her, his expression pained.

Out of the blue, the lightly healed scar of Vance's hasty departure scratched open.

"No. I'm not married." Her voice wavered defensively, reeling from the unexpected sting. His gaze took her in, uncertain. "Not anymore," she admitted.

Embarrassed, she flushed. She felt the guilt like a slap. She should have told him, answered with the truth when he asked on the courts. Now she backpedaled, understanding the weight of this moment and hoping that her honesty now would be enough.

"I'm— Oh my gosh. I'm so sorry. I should have said something." She blundered on. "He . . . left me. We haven't been together for months—"

"You don't have to tell me—"

"I want to. I mean, honestly." Her words spilled out, hot and fast. "We're officially divorced. It's over. But I should have told you . . ." She trailed off, feeling wetness spring into her eyes.

Why, really, had she avoided mentioning her recent divorce? She tried to shove down the guilty answer, but it bubbled up again. She was ashamed to admit that her ex had viewed her as unworthy. That was the crux of it. She wished then for a time machine—to go back to the courts, so she could explain to Ethan that she was recently out of a marriage, or back even farther, and not marry Vance to begin with. Meg winced. *Stop that*, a voice inside her whispered. *Stop beating yourself up. You are not less than you are.*

But still, her thoughts fled to her unfinished phone call with her mom. Her parents had been like sea horses or shingleback skinks. Mates for life. Why couldn't her love life be easy, like theirs?

In her heart, she knew the answer. And the truth was the only way to mend this rift.

"My marriage was . . . Well, we never really fit right, you know what I mean? When my dad died"—she tensed with emotion, feeling the ache of it still—"it took my mom years to get back to herself. They just belonged together. But my marriage? It wasn't like that.

"My ex was . . ." But she bit back the easy route. "*I* was . . ." And then it came to her, clearly. "I guess it was easier for me to be with someone who was a little wrapped up in himself. You couldn't really get too close to him."

She was five toes into the water. This was wading, but if she wanted to make this right, she had to dive in. "The truth is, I never had the guts to open myself up enough to find a partner who balanced me. The real me, making a real connection. Like my mom and dad had."

He had been regarding her with such intensity she felt she might melt like wax right into the fire. She stalled, heart in her throat, watching for his reaction.

"You seem pretty authentic to me."

The tenderness in his voice washed over her, and she grabbed on to this bit of forgiveness. It struck her that she and Vance may never have had a truly honest conversation. Like this.

"Wait a sec." Her eyes narrowed. "How did you know I'd been married?"

She startled when he rose from his rock. Ethan strode the few feet around the campfire and eased beside her on the log. Without a word, he laced his fingers through hers, and the simple brush of his knuckles against her skin awakened her senses. Gently, Ethan lifted her hand toward the firelight and traced a fingertip along her finger.

Then she saw it. A ring-shaped tan line.

"Oh," she breathed.

"Hey." He squeezed her hand and caught her eyes with his, a small gesture, but filled with understanding. His steadiness sank into her like water into sand. "I'm sorry about how I reacted back on the courts. How I cut you off without any explanation."

Emotion welled in his eyes. It pressed her lungs against her rib cage to see that he was hurting, too. "When I saw that ring mark, my head jumped to the worst conclusion, and I couldn't drag myself out of it—" He sighed. "That's why I took Rooster up on his offer when he said he was going hiking. I thought he and I would hike up here, and I could spend a night or two in the woods, and the fresh air might clear my head. I . . . shouldn't have assumed."

"Oh, Ethan." Remorse coursed through her for withholding,

with or without intention, the history of her real self. "I'm really, really sorry."

"Well." Ethan stared into the dwindling fire and nodded his understanding. "I'm just glad you're not married." A puff of a laugh escaped his nose. "The whole hike, I went over and over it in my head. I kept telling myself to get over you. But in the back of my mind, I kept thinking: dammit, I really like you."

Above the hum of his uncertainty, *I really like you* boomed through a megaphone. Her heart somersaulted. He really liked her! "Me, too," Meg managed. "I *really* like you, too."

And when she matched his firelight-flecked gaze, Ethan smiled, full on this time; a smile that reached his eyes and said, *I forgive you. I understand you.* Little ice crystals around her heart tinkled as they thawed.

A sizzling hiss and a pop sent a spark shooting from the fire. Overhead, the sky had darkened to indigo, and two stars poked through the blanket of the night. Light as a feather's touch, his hand rested on hers, his fingertips folding into the soft skin of her palm. Each of them stilled, listening to the amplified crackling of the fire and the harmony of their synchronized breathing. She felt the delicious charge trickling like electricity between them.

For a long moment they watched the dwindling fire. "Look at those coals," Ethan said, his voice hushed as a heartbeat. His lips were near enough to her hair that her scalp tingled with arousal. "It's like a light show."

When he turned his face toward hers, she could hardly bear it. She longed for a kiss that would heal their hurts and seal them together. But she did not move toward him. Not yet. She wanted to hang on to this moment. She did not want to stir the stars.

And then Ethan drew back, leaving a sensory shadow on her hand. "You ready to get settled in for the night?"

She kept her voice light while her body fought off the adrenaline. "Sure."

"Good." Rising to his feet, Ethan doused the fire, simultaneously extinguishing her hopes for rekindling the fleeting fire between them. He stepped into the thick blackness of the woods behind her. "I'll be right back."

Meg stood there listening to the crunch of his footsteps behind her, feeling every bit as charred as the smoldering logs, wondering, as she waited, why she had withheld such an important sliver of her past, how she had splintered the trust between them so easily, and how difficult it would be to repair the damage.

Ethan spoke, his voice carrying through the trees.

"Okay. You can turn around now," he said, and she twisted to look behind her, amazed by what had been there all along in the darkness.

TWENTY-TWO

Meg blinked to assure herself she wasn't hallucinating. As her eyes adjusted to the light, she squinted, trying to make sense of the view. Where there had been a dark mass of forest, there was light. Bracelet upon bracelet of fairy lights twined around the boughs of an enormous big-leaf maple, a tree so massive that eight trunks emerged from one colossal stump.

And as she pieced together what she was looking at, Meg shook her head in wonder.

Supported by eight sturdy fingers, a bungalow tree house sat cradled in the palm of the tree. In front of the rustic door, a cozy porch jutted out, complete with a table and chairs hewn from downed forest wood. Meg's heart thudded at her rib cage—it was perfect: Function plus beauty. Art. The final touch was the colorful hammock beside the camp, swaying in the light breeze.

"Solar lights," Ethan said, holding up the switch, as if that was the cause of Meg's astonishment.

Meg found her voice. "What is this place?"

"My cabin. Well, my family's cabin. We're just outside the national park, so we usually get a lot of action here as a rental. But it's not rented tonight." He shrugged. "So I had planned to stay here a night or two and give myself some space to think." He gestured to the plank steps. "Go ahead."

She climbed up, and when her view leveled with the bungalow's interior, her eyes widened. Inside, there was room for only a bed. It sprawled out like a reclining prince, replete with a deep mattress and topped with a multicolored quilt. A parade of pillows marched along the wooden headboard. Her fingers unthinkingly touched the corner of the soft sheet. The bed was just the right size, cozy and perfect for two. "Wow," she breathed. "Just for future reference, I think 'roughing it' undersells it."

He said, "It's a nice night. I can take the hammock. Give you your space."

She did not need her space. In fact, she wanted to be as close as two humans could get. But instead of suggesting the mountain cabin snog-fest she craved, she heard herself say, "It's your cabin. You shouldn't have to sleep outside. I can sleep in the hammock if you—"

"You take the bed," he insisted. "You can't tell me that after all we've been through today, you're not wiped." He gave a nod to indicate that his decision was firm.

But his eyes spoke otherwise, and instead of leaving, he stood in the doorway. The sound of the nighttime toads and the rustle of wind in the leaves snuck between the wooden cabin walls. Neither of them spoke, but his glance caught her hips and traced her contours until he reached her face. Then he sighed and rapped softly on the doorpost with his knuckles. "G'night, Meg."

Meg flopped back on the bed and stared at the rafters. "Grr," she groaned, tapping her brow with her fists. "Grr."

Meg retrieved her cell phone from her bag. With little faith, she pressed it on, and, miracle of miracles, the screen came to life.

She bolted upright and texted Rooster. I'm safe. How's the hand?

In response, her phone rang. Rooster's voice sounded distant, tired. "Where are you? Are you all right? We were so worried . . ." He paused. "It's Meg," Rooster's muffled voice translated to Annie.

"I'm fine. I'm fine."

"Thank heaven and the saints. Can't tell you how glad we are to hear you're okay. The hand's okay. I'll have to cancel my harp concert at Carnegie Hall, but it'll heal. Where are you? Is Ethan with you? Are you already down the mountain?"

"No. Listen. It's a long story, but Ethan's here with me and we're both fine. I'm safe. I'll be down in the morning, and I can tell you all about it."

"Okay." He hesitated, his Papa Bear radar perking up. "If you're sure. You know how to reach me if you change your mind. Annie and I found motel rooms for the night in Port Angeles. Text us when you're down and we'll pick you up."

Meg sighed as she packed her phone away. Here she was in a lovely, romantic cabin. The man she craved was only fifty feet away, but he may as well have been in Alaska. She pulled off her hiking clothes, including her campfire-scented fleece. Investigating the contents of her pack, she was pleased to find an unworn, lightweight thermal shirt, which she tugged on before snuggling beneath the cozy comforter.

She should sleep. She should be exhausted. But instead, she lay there, engaged in a rafter-staring contest. Her thoughts pingponged between steamy—the hot man lying in the hammock outside—and depressing—Rooster's mangled hand. She tossed onto her side. She flopped onto her belly. She groaned into her pillow.

The steamy thoughts won out.

"Enough already." She kicked aside the comforter and slid her bare feet into her hiking boots. Clunking across the wood floor, she groped her way to the door, pushed it open, and stood on the landing. Her eyes adjusted. Overhead, the night sky glittered with a creamy wash of starlight, but the creature sounds of sunset had ceased. The mountaintop was silent save for the hushed crinkling of leaves pushed by the wind. Below, she made out the wonky slope of the plank stairs. Steps away, there was the hammock. Just a short walk across the earth, and she would be there. She could stand on the landing till her feet grew roots. Or she could stride across that dark expanse and take control.

Screw it, she thought, her feet carrying her down the stairs. Meg Bloomberg was tired of waiting for someone else to make her life happen. In her eagerness, her fingers missed the handrail, and she tripped down the lopsided steps. "Ow," she said quietly to the dirt at the bottom. Righting herself, she tromped over the roots, circumvented a stump, and skittered over the pebbly ground until she found herself standing behind the head of the hammock.

She froze there, heart pulsing in her ears, wondering if she should turn and go back. This was silly. Maybe it was too soon after getting their wires uncrossed. He could have made a move in the cabin. But that whole "give you your space" thing could have meant he simply wasn't sure if he wanted the high-maintenance job of being the postdivorce rebound dude. On the other hand, maybe he was lying awake thinking about Meg. He *had* said he really liked her. Quietly, very quietly, she decided to check in on him.

"Are you asleep?" she asked, her words thinner than a whisper.

"Are you kidding? I thought you were a bear."

Smiling, she came around. He lay on his back, eyes wide. She saw he was smiling, too. Ethan patted the space beside him.

Meg kicked off her boots and slid into the hammock. Side by side, they lay together, their hands clasped over their chests like twin statues. They stared up at the spreading boughs, at the canopy of leaves that trembled like lips on the verge of speech. Neither of them said a word. Meg was acutely aware of each spot where his body met hers; their calves pressed together, thighs touching, his hip resting on hers. The midnight scent of his skin dizzied her with desire, but she would not break the spell, because lying perfectly still beside him was arousing her in a way that made every molecule of her blood press against the surface of her skin. If he touched her, if he even moved an inch, she imagined she would combust.

He turned his head and spoke low near her ear. "I'm glad you're here." The hammock swayed in the soft breeze. He breathed against her temple, stirring her hair, and she closed her eyes to absorb the intensity of his nearness.

"I still feel bad about pushing you away like that," he said. "That whole thing. That had nothing to do with you but with—" He stopped, and Meg got the sense he was choosing his words with care. ". . . It was all stuff I've been carrying around for years."

He closed his eyes. She watched him, waiting for him to go on. The wind pressed strands of his hair against her cheek. The silence went on for so long she wondered if he had fallen asleep. Then he opened his eyes and spoke in a voice barely above a whisper. "You know how I told you my dad was out of the picture?"

Ethan continued. "Growing up, it was just me and my mom. My bio dad, I barely remember him, but apparently, he was a pretty convincing bullshit artist." He stared at the branches and shook his head, still affected by the memory. Meg listened, not daring to budge. "When I was three, my ma found a ring in his wallet. He had this whole other family. And he chose them over us."

Meg absorbed his words. "That sucks."

He chuckled bitterly. "It does suck. So I guess you could say I have trust issues. Doesn't excuse my behavior; just history."

She felt it then, the sensation of opening. Of one person making their heart vulnerable to another and accepting the invitation to do the same. "I bet that was hard. On both of you." Listening to the rise and fall of his breath, she watched the leaves shimmer in the dim moonlight. "I have a giant hair ball of trust issues of my own, obviously. Though mine are more recently acquired," she said, trying to make light of it.

He said nothing, but she could feel the movement of the hammock as he nodded and gave her the space to continue.

"Sometimes," she said, "I feel like I wasted this whole period of my life. I thought my marriage was this partnership. Everybody has to make compromises, right? He spent years in dental school, and I gave up painting so I could support him. So, for two years while he got his dental practice off the ground, I beaded and felted cat collars. Don't laugh."

"Wasn't going to."

"Anyhow. As you know. He left. And I'm still not sure what the full story was." She shrugged, although it still did not feel like a shrugging matter. "The whole time we were together, secretly I kept blaming him for making me give up painting. But he never did that. I did that." Shame welled in her chest at having put herself aside for another person. It was one thing to be supportive and open, but quite another to give up on oneself.

He lifted his hand between them, and she linked her fingers through. "You don't make it into your thirties without dragging a few anchors in your wake," he said softly.

She nodded, his words hitting home. She understood what it felt like to carry around an anchor. Understood that trust was fragile and breakable, only because gaining it was such hard work.

But with Ethan? She felt a lifting of the burden. A possibility.

"But I know what you mean," he said. "Sometimes in my

business, the people I work with say they want to be environmentally friendly, but they don't actually want to change the way they operate. Everyone wants an easy fix, but sometimes you have to, well, take out the courts, so to speak. Raze the field. Do a controlled burn so that new growth can appear."

The mention of the doomed courts pinched at her, but maybe Ethan had a point. There was no easy fix for blunders made in the past, and the closest anyone could come to redemption was to move forward with good intent.

The stars winked between the boughs, and the leaves reacted to the wind. She guessed then that commitment didn't come easily to him, that he stepped lightly into relationships for fear that they were delicate, untrustworthy things. That he waited to see if they took root and blossomed. And she was—or always had been—the opposite. Meg fell into trusting too willingly. She could free-fall, eyes closed, and she believed trust would catch her. Perhaps they both were going to have to change the way they operated.

As if coming to the same conclusion, Ethan tipped his body so that it faced hers. The hammock shifted, and she let the movement roll her, cocoon them. Their faces were so close. The strain of the past couple of days had left her body thirsting with the desire to reconnect. And from the way the points of their bodies touched in all the soft and hard places, she knew he felt the same.

Their chests rose and fell against each other, her eyelashes fluttering at the touch of his warm, sweet breath. Brimming with delicious wanting, she gave just the smallest tilt of her head. He pressed toward her, his lips first, and his hands following. His fingers skimmed the hem of her shirt and, lightly, he traced the skin up her rib cage. Her thumbs caressed the hollow of his hip bone and threaded along his boxers. Her greedy fingers pressed down his abdomen.

"Mm," he groaned, licking a line with the point of his tongue from her collarbone to her ear. He combed his fingers up her scalp, lifting her hair against the grain.

Both hands in her hair, he stopped. Ethan pulled her face away and regarded her.

"What?" her lips whispered. "What is it?"

"You," he said. He lifted her hand to his lips. Gently, he kissed the pale line below her knuckle. "What a fool he was to let you go."

The words touched her core. She could feel the pull between them, a tension so sweet it was nearly unbearable. When she could deny the magnet's tug no longer, their lips came together—at once relieving and inflaming that lovely ache. This was not the lusty need of their seat belt kiss, nor the giddy infatuation from the hotel porch, nor the public smooch on the practice court. This time, the press of his lips felt like a completion, the final note in the symphony.

And then Ethan's mouth was in her hair, and she stretched her face to the sky, exposing the innocent, moon-kissed skin of her neck. He lifted her shirt, and his lips grazed a trail down her body. Weightless, she slipped through the hammock to the center of the earth. She kept free-falling, falling and falling and falling without a net in sight.

TWENTY-THREE

Last night, dizzy with the residue of desire, they pad-footed along the rough earth and climbed into the tree house. Without the gymnastics necessitated by the hammock, they took their time, relishing the luxury of drawn-out pleasure. Afterward, beneath the cozy comforter, she snuggled against Ethan and dropped into a sleep so satisfying and luxurious she wished she could bottle it and save it for a restless night. Now an Ethan-shaped indentation lay beside her, the bed so recently abandoned that his scent still hovered. Making slow circles with her ankles, she enjoyed the texture of the smooth sheets.

On the rustic nightstand, Ethan had left her a folded, fresh T-shirt. Smiling, she dressed and skipped down the cabin steps, looking forward to pouring boiling water into a pouch of dehydrated scrambled eggs. What a brilliant invention. Perhaps she should switch to buying all her food dehydrated. She hoped Ethan had coffee; then again, if he traveled with pasta Bolognese, he surely stocked up on the roasted beans. A Northwest morning without coffee was like an air sandwich.

She found him reading in the hammock, and when he noticed her, the sly lift of his lips brought back the memory of last night's intimacies. Meg reached for his paperback. "Check the page number," she said, and gave him an instant before she snatched the book and tossed it to the ground.

"Mmm." His hand slid down her side until he reached her hip. Yanking her toward him, he murmured, "Good morning."

More than a little aroused, she coiled her arms around him, hammock and all, and slid on top of him for a kiss that would have shocked her former self. The wind picked up and set the hammock swinging. Coming up for air, Meg caught a flutter of paper in her peripheral view. "What's this?" She hadn't seen it in the darkness last night. Meg unclipped a deck of laminated cards from the suspension rope.

Ethan sat, as best as he could, and peeked over Meg's shoulders. The back of each card read *Hammock Fun at the Mountain Love Shack*.

"What *is* this?" she asked again. This time it was a mock accusation. She flipped through the first few cards, her eyes widening. Each card featured a racy cartoon image complete with captions and instructions. "This is your *family's* cabin?"

Ethan had turned an adorable shade of red. "This is . . . I have not seen this before. This was not here the last time I was here," he protested.

She sifted through the cards. *Pigs in a Blanket: Self-explanatory. Night at the Improv: Anything for a laugh. Zipper: Has teeth. The Candelabra: One foot on the floor and the other limbs raised to the sky. Brace Yourself, Franny: See details in image.*

"This is like the hammock *Kama Sutra*," she observed.

He reached over to keep her from flipping to the next card. "This looks interesting. I suggest we try the Cheeky Chipmunk."

"Oh, do you?" Shifting, Meg straddled him. She cradled his face in her hands and kissed him.

His hands glided down her backside and he squeezed two handfuls of Meg. "You are cheeky, aren't you?"

"I am," she smirked, and pressed herself against him. "Ooh. Paddle up." Their kiss, soft and playful at first, quickly devolved into a sense-obliterating crush of passion.

"Oopsie! Don't mind me."

Meg jumped at the approaching voice and swiveled to see a round-faced, cheerful woman in her sixties.

As he bolted upright, Ethan tipped Meg from the hammock. He grabbed her arm, steadying her landing. "Mom!" Ethan gasped.

Her eyes crinkled in apology. "So sorry. So sorry, sweetheart. Hope I'm not interrupting." She set down a stack of sheets on the picnic bench and gave Meg a friendly wave. "Hello," she sang before reaching out her hand. "I'm Babs. Babs Fine. Ethan's mom."

"Ma. What are you doing here?"

Meg's head whipped back and forth between the pair. Now it was her cheeks that she knew were sprouting a pink blush. His mother?

Babs smiled and nodded at the linens. "Changing the sheets. Do you think they change themselves?" Turning her attention to Meg, she asked Ethan, "Who's your friend?"

"This is Meg, and we were just packing up—"

"Is that what the kids are calling it these days?" Babs's lips lifted with her sidelong glance. "I've made you your breakfast, pumpkin, just like you like it. I wasn't expecting company, but there's plenty for the both of you. Let me just get these sheets on." Still mastering her surprise, Meg moved out of Ethan's mother's path. "Meg, do you want a latte? A half-caf? I'll call Henry and let him know. He likes to be prepared."

"Henry's Mom's boyfriend," Ethan clarified, as if that was the part of this scenario that needed explaining.

A latte? In the wilderness? Meg stuttered, "Um. A mocha? Soy if you have it."

"You got it." Turning to her son, she said, "You should get a move on. We have our appointment at ten, remember? And Ethan, honey?" She waggled a finger at her son's boxers. "You might want to put on some pants." Babs trundled into the cabin, humming the theme from *Star Wars*.

With an apologetic glance at Meg, Ethan wriggled into his jeans.

"Oh my god," Meg whispered. "Your mom . . ." Her eyes flew wide as she listened to the rustling of the bed-making inside. "Oh no! The garbage can . . ."

"She'll leave that for me—"

"Ethan, sweetheart, where do we keep the spare trash bags?"

"Oh god," Meg murmured. "I might die of embarrassment."

"Never mind. Found them," Babs called from within. "Three! Good for you. Always a good idea to use protection."

Ethan cocked his head. "Burial or cremation?"

"Just chuck me off the cliff, please."

"All set," Babs announced, emerging from the cabin a few minutes later. Apprising Meg and Ethan's readiness, she nodded her approval and headed off into the hemlocks. Meg followed, too dumbstruck to wonder where they were going. In the span of minutes, Meg had gone from feeling like a grown-up taking charge of her sexuality to a teen caught with weed in her sock drawer. She did not ask if they were headed toward the main trail or back down the route she came. In fact, she wouldn't have been surprised to find a helicopter waiting behind the ridge.

As they trod the worn trail, Ethan placed a hand on the small of her back. They walked for several minutes along a widening path, and Meg noticed a subtle change in her surroundings: the chirping of the birds was replaced by the noise of . . . what was that? Cars? With a mounting sense of the surreal, Meg heard a car horn, then spotted a telltale sign of civilization: the peak of a cell tower.

Steps later, they emerged from the woods to a subdivision and marched through the backyard of a contemporary home. "Casa, sweet casa," Babs declared.

Catching on to Meg's confusion, Ethan explained. "The cabin and the maple stand, that's all part of my mom's property. This is Olympic Heights." He directed her up the porch steps of a colonial craftsman. A golf cart sat parked in the driveway. Her mouth dropped and she resisted the urge to hit herself upside the head. The goat, the cliff crossing, the fear of freezing to death with gummy worms stuck in her teeth. She had been so close to civilization and had not even known it.

Bewildered and feeling not just a little awkward, Meg allowed herself to be led to the dining room. A breakfast of scrambled eggs on toast graced the table.

"Wow," Meg managed. "This looks amazing." Babs and Ethan dug in, and Meg twirled the fork in her hand. She nibbled at the eggs. They were fluffy and rich. "These might be the best eggs I've ever had."

"They're fresh from Ethel Mae. She's our best layer," Babs said. She ruffled her son's hair and beamed at him. "Speaking of laying, that reminds me—" She nudged Ethan. "What did you think of my Love Shack cards?"

"Mom—" Ethan started.

"Henry and I got the idea when we were enjoying a little camp-out in the hammock one night and . . . Well, never mind. In any case, Pigs in a Blanket comes with very high reviews." She winked theatrically at Meg, who glanced to Ethan for help.

"Didn't you say something about coffee, Ma?"

On cue, a fit older man approached from the kitchen. His wavy long hair was wrangled into a ponytail beneath a cap that read *I Speak for the Trees*. He carried a delicate teacup balanced on a saucer. "A soy mocha gal, huh?" he said, setting the piping cup on the table. A chocolate syrup heart was swirled into the foam. "Shoulda guessed. For Ethan, it would have to be that or an almond milker." Meg did not know what to make of that, so she made nothing.

Ethan chuckled uncomfortably. "Can we try *not* to scare off my friend in the first few minutes, please?"

Henry guffawed. "She don't seem the type to scare easy." He arched a bushy brow.

Ethan told Meg, "Mom met Henry on the Founders Courts. Actually, he was the one who taught me and Mom how to play."

"Are you a pickler, too?" Babs scooted onto the chair beside Meg and rested her chin on her clasped hands.

"She is," Ethan answered. "She's good." Meg beamed, flattered.

Henry said, "In that case, you've come to the right place."

Henry motioned for her to join him at the kitchen window, and he directed her attention to the backyard. There, a portable net sat over a sport court neatly painted with pickleball lines. Her laugh spilled out. Seemed everybody and their uncles were turning parking lots and driveways into pickleball courts.

"What a wonderful coincidence," Babs exclaimed, sipping from her cappuccino, which was more foam than coffee. "We could use a fourth this morning. I'd rather sit out. My back could use a rest after last night." She and Henry exchanged a lewd glance.

Ethan hung his head. "I'm gonna need some more therapy."

"What do you say?" Babs asked. "Can you sub in? Henry and you against Ethan and his Picklesmash partner." She looked down at her watch. "We're supposed to play at ten."

"I'm in," Meg said, nodding. "And it will give me a chance to meet this mysterious pickleball partner of yours. What's his name?" she said, turning to Ethan.

"My partner?" he said, taking a bite of eggs. "His name's Michael Edmonds."

The name tunneled into her like a freight train. Or a sock to the gut with a bowling ball. Or the blow of a safe tied to a piano and chained to an elephant and dropped from a twelfth-story window. Michael Edmonds, the advanced player from Lakeview, planned to ditch Annie to play at the *beginner* level for Bainbridge? With Ethan Fine. *Her* Ethan.

At last, sound sputtered from her lips. "Your partner is Michael Edmonds? Michael? Edmonds?"

"You know him?"

"Wait." Her hands flew out in front of her. "Are you saying that you and Michael Edmonds are practicing so you can compete in the *beginners'* slot at Picklesmash?"

"Oh, so you *do* know him," Ethan said. "Then you get it. It's our sneak attack plan. It's going to take some work to make a convincing beginner out of him."

Meg gaped, flabbergasted. Bainbridge! How dare they cheat with such impunity? And Ethan! How could he willingly participate in this charade? She struggled to get her fury under control. This was the same guy who, just last night, she'd bared her soul to. The guy she'd trusted with her private truth. How could he dare to pose an A-lister as a beginner for the sake of a tournament win? Was this some kind of April Fool's prank? In July? Her heart begged for a misunderstanding.

But then, look at him, all smug with his half-caf breve perched between his hands, untouched by guilt. That conniving, smarmy, pickle-partner-stealing jerk.

And poor Annie. Meg had been holding out hope that maybe she was wrong about the partnership. But here was more evidence of his betrayal. How would she break the news that Michael not only did not want to date her, but he would not even play with her? That Michael was jumping ship to pickle with the enemy? It would break her friend. She balled her fingers into fists and dug her nails into her palms. The pain did little to stanch her fury.

Michael Edmonds is Bainbridge's secret weapon. Marilyn had spilled those beans out on her backyard court. But Michael wasn't just helping the Bainbridge folks with his experienced advice. Michael Edmonds was playing down to ensure that Bainbridge would bring home the Picklesmash trophy—and therefore a bucketload of cash. Which, Meg noted, the Founders didn't even need! That double-crossing, two-timing creep.

The wheels of her brain spun so furiously she could smell the burning rubber. Did Michael plan on lying in wait until tournament time, just so he could pull out his A game against Lakeview's weakest team? What a phony! A charlatan. What kind of jerk screws his own league out of a fair shot? And what kind of asshole trains a guy to look like he's crap at pickleball in order to attain nefarious ends?

Ethan Fine, that was who.

The sound of tires on gravel interrupted her thirst for revenge. Babs waddled toward the front door. "Here he is. How 'bout you all warm up together while Henry and I clean up in here?"

There had to be an explanation. Maybe this was a different Michael Edmonds. It was a common name, right? Both Michael and Edmonds. Meg inched toward the window and lifted the curtain to the side.

Her breath caught. Yep. No doubt about it. It was him, all right, the same man who shouted his own name in victory after a winning point. The same guy whom Annie had finally mustered the nerve to kiss. The same Michael Edmonds who was faking his beginner's status to help Bainbridge win. Michael Edmonds in the flesh.

That two-timing skunk parked his car in the cul-de-sac and began moseying toward the house.

Meg fumed, lumping Michael together with Ivan the Terrible and Vlad the Impaler. And Ethan the Untrustworthy! She should have seen this coming. Now she could see how he had reeled her in, only to stomp her beneath his laterally stabilized pickleball shoes. All along, Ethan had known she played for Lakeview, but had hidden his own pickleball expertise. And now this! How easily she had fallen for him. How well he had hidden his true nature.

She had to get out of there. Now.

Meg looked left. Henry was offering her a paddle. To the right, Babs had refilled her mocha and was spooning in extra foam. Ahead, Ethan smiled, pleased with himself at his cruel deception.

Her thinly maintained veneer cracked, and her venom erupted. "I can't believe you," Meg fumed. Her whisper was more an indictment of herself than of him. "I can't believe I trusted you. I am so outta here."

Ethan's brow dipped as he was caught in his dastardly betrayal. "Meg. Wait!" he cried, leaping up from the table and knocking a wave of breve from his cup.

Oh, he was good, pulling off that innocent-guy act she had bought all along.

But she would not wait. She threw on her pack, knocked into a chair, banged her knee on the end table, opened the closet, realized it wasn't the exit, and finally managed to storm out the back door without glancing behind her.

With no plan in mind, she strode past an unflinching Michael Edmonds, out to the gravel road, and down the hill. She could feel the flush in her face and the hot wetness stinging her eyes.

Damn him. She really liked Ethan. What a jerk. She would march all the way down the mountain if need be. Or better still, she would hitch a ride down and get the hell away from there as fast as possible. If only there were any cars at all passing by on the top of this miserable mountain.

At last, she heard the rumble of an engine ahead. Meg picked up speed, jogging to catch up with the vehicle. Spotting her in the rearview, the driver slowed to a stop. Meg was panting by the time she reached the truck. "Can you give me a lift to Port Angeles?"

It was unconventional, but, judging the state of her distress, the driver acquiesced and passed her a vest. "We can't fit you in the cab, but you can hang on to the back and we'll take it slow."

And that was how Meg Bloomberg endured her ride of shame: wearing a fluorescent vest and a hard hat. As she bumped down the mountain cursing her lack of sports bra, Meg clung to the rail of the recycling truck and thanked her stars it wasn't garbage day.

THE BACKSPIN

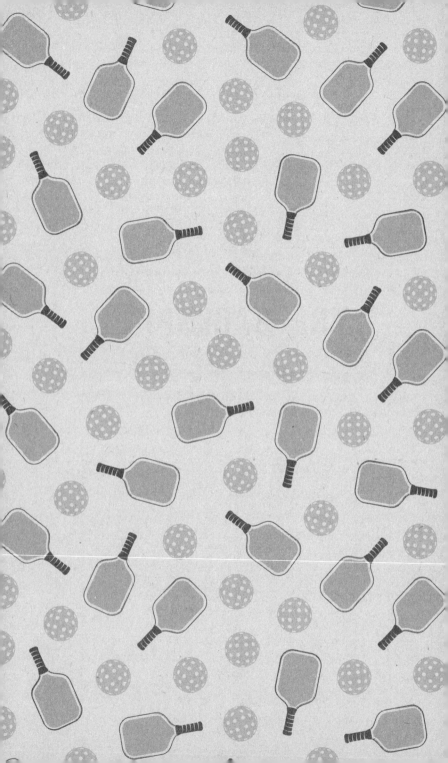

TWENTY-FOUR

At a gas station outside of Port Angeles, Meg retrieved the keys to the blue hatchback. "I only put a couple of dents in the rear, but you can hardly see them," Annie joked before jogging off to the restroom. Meg tried a weak smile, but her heart was not in it.

Rooster used his good hand to chuck Meg on the shoulder. "Buck up," he said. "It ain't over for you. You're a pickleball powerhouse."

He raised the plastered finger and thumb and said, "They did an all right job, don't ya think? And on the plus side, I can do this," he said, lifting his L-shaped cast to his forehead. "Loser! That's the sign I'm gonna make for the other team when you find another partner and kick their butts."

Her deflated heart pushed out an appreciative smile. Later, Meg promised herself, she would tell Rooster choice parts of the story that had led to her discovery that Ethan and Michael were both behind cheating in the tournament. But now, all of them were hungry and tired and a long way from Bainbridge. And she owed it to Annie to tell her the truth, privately, first.

Besides, a nagging voice in her mind warned that her gullibility with Ethan spoke of a deeper defeat. If she couldn't trust herself to know whom she could trust and whom to distrust, how could she trust herself? Her circular self-deprecation was giving her a headache.

"You can get a better teammate than this old coot, anyhow," Rooster was saying.

"Actually," she mumbled, "I think I'm going to take a break from pickleball. Maybe it's not for me."

"Maybe you're right." Rooster kept his eyes pegged on hers and nodded solemnly. "Maybe you should just quit."

A silence followed. In that instant, her private suspicion was confirmed. She *did* suck at pickleball. How long had she been fooling herself?

Rooster snorted. "I was messing with you, kid! For cryin' out loud, what are you thinking? You lost your partner. So what? You have one lousy obstacle thrown in your way and *boom!*" He snapped his fingers. "You quit? You think success is easy? Did Einstein give up when he wanted to find the theory of relativity? Did Michael Phelps stop swimming after one gold medal? Did Marie Curie stop working on radiation when . . . Well, maybe she should have, but that's beside the point. No. The best ones never stop. They keep trying. All those little pebbles of failure along the way . . . they make stepping-stones to success. Because there's one thing all the greats have in common: they've got nerve, all of them. Right?"

Meg nodded, only half-convinced.

"Right?"

"All right. All right. I'll keep it in mind. Like I need advice from you. You look like you're about to rob a bank." She smirked and mirrored his bandaged hand. "Stick 'em up."

"You think that's funny, huh?" Rooster countered.

Meg pointed her finger gun at herself. "Who? Me?"

"Watch out, lady," Rooster said, and flashed two fingers and a thumb. "I'd flip you the bird, but my fingers are having technical difficulties."

"We're gonna grab a bite before we return to the Outlook," Annie said to Rooster as she marched back toward them. "You sure you won't join us?"

"Let me just check." As he tapped in his wife's phone number at a glacial pace, he told the ladies, "Vernie and I have plans for an all-night Scrabble tournament with Lulu."

Laverne's greeting echoed over the speaker. "How's our Lulu doing?" Rooster asked in a voice that could be heard in Oregon.

"We've been having some excitement." Laverne matched his volume. "She had a contraction." Rooster sucked on his teeth, and the group exchanged glances. Lulu was still two months before her due date. "Cool your rocket blasters, sweets," Laverne continued, "Probably a false alarm. She's at the clinic getting a check, just in case."

The instant he hung up the phone, Rooster squeezed them both into a quick hug and hopped in his Buick. "I'll let you know when I get another hall pass, ladies." Smiling, Meg rolled her eyes. Rooster pointed his bandaged fingers out the window. "Kapow, kiddos. See you soon."

By the time Annie and Meg rolled into Bainbridge an hour and a half later, the last golden rays of sunset glowed against the facade of the Greens Grill. Annie, hangry and determined, followed the hostess at a clip to an out-of-the-way table on the outside deck. In distracted silence, they glanced at the menu and sipped at their waters. Annie scrolled through her phone and researched Bainbridge hospitals with facilities for preemies. Meanwhile, Meg racked her brain, considering how to tell Annie that Michael had turned out to be a double-crossing tournament thief.

So she stalled. When they reached for the last of the breadsticks,

Annie caught Meg's eye and glanced away quickly. If Meg hadn't known better, she would have thought that Annie was keeping an uncomfortable secret from her as well.

"We need a drink," Annie urged.

Meg narrowed her eyes. Annie rarely drank anything stronger than mint in her lemonade. "Okay," she said, suspicion lacing her response.

Annie waved over their waiter. "Two margaritas, please." As he moved to leave, she tapped his arm. "And two tequila chasers." Now Meg's curiosity shifted into overdrive. Something was definitely up.

Annie waited until the drinks were in front of them. She took a sip, steadied her gaze, and said, "Reflux Dave texted me . . . I'm so sorry, Meg," she sighed. "They gave the beginners' slot to Vance and Édith."

The effect was more like a dull headache than a stab to the gut. Not sharp, not unexpected, just disorienting. She understood it. She did. Without Rooster, she couldn't compete anyway. Even so, she felt the sting of her old league's decision. They hadn't even given her a shot at challenging her competitors. More than anything, she felt as if Vance had robbed her—stolen away something that should have been hers.

Meg tapped her forehead on the tabletop, not hard, but enough for theatrical effect. This morning, the guy she'd crushed on had crushed her. Now her pickle peeps had kicked her to the curb as well. All that remained was an ex-partner with a finger gun and the hammock indentations on her left buttock.

And knowing that the bad-news dump had only just begun, Meg exhaled through her nose. She wished she could protect Annie from the truth, but it was time to open up a bag of jerky.

"I saw Michael Edmonds," she started.

Without preamble, Meg shared the sorry saga of Michael's

betrayal: from trying to pry the scoop from Marilyn, to seeing him with paddle in hand creeping into the enemy camp. "Michael Edmonds plans to skip out on you to play for Bainbridge. Worse, he's playing down and pretending to be a beginner. I'm sorry, Annie. But I saw him with my own eyes."

At first, Annie said nothing, and Meg wished her empathy were a magic trick that could make Annie's hurt vanish. "I can't believe it," Annie whispered, her voice warbling with emotion. "I can't believe he would do that to Lakeview. I just can't believe—he would do that to me!"

"I know. I am so sorry."

"Wait." Annie gripped Meg's wrist. "You saw him playing? Who was he playing with?"

"Well, that's the other thing," Meg confessed, her heart rate accelerating. "Michael's partner in crime?" It hurt so much she could hardly say it. "Ethan Fine."

"No."

Meg nodded soberly.

"Your Ethan? Shirtless Wonder Ethan?"

"Yep."

"Ethan?" Annie shook her head, as if her disbelief could make it un-so. "Close-down-our-courts-and-totally-screw-us Ethan?" She side-eyed the tequila shot. "Aw, Meg. Shit. Excuse me," she said, automatically apologizing for her language. She clinked the glass against Meg's and threw it back. Then she snatched Meg's shot glass and downed that as well. "Shit," she repeated.

"There is something very wrong in the world," Annie continued, "when your Shirtless Wonder is a conniving asshole and my Michael Edmonds is a"—she looked over her shoulder for the bad-word police—"a fucking teabagger."

"I'm pretty sure you mean sandbagger."

"Teabagger," Annie said, downing the rest of her margarita.

• • • • •

Two margaritas in, Annie suggested they move indoors to sit at the bar. "I need to cut out the middleman," she explained, and scooted into one of the captain's barstools. Her mood over the last hour had gone from fury to self-pity to vengeful indignation. Annie gritted her teeth. "I can't believe those guys. It is just not right. We need to do something about this." She threw as much force behind her squeaky voice as she could. "I'd like to pickle their balls."

"Now, that would be something."

But Annie was already nixing the idea with a shake of her head. "On second thought," she amended, "testicular pickling is not a long-term solution. Because . . . Scrotox."

"Say what?"

"Scrotox. You know. Botox for the scrotum."

"That is not a thing."

"It is totally a thing. Scrotox," she repeated, enjoying the sound of it way too much. "I heard about it from one of the nurses. Smooths while it plumps. It's real. I'm gonna look it up." Annie jabbed at her phone for proof and shared the screen. "See?"

"Ack! Make it stop!" Meg buried her eyes in her palms.

Snatching the phone back, Annie whisked away the website. "Blech. You can't unsee that kind of thing."

Annie tipped back the last of her margarita. Before long, she started to swipe at her cell again, and Meg began to wonder at the sober change on her friend's face. "What are you doing?"

Annie's sigh dropped so heavily she could have broken a toe. "I hate that I'm doing this. But I can't stop."

Over her friend's shoulder, Meg glimpsed images as they swept past. Michael Edmonds kayaking with his fiancée. Michael

Edmonds laughing over a latte. Michael Edmonds counting out change. By the umpteenth image, Meg pulled the phone away from her.

"Gimme that. That can't be healthy," Meg said. She glanced down and gawked at the last image on Annie's cell. Michael Edmonds on Marilyn's asphalt pickleball court. With Ethan. How dare those bullshit artists blaspheme the original courts with their sandbagging presence? She tossed the phone back to Annie. "That pisses me off."

"Better to be pissed off than pissed on," Annie declared much louder than necessary.

The bartender appeared. Swishing her bar rag across the surface, she lifted their empty glasses. "How 'bout I get you two some soda or juice for the next round?"

Annie said, "I think we're being cut off." Resigned, she nodded toward the side, where fruits and veggies were piled in a bowl beside a blender. "We'll have a couple of smoothies. And some water."

The bartender filled two glasses with ice water. Annie sipped at it and chewed on the ice. She leaned into Meg, her eyes glinting with mischief. "I have an idea. If Michael can post all of the wonderful and fun things he's doing with his stupid fiancée and his stupid pickleball paddle, why can't we?"

Meg had drunk just enough to believe that this was a very good idea. "We should make them jealous and sorry that they messed with us, show those boys what a good time we're having," she said, aiming her cell at the bartender, who was blending up a healthy-looking veggie shake. She hit record. "Blend it up. Vroom!" Meg cheered before hitting the post button. "See? We are fun and wonderful. Right?"

"We are. We are won and funderful." Annie cocked her head. "That is not right."

"Okay. One more of us." Meg snapped a selfie of their cheeks pressed together. Annie's lopsided grin was cut halfway out of the shot. "What should we caption it?"

"I dunno. Say: We're having so much fun. We are . . . eating caviar and drinking champagne. And tomorrow we're going out to the beach and we're getting on a cruise."

"First of all, that is way too much to type. And second of all . . ." She forgot the second of all. "Say something short. And true. Everybody knows there aren't any cruises from Bainbridge," she clarified, impressed that her brain was functioning in such a rational manner.

"No cruises? They should have cruises. Maybe we could find a big ship . . ." Annie countered hopefully. Grabbing Meg's phone, she voice texted. "Today drinking 'ritas. Tomorrow taking a big ship on the beach. Ta-da! Captioned and posted. Now Michael will be very jealous that we are having so much fun while he is teabagging in a pickleball tournament and marrying some stupid . . . other . . . person—" The end of Annie's sentence was lost to the sob.

Meg took a sip of the foaming, chunky green liquid. It tasted as unpleasant as chewing tinfoil, or finding out the guy you opened your heart to was a duplicitous, backstabbing weasel.

TWENTY-FIVE

Meg woke in the pitch dark. There was a half moment of sea-legs confusion before she made sense of her surroundings. She was in her bed at the inn, still fighting the drunkenness and leaning toward hungover. The clock read three fifteen A.M. She tried to fall back to sleep, but instead, her brain began a comprehensive list of her failures: She'd blown her shot at kicking Vance's ass on the courts. She'd lost her chance at finding solace in Ethan's arms. And to boot, inspiration refused to strike on the fence that lurked out there in the night, mocking her with its blank pickets.

Annie snored softly in the other bed, and Meg concentrated on listening to her friend's measured breathing. The sound helped her relax. As she walked the bridge between wakefulness and sleep, her mind found its way out of the maze of self-pity.

Seventy percent asleep, her imagination threw splashes of color onto the empty fence. Her freely associating brain erased them, tried geometric shapes, and rejected those, too. A dream paintbrush laid down a realistic, pebble-filled shoreline that blended into the landscape. A sort of trompe l'oeil that blurred the lines between art and reality. A bucket of water washed it off. Next, her imagination painted a Rousseau-reminiscent fantasy, set in the rainforest rather than the jungle. Then an expressionist design: jolts of color like street-art graffiti that came to life with its vibrant story. It wasn't fully formed, but she felt the muse within her stir, and the seed of that idea soothed her to sleep.

She woke to the jingle of her ringer. Jumping on it before Annie startled—of which there was little likelihood, with the way she was snoring—Meg answered.

"Hello?" Her greeting came out raw and scratchy. Her head pounded.

"Who is this?" the voice on the line demanded.

"Mom? It's me. You called me," Meg clarified.

Dina Bloomberg softened. "Oh! I thought you were a man. You sound terrible."

Meg squinted into the light that poured into the room. What time was it? Before she could orient herself, her mother barreled forward. "I saw your post last night and I thought to myself, Dina Bloomberg, your daughter is having a crisis. And when a girl has a crisis, she needs her momma."

Meg rolled her neck to the side and felt a sharp pinch. Stars danced in front of her eyes. The embers of a dream flared up in her head. Something about the fence. Had she come up with the idea? Had her dream offered her the solution and now all she had to do was reach back into her memory and—

Dina said, "And I hope you brought a shovel to the beach this morning."

Meg sat upright in bed. "What?" She was fully awake.

"According to your post, yesterday you drank margaritas. And today you were going to the beach to—"

Oh no. "Hold on." *Oh please, please, please,* Meg thought. Her fingers stamped at her phone, and she pulled up the post. Oh no, no, no, no. The cruise ship plan. The post read, *Tomorrow taking a big shit on the beach*. Drinking and texting. Surely there was a lesson there.

"And don't get me started on that video. What are you and Annie getting up to?"

"Hold, please." Again, Meg switched to her post. The camera swayed as Meg videoed from her barstool. In the glass blender, a peeled cucumber stood upright, with two small tomatoes cradling the base—until the machine whirred the contents into mush. "Blend it up. Vroom!" Meg's voice slurred through her laughter.

"Mom." Her stomach churned like the contents of the blender. "I have to go. But I'm fine. I'm glad you called."

"I can come home. If you need me, I'll come home."

"That's sweet, Mom. I'm fine. Don't worry about me." Of course, she did want her mom to come home and comfort her and hug her and tell her she'd always suspected that Vance was a horse's ass and that one day she would find love again and that her whole future was promising because she was strong and smart and resourceful.

But she also wanted her mom to live the life she'd never gotten to experience when she was nursing Dad at the end while raising Meg and working full-time. At last, her mom was living the life she dreamed of. Dina Bloomberg might be thousands of miles away, sleeping in a village where the nearest cell tower was an hour's ride through the jungle on an ancient motorcycle, but . . .

"Wait a minute. How are you getting through? Where are you?"

"It's a funny story, actually. So, months ago, Annie friended me. You know I get online whenever I can. And I've been following her story. All that pickleball. It looked like so much fun I thought I'd try it." Her mom paused before the big reveal. "I'm on a pickleball vacation in Arizona! What a hoot. I am an absolute addict."

At last, Meg's smile broke through her hungover haze. Only one person in the world had worse hand-eye coordination than Meg Bloomberg, and her name was Dina Bloomberg.

"So how 'bout it? Should I come back to Seattle? I can hit it around with you."

Meg hated to get her hopes up. Since her dad's death, her mom's behavior had been so unpredictable—one day she might say she would return to Seattle; the next morning she would change her mind. But if she did come . . .

Meg visualized hitting a pickleball to her mom. Dina would smack it into the net or send it over the fence or whiff it altogether. It sounded wonderful.

"I'd like that, Mom," she said. "I'd really like that."

· · · · ·

How many people had already seen that post? While Annie was still downed like pre-Roosevelt, old-growth forest, Meg deleted both posts. Annie would be none the wiser—unless one of the 341 people who'd liked the post had already reposted it. But that was unlikely, right? Next, Meg waffled for several minutes before opening the string of texts from Ethan. Her stomach twisted the moment she read the first sentences. *What happened? Did I say something that upset you? I thought we were . . .*

How dare he pull the innocent act? She tossed her phone onto the bed.

Meg's temples pulsed. Her dreams were spinning away from her. She inhaled, a long, slow pull through the nose, and stilled her mind. When she felt at odds like this, she tried to focus on the things she could control.

The fence. That was one thing entirely in her own control.

With heroic effort, Meg dragged herself from her bed and hobbled out to the yard. She surveyed the task before her. *You can do this*, she reminded herself, and gathered her brushes and paint from the shed.

She sat on the cool grass and leaned back on her palms. Squinting at pickets, Meg concentrated until her eyeballs began to jitter. In this outwit-and-outlast fence vs. Meg contest, the fence was winning. The damn thing had not suggested a single idea of its own. Beside her, the hardware from the dismantled gate lay on the lawn. Mayumi had given her free rein to do as she pleased, and although she still did not have a vision for the big picture, she knew it had been necessary to remove the concept of an enclosure from her makeshift canvas. Now that the gate was out of the way, maybe an idea would strike her.

"How's it going?"

Meg sprang to her feet to find Mayumi ambling across the lawn. "It's going," she said, feeling like she'd been caught tiptoeing through the back door after curfew. Here she was, entrusted with this worthwhile project, and she had made not an iota of progress. Unless she counted taking apart the gate. Which, really, was more about destroying than creating. Essentially, she was making backward progress.

Mayumi sidled up alongside her. Hands clasped behind her back, Mayumi nodded at the blank fence. "When I'm stuck on something," she said, "I like to step away from it for a bit. Then come back to it fresh."

Meg didn't have the wherewithal to reveal that she had stepped away from it plenty, to climb a mountain and be inspired by nature, but that sidetrack had resulted in nothing more than a cringeworthy morning after and some misguided drunk texting. Mayumi said, "Or sometimes a cup of tea helps. How about it?"

"All right." Grateful, Meg followed Mayumi up the porch steps and into the bright kitchen. When the green light appeared on the electric kettle, they chose tea from a tin and took the steaming mugs to the table. Meg's eyes followed Mayumi's gaze to the evacuation photos and documents displayed beneath the glass.

Mayumi swallowed her tea, her eyes rife with emotion. She tapped the photo of the mother and her preteen daughter. "You are probably about my grandmother's age in this photo. And my mom was only eleven." Meg glanced up in surprise. "My grandmother died not so long ago at a hundred and three, can you believe? I would think it would be hard not to be angry, but instead, she channeled her energies into higher purposes. After the war, she became an activist."

Meg looked at the girl in the photo and saw traces of Mayumi's chin and lips in the image. "So your family came back here, after the war?"

"It was our home. No matter what. You can't just give up on something because parts of it caused you pain. If it's worth it, then you work on it. That's how my mom felt about this home. She wanted to bring it back to life." Meg blew on her tea, and then, together, they sipped. When the cups were empty of tea, they sat longer.

"My friend Marilyn says you are a pretty good pickleball player."

Did everybody on this island know one another? "I wouldn't say I'm good. I'm working on it." Meg shrugged.

"I'm sure you're being modest."

Letting out an awkward chuckle to cover her discomfort, Meg muttered, "Thanks," but she did not feel like a good player. Or a good painter. Or a good anything right now.

When the guest bell at the front desk dinged, Mayumi excused herself. Meg wandered back outside. Stalling, she plopped down on the grass and scrolled through her photos, viewing different angles of the fence and noting how it settled with the landscape. This time, when she arrived at the photo of her failure face, she saw something new.

Behind Meg's misery in that very same photo, the courts were alive with the vibrant joy of pickleball—players consumed with passion, absorbed by the moment, and carefree.

Like Rooster had suggested, she tried now to connect to the memory, not of her own pained expression, but of the photo's background players. To remember the way she felt on the courts when she hit a great shot, or when she won a point. When she played well, everything else faded. Pickleball was rejuvenating. It was thrilling. It was downright fun. And, like Marilyn had said, wasn't that the point?

She had forgotten fun. Forgotten that one could *have* a fresh start. Six months ago, she'd never imagined that she would be here on Bainbridge, playing pickleball and working on a legit painting project. But here she was, doing it, starting anew, making progress— even after her wasted years of marriage and the setback with Ethan. Like forests that burned to make way for the green saplings; like Mayumi, who had preserved her family's painful history beneath the glass and still rebuilt her home into a place of warmth and welcome.

Hard things happened, but good things could come of them.

When Meg glanced up again at the blank pickets, the tabula rasa no longer caused her angst. The empty canvas was a fresh start. She closed her eyes and inhaled, allowing the crisp scent of grass and the cool air on her cheeks to wake her senses. Meg pictured the fence on the canvas of her eyelids. She could sense the muse's approach. Inspiration knocked. Meg let the door swing open.

In her mind's eye, she grabbed hold of the phantom mural before it got away. Her brain sharpened the images and shaped her vision. With each stroke of her dream brush, the colors grew bolder until her vision solidified, and the mural appeared as clearly and completely as if she stood beside it. Invigorated by her creative awakening, she let a smile twitch in the corners of her lips.

Mayumi had given her a gift today. She knew exactly what she would paint.

TWENTY-SIX

Annie appeared just after nine in the morning, puffy eyed and groggy. In a great tribute to their friendship, she trundled up to Meg and offered to help with the grunt work. And in an even greater commentary, she deigned to appear in a T-shirt and—here Meg's brow angled upward—were those sweatpants?!

The fence's muted blue foundation didn't fit Meg's new vision, so together they began the arduous task of stripping the paint and applying a gesso primer. Side by side, they worked for three hours, and when Annie left to get them some lunch, Meg remained immersed in her work.

She traced guidelines in a muted yellow that she would paint over another day. *Finally*, she thought. A project that sang to her. The electric current of her creativity hummed in her veins, her hangover a forgotten fog. Meg's instinctual brushstrokes swept wheat-colored lines and swoops onto the close-set pickets of the fence. A voice in the back of her brain whispered: *Right here. Right now. This is me.* Inside her chest, she felt a garden blooming.

The morning sun did its work and dried the paint in five pickets' time, and before the spell of her enthusiasm wore off, she had finished the circuit of guidelines. Beads of sweat trickled down the back of her neck and, satisfied, she relished them as proof of her hard work. The sketch was laid out.

On a roll now, she drove into Winslow on a paint run. Meg strolled through the rainbowed rows of paints, dragging in the pungent scents of oils and new paper. She loved an art store. Picking out supplies was a treasure hunt, a precursor to endless outcomes. Up and down the aisle she wandered, holding the bottles at arm's length to check the colors. No flat-bodied mural paints for her. And even though she was going for a contemporary vibrance, she avoided the too-flashy brilliance offered by spray paints. Vivid acrylics would allow for the glossiness of spray paints, plus she could apply the paint with a brush to blend and distinguish her hues. Yes. Those would work perfectly.

With her cart brimming, she snapped Mayumi's credit card on the counter. For the first time in a long time, Meg had free rein both financially and creatively over her artistic vision. Satisfied with her purchases, she folded the receipt into her wallet.

When she returned, as she lugged the new paint supplies to the shed, she spotted Annie on the lawn. "Admiring our handiwork?" Meg asked. But as she neared, she noticed her friend had been staring at the departing figure rounding the bend down the beach.

"*He* came by looking for you."

Meg's heart ka-thunked against her rib cage. She wanted to call out his name and break into a run after him. Leap into his arms and kiss him. Or kick him in the nuts. She wasn't sure which. Instead, she said, "Oh?"

Planting her hands on her hips, Annie jutted her chin. "I told him to get lost." Then, seeing Meg's stricken expression, Annie groaned, "Oh no. I said the wrong thing."

"No. No. You said the right thing. He's a conniving rat." But her insides folded up like origami. Dagnabbit. Why did she still have such a soft spot for the guy? Against her better judgment, she asked, "What did he want?"

"Said he just wanted to talk to you." Taking in her friend's mute reaction, Annie scrunched up her lips. "Dammit. I did say the wrong thing, didn't I?"

"No. No."

"If you have to say it twice, it means yes. Aw, Meg. He looks miserable. I mean, he looks great, but he seems miserable. Maybe you should . . . you know . . . hear him out."

A current of conflicting emotions tumbled through Meg. Even catching a glimpse of Ethan like this made her pulse skip with hope. On the other hand, Meg's patience for the ups and downs of Ethan's behavior was growing thin. It was like playing with one of those light-up yo-yos that's supercool until the string gets tangled and the battery dies.

"You know what? Forget him," Meg said. "I can't keep stressing out about that . . . situationship. I could use a break from him and all the—"

"Sulking?" Annie finished.

"Yeah. That. We need a pick-me-up. And I've got an idea."

"Does it start with *p* and end with *ickleball*?"

Meg could already feel her spirits lifting. "Yah. You betcha."

· · · · ·

Annie may have painted a fence that morning in sweats, but there was no way she intended to show up to the courts in less than a black tennis kit with fluorescent orange piping. Visor and shoes to match. As Meg dragged her through the silver arch at the Founders Courts, Annie grumbled, "Remind me. Why are we doing this?"

Meg shrugged. "For fun." Just because neither of them had a partner for the tournament anymore didn't mean they couldn't have a good time hitting it around.

"For fun, huh." Annie tugged her high-end paddle from its protective case. "Hmm. That's new."

They made quick work of their stretches and warm-up. Eager to play, Meg set her stance. Her serve came off the paddle without a thought for grace or style. It felt good to throw all her conflicted emotions about Ethan into walloping the ball, rushing the net, and returning Annie's smokers. Meg danced on her feet, hot-coals style. She raced to cover the half-court as they cracked the ball back and forth, both of them slugging the ball harder than usual. Meg kept up, returning everything Annie could give her. And in an instant of clarity that surprised even her, Meg lobbed one to the back corner while Annie waited helplessly at the net. Both of them stopped, mouths agape, to watch the ball hit the baseline paint.

"Did you just win that point?" Annie asked, incredulous.

"Don't act so shocked. I've been taught by the best."

Annie marched to meet her friend at the net. She screwed her face up into a curious expression. "I was thinking."

"Oh. Good. I thought maybe you were farting."

"Nope. That was right before I got out of your car. I left it in there to miasmatize."

"I'm certain that's not a word."

"It is now." Annie grinned and placed a hand on her friend's shoulder. "I just had an idea. Why don't you and I play together in Picklesmash?"

Touched, Meg soaked in the comfort of Annie's kind proposal. But the fact was, Meg's basic game was a long escalator ride down from Annie's sophisticated play. "I would have to play up. That would put you at a disadvantage."

"So what? So we don't win. I would be okay with that," Annie said, shrugging. "You said yourself we should play for fun. And it would mean you would get to play your first tournament. You don't have to decide right now. Just think about it." Annie stepped back behind the kitchen line and tugged a 2Win tournament-quality ball out of her pocket. She dropped it onto her paddle and sent a perfect dink over the tape.

As they tapped the ball in a kitchen drill, Meg considered Annie's suggestion, wavering back and forth each time the ball arced over the net. It would be fun, but it would mean she would have to move up to Annie's advanced status and play against an A-level team. They would enjoy partnering, but they would lose every match. That wasn't pessimism, it was the way the odds stacked up. Not to mention that Jeannie the rabid school counselor would have a conniption if Meg stepped into Michael Edmonds's place—a spot that should go to one of her minions. As much as Meg would enjoy having a shot at playing in the competition, she shook her head.

"It really is sweet of you. And I appreciate it. But I don't think it would be fair to either of us, not to mention to Lakeview."

"Okay. Something will work out. We just have to be open to the possibilities of the universe."

The afternoon cooled, and they paused in their play to don light jackets and to scarf down handfuls of peanuts and raisins. In the distance on the converted tennis courts, they watched Coach Chad, fully recovered, instruct a crew of seniors in the art of the drop serve. Plastic balls sailed in all directions except over the net. Chad, on his guard, thrust his arm toward his head anytime a ball came within three feet of him. Meg's gaze traveled beyond the lessons to the pickleball courts in the distance.

At first, she did not register anything unusual about the pair of players. Just two men sharing a wildly uneven game.

Hold on. Meg let Annie's shot bobble past her. *What?!*

She couldn't be seeing what she thought she was seeing. Could she?

Stepping to Annie, Meg nodded her chin toward the far court. She heard her friend's sharp intake of breath.

Their attentions locked on the pair. They stared, unspeaking, their suspicions rising. With a glance of agreement, Meg and Annie left their paddles on the picnic table. Drawn to the strange, uneven ballet playing out on the court, they wandered toward the two players engaged in a singles match.

When they were close enough to make out the players' faces, Annie threw her hand out to stop Meg's advance. "Oh my god," she gasped.

"Oh my god," Meg repeated.

"Is that?"

"It is."

There, on the court, playing his A game against some under-skilled C-team benchwarmer, was that snake Michael Edmonds.

Meg's ire threatened to explode out of her ears. "I am going to lose it with that guy. Hold me back before I bust his 2Win tournament-quality balls," she said, although she had no intention of allowing herself to be restrained. Speed-stepping, Meg marched to the courtside bench. Annie followed cautiously, as if approaching an unfriendly dog or a tax auditor.

Michael Edmonds continued to strike the ball, oblivious of his impending ass-kicking. He swooped and struck and outplayed his lesser adversary with clean technique and practiced finesse.

Meg balled her fingers into fists. Her rage flared and she turned to Annie. "That 'I'm a beginner' bullshit is ending now. Look at how he's creaming that poor guy."

Michael Edmonds did not notice the ladies' approach. He was

focused on his play, hitting easy gets to his opponent, drawing him in for a bigger kill. After a few weak crosscourt attempts, Michael's opponent blundered his lob, sending the ball directly to Michael's forehand slam hand.

Wham! Michael smashed the hard plastic ball into the weaker player's chest. Meg winced sympathetically. That was exactly why she always wore a padded bra while playing.

"Oof!" Michael's opponent groaned.

Michael Edmonds rushed the net. "Oh shit. I swear I was aiming at your feet."

"You're supposed to be helping me, not beating the crap out of me. Ow!" The injured man rubbed at his sternum and lifted his head.

Meg gasped.

"Michael Edmonds!" Annie exclaimed.

The two men, mirror images, answered to the name.

TWENTY-SEVEN

Two Michael Edmondses? WTF? They were *twins*?

"Annie! What a surprise." The skilled Michael Edmonds smiled placidly. Like he was greeting her with a cup of tea. As an afterthought, he added, "Oh. Hey, Meg."

For Meg's part, no response was forthcoming.

The other Michael Edmonds, the wounded one, prodded his chest and winced. When he lifted his head, his gaze lit on Annie. Their eyes met, and a palpable charge exploded between them. Overhead, clouds drifted apart, leaving a sliver of space from which a dramatic beam of light cast a ray of golden splendor over their gaping expressions. The air rang with a celestial chord.

Injured Michael spoke. "It's you," he uttered reverently. "Passionate . . . abandon."

"You're hurt!" Annie sprang toward him. "Let me . . ." She helped him raise his shirt.

There, at the center of Michael 2.0's chest, a round bruise was forming, the center of it a gaping space left by one of the pickleball's holes. As Annie's fingers traced the red mark, he stared at her dreamily. "I was hoping I'd see you again," he said.

"Holy crap," Michael Edmonds the First interjected. "*Annie* is the doctor you've been going on about. The one who Heimliched the grape eater. The angel who kissed you out of the blue. Annie Yoon. You're kidding me."

Lakeview's A-team player turned to Meg. "I don't believe this. He's been talking about her nonstop, like she was some angel sent from heaven. And all along it was *Annie*?"

Meg's voice box unlocked. "What the hell is going on, Michael?"

"Michael?" said the wounded man. Only now did injured Michael break his gaze-meld with Annie. "You told them *your* name was Michael? *I'm* Michael." His face turned toward his twin. His brow furrowed in frustration. "What the hell— Do we have to share everything?"

"Whoa. Hey. Cool it, bro."

"You cool it, bro." A long, tense pause ensued. Then, both Michaels broke into laughter.

"Hey!" Meg fumed, indignant. "What. The. Hell. Is. Going. On?"

She turned her fury toward First Michael: Mr. Pickleskills. He who'd abandoned Annie weeks before an important tournament to rush off to an island and propose to some woman who Meg had never known existed. Why Meg felt abused by this betrayal, she did not fully understand. But on Annie's behalf, she warned, "You better tell us what is happening right now."

Hands up in surrender, Lakeview Michael apologized. "Okay. All right. I see that the jig is up." He pressed a palm to his T-shirt and adopted a conciliatory tone. "Annie. Let me reintroduce myself. I am your partner in pickleball: Dave Edmonds."

"What?" Annie cried. "Dave?!"

"I hope you can forgive me. The Lakeview league just has too many Daves. I didn't want to be another one."

He turned to his twin and explained, "They can be cruel. You have no idea. I had no choice." He appealed to Meg. "Look at poor Reflux Dave. What if they zeroed in on my pointed incisors?

Dracula Dave? No. I couldn't take that chance. So when I first started playing, I borrowed my twin's name. You can imagine how hard it was to remember to answer to Michael. I had to keep reminding myself that I was him."

"And that's why you kept yelling 'Michael Edmonds' every time you scored a point," Meg realized.

He nodded.

"So," Annie cooed, tilting her head to soak up the goo-goo eyes of the man delighting in her nearness, "*you're* Michael Edmonds."

"All along," the real Michael replied.

"All along," Annie repeated numbly, as if the obviousness of this truth had been set in motion a lifetime ago.

Meg narrowed her eyes, the whole scenario unspooling before her. So it was Dave Edmonds who'd gotten engaged out of the blue. Dave Edmonds who still planned to play for Lakeview in the advanced pickleball slot with Annie. And it was Michael Edmonds whom Annie had kissed. The one Annie believed she'd had a connection with. Because, it turned out, she had.

But the real kicker was the revelation that Michael Edmonds 1.0 actually *was* Bainbridge's secret weapon, the newbie player they'd pinned their hopes on to partner with Ethan . . . if they could only bring Michael's play *up* to a beginner's competition level.

"Oh no." Blinking with the realization, Meg glanced at Annie. "Ethan," she moaned.

She had lost her temper and marched out on him, ignored his attempts to get in touch, and built a case of onerous despisal against him. And now the real basis of all that venom—Ethan's duplicitous support of a faux beginner—was the true lie. Her brain wrestled with the overabundance of oxymorons. But more pressingly, she wondered how to take back her unkind words, the snubbed texts, and the cucumber in a blender.

Her stomach did a regretful little flip. Love had appeared on her doorstep, all cuddly and sweet. She had taken it in and given it spoonfuls of warm milk. Then, for no good reason, she had locked love out in the rain and called it a lying, deceitful dream-crusher.

She hoped with 110 percent of her mathematically challenged heart that Ethan could forgive her.

TWENTY-EIGHT

Meg had not stopped fretting since Michael-Edmonds-squared had appeared yesterday. Her texts to Ethan went unread, her apologies and explanations unacknowledged. Annie did her best to divert her attention. Twice, they played on Marilyn's nearby courts. While she played, Meg's spirits lifted, but the instant she walked away from the court, her energy flagged. Without the closure of Ethan's forgiveness, she found it difficult to paint, difficult to harness that creative momentum that had come naturally to her days ago.

Meg looked up from the newsprint sketch pad to find Annie refolding a T-shirt into a vacuum bag. Annie's usual effervescence bubbled over with her newfound romance, but for Meg's sake, she had tried to rein it in. Still, after deflating the shirt bag with a hand pump, she gave the plastic a satisfied pat and packed it into her suitcase. "I love vacuum seals," she chirped. Quickly, she shot Meg an apologetic glance.

"Annie," Meg suggested for the umpteenth time, "it's okay to be happy around me. I'm happy for you."

"You sure you'll be okay staying here on your own? I can see if I can stay another day if you need." But already their vacation had extended for more than a week, and Meg knew her friend would be needed back at the hospital come Monday.

"I'll be fine. It's just till I finish the fence." She flipped through the pages of her sketch pad. The design was tight and the idea well-developed. All she needed was to pull herself out of this funk and get paint on pickets.

The mattress shifted when Annie plunked down beside Meg. "If you want to talk to him, go talk to him. Find him. Ask Marilyn where he is. Otherwise, you're just sitting here, feeling sorry for yourself. What are you waiting for? A runway flagger?" She waved her arms at an imaginary plane. "*Now approaching Gate 17. Right this way.* Find him. Maybe his phone is dead. He's probably sitting around waiting for some word from you. You both could grow old together, waiting for signs."

Easy for her to say. Within hours, Annie and Michael had bent toward each other like two plants, each one reaching for the sun; an uncomplicated and obvious attraction. "I was beginning to think I was imagining things," Annie had admitted.

Annie's discovery of the Edmonds twins had been a huge relief. Of course Annie gave Dave Edmonds her brand of pixie hell for going AWOL. Dave confessed with profuse apologies that because of his allegiances to Lakeview, his trip to Bainbridge to help his brother had been hush-hush. And while Dave Edmonds dug into the job of regaining Annie's trust as a dependable partner, the real Michael Edmonds was head-over-laces infatuated with her.

"I'm gonna miss you," Meg said.

"Me, too." Annie circled her arm around Meg. She leaned her head on her friend's shoulder. "Don't forget about our meetup at the Founders Courts this afternoon, okay? One last set before I head back."

"Okay. But you have to play left-handed."

"I am left-handed."

"Okay. But you have to play with a frying pan."

From the corner of her eye, Meg watched Annie as she packed. Despite her attempts to convince herself otherwise, a pang of unexpected jealousy crept up on her. Annie had found her certainty so easily. Working on the fence was a step in the right direction. But it would be hard work to keep that energy going when she resumed her humdrum Seattle life.

Setting down the sketch pad, Meg stood. "I think I'm gonna take a walk and clear my head."

"You do that." Annie shot her a meaningful look. "I hope you find him."

· · · · ·

Meg meandered down the pebbled beach and then onto the road lined with gingerbread homes. At last she reached the western hemlocks that towered above Marilyn's cozy ranch house. Marilyn, the hub of the island's wheel, would know how to find Ethan. There was no car in Marilyn's driveway, and nobody answered the door, but it was a long walk back to the Outlook, and besides, it bummed Meg out to watch Annie pack. Better to hang out here. If Marilyn had left some pickleball equipment outside, Meg could occupy herself until she headed to the Founders Courts.

She cut in along the side yard and treaded carefully around the ubiquitous blackberries beside the house. A metal pail was tucked against the siding. She pulled the cobwebs off two worn balsa-wood beginner paddles. And at the bottom of the bucket, she spotted a 2Win tournament-quality pickleball.

Readying her stance, she eyed the opposite side of the court, tossed the ball, and swung. Her serve sailed over the net and rolled toward the wild yard. She collected the ball and tried again, this time from the other side. And then again. Her serve had come a long way from the tentative, off-target shots she'd made months ago when Annie and Rooster had begun coaching her. Now she hit with certainty, using muscle memory as a guide. She swung, and her ball landed hard and fast right at the baseline, flew off the court, and bounced deep into the woods.

Great. Now Marilyn's ball was lost to the savage wilderness. Meg squinted at the blackberry brambles beside the courts. She took a dubious step off the asphalt and peered beneath the ferns, surveying the damp, coffee-colored earth. Scanning the foliage and weaving between the pines, she searched for a flash of neon green. Stumped, she stopped and stood, hands on hips. Where was that ball?

At last, she spotted something.

It was not her pickleball. Beyond the low salal shrubs, she noticed a mound of white stones. They must have been moved here from the shoreline—they were rounded by the sea. The center of the pile was topped with a wooden plaque. A child's wobbly hand had seared a name into the grain. *Pickles.*

"Pickles!" Meg uttered, and bent down to examine the plaque. Seating herself on a fallen log beside the marker, Meg whispered "Pickles" again, and this time her voice was thick. In her imagination, she pictured Rascal, the sweet dog of her childhood: a mischievous, cream-colored poodle-terrier with boundless, cheery charisma. A lump clogged her throat: a twinge for the memory of Rascal, but also something deeper.

Pressing her lips together, she stared at the careful pile of rocks and felt the weight of those stones squeezing her chest. Unexpectedly, her eyes filled with emotion. A rogue tear threatened to tip over her lid, and once it fell, she saw no point in holding back. It felt good to cry, so she entered into it with gusto, enjoying the private luxury of feeling immensely sorry for herself.

She bent over, keening. She cried for the family who'd lost

Pickles, and for ten-year-old Meg, who ached with missing Rascal. And for grown-up Meg, too. For these past months of keeping it together because she thought that was what she was supposed to do. Her gut squeezed like a towel being wrung out—she sobbed for the unfairness of her mom's distance when she needed her mom sometimes, and was that so wrong? And what else? Surely she could think of more things to be sad about. There was the bullshit she had told herself when she'd given up painting and pretended it was Vance's fault. Was it okay for her to be a little jealous of Annie, too, for her good fortune? Sure. She gave herself permission to cry over that, too.

The best, she saved for last. Because mostly, she felt really, really, really sad that she'd messed things up with a pickleball hottie whom she genuinely liked.

That final truth snapped the last holds of the dam. Giddy with release, she indulged in a real sob-fest. A pity party for the ages.

Minutes later, she finished it off with a few shuddering heaves. Her face hurt and her sleeves were wet. She was pretty sure her stomach muscles would be sore in the morning. But she felt absolutely refreshed. She had earned that cry, and she congratulated herself on taking full advantage of the opportunity.

Rational Meg resumed her rightful position in her brain. Healing took time. Life didn't have instant solutions, no easy wins. She smiled sadly at the old Meg, the kind of gal who secretly fantasized about fairy-tale endings, who believed in the Golden Pickledrop, the easy win. The shot that would send the ball spinning along the top of the net and dropping into the kitchen at the opponent's disbelieving toes. What a crock. If there was one thing to be sure of, it was that there were no sure things.

"Oh, Pickles," she sighed. Her finger traced the curve of the smooth stones. "It doesn't even exist, does it?" If only it were that simple, as if this immortal pup could point her way to success. Face it, she thought: finding the right path would not be easy.

Pickles answered, "It's right here."

Frozen in place, Meg stared at Pickles's name plaque. Her heart rate thrummed, pulsing with an electric rhythm that resonated all the way into her thumbs. Could Pickles be right? Could the ungraspable solution live right here, inside of her?

"Meg?" The voice spoke again. "Is this yours?"

Slowly, she turned. It wasn't Pickles's voice talking. She knew that voice . . .

There he stood, holding a tournament-quality, neon green ball pinched between his fingers.

"Ethan!"

"I went back to the Outlook to look for you. This time Annie told me you'd probably be here. Are you looking for this?" He held her ball aloft.

"Oh, Ethan." Pickles. Talking! Shaking her head at her imagination, she swiped at her puffy eyes. Dang! What she wouldn't give for a couple of cold cucumber slices.

He stood close enough that she smelled woodsmoke on his shirt. Her heart raced. She wanted to fall into his embrace, wanted to tell him she had been a fool to doubt his kindness. With every ounce of her being, she hoped that he could accept her apology.

"Sorry I've been out of touch. I stayed at my mom's hoping to hear back from you, but when I didn't, I moved into the cabin for a couple of nights, trying to sort things out." Ethan shuffled his feet. When his eyes left hers, her chest clenched. "I couldn't understand why you . . . up and left like that."

"Ethan. I—"

He raised a finger in the air, stopping her words. His eyes were smiling. He said, "But then . . . I heard you got quite a shock. Two Michael Edmondses."

Shoving him playfully, Meg laughed with relief at the lightness in his voice. The last of the stones that had pressed on her chest crumbled, and bubbles of hope replaced them. "It *was* rather shocking." Checking his reaction, she continued, "How did you hear about that?"

"Bainbridge is a small island." He handed her the pickleball and gestured at the wooden plaque. "I didn't mean to interrupt your discussion with Pickles."

"We were having a lovely chat."

"I see that." He leaned toward the stones. "How's tricks, Pickles?" Ethan paused, ear to the rocks. "What's that? Yeah. Okay. Will do."

"What did he say?"

"He says to tell you your shirt's on inside out."

Meg looked at her shoulder to see the seam of her shirt. Ethan shrugged. "Pickles suggests that I help you remedy the situation." He lifted an eyebrow lewdly.

"I'm pretty sure I can handle it." Turning her back to him, she raised the shirt over her shoulders and put it back on properly. When she swiveled back, Ethan's wry smile marked his face.

"What are you grinning at?"

"Your bra is hooked all wonky, too."

"I am not taking off my bra, if that's what you're after."

He pointed at himself in mock offense. "Not me. Pickles. He was quite insistent."

"Pickles should try a more subtle approach." She grinned. Then her smile faded. "I'm so sorry, Ethan. I should have trusted you." How vulnerable it must have felt for him: to finally be on steady ground, and then she'd up and left without explanation. "I'll have to work on that."

"We probably both have some work to do in the trust department," he admitted.

"But anyhow, I'm sorry. I shouldn't have walked out like that, without any explanation."

"No sorrys in pickleball." He reached for her. "If we're going to work it out, though, we're going to have to spend a lot more time together."

Tugging her toward him, he made a play for her lips. She pulled back, toying with him. "Aw, come on," he pled, and went for her again. This time, she allowed it, tangling his lower lip with her tongue and then with a soft bite.

Suddenly, Meg pulled away. "I think Marilyn has one of those Ring cameras."

Ethan spun toward the house and waved. "Hi, Marilyn." He kissed Meg saucily and offered the camera a cheeky smirk.

"Okay. Show's over," he said, and with that, he scooped up the pair of beginner paddles. "Come on. Let's knock it around a little."

"Only if we can knock it around more later," she teased, relief making her giddy.

He pinched her hips playfully. "I like the way you think."

· · · · ·

Stance at the ready, Meg waited for Ethan's return. The ball flew toward her, and Meg spent a millisecond too long wondering if it would make it over the net. Suddenly, *zing!* the ball curved over the net into the kitchen. It hit the ground and spun back toward the net.

She ran for it, cursing herself. Once again, Meg had left herself vulnerable to Ethan's cutting backspin. She'd barely reached the ball when it bounced off the edge of her paddle and rolled toward the thorny blackberries that lined the court.

He jogged to retrieve it and waved her toward the net. "You keep letting me beat you."

"You're better than me. Of course you're going to beat me."

"Listen," Ethan confided. "All you need is consistency. Focus. Just hit the ball over the net and keep it in bounds. You don't have to do anything fancy. Let your opponent make the mistakes. Let me beat myself."

She sighed. Tightening her grip on her paddle, she focused on the ball. This time, she watched her serve soar past Ethan.

"I thought I said don't try to beat me. And then you aced me."

"Yes, but I wasn't *trying*. I just . . . did."

A right-sided grin crept up his cheek. He walked toward the net. She met him there. His hand reached for her across the tape, and he pulled her hips toward his, crushing the net between them. He grazed her lips with his and she leaned in, hungry for his kiss.

"I missed you," he said low in her ear.

Their lips connected. "I missed you, too."

"I have an idea."

"And what would that be?" she asked, innuendo lacing her question.

"Why don't you and I team up? For Picklesmash."

Drawing back to take him in, she asked, "Picklesmash?"

"Look. Rooster's injured, and I—"

"But you already have a partner. What about Michael Edmonds?"

Ethan released an exasperated sigh. "Michael Edmonds is not you. You should play with me. We play well together. If you would consider it—"

She hesitated, not wanting to say no outright. And not ready to say yes. A concern had been building in her brain. Earning such a large cash prize was an unheard-of reward for winning a few rounds of oversized Ping-Pong. Since the day she'd learned that Bainbridge would compete in the tournament—a contest with a lot at stake—she had wondered: Why would Bainbridge need such a prize? The Founders Courts were already perfection: possibly the sleekest, smoothest, best-kept courts in the nation.

If she and Ethan were going to make a go of it, she needed to start practicing honest, open communication. And hadn't they both wasted enough time not being frank with each other? She risked offending him, but she had to score a point for fairness. Inhaling, she braced herself.

"Listen. Can I ask you something? You and Marilyn and the whole Bainbridge crew. Don't you think it's a little . . . unnecessary? To train your league and try to win all that cash when you guys already have, like, the nicest courts in the Pacific Northwest? Why take that prize money away from a team that might need, for example, new courts?"

"Yeah." He nodded amiably. "Yeah. I can see how you could see it that way. But we're not planning to spend the prize money on our courts. We want to win so we can donate it all to charity. That's the project that Marilyn's been spearheading for the past few weeks. We've been researching worthy charities, and then voting on where the donations should go. If we win."

If not for splinters, Meg would have thunked her head against the balsa-wood paddle. Charity! All this time Meg had imagined that her quest to help Lakeview gain a fancy, smooth-surfaced court was a noble one. And here was Bainbridge, playing for the good of others. What a knucklehead she was.

Ethan continued. "Marilyn wants the funds to go to one of the pickleball recycling campaigns. I like the idea, but I'm partial to splitting the winnings for different sports charities. There are some great ones out there that donate equipment to kids in need or provide opportunities for people with disabilities. One that I like sets up sports leagues in divided neighborhoods and helps teens unite by teaming up together instead of ganging up against each other. There are even pickleball training camps popping up for kids who could benefit from some outdoor fun."

"Huh." She gathered her thoughts, balancing this new info with her loyalties. "Don't get me wrong. All of those are great causes." But she could feel the shift within her, an understanding that Ethan's intentions—restoring the wetlands, supporting young athletes—were well-founded. But there was still the issue of her home courts, and her allegiances tugged at her. "I guess I just feel bad. I mean, if Lakeview wins, they still couldn't build a dedicated space. Even if the money came through, where would all those players—" Out of the corner of her eye, she caught him smiling. "What?" she asked. "What are you smiling about?"

"Let's just say I made some calls and I've got something in the works. Nothing solid. But a possible, repurpose-able space. If Lakeview can find the funds, I can help find a place you can put your courts."

The thoughtful gesture pushed her one foot closer into Ethan's court. Maybe her home team would find a place to land after all. And at least the possibility made for a fair fight, especially since Lakeview had handed off her shot at the beginners' spot to her ex.

And helping disadvantaged teens. Well, that was a no-brainer. Facing off against Vance and Édith would be the bonus. She had enough *L*'s on her scorecard. She wanted a *W* in her column. And if it took every ounce of luck and skill she could muster, she would earn it on the pickleball court.

"Okay," she said. "I'll partner with you."

He smiled with his whole face. "You will? You will? That's great." Exuberant, he took her hands and pulled her close. "That is so great. I'll work it out with Michael. I'm telling you he'll be happy about it; trust me. He never wanted to play in a tournament. He was only trying to help Marilyn and the team—"

Meg planted her lips on his. "Less talking. More kissing."

He muttered something into her mouth.

"What?"

"Pickles approves."

She smacked him hard on the chest.

"Mm. I like it," he whispered into her neck. Their paddles clattered to the pavement.

· · · · ·

After a pleasant make-out session, Ring camera be damned, they headed to the Founders Courts to see Annie off. Ethan borrowed a pair of paddles from the doghouse supply shed, beneath a bone-shaped sign reading **PICKLES**. On the near court, the real Michael Edmonds sat beside Annie on the bench. Their fingers were intertwined, and their gazes were so glued to each other that their eyeballs were practically touching.

Ethan slung a friendly arm around Michael's shoulder. "Hey, buddy. I hear love is in the air."

Michael Edmonds turned. "Ethan! I'm glad you're here." Michael's expression was ringed with something unreadable, somewhere between apologetic and nervous. "I've been meaning to get in touch with you."

"Yeah. We should talk. About the tournament . . ."

Michael winced.

"What would you think if Meg here filled in for the beginners' slot for Bainbridge?"

"Do you mean she would partner with me?" Michael asked.

Hesitating, Ethan admitted, "No. With me." Brimming with tension, Meg waited.

"So, Meg would take *my* spot?"

Ethan's slow nod confirmed it. Michael looked from Meg to Ethan and back again.

"Well, thank heaven for small miracles. That's exactly what I was going to ask you." He clapped Ethan on the back. "Nothing worse than being publicly humiliated in front of a crowd of strangers."

"Outstanding," Ethan said. "I figured you'd be all right with it."

Bainbridge's Michael Edmonds gave a long, relieved exhale. "Don't get me wrong. I do want to improve my game. But I'm not ready for a tournament." His gaze roamed back to Annie, whose cheeks were fresh with color. "Maybe all I need is a patient teacher."

"Or a doctor teacher." Annie giggled. "Get it? I'm a doctor." To his credit, the real Michael cracked a goofy grin.

From the courts where he was practicing his serve, Dave Edmonds said, "This is painful. I feel like I'm in a cable special. Are we gonna play or what?"

Meg nodded, and a thrill traveled up her arm when Ethan looped a pinkie finger through hers and led her to their side of the net.

Michael Edmonds sat on a sideline picnic bench, one lean leg crossed over his knee as he watched the two teams practice. His attention rarely left Annie, who partnered with Dave and played as well as ever despite the distraction.

Meg played hard, pushing herself. Playing "up" against a stronger team raised her accuracy and consistency. Annie and Dave whupped them 11–4, although at least one of those four points was earned when Annie hit a ball out-of-bounds on purpose, just so she could retrieve it from beneath Michael's bench.

During the second game, Meg noticed her confidence building. Her hits were softer, more directed. By the fifth game she was in the groove. Meg and Ethan found themselves playing it out until they squeaked past their opponents with a win by two points at 13–11.

Dave Edmonds held a hand up in a gesture of defeat. "All right. I'll admit it. You two play well together," he remarked, reaching over the net to tap paddles. Annie and Dave had taken it easy on them; that was obvious. But it was a solid game all the same.

"That was fun, wasn't it?" Ethan asked, gazing at Meg in a way that made her insides all squiggly. Grinning, Meg nodded her agreement. Because it *was* fun. And that was the point.

TWENTY-NINE

Meg shielded her eyes from the afternoon sun and surveyed the fence. After twelve days and fifty-four bottles of acrylics, she had laid the final brushstroke. She blew a long tunnel of air from her lips, fingers still buzzing from holding a brush steady hour after hour. She wiped a smudge of paint from the back of her wrist and let her eye travel along the posts.

Her feet carried her along as she circumnavigated the fence, allowing her mind to take in the entirety of the project. There was a kinetic feel to her work that moved the viewer from one moment to the next. When she arrived back at her starting point, Meg paused. She rested her hands on her hips and allowed the satisfaction to ripple up from her toes to her aching shoulders. Despite the pain in her body, she was elated. Her smile erupted naturally. It was the best thing she had ever painted.

And to top off her excitement, any minute now, Ethan would arrive. She had kept him away from the inn all week. They had practiced together, but nothing more. And each day, their weeklong agreement became more and more challenging.

Their contract had begun the day after Annie's departure. Meg had twirled her glass between her fingers and sipped at a gewürztraminer: a wine that they'd both agreed they would rather drink than spell. When Ethan had reached beneath the table and skimmed his hand along her knee, she'd found herself stopping his fingers. "Okay. I've been thinking about this, and you're not going to like it any more than I do, but . . . you are bad for my concentration."

Ethan's laugh was closer to a cough. "Am I distracting?" His face struck a runway model's serious-sexy pose, which looked a little like his lips had been smushed against a windowpane.

"I'm serious," she said, smacking his sneaking hand off her thigh. "All I can think about is how much I want to touch you. And I need to be thinking about the painting. I think we need a ban. On everything."

"Everything?" he asked, incredulous.

"Sex," she whispered. "And any related temptations. Until I'm done with the mural. I'm telling you. I can't concentrate."

"I don't need a ban. I can resist temptation," he said, and took a huge bite of the chocolate bombe cake. "This is delicious. Let's order three more."

Still, that same evening when she leaned toward him, he stepped back. "Nope," he admonished. "I'm gonna do everything I can to support you in your painting. And if that means that I have to take cold showers and visit my friend Mr. Handy, so be it. In fact"—his gaze twinkled devilishly—"I think we should up the stakes." She eyed him, suspect. "You know that all the best athletes lay off drugs, alcohol, and sex when they are prepping for a big game. We do have a tournament coming up . . ."

Now it was Meg's turn to balk. The painting would be complete within the week, but the tournament was still three weeks away.

"Imagine our energies singularly directed," he said. He spoke so close to her cheek she sensed the heat of his lips on her skin.

"Ack. You're not helping."

Still, they sealed the pact, confirming it with a chaste handshake.

Day by day, the plan worked. Without the compelling distraction of Ethan, she hunkered down and threw herself into her tasks. Her days were consumed with painting and pickleballing. Pickets and pickles. She breathed for them, ate for them, and dreamt of fenceposts and dink shots. Meg loved waking at sunrise, alert and attuned to her creativity. The early mornings offered her painting project the added benefit of softer light. At lunch, she shared her progress report with Mayumi at a shorefront picnic table beside the Outlook Inn. When she wasn't painting, she drilled with Ethan or with Marilyn, whose age was no deterrent to her tenacity. Meg developed a routine and found that she was a strict taskmaster; once dedicated to either practice, she could not be diverted.

Now, standing back from the fence, she felt a tug of sadness at the end of such a momentous project. It had been a challenge, but looking at her accomplishment, she felt immense pride.

Her phone pinged. Here, Ethan's text read.

Moth wings fluttered against her stomach lining. Now that the big reveal was imminent, her nervous excitement mounted. Adrenaline buoyed her as she jogged to greet him in the parking lot. She wanted the effect to be a total surprise, so she tied a scarf around his eyes and steered him around the uneven lawn toward the back of the fence.

"Boy. This is so rife with the opportunity for innuendo. I like it."

"Hey. No innuendo. You promised."

Meg positioned him so that he faced the fence. Her nerves did jumping jacks; it was a personal thing, showing off one's artwork. She felt vulnerable, exposed, naked. She did not need his validation to prove that her work was quality. She felt that truth, right down to her bones. But she sure hoped he liked it.

"Okay. You can look." She undid the knot on the blindfold. "I want you to get a feel for the whole story, so you have to start from the right angle." Ethan blinked, his eyes adjusting to the sunlight. She watched him take in the mural. He did not speak, did not alter his expression while she worried the blindfold between her fingertips.

There at the rear of the inn, her artwork's story began. In near-mirrored images, the mural created a progressive story that wrapped around the side yard and met at the hotel entrance.

The first segments near the back socked the viewer with the power of two clenched fists—modern, kinetic images in purples and browns. The matching, balled hands were squeezed tight, the blood disappearing from the skin, as if the hands were afraid of allowing enclosed secrets to escape.

Ethan's head shifted to the right, in the direction he would "read" her piece. She'd designed it that way. English readers trained their gaze to measure visual cues from left to right. Ethan moved toward the next vibrant piece: an orangey hand, tight, but allowing the release of a glimpse of bright blue light.

He stepped at a deliberate pace, following the U of the fenceposts from back to front. She followed, keeping her distance to avoid breaking his focus, while he paused at another hand, in shades of pale yellow and ochre. The fingers opened slightly to reveal a portion of an indiscernible word. In the next image, he studied the burgundy hand covered in scars. The hand looked frozen on the brink of releasing a sunset-tipped rosebud.

Discreetly, she had scrutinized the hands of her friends and copied them here, not in realistic hues, but faithfully. Her stylized work captured the essence of Mayumi's long fingers carrying the pain of her parents' deportation; of Annie's struggle to release her workaholic habits; of the roughened skin of Rooster's self-destructive past. Along the way, the images changed—first pent-up and closed, then relaxed with the release of the torment and the secrets enclosed within their palms.

She followed Ethan as he viewed Rooster's hand, at the back of the fence, scarred and broken, to where it reappeared toward the open gate in the front of the inn. In the latter painting, once unbandaged, his exposed skin bore images symbolizing his love for Laverne, his yearning for his unborn godchild. Mayumi's hand, clasping the hand of her mother and her grandmother like nesting dolls, at first painted in blueish gray, resurfaced later in sky blue. In the latter image, her grandmother's pain was lifted away on butterfly wings. At last, where the gate used to be, two open hands reached toward each other. On one side of the opening, a hand marked by a small freckle at the base of the thumb reached toward her own, both palms and splayed fingers welcoming visitors to explore the space between them.

Ethan shook his head and opened his mouth. In that elongated moment, Meg could hear the stampeding hoofbeats of her heart. What if he didn't like it? What if he took offense? What if . . .

"It's so powerful," he said. And in the rawness of his tone, she knew she had moved him. "I didn't know . . . what to expect. Something decorative and pretty, I guess. But this—" He closed his eyes in a long blink. "This is so much more than that."

Meg allowed a slow smile.

"It's such a clear story. All these people. Real people. I can see the pain they carried, and here"—he pointed to the first hand where a puff of dust escaped—"here is a person trying to let go of it."

His eyes glinted with emotion as he turned to her, and Meg thought of his father's disappearing act, and wondered what other private histories Ethan concealed beneath his confident appearance. She hoped that over time she would come to know all the dips and rises in the road of his life. He said, "We all do it: hold it in, keep it bottled up. But look how powerful it is to release that pain."

"That's what I tried to capture. There's power in owning your past, even in the agony and the mistakes. And here"—she gestured toward the open gate—"that opening is like an escape hatch—the release spot. The place you can look back on and say, 'Wow, I got through that and here I am.'"

"I can relate to that."

She beamed, pleased that he connected to her art. Now she was certain: the fence had been the perfect canvas for her project. A fence could be an enclosure, meant to keep people in. Or a barricade to block people out. But her fence, this fence with the gate removed, acted as a reminder. It offered permission to escape the prisons where people stored their pain. Now the fence was less like a barrier and more like a bridge, designed to welcome people in.

He reached his hand toward hers. Meg's skin slid against his, their thumbs fitting like puzzle pieces. His freckle winked up at her, and she glanced at its twin on the fenceposts, all the while thrilling to the sensation of his skin against hers. The fence was complete, but there was still a tournament to win. Holding hands was within the boundaries of friendly behavior. Nothing sexual about handholding, she had to keep reminding herself.

They strolled the beachfront, their feet crunching against the pebbles. The sun took a dive into the pink water and a couple of blinking stars pressed through the evening sky.

"I can't stop thinking about your painting. Not just about how it affected me, but about . . . you. You have that in you. I've never met someone who can imagine something like that. Something creative that touches people."

She heard herself clear her throat, embarrassed by the sweetness of the sentiment. "Now, if only I could play pickleball that well."

Ethan halted and clasped her hand. His eyes hit her. "You can. You do. You just have to believe it."

Meg offered a tiny shrug. "I do. I believe it," she said, but a puff of disbelief escaped her nose. True, she might be able to pull off a win. On the other hand, she might be humiliated by her ex-husband and his gorgeous, athletic partner.

"No. Really." He tucked his chin, catching her eyes. "Have you ever heard of a thing called the Golden Pickledrop?"

She rolled her eyes. "Of course I've heard of it."

"People always think that a single winning stroke is out there, a fast path to success if they can only find it. But the only Golden Pickledrop is here," he said, and he touched a finger to her chest. "The sooner you believe it, the sooner you can play like you paint."

He pulled her close and she fit perfectly into all the negative spaces. His embrace was the kind of hug she felt in her toes. His lips on hers were warm in the cool of the evening, turning her thighs to quivering jelly and making her nether regions tremble like june bugs near a lightbulb. Craving more, she dug her fingers into his back, her body alive with desire.

He groaned with frustration. "I want you."

"Well. The fence *is* finished . . ."

"You know, if we want to kick some butt in that tournament, we do need more practice at working together . . ."

She smirked. "I thought you said that the best athletes abstain before the big game."

"Meg. Those people are professionals. We can't hold ourselves to those standards."

"You make a good point. Okay. Pact over."

"Oh, thank god."

They stumbled, still clinging to each other, toward the shadowed bench high up on the beach. Sheltered by the pines that edged the shoreline, they tumbled onto the bench, groping each other. As his hand wandered up her shirt, her back pressed against the metal armrest. "Ow. Ow!"

"Here." He shifted to seat himself on the wooden slats and lifted her onto his lap. They made out, deeply, passionately, rediscovering each other's lips and tongues and . . .

"Ah!" he shrieked. "Leg cramp!" He shoved her off his legs and onto a patch of dark, dry sand below the bench. "Sorry," he cried, and stretched out his calf. "Leg cramp. Are you okay?"

Laughing, she brushed off the sand. "Maybe we should . . ."

"Go inside?"

"I have a nice bed . . ."

"Come on." They made their way up the beach and hustled up the porch steps of the Outlook Inn.

At the front desk, Mayumi perused a pile of receipts, her reading glasses set low on the bridge of her nose. When she spotted them, she peered curiously over the frames.

"Hi, Mayumi," Meg said as they raced past.

"Hey, Mayumi," Ethan echoed. Mayumi's brows crept upward. She said nothing.

They took the stairs two at a time and spilled into the room like a tsunami.

· · · · ·

Later that afternoon, as she curled into the curve of Ethan's body and drifted toward a delicious nap, Meg's mind wandered. But instead of dreaming up a fence design, her brain played out a pickleball match. The details were so clear that she felt the wind, heard the tick-tock of the ball bouncing, noticed the stretch in her Achilles. Bending her knees, she scooped, keeping her toes just outside the kitchen line. She dinked from corner to corner. Plink, plink, plink. Until at last she spotted an opening. Meg aimed. She swung. Her arm lurched upward, thwacking at her dream ball and whacking against the headboard.

"Mmph," Ethan muttered, dragging his arm out of the danger zone.

As she shuffled her pillow closer and her heart rate slowed, Meg smiled to herself. She imagined players around the globe smacking their lovers in the forehead while their sleeping minds returned a serve or volleyed at the net. There must be hundreds, no, thousands upon thousands of pickleball fanatics. And now that she had dreamed the pickledream, she was one of them. Even her subconscious knew it.

She snuggled against the comfort of Ethan's sleeping form. For the rest of the luxurious midday snooze, pickleballs and sex filled Meg Bloomberg's sweet dreams.

But not at the same time.

THE PUTAWAY

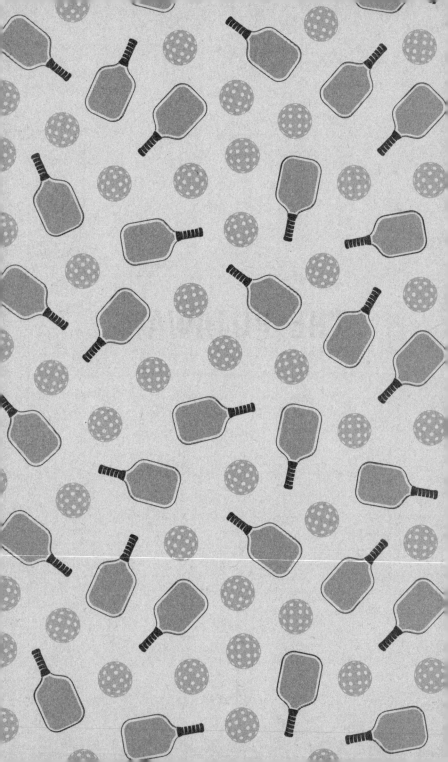

THIRTY

Three consecutive weeks of sunshine had to be a record in Seattle. Despite the sixty-five-degree August chill, the fans and players gathering outside Everest Park sported summery gear: shorts and T-shirts emblazoned with kitschy pickleball greetings like *Day Dinker* and *My favorite game is the next one*. Excitement built as the crowd clamored to enter the grounds of the Northwest Picklesmash Tournament.

Treading through the entrance gate, Meg swallowed her trepidation. Everest Park was known for its first-rate surfaces and for the fenced dividers between courts to keep balls from running away. Mainly, it was recognized for the kind of attitude a court can project when it knows it is one of the highest-class facilities in the county—nearly as expertly designed as the Founders Courts. Bleachers set up especially for the tournament offered perfect views of the twelve pristine courts.

Meg clutched her paddle to her chest; a blended cocktail of emotions whirred through her veins. Sure, she hoped Bainbridge could bring in a win for their charities, but she would be happy, too, if Lakeview won cash for their new courts. As for Vance, as nervous as she was, a big part of her wanted to face off against him. And win.

Meg moved with relief when she caught sight of Annie waving

her paddle. Seated beside her friend, the real Michael Edmonds lifted a hand in salute. Meg made her way through the bleachers, stepping over legs until she reached Annie.

"Saved you a spot," Annie said, removing a baseball cap from the bleacher seat.

"Any sign of Rooster?"

Annie hesitated. "He sent a text to the group chat." She tapped at her phone and displayed the message. Would love to be there to support you but having issues here. Good luck.

Meg matched eyes with Annie. "Hope everything's okay." Rooster had asked them to give it some time before visiting the newborn preemie, but they were hoping Lulu and her little one were out of the woods.

"I'm sure everything's fine. He wouldn't want you to worry."

It was true. Meg had Annie and Ethan to thank for helping her reach this moment, but Rooster's faith in her had started it all. He would want her to focus on doing her best. Taking a cleansing breath, she wrangled her attentions toward that purpose.

When she looked up, there was Ethan moving toward her, scooting between the bleacher benches with his smiling eyes set on her. The warmth in his gaze made her feel like she was the only one, the most important person in this giant crowd of players and spectators. She stood and kissed him in greeting, lingering longer than a hello warranted. They sat, their hands clutched together, grinning like satisfied cats.

On the bleachers around them, their neighbors began to stir and murmur. A few spectators stood, craning to see the courts below. A man dressed in cowboy boots and a pearl-buttoned shirt cruised across the courts to a small stage where a podium had been set. He yanked a microphone from a stand and cleared his throat.

"Ladies and jelly beans! I wanna welcome you to this year's

Picklesmash Tournament." A pounding of eager applause rippled through the stands. "Wow. Now that's a spirited bunch. I'm Carl Dewitt, and you might recognize me as a four-time champion cattle caller from the Puyallup Fairgrounds. I'm gonna tell you right now, I don't know the first thing about pickleball, but I sure was excited to learn that I could get paid good money to shoot my mouth off about whatever y'all are doing here. What a gig. I'll do my best not to disappoint. Let's get 'er done."

Meg shifted to see the cause of the fresh excitement that bubbled through the crowd. "Who's that?" She pointed at the relaxed athlete waving to the crowd.

Carl fished a shred of paper from his pocket. "All righty. Let's all clap our hands together. First up is the professional pickleballers showcase. Let's see who we got here." He scrutinized the scrap. "Nope. That's my grocery receipt."

"That's Phil Chow," Ethan said. "Twenty-two years old and he's on the up-and-up. And I wouldn't be surprised if you knew the other guy. In the tennis whites."

Instantly the crowd was on their feet, cheering. The pro dressed in all white stormed onto the courts like he owned them. "He's kind of a local celebrity," Ethan said. Meg could see why. With his arms boasting muscles and tattoos and with his wavy black hair pulled into a man bun, the guy had style and looks, and the crowd was eating him up. "Tyler Demming. Lives right nearby."

"Really?" Meg said. "You're not gonna believe this, but that guy played with me a couple months ago. He saw me waiting for a game at Lakeview, and he offered to partner with me."

She remembered admiring his play, awed by his easy grace. She hadn't been aware that he was a pro until after their game. "I'm a beginner," she had warned him. "Are you sure you want to partner with me?"

But Tyler Demming had assured her that above all, they would have fun. During the game, when she'd hit a well-angled dink, he had said, "Great shot. See? You belong in this game."

She told Ethan, "He set everything up so I could close the point. It was like he knew exactly what would happen three shots down the line."

"He does that. He goes to area clubs and joins in with the peasants. No offense."

"None taken."

"Did you win?"

"Of course."

The showcase game began, and the spectators leaned forward, enraptured by the fluid play of the pros. Meg marveled as, leaping and sliding, the opponents battled one-on-one. In rec play, Meg raced around, busting her butt to get to the ball on a doubles court. These players covered the full singles court with ease. There was no banging back and forth, just calculated placement and point-ending finesse.

"Wow." Behind her, Dress Shirt Dave was shaking his head in wonder at the pros' talent. When he noticed her, he grinned. "Oh. Hey, Meg. I hear you're playing for Bainbridge."

Her lips parted as she prepared to defend herself, but Dress Shirt Dave presented his fist for a bump. "They're lucky to have you," he said.

Below on the courts, the demo match ended. Tyler Demming tapped paddles with his opponent, and with his winning grin, he raised both hands in victory. Tyler's victory sparked a near collision among a couple of female fans who rushed down to the courts, Sharpies in hand, presumably to get their paddles signed. At least Meg hoped it was their paddles. Meanwhile, tournament volunteers swooped onto the playing surface. Armed with brooms and garbage bags, they removed freshly fallen leaves and pine needles from the courts.

In the stands, people began to murmur at a new development. Several rose to their feet. Meg followed their attentions and caught sight of the glamorous couple striding through the gate.

The man moved effortlessly, his blond, wavy hair bouncing with his step. The woman's bronzed, toned legs rose above her invisible socklets and disappeared beneath a sleek fuchsia skirt. With each pace, the skirt rose and dipped, offering a peek of the curve of her buttocks. Her breasts levitated beneath a white scoop neck worthy of a parental advisory rating.

Meg took in the slo-mo runway walk of the eye-catching pair, and her bitterness surprised her as it breached the surface. Vance and Édith waved at the crowd. Waved! Ethan, with his attention pegged on the pros' match, took no notice. But Annie tapped Meg and whispered, "Doesn't matter. Just focus on your game."

"Do you think those are real?"

"Hey." Annie's gaze caught Meg's. Evenly, she said, "You. Focus. Lemme check the matchup schedules. If you play Lakeview first or second, you can get it over with."

Sixteen Northwest clubs from around Washington and Oregon were slated to participate, from the Canadian border-town league, the Bellingham Ballers, to the state's southernmost club, named Vancouver: The One in Washington.

The morning matches were already arranged. Annie and Dave Edmonds, back with Lakeview, were scheduled to play their first round in an advanced match against Bainbridge's Juanita and Sebastian. But Meg did not recognize any of the players she was slotted to compete against before lunchtime.

As the organizers set up the first matches, the players and spectators mingled on the soccer fields beside the courts and at the sheltered picnic area. Hand in hand, she and Ethan strolled around the outskirts of the playing area.

Across the lawn, Meg spotted a cluster of Lakeview players collecting near the drinking fountain—several of the Daves, the guy who wore sports glasses with the lenses popped out, Mustache Steve deep in conversation with Did-I-Mention-I'm-Single Steve, and Jeannie and her minions—all stood clumped together. As she neared, she noticed they'd gathered around Reflux Dave, who, with uncharacteristic exuberance, was regaling the gang with a story.

Reflux Dave's face glowed. "And then they gave me this. Look!" He thrust a plastic bag at the rapt crowd. "A quarter and one penny, both dated 1996. That's what they pulled out of me!"

A collective gasp traveled through the group.

"Yeah. They let me keep 'em. Now I feel great. I can't believe those were in my intestines all those years. Musta been some crazy game of quarters. I have no idea how the penny got in there. Imagine. All that misery was twenty-six cents."

"26 Cent," Mustache Steve said. "Hey. That's your new name."

Dave's sudden smile nearly busted his cheeks. "Yeah! 26 Cent. That's so much cooler than Reflux Dave. 26 Cent. That's me!"

"26 Cent," the others echoed. A stampede of hands pounded him on the shoulder in congratulations before collectively turning toward Meg.

"Hey!" Jeannie shouted, noticing her. "If it isn't Little Miss Turncoat. Or should we call you Meg 'Benedict Arnold' Bloomberg? We hear you're sleeping with the enemy. And worse, you're playing pickleball with him." Cringing, Meg stopped in her tracks and swiveled to Ethan, but he was out of earshot, filling his bottle at the fountain. Jeannie took a step too close. "How does it feel to cross over to *the dark side*?"

What was Jeannie's problem? Wasn't Jeannie the one who'd

convinced Lakeview to replace her? But Meg worried—would her whole tribe turn against her now that she planned to play for Bainbridge?

"Look, you guys," Meg stuttered. She wanted to play, wanted to win even, but it wasn't worth losing these friendships—if that was what it came down to. "If you feel strongly about it, I don't have to . . ." Her voice faded away, fighting against completing that dreaded idea.

Jeannie's cackle cut in. "Take it easy, Meg. I'm just giving you shit. Ethan!" she shouted, pegging him in her sights. Jeannie's expression morphed into a genuine smile. "I was looking for you. Check this out." Jeannie riffled through her gym bag and came up with a pocket-sized journal titled *Birds of the Northwest*. Striding to the drinking fountain, she strong-armed Ethan and pointed eagerly at an entry in her book. "See? This book you gave me is great. I checked off the red-tailed hawk, a juvenile bald, and an osprey, too. Ospreys are easy. I spot like three a day."

"I know. I saw your post on the birding chat. And great sighting on that breeding loon—with the checkerboard visible in the shot."

"Can't believe I caught that. Right?" Jeannie agreed. "Just south of his usual breeding ground. That was a lucky find."

Unsure if this was a stress-induced delusion, Meg blinked hard. "So, you're okay with the wetlands project?"

"Meg. Did you not hear? I'm beating Ethan on my bird count already and I've only just started." Leave it to Jeannie to make a competitive sport out of watching nature. "This guy's not such a rat bastard after all," she added, clocking Ethan on the shoulder. "He's helping us work out the permits for a new space."

Meg looked to Ethan for confirmation. He gave a modest shrug.

Jeannie gave Ethan's shoulder a motivational punch. "Tell her," she insisted. But before he could say a word, she jumped in. "So,

Ethan here," she recounted, friendly as can be, "goes and contacts the city and gets permission to repurpose that empty shopping mall space for indoor and outdoor courts. If we can raise part of the funds, the city's gonna help us convert it all into a massive complex. Lights. Coverage in winter. And bathrooms for all!"

Meg let out a puff of relief. "That's great news," she said, taking in Ethan with newfound respect.

"Besides," Jeannie continued, "we're gonna stomp Bainbridge into the dirt today. You don't stand a chance against Vance and Édith. They're like those superhero teams in the movies. Know what I mean? If the world was about to explode, they would be the couple who would save us all. And they'd look great doing it." Jeannie slapped Meg on the shoulder. "Lakeview's gonna win us some shopping mall courts. But good luck with your matches, killer." She pointed a finger at Ethan. "And you. Expect an ass-kicking this season on your pied-billed grebe count." Snickering with her underlings, she marched off.

That was the Jeannie Meg knew and sort of loved. Playing pickleball made people happy, but it did not necessarily make them nice.

While she and Ethan strolled toward the stands, Meg recognized the win for what it was. So what if Jeannie was supporting her ex in this epic battle? Little by little, Lakeview would climb on board with the wetlands, and that was progress.

"That went about as expected," Ethan said when they were alone. "What do you say we hit a couple before our first game? Do we have time for a quick pickle break?"

"I'd like a quick pickle break," Meg murmured. Tugging him to her, she smooched him. Then, for good luck, she threw in some moderate grinding.

Pulling away, Ethan put on a scowl. "Meg. I'm shocked. I meant a quick warm-up." His eyes said otherwise as he traced a languid finger from her chin to her belly button. "You're a terrible distraction. Now I have to go find some ice."

"For tennis elbow?"

"No. To bathe in. You're driving me crazy." As he disappeared toward the concession stand, her smile felt so explosive that her cheeks hurt.

By the time Meg hurried back to the stands, the advanced and intermediate rounds had already begun. On court F, Annie and Dave Edmonds spun the hurtling sphere back and forth against their opponents from Bainbridge. She cheered for Annie, but secretly her heart rooted for Bainbridge: the new team that had accepted her with open arms. She wished they both could be winners.

The smell of hair product and subtle perfume appeared before Marilyn did, sporting a metal pickleball association pin tacked to her fitted blouse. "Yoo-hoo! I have the matchups," she called. She straddled knees and avoided feet as she squeezed toward the spot beside Meg. Marilyn planted herself, concentrating as her French-manicured nails scrolled through her phone.

"I already saw the schedule," Meg said. "Ethan and I play Shoreline at ten. They posted all the morning matches."

"Right," Marilyn agreed. "But I'm a club administrator. So, I have the full day's lineup. I thought you'd want a heads-up."

The sliver moon of Marilyn's white-tipped nail pointed at the final slot of the day. When she read the matchup, Meg's tongue dried to dust.

"You're kidding. The last game of the day? The last one . . . and it's me against my ex-husband?" By now, Ethan knew the whole story of her history with Vance, as did Marilyn, who rubbed Meg's shoulder blades like she was giving her a good sanding. "You're gonna be fine. You've practiced. You've worked hard. You are a solid player. Remember. There's no reason they would have any advantage over you. They're beginners, too."

It was true. For each of them, this was their first tournament, the first time playing with the tension of spectators and a sizable prize on the line. Meg said, "It's just a lot of pressure. To pit us against each other for the final game of the tournament."

"No more nor less than any other game you play today. There are no brackets, so no eliminations. Just a round robin. Each team plays an equal number of times," Marilyn explained. "The clubs are given points based on the cumulative match scores. Meaning, if you and Ethan win 11–2, Bainbridge gets nine points. At the end of the day, whichever club has the most points wins. With more than fifty games being played today, one match is not going to make or break the tournament. I'm just letting you know ahead so it's not a shock."

Meg mulled over her strategy until a cheer roused her. On the courts below, Annie and Dave tapped paddles in victory. As she threaded her way through the crowds, she set up a personal strategy. She would play hard before the lunch break, but she promised to pace herself and reserve some power for that last game.

Ethan appeared beside her courtside, just as Carl Dewitt announced, "Beginners' round one: Shoreline vs. Bainbridge."

Sliding an arm around her waist, Ethan squeezed her hip bone. "We got this."

. . . . .

Their first game began.

Climbing parallel ladders, Ethan and Meg, and the Shoreline beginners, Lydia and Dimitri, inched upward. Lydia was a popper, and Meg could see the high balls coming, but Dimitri was a banger, which made it hard for her to take the power off. They matched points at every step. Three to three. Five to five. Seven to five. Double eights. Meg pressed herself to keep her focus. Already, the volunteer ref had called her on a kitchen fault when her foot had slipped a quarter inch over the line.

Soon enough, the score was 11–10 in their favor, and although eleven points generally took the victory, the win-by-two-points rule was in place. Meg looked up to the crowd and caught Annie's eye. Her friend jumped to her feet and cheered vigorously.

Ethan served, and Meg thrilled when she managed a third-shot drop. But Meg had telegraphed her target. Lydia from Shoreline stepped easily into the kitchen, waited for the bounce, and returned cross-net. Lydia's shot, however, sailed higher than intended, and Meg pounced, smacking the ball down the center. Both Lydia and Dmitri went for it, clashing paddles and sending the ball flying off the court. Meg's hit won the match point. *Down the middle solves the riddle*, she thought.

Paddles were tapped all around with polite sportsmanship, but the moment they strode off the court, Ethan lifted Meg off the ground and twirled her around. "You played great!"

Game followed game. Despite their efforts, they lost by four points to the beginners from Phantom Lake, but Meg had expected to lose to them. It was rumored that although the teenage sibling team had never played in a pickleball tournament, both had starred on their high school tennis team. For the remainder of the morning, however, Ethan and Meg narrowly inched out their opponents from Portland and Spokane, and even kicked some Kirkland bootie right on their Everest Park home court.

At lunchtime, Annie and Meg found a spot in the shade of the picnic shelter. On the horizon, a dense curtain of clouds formed, contrasting the blue-sky microclimate overhead. But here, on the green lawns of the park, the sun pounded down on the sweaty participants and spectators, while Bainbridge and Lakeview players mingled amiably at the wooden picnic tables.

Meg drew out her tuna sandwich. Annie opened the lid on a tofu-chickpea salad. Surprised to see her friend depart from her steady Bainbridge diet of burgers and brownies, Meg narrowed her eyes at the preponderance of veggies in Annie's meal.

Annie shrugged. "I'm just happy that hotel rooms don't have scales. Otherwise, it wouldn't have been a real vacation."

They ate their portioned lunches: enough to fuel their games but not so much as to double over with cramps. After Annie managed to get her fork into the last rolling chickpea, Meg leaned in. "How's it going with the real Michael Edmonds?"

Her friend's grin took over her whole face. "Fine . . ." Her sing-song indicated there was more to say.

"So you like him."

"Oh, Meg." She rolled her eyes heavenward. "I know it's cliché, but he's perfect." Her voice dropped into the confidential zone. "I think I'm in a serious relationship."

"You mean, you never laugh?"

Annie groaned. "And on that note . . . I'm gonna head over and practice once more with Dave." She hugged her friend's arm. "You're gonna do great in your game against Vance. Don't let them psych you out. You got this."

Meg settled herself onto the picnic bench. To help push away the nervousness about the impending game, she set about distracting herself with a daydream that involved Ethan, coconut-scented sunscreen, and marshmallow fluff. She hadn't even gotten to the good part when she felt the bump on the bench of someone sitting down beside her.

Glancing up, she found Vance, his smirk knocking her vibe right out from under her.

THIRTY-ONE

"Megs!" Vance announced. His teeth gleamed like piano keys. "Fancy meeting you here." He leaned in close. "Pickling for the enemy, are you? I like it. That's spunky. I'm jumping with nerves."

She breathed in through her nose. "Hello, Vance," she said evenly.

He chuckled. "Playing it cool, eh?" He smoothed his hair with his fingers. "Looks like we'll settle things on the battlefield." He winked. "Not to worry. We'll take it easy on you."

Her jaw moved to speak, but she had no response. No clever comeback that would put him in his place. Like a Pacific banana slug camouflaged by nerves, she remained unmoving in the perfect spot to be stepped on.

"All right. Well. No hard feelings." Vance petted her shoulder patronizingly.

"No hard feelings?" She knew it was pointless, but she had to say something. Her voice shook with pent-up anger. "You broke off our marriage on the back of a Home Depot receipt. What the hell, Vance?"

"Yes. Well. In my defense," he confessed solemnly as he stood to leave, "I did look for a notepad."

That. Was. It.

The straw broke with such clarity she heard it snap. "Wait," she enunciated.

He halted at the sound of her voice. A smirk formed on his lips at being called back. Typical Vance. He believed he still had some hold on her. "I've been practicing," she said, keeping it together. "You better bring your A game."

"That's the spirit. And good on you for making it this far. You never were much of an hand-eye-coordination person, right?" Meg swallowed hard. Logically, she knew he was taunting her on purpose, trying to get into her head, but still, it hurt. She knew exactly where he could put his $7.99 caulking gun right now.

He tapped the table. "See you on the courts. And best of luck, buttercup."

Meg raised her voice as he departed. "And good luck to you. Butter—" No. It didn't make sense to call him buttercup. She glanced around at the smattering of picnickers, but the few remaining at the table paid her no attention.

Meg popped the last of the tuna sandwich in her mouth just as Ethan sat down across from her. "Butter?" he asked wryly. But then, following her line of vision, he turned back, and his voice was gentle. "That's him, huh? Your ex?"

"Yep. That was Vance." Over the last few weeks, as their relationship had strengthened, Meg had outlined the silhouette of her brief marriage. In the telling, she had been generous, taking responsibility for her gullibility and permissiveness. She couldn't blame her participation on naïveté. She had made a choice to be with Vance, but at least now she was out of it.

Ethan shook his head. "Well. Good riddance to that loser. Puts everything in perspective, though. I don't even need to beat him on the court. I already got you." The light in his brown eyes showered her with affection and washed her clean of her past.

"Cheeseball. How do I put up with you?"

"Don't worry. I still plan to kick his ass on the pickleball court."

Starting suddenly, he said, "I almost forgot!" Reaching into his back pocket, he pulled out a business card. The simple text was embossed in neat block letters that read *The Welcome Inn*. "For you."

"What's this?"

"It's from Mayumi. She told me they've been getting crazy publicity: in the local news, on the hotel's social media. Your mural is blowing up on Bainbridge."

Meg felt the warmth spread across her chest. "Really?" She re-read the name printed on the card. "Welcome Inn? What happened to the Outlook Inn?"

"She's changing the name. 'Cause of your fence. I'm telling you, you should see it. Tourists are checking it out like it's a Picasso. And . . ." He turned the card for her to see the writing on the back.

"Who's this? Jim Loeb?" she asked, scrutinizing the name. WSDOT. The Washington State Department of Transportation. She read Jim Loeb's hastily scribbled note. *Saw your work. Impressed. Please get in touch.*

"Mayumi says he's the marketing guy for the ferries." He smiled. "I think it's a commission."

A commission! She played it cool. "You think? Hmm. That would be something to consider."

He saw right through her guise. "Are you kidding? Meg. The DOT. You know what that could mean?"

She did. The ferries weren't just transportation. They were symbols of Seattle. And to an artist, ferries offered yard after yard of flat canvas. Wouldn't that be something? Meg contained it, the hope, the possibilities, because what if the job didn't pan out? What if she was letting her dreams run away with her?

Ethan wrapped his arm around her shoulder and shook her. "Meg's gonna paint the ferries!"

His optimism was contagious. Why not grab ahold of that kite tail and fly with it? The sheer happiness of being seen and recognized for her talent brought a huge grin to her cheeks. "Wouldn't that be great?"

"It would." He tipped his head toward Vance and Édith, who had attracted a small crowd of gawkers to watch them stretch. "What kind of name is Vance, anyway?" Ethan asked. "It's like his parents couldn't decide between Vince and Lance, so they split the difference."

"There you are." Meg heard her friend's chirpy voice before she spotted her. Jogging toward them, Annie was pointing at the sky and panting, "Have you seen the clouds?"

They followed her finger. Overhead, dark clouds gathered and pressed toward the courts.

"They're starting the final games early to beat the rain. Marilyn just told me. They're making the announcement."

"What do you mean?" Meg asked.

"Your attention, participants," Carl Dewitt announced, poking his cowboy hat off his forehead. "I hate to cut your lunch short. Vittles are vital, y'all, but pickleball calls. Due to the threat of rain"—he gestured at the darkening sky—"we'll be skipping the rest of the break and jumping right into the final matches."

"The last match!" Panic lit Meg's face. "Now?"

Ethan squeezed her hand. "You and I are gonna do great. Don't let them get in your head."

Behind them, a gruff voice cut into their conversation. "You got that right. They should be the ones worried about *you*."

Meg spun to find the shiny glint of her favorite bald head. "Rooster! You made it. I was worried . . ."

She paused midsentence, silenced by amazement. Cradled in Rooster's arms was the teeniest, pinkest, purest bundle of baby that Meg had ever seen. The eensy-weensy fingers curled like flower petals; the fingernails glinted as delicately as a minnow's scales. The sleeping three-week-old's creaseless eyelids expressed an impossible level of peacefulness.

"Meg Bloomberg. Meet Zoe Gardner. Ain't she beautiful?"

"Oh! She's perfect!" Meg's face opened with genuine happiness for her friend. "And I'm so relieved to see you. When you texted that you were having issues, I thought . . ."

"Oh, that!" Laverne rushed toward them, toting a diaper bag packed for an escape from civilization. "That was only a temporary disaster. Would you believe Rooster bought toddler-sized diapers? For an infant! Poop was everywhere."

"How was I supposed to know they came in different sizes?"

"Where's your goddaughter?" Meg asked.

"Lulu? She's napping in the car." Rooster smiled the relieved grin of a tired parent. "Papu and Nam-nam get Zoe all to ourselves." He chirped at the sleeping baby. "Right, pumpkin? Are you my little pumpkin-wumpkin?"

Meg laughed at seeing big, tough Rooster turned to mush by a girl the size of a football.

"I'm so glad you're here."

"Wouldn't miss it," he said, not taking his eyes off his precious charge.

Carl's voice boomed over the loudspeakers. "We're ready for the games to resume, ladies and jujubes. The scores are as tight as a belt after Momma's Sunday brunch; a couple of the clubs are neck and neck. I sure am excited to see which team comes home with this very generous prize. Good luck to all. Now . . . let's get 'er done!"

Meg placed a pair of fingers against her throat to check the thud of her heartbeat. There was no time to be nervous. Just time enough to get in the zone.

She clasped Ethan's hands in hers. "We *have* to win," she said, and she squeezed his fingers for emphasis. "I really want to beat him."

Ethan lifted his brow, apprising her anew. "I don't think I've ever seen this side of you."

"The kick-some-butt side?"

He nodded his approval. "I could get used to this butt-kicking version. In that case . . ." He imitated Carl's drawl. "Let's get 'er done!"

· · · · ·

Marilyn stormed toward the picnic area. Inching between them, she cuffed Meg and Ethan by their elbows and dragged them toward the court. "We don't have much time, so I'm gonna give it to you straight. The competition is tight. I've been keeping tabs on the matches."

She halted and pulled out her phone to display a series of organized columns on a spreadsheet. How she had managed to build such a complex document on her cell phone was a mystery, but Marilyn was Marilyn.

"Here's the thing. Lakeview is ahead, but barely. Just two points overall. It's up to you to squeak them out. Beat them by three or more points, and we win this whole thing."

Meg squinted at the phone and gave the teeniest shake of her head. "Three points?" Meg grimaced. "It's Vance and Édith. They're . . . they're good."

"And so are you. And, you have all of us supporting you. In fact"—Marilyn waved over the woman who had been lingering in the background—"look who I found wandering around courtside. I took one look at that face, and I subtracted thirty years—"

"Twenty-five," the older woman corrected.

Meg's face lit. "Mom!"

"So excited for you, darling." Dina Bloomberg gathered her daughter into a bear hug, and Meg swallowed the happy lump in her throat. "I just arrived," Dina gushed. "But I don't want to distract you. We'll catch up after. I'll be cheering you on from the stands. You go out there, and you win this."

"For Bainbridge," Marilyn said.

"For kids who need sports equipment," Ethan pitched in.

Dina Bloomberg added, "For your mother."

"By at least three points. No pressure." Marilyn squeezed Meg's arm with a considerable amount of pressure. "Now, go pickle their asses."

They hightailed it to the appointed court. Already, the stands were crammed with fans. Normally, a beginner's match would attract little attention, but word of a tight finish had threaded its way through the masses, and now a crowd gathered to watch the spectacle. The weight of her responsibility and the anxiety of proving herself against her ex pinched her stomach. She strode onto the court.

There was Vance, and behind him, Édith. Her long legs led her torso like she was a giraffe galloping on the savanna. Her hair bounced behind her like an ad for a creamy conditioner made with minerals from the Dead Sea. They conferred, switching between English and French, before selecting a spot on the court on which to stretch. With more grunting than Meg thought necessary, they tugged and wrestled each other into a pretzeled tantric pose. She tightened her ponytail in determination.

"Hey, guys. Guess what?" Meg's old pal Peter, dressed to match his wife, Portia, in a neon ref outfit, appeared beside Meg and Ethan. "We're reffing your game! Well. Portia is. I'm here for moral support."

Ethan tugged Meg aside. While he rolled a pickleball between his fingers to check for cracks, he asked, "What do you think about that? Peter and Portia play for Lakeview, right? She'll be biased."

"I wouldn't worry about it," Meg said. "I don't know any two people who are as fair as Peter and Portia. They're like King Solomon. And Queen Solomon."

"Excuse me." Peter and Portia reappeared, unnaturally close. In a low voice, Portia mentioned, "We just wanted to say that we heard your Bainbridge league plans to donate their winnings to youth sports charities—"

"So," Peter's voice trailed off to a conspiratorial whisper, "I'll be on the sidelines . . . rooting for you."

"Good luck, you two." Portia winked and marched to the net, measuring tape in hand.

"On the other hand, it might be okay if our ref were a little biased," Ethan amended.

Portia gave a wary glance at the gray-black cloud stomping on the horizon. Then she got to work measuring the net height. She tweaked the crank, adjusting and remeasuring until the tape read thirty-four inches at the center and thirty-six at the posts. Satisfied, Portia waved to all four players. "Players. Approach the net."

Portia refreshed them on the rules, and all parties nodded their understanding.

"*Bonne chance*," Édith offered, her voice imparting equal parts generosity and smugness.

Sweat collected beneath Meg's grip as she strode to the baseline. She wiped her paddle hand on her skort.

Portia lifted her hand. "Begin."

THIRTY-TWO

Meg's head whipped up in time to see the ball hurtling toward her. Before she had a chance to untangle Édith's smugly generous *Bonne chance*, they were in the thick of the volley. On her fourth hit, she swung hard and knocked it right out of the park; a great hit for baseball, but alas, this was pickleball.

Ugh! The shock of a rough start shook her. Already, Meg's faulty focus had cost them a point. She had not yet recovered her composure when Édith's next serve zipped past her.

Not a full minute into the game and they were down by two.

"No worries," Ethan mouthed, reassuring her.

Still, Meg grunted with frustration. She had given away the points, offered them up on a platter with a mint garnish and a lemon squeeze.

"Sorry. My fault."

"No sorrys," he reminded her. "Just play your game."

Édith, confident now, sent another rocket across the net, but this time, the ball skipped just beyond the baseline and careened into Meg's foot.

"Long," Portia called. "Side out."

"Long? *Non*," Édith cried. "The ball. It hit her foot! It is our point."

"It hit her foot . . . *after* it landed out," Portia countered. "Side out."

"*Merde*," Édith muttered. In high school French class, Meg had earned a lunch detention for uttering less.

Recentering herself, Meg set up her serve and swung, but the moment she made contact she could tell her racket was misaligned. The serve landed midcourt—a basic mistake, and easy pickings for Vance. When he returned her weak shot like a missile, Meg smacked the ball when she should have tapped it. She winced as her ball soared right into Édith's forehand slam. Ethan served next, but Meg's third shot flew out-of-bounds. And just like that, it was side out.

"Oh my gosh. They return everything," she said.

"You're doing fine. Remember. Reset after each point. It's like a coin toss. The points don't follow a pattern; there's no such thing as a bad run of luck. Each point is unique."

Regaining the advantage, Édith made her angled slice serve look easy. Meg popped it too high—where Vance waited for the bounce—and slammed it into Ethan's thigh.

"Well done, babe." Vance tapped his girlfriend's butt with his paddle. "Your serve set me up perfectly. I remember the last time you used that move!"

"Ah!" Édith remarked, her eyes wide with understanding. "*Exactement! Comme lorsqu'on a gagné le tournoi.*" The significance of Édith's comment clicked into place.

"*Un tournoi*," Meg whispered. A tournament! *That time we won the tournament.* That was against the rules. Beginner competitors weren't allowed to have competed in a tournament, much less have won one.

"Time out," Meg called. Portia raised a hand, allowing it. Meg whispered to Ethan, "She just said they won a tournament. That's against the rules! They can't play in the beginners' spot!"

"What do you think? Do you wanna tell Portia what you heard?"

Meg thought it over, waging an entire internal battle over the course of seconds. Soon enough, she came to her conclusion: If Vance and Édith needed to cheat to win, then that was on them. The fact that they'd played in a tournament had no impact on this game right here, right now. She was going to fight a good fight and use the skills she had built with hard work and determination.

She shot Ethan a side glance. "You know what? Forget it. We got this. Let's take them down."

They bumped fists. The moral high ground spurred Meg's purpose. Overhead, a gray screen slid over the last corner of sunshine. She read the clouds.

Rain.

A teeny droplet splashed against the pale green pavement. Another hit her visor. Another smacked her forearm. *Hold off*, her eyes begged the charcoal sky. *Give us time to turn this around. Just let us beat them. By three points. And then you can flood the place.*

Portia signaled a return to play.

The light mist cleared Meg's head, and this time when the ball came, she was ready. Instead of smashing, she angled her paddle and yanked backward to add topspin. The bounce took Vance by surprise. When he missed the shot, Bainbridge regained the serve. Encouraged by the small victory, Meg straightened.

Get a point, she told herself. *Get one point.*

Ethan served and the volley began. She readied herself, still half hoping the ball would not come to her so that she wouldn't screw it up. But when Édith's too-low lob came to her wrapped up in shiny paper and a bow, she tore into it and . . . *bam!*

She scored a point!

Positivity tingled at the back of her scalp. At least she hoped it was that, and not lice.

"Way to go, partner," Ethan whispered. "Great shot."

They were on the board, and thanks to Ethan's patient dink rally, in minutes, they doubled their score. Even when the serve went back to the other side, Meg felt satisfied. Their foot was in the door.

Vance and Édith worked together to shove that door shut once and for all. They advanced another point. With the score at 8–2, the glamorous pair inched closer to the winning eleven points. Then, by some miracle, Édith served right into the net and Vance whacked one way out.

Meg's mind percolated with an iota of optimism. She had seen teams come back from 2–8, hadn't she? She must have.

Readiness buzzed inside her like a current. Ethan served, and Meg achieved a textbook third-shot drop. It was such a lovely hit that Meg almost dropped her paddle in surprise.

"Whatta shot!" Ethan marveled.

One small success begot the next and another followed. While the sparse droplets turned into a light mist, Ethan and Meg's score increased. Point by hard-earned point, she pushed herself. Rather than dampening her play, Meg felt spurred on by the fresh drizzle. Before long, they were only down by one.

Striking distance.

Édith blinked the rain away. She bent forward to adjust her boobs and tugged her shirt away from her bra. "I wet myself!" she cried. Édith's normally silky hair frizzed out like an old broom and her dripping mascara gave her a stoned panda vibe.

Vance looked nervous. Forming a T with his hands, he stormed toward Portia. "Time! Time out. It's going to pour. You have to call it, ref."

Portia looked to her husband uncertainly. Peter shrugged. "Your call."

"Yes," Édith pressed, her chest rearranged back into matching torpedoes. "You should stop this game. The courts will be slippery. We could be hurt."

"It's really just sprinkling," Meg said. "The surface is hardly wet."

Peter jogged over to confer with Portia. It was true: if the rain got any stronger, the courts could become slick and dangerous, and no tournament prize was worth slipping and wrecking a knee. Meg had seen it happen, and she knew how painful an injury like that could be. And worse, it would mean no pickleball for at least a month.

Still, she had played on wetter. Meg looked up at the sky. A thin line of light was stenciled at the base of the clouds. Maybe it would clear. Alternately, maybe it would pour. Either way, they ought to play fast.

"Continue play," Portia decided.

Clutching the ball in concentration, Meg calculated. They were down by only one point. 8–9. If by some miracle they managed to win, they still wouldn't have the requisite three-point lead to take the tournament.

But suddenly, it didn't matter. Her goal was as obvious as a porcupine in a pillowcase. She wanted the win. Not just to beat Vance. *She* wanted this. For herself.

When she swung, her ball flew deep and crosscourt to Vance, exactly as planned, and when it came back, she dinked to the kitchen corner. That gave Ethan time to run forward to the center of the no-volley line. Édith returned right into the trap, and Ethan poached the ball and sliced it at the perfect angle. It struck the pavement behind Vance.

"What were you thinking?" Vance yelled at Édith. "Don't just whack at the ball. Use your head! You put it right to his forehand paddle! You lost us that point."

"Me?!" Édith retorted. "It was your weak return. You set it up. The point was lost two hits ago. Just like what Coach Zach says. You need to support me."

"Coach Zach says *I* need to support *you*?" Vance's face flushed red. "Who the hell does he think he is? Is he your bloody psychiatrist now? Or is it more than that?"

"Language!" Portia called. "Please. Watch your language."

From across the net, Vance glared at Meg in disbelief. He must have thought they would be easy pickings. But no. They had tied it up at 9–9. Two more points. Two more points for a win.

Meg's mouth hardened into a tight line. She gripped the paddle, swung her arm like a pendulum, and *wham!* served high and deep. "Out!" Édith cried before the ball landed right on the baseline.

"The line is good," Portia countered. "Point goes to Bainbridge. 10–9."

Vance's coloring climbed up his neck and reddened his forehead. He looked like a blond tomato. In his fury, he turned to Édith. "You should have stayed back. That's your third unforced error. Get it together." He grunted while modeling a powerful swing. "Like that. Same thing you did in that *tournoi*. Like Christmas in Cancún."

His comment landed like a boulder tossed off the high dive into a cup of water. Meg went numb with the weight of it. Cancún. Last winter? Her mental calculator subtracted the months. Meg had still been married to Vance last December. He'd claimed that trip to Cancún was a dental seminar. "Very boring," he'd warned her. "I'd ask you to come along, but it's all incisors and impacted molars."

Indignation rolled through her. Cancún at Christmas? It was one thing to cheat in a tournament, but quite another to cheat on one's wife. She glared at Vance, at his self-satisfied smirk. Meg lifted the ball for her serve and powered up, dead set on vengeance.

Then for an instant she was outside her body. She stared down at the other Meg, at the one from that painful photo, her face drawn and miserable with his betrayal. And as she revisited that old ache, a rush of warmth brushed her cheek. The sensation felt so palpable that she turned toward the stands to face the source.

Meg's breathing grew slow and deep. Behind the gray cloud, the sun struggled, casting a veil of hazy light onto the smiling group. A spotlight illuminated her unwavering fans.

Her friends.

There was Annie—all logic and science—who'd swum into love's deep waters moments after she dipped her toe in. Meg glanced at Rooster, who cuddled his granddaughter, trading his addiction for a fresh start. Beside him, Meg's mentor Marilyn leaned forward, her face shining with encouragement and pride. There was her mom, Dina Bloomberg, who hopscotched across continents and loved without borders. And beside her, Meg could feel Ethan's solid presence like an anchor—not dragging her down but grounding her. She looked at those good people and her eyes stung with emotion.

She reached for the 2Win tournament-quality ball beneath the stretchy liner of her skort. When her fingers brushed the business card she had placed there, pressed against her thigh, her touch sent a visceral ping to her brain. The scent of acrylic paints filled her nose, and she let her fist uncurl, releasing the pain and need for revenge. Conceived and born from her creativity, her resolve alone had brought that fence to life. That was all her. She had done that.

She could do this.

Meg twirled the ball between her fingers and felt her strength build from her toes to her scalp. All she knew was this moment: the ball and the paddle and the vapor steaming off the courts that smelled like victory. Meg drew herself to her full petite stature.

Rooster's advice bounced back to her: *Remember. There are only two things out here that matter. You and the ball. And the ball doesn't really matter.*

She served.

This time when Édith returned deep, Meg's body and brain were engaged. Her third-shot drop landed perfectly. The four players ran to the kitchen line, where the pickling began. Diagonally and repeatedly, the ball hopped low over the net, Meg vs. Édith, Édith vs. Meg. Back and forth. Back and forth. She could keep it up forever. Until . . . Meg's dink bounced too close to center. Vance took advantage of the opening. He reached into the fray with an underhand hit.

The lob arced over Ethan's head.

Meg reacted instinctively. She spun and raced to the baseline. Twirling toward the net and screeching to a halt, she spotted the ball with a pointed finger and lined up her shot. Following the parabolic descent of the green sphere, she waited for the right millisecond. Only the ball, the ball, the falling ball, filled her brain.

And . . . now! Flicking her wrist, she heard the perfect sound of the ball connecting with the paddle's sweet spot.

High above the courts, a thinning cloud shifted. A ray of light as clean and pure as the dawn of earth poured from the heavens. Vance, Édith, and Ethan stood shocked and immobilized as the beam found its mark and illuminated the strange trajectory of the neon ball. The universe contracted into a single pinpoint.

The spectators leaned forward in their seats. As if lit from within, the ball slowed and hovered at center court. The seconds stretched, becoming as long as days while the plastic sphere made up its mind. It swooped toward the tape. It made featherlight contact. Skimming the vinyl, the ball whistled as it spun and balanced on the ridge. It rolled, dancing along the narrow tightrope, following an impossible path. At last, it twirled in its sunny spotlight and, suddenly aware of its own gravity, dropped straight down into the kitchen.

Ungettable.

Meg's breath halted. An instant passed while the initial shock wore off, and then she rushed to the net and skidded to a stop. In a puddle on the other side of the net, her ball still spun and twitched.

A hush descended on the watching throng. The birds stilled on their branches. In Puget Sound, a giant octopus blew a bubble, but other than that, nobody moved. A silence as vast as the galaxies permeated the stands, the courts, the nearby trees.

And then . . . the crowd erupted in cheers.

"Game goes to Bainbridge." Portia lifted her voice above the din. "11–9."

Meg's heart thudded in her throat as reality sank in. She had done it. The unicorn of pickleball was hers.

Meg Bloomberg had executed the Golden Pickledrop.

THIRTY-THREE

Elated with the ecstasy of victory, she and Ethan fell together. "We did it!" she said. "I can't believe it—"

Ethan jerked from her grip as the throng of spectators jostled them apart. Hands reached out to pat her on the back, to squeeze her arm. From out of nowhere, Boring Dave, Knee-Brace Joe, and 26 Cent appeared and swept Ethan forward. He was swallowed by a mass of well-wishers. It was a crazy, noisy moment, but Meg held completely still. Eyes taking it all in, she captured a mental picture of the scene. The sun pushed through the last of the gray and washed across the courts. Already the damp spots were disappearing, while the smell of recent rain freshened the air. Players and spectators alike pressed down onto the courts to join in the excitement.

"Pardon me. Excuse me, folks." Carl edged his way toward the platform beside the courts. "Let me get through here so I can see you all." Meg noticed the flash of a white envelope clutched in his fingers. The results!

Ethan was no longer anywhere in sight, but she could make out the back of Annie's head near the podium. She began to inch her way through the crowd, trying to take advantage of Carl's wake.

"It's her," a voice whispered, and some of the folks near her turned to see.

"Hey! It's you." A sporty teenager in blue braids touched Meg's elbow. "Congrats."

At that, several heads swiveled. "Wow. That was something." "I've never seen anything like it." "Where'd you pick up a shot like that?" A guy with a *Dinking Problem* T-shirt tapped his paddle to Meg's, saying, "Maybe some of that picklemagic will rub off on me."

Jeannie appeared beside her, flanked by her girl goons. The school counselor's expression twisted with conflict. "Hey." Jeannie shook Meg's hand with awkward formality. "Good playin' out there."

Meg's "Thanks" was heartfelt. Jeannie's congratulations meant all the more to her—knowing how hard they must have been to offer.

The buzz rippled through the group. People parted to let her pass. As she marched, more onlookers tapped paddles with her or gave her a thumbs-up. Meg absorbed her sudden celebrity with happy embarrassment. By the time she made it to the front of the throng, Ethan was still nowhere to be found, nor Annie nor any of the Bainbridge crew. Instead, she stood crunched beside a group from Vancouver, the Washington One.

Carl raised a hand for attention. "What a sport! Looks like so much fun I think I'll give pickleball a try myself."

A chant rose from the back of the crowd. "Pick-le-ball. Pick-le-ball."

"Pick-le-ball. Pick-le-ball," Meg joined in, carried away with the energy of the throng.

Carl lifted a hand for silence. "That being said," he drawled, "a tournament is a tournament. There are winners and there are . . . well, there're no losers here. You're all winners today."

The group roared their approval.

He lifted the envelope to the sky. "But there are people who actually won this thing. So let's get 'er done." With a theatrical flourish, he raised the flap and extracted a slip of paper.

An expectant hush blanketed the crowd in anticipation of the announcement. By Marilyn's calculations, Bainbridge needed three points for the win. Meg's match delivered, but only by two. And despite the thrill she felt in beating Vance, she fervently wished her efforts were enough to pull in a win for the sports charities.

Meg sensed the heat of someone's gaze and turned her head. Across the crowd, she spotted Ethan: his kind, golden brown eyes framed by impossibly thick lashes. His smile captured her and erased the crowd around them. It was the sort of stare that went in deep, a smile meant for only her. She felt their connection in several parts of her body at once.

"The winner of the Picklesmash Tournament and the recipient of this here generous check is"—Carl squinted at the small card between his fingers—"the Lakeview Pickleball Club of Washington."

While cheers rang in her ears, Ethan smiled at her and shrugged. She returned his sweet gaze, lifting her shoulders in a matching gesture. Never mind the title. Meg was a winner.

"Hold up. Hold up," Carl called. A slender woman in red-framed glasses was pushing her way toward the microphone. She hopped onto the small stage and shared her phone's screen with Carl.

"Will you look at that?" He took the phone from her hand. "Our anonymous patron says that we had a very close contest, and that they would like to . . ." Carl paused to read the passage to himself before announcing to the crowd, "The sponsor would like to award a commensurate amount to youth sports charities in honor of the runner-up team from Bainbridge Island."

A whoop exploded around them. Meg, connected by an invisible thread to Ethan, felt her spirit soar with the pride of accomplishment and the satisfaction of knowing she had given it her all. Everything escaped her mind except their victory and the elation it brought her. She came, she pickled, she conquered.

Players congratulated one another and joined in the happy spirit of pickleball camaraderie, all rivalries forgotten. Cheers and hugs erupted around her until, little by little, the crowd began to break up. Her head swiveled, trying to catch sight of her Bainbridge crew, but instead, Meg heard a familiar brash voice.

"Édith! Please. Wait!" Vance pled.

Meg turned to find her ex at the edge of the throng, stomping after his rain-drenched girlfriend. As she absconded toward the parking lot, her electrified hair gave her the appearance of a woman possessed with supernatural rage. Vance chased after her. "Édith! I said stop."

At the sound of his booming voice, the departing fans turned toward the spectacle.

"You"—Édith spun on him, lit with fury—"are not a nice person," she seethed. "You only care about winning your silly pickleball. I will not play pickleball with you again. *Jamais.* We are *finis*! When I get home, I am crushing your balls." She stood nose to nose with him and raged, "From now on, you can pay your own rent. You can buy your own car. And I am *certainement* not paying for your Scrotox."

A laugh escaped through Meg's nose. It felt as satisfying as permitting herself a sneeze she had been holding inside for months.

While the remaining picklers and spectators pressed toward the exits, Meg scanned the area again for Annie and Ethan, hoping to share her excitement. But there were too many tall people around her. So, she wandered toward the parking lot guessing she might bump into them. Her brain felt so overfull she couldn't even remember where she'd parked her car.

Clicking the key remote, Meg listened for the answering chirp of the blue hatchback. She was completing her second circuit when she heard "Meg!"

Instantly, she recognized the good-looking player in white from the pro showcase. "You're Tyler Demming!" she said, flattered that he had called her by name. She grinned and could think of nothing more to add until an idea came to her. "I played with you once. At Lakeview. We won."

"Is that so?" he said, nodding.

"And we had a lot of fun."

He grinned. "Now, that's what I'm talkin' about. Fun is the point, right? Hang on. I wanna grab something from my car. Do you have a minute?"

She followed a few steps behind to his coupe and she fidgeted while he rummaged in his trunk. At last, he came up with a plastic bag and a slim black marker. He reached into the bag.

"Ta-da!" With a showman's fanfare, he pulled out a plywood pickleball paddle, the kind that came in pairs in a beginner's kit. Except this one was spray-painted gold.

"Meg . . . What's your last name, Meg?"

"Bloomberg?"

"Meg Bloomberg. Executer of the elusive Pickledrop, I bequeath to you the Golden Picklepaddle." He passed it to her with the gravity of bestowing knighthood. "Congratulations."

She marveled at the paddle. A smattering of scribbled signatures, including Tyler Demming's, covered the surface. "So, I sign it?"

"Of course. You earned it."

"And when I see someone else make the Golden Pickledrop, I give this to them?"

"*If* you see someone make the Golden Pickledrop. Ever again."

"Do you think I should play with it? Once in a while?"

Tyler shrugged, his long hair loose now and skimming his shoulders. "It's yours, Meg Bloomberg. Use it as a cutting board if you want," he said, and ducked into his car.

She would never desecrate the Golden Picklepaddle. It was like receiving Excalibur. Like King Arthur would ever have considered using his famous sword as a cutting board! It was not only illogical, but also impractical. She clutched the paddle to her chest, swelling with pride, and returned to scanning the lot for her car.

In the next row over, Rooster leaned against her blue hatchback.

"Been waiting for you. Did you lose your car?"

"No comment."

He squinted at the plywood paddle. "What's that you're haulin' around?"

Meg held out the paddle for Rooster to see. Despite her attempt at modesty, her huge grin gave her away. She tried to sound casual. "It's the Golden Picklepaddle. Tyler Demming gave it to me."

"Tyler Demming," he said with reverence. Rooster touched a finger to the edge of the paddle and jumped like he'd received an electric shock. "Yowch. Good for you. I knew you could do it."

Bathed in Rooster's praise, Meg stood there beaming.

"Hey. Give me your phone. Go stand over there and let me get a selfie of you with that thing."

Her lips parted to repeat that a selfie could be taken only by oneself, but Rooster cut her off. "I'm just joshing with you. Come on. Hold that thing up."

He snapped it, and the two of them peered at the screen to see the result. "Now, that's true beauty."

"Aw, Rooster."

"I didn't even notice that rainbow in the background till I saw it in the photo."

She turned to see a hazy prism in the distance and punched him gently. "Thanks a lot."

"Now, don't you dare delete that, darlin'." He pulled her into a bear hug. "That one's a keeper."

MATCH

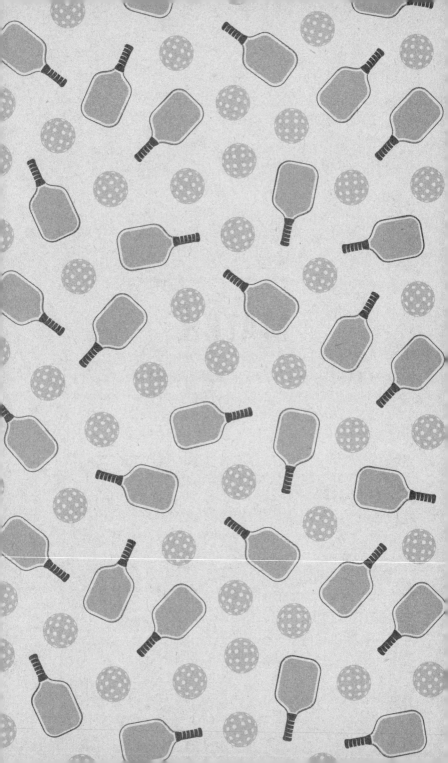

THIRTY-FOUR

ONE YEAR LATER . . .

On the horizon, Seattle shrank to the size of toy buildings. Ethan hooked his thumb into the belt loop of Meg's white jeans. Taking in the green glint of Puget Sound, Meg melted into him, grateful for the calm waters today in the channel between Seattle and Bainbridge. When she traveled via the solid weight of a ferryboat, she never felt so much as a ripple, but with a smaller boat like this one, any wave sent up by a passing speedboat could send their vessel rocking. The catamaran—a yacht posing as a sailboat—skimmed past the rocky outcroppings and feathery evergreens that marked the passageway into the Olympic Peninsula.

"This sure beats the ferry." Ethan smiled. "No waiting in the car line, no ticket fees . . ."

"But no clam chowder," Meg put in.

"Ah. That's true. But the champagne is free and flowing." Lifting the bottle from the sidebar, he tipped more bubbly into her flute.

"Michael? Annie?" He proffered the bottle.

"None for me," Annie said, reminding him by patting the small bump of her belly. "But I'll take some more apple seltzer." She swigged a mouthful. "This stuff is so good. Sweetheart? Let's get rid of all the water and replace it with apple seltzer."

"Anything for you, my love," the real Michael Edmonds agreed. He planted a peck on her lips before spinning back to yank on the jib line.

Meg gave Ethan a sly grin and snuggled closer, their backs turned away from the breeze. This was the life: sailing across the Sound, the sun shining on her tan shoulders. The champagne didn't hurt, either.

"Check it out!" Ethan pointed at the silent ferry skimming the Sound. "There goes one of Meg Bloomberg's floating masterpieces."

She gazed out at the majestic queen of the waters, flushing with the rush of accomplishment. "When you're on the ferry," he said, his lips vibrating against her neck, "it's hard to see the whole thing. From here, you get such a sense of the scale and perspective. It's marvelous, Meg." The compliment was for her ears only, and her skin warmed with his attentions.

What an unexpected pleasure it was to work with someone she loved on something she loved. Ethan's environmental company consulted with Washington State Ferries on their Go Green project to convert Seattle's iconic vessels to hybrid electric boats. During the continuing project, Meg contributed a series of designs and headed the teams that painted the murals onto the ferries: vibrant, active images that highlighted the region's natural resources.

The wake from the ferry crossed beneath their boat, thrusting Ethan closer. Taking advantage of the opportunity, she tilted her face to his lips.

"Get a room!" Annie shook her head in mock disgust. She tipped back the last of her seltzer. "Hey! I just realized. Guess what today is."

Meg resisted rolling her eyes. "Let me guess. Isaac Newton's birthday? No? The anniversary of the day molecules were invented."

"Nice try, but Isaac Newton was born in January. And I'm not even going to acknowledge that other comment. No, I'm talking about one year ago today: that's when we left on our big trip to Bainbridge."

A wistful nostalgia built in Meg's throat. Annie slung her arm around her and squinted into the distance. "Doesn't Seattle look tiny from here? Just look at all those miniature trees. It's so beautiful, our Emerald City," she mused.

Michael called, "Coming about," and they all ducked out of the way as the boom swung across. Ahead, Meg spotted Annie and Michael's property in the secluded bay.

Although the four friends met up regularly at Ethan's place in Winslow, she loved visiting Annie and Michael's magnificent Bainbridge home on the rustic side of the island. At Thanksgiving when the rain pounded the Sound, or in May when the pink dogwoods reflected in the waves, Meg marveled at the changing view. First came the caw of the seagulls that swooped and whirled above the boat. The sound mingled with the scent of seaweed and cool air. On land, the salt water washed up onto a dark sand and gray stone beach, but beyond that was the real showstopper. The Edmondses' home, an upscale cottage, was built to blend in with the natural setting. The architect had balanced a perfect mix of luxury and quaintness. It sat upon a wide, green lawn bordered with old-growth pines that blended with the rocky hillside behind them. Beside the house, the couple had installed a state-of-the-art pickleball court.

Meg still couldn't get over Annie's new, opulent lifestyle. The Edmonds twins, it happened, were not just mansion rich or fancy-cars rich. They were let's-buy-a-private-island-resort rich. They had built their athletic supplies startup into the mega-successful 2Win Industries. Tournament-quality pickleball equipment turned out to be big business. It wasn't long before Meg figured out that the anonymous sponsors of Picklesmash—who allotted the funds for the tournament prize and donated generously to youth sports charities—were those same 2Win-twins. Annie, who was used to spending waking moments snagging bites of power bars in between treating patients, now had time to run her pediatric clinic free of charge and even enjoyed the luxury of regular sit-down meals.

Michael steered expertly into the cove and parked the catamaran in its slip without jostling the dock even once. Knowing that his wife bristled at bridges and gangplanks, Michael had built a slip that made disembarking a cinch. As Annie stepped off, he nodded his chin to the side of the catamaran, where the boat boasted a new name: *Anniething 4U*.

"Perfect," Meg agreed.

From the dock, Ethan pointed to the new addition to the landscape. "Tell me that's not your helicopter."

"It's not our helicopter." Michael looped the ropes through the grommets on the dock and cinched them tightly. "Okay. Yes. It is. Annie's idea. I love to fly, and she loves to help people."

"It's not what you think." Annie waved her hands to wipe away any misconception. "We bought it for emergency pediatric flights. We can get kids in the remote areas to the mainland hospitals faster than the ferries. Michael pilots, and I take care of the patients on the way. We have the money, and I figured . . ." Annie shrugged, embarrassed. Having oodles of spare cash was new to her; she worked tirelessly to find ways to donate her time and funds.

Meg tried to imagine herself in Annie's place—spectacularly wealthy and starting a family. Despite the glamourous lifestyle, Meg did not feel a pinch of envy. She and Ethan split their time between her downtown Seattle condo and the island; she could walk right onto the ferry and sail to the waterfront house Ethan rented outside of Winslow. The owner of Ethan's place was looking to sell, and with their contracts with the Washington Ferries nearing completion, they talked about putting in an offer. Just the vision of sharing that cozy home with him, windows open to let in the salt air, gave her a thrill. Her life was just right; one day at a time, waiting for the next one to unfold. Although, she had to admit, it didn't hurt to have wealthy friends who owned a waterfront pickleball resort.

A chorus of barking dogs bounded down the lawn. They jumped and raced in circles to celebrate the group's arrival.

"Down, Relish," Annie cried to the golden retriever who was making a meal out of Ethan's belt buckle. The other two dogs, Pickles the poodle and Gherkin the Chihuahua, barked and bounced. The dogs meandered between the visitors' legs in crafty attempts to knock the guests off their feet.

The light in the sky pulled off a convincing impression of three o'clock in the afternoon, although it was nearing seven by the time they sat down to dinner. In between the salad and the grilled salmon, there was laughter as phones were pulled from pockets to compare videos of baby Zoe waving hello while Rooster cheered. During the crème brûlée, the conversation hopscotched to the city council's decision to fund the remodel of a defunct shopping center and turn it into a PickleMall. Once Ethan had given the good news to the Lakeview crew, Jeannie had run with it. Now a birder as well as a baller, Jeannie convinced the league to donate their prize money to build a boardwalk over the wetlands.

"Speaking of pickleball," Annie mentioned as she piled the glasses onto a tray, "who's up for an evening pickleball match? Or are you afraid to get your asses whupped by a pregnant lady?"

"You're on." Meg was always up for pickleball. "Let me help you guys clean up."

"Nope. We got it." Michael headed to the sliding door with the stacked plates. "You two go take a walk. Unless you'd rather warm up on the courts." He gazed at his wife appreciatively. "You do not want to underestimate the athletic prowess of a woman with pregnancy hormones surging through her," Michael commented, and disappeared to clean the barbecue. Annie opened her laptop to consult with one of her patients, leaving Meg and Ethan to stroll the beachfront.

Fingers interlaced with his, she breathed in the fresh sea air and relaxed. Threads of clouds streaked the sky. They glowed with pastel pink and purple shading at their bases, like they were dabbed in watercolor paints. Puget Sound looked flat and still, making a mirror of its surface.

A ferry appeared in the channel. Wordlessly, they witnessed its slow, smooth passing. When at length the ripples that marked its existence vanished, Ethan turned to her and slid his fingers along her waist. Her skin tingled with the deliciousness of the sensation as he enfolded her in his arms. Even after a year of his companionship, each time they touched she felt both a fresh sense of excitement and the comforting sensation of being home.

"We make a great team." He spoke into her wind-tangled curls. "Don't we." It was more of a statement than a question.

"Mm-hmm." She wanted to stay like this till morning. Her head on his chest. His breath in her hair.

"You're always imagining, dreaming, creating things. I could never begin to do anything like that, but you . . ."

"That's 'cause you're more logical. And spatial. Like how you have such a good sense of direction. You know me. I can't find anything. Without my phone I am lost. I can't drive anywhere; I can't—"

"Meg," he interrupted her. "Meg Bloomberg . . ." He said her name with reverence, like she was the only human in the world.

Meg yelped. Something touched her leg. Relish, the golden retriever, was poking his snout at Meg's calf. The retriever toyed with a pickleball in his mouth. He flung his paws up on Meg's thighs. "Get offa me, Relish. Down, boy."

"Hey. Whatcha got there?" Ethan asked, tapping at the slobber-covered, neon green pickleball. The frisky pup refused to relinquish his prize. "Come on," Ethan said, tugging at the slimy pickleball.

"Drop it," Meg commanded, and Relish plopped the ball at her feet. Without hesitation, she scooped it off the ground and tossed it. "Fetch, Relish!"

Relish scampered away but skidded to a halt when the ball bounced on the grass, busted in two, and flew apart like a mermaid's coconut bra gone renegade.

"Shit." Ethan ran toward the broken shreds of plastic. "Shit."

"They own the company, hon. I'm sure they're not gonna freak out about one cracked— Hey. What's this?"

Meg squatted on the grass and sorted through the blades. She picked up a delicate ring. Tiny diamonds surrounded a light blue aquamarine gemstone. To match her eyes.

In a sensation that could only be described as the Golden Pickle-drop, her heart skimmed along the top of the tape, spun full circle, and dipped toward her toes.

"Is this?" she asked. "Is this . . . ?"

"Hold on." Flustered, Ethan loped to where Meg knelt on the lawn holding the ring. "Here. This is not— Hold on. Switch with me." He reached out a hand and lifted her to her feet. Bending onto the grass, Ethan took her spot and steadied himself on one knee.

The dog, taking a cue, lay down expecting a belly rub.

"Can I . . . ?" Ethan gestured for the ring. "I had this whole thing set up. I was going to make a speech and . . . but now—"

"I would like to hear a speech."

"Oh." Ethan shifted his weight. "Okay."

He took a steadying breath. "Meg Bloomberg." He swallowed, his Adam's apple bobbing sexily. His eyes were damp with sincerity, and, seeing it, Meg felt hers prick with tears, too. The pause hung expectantly between them and they both laughed, overfull with emotion.

"Meg Bloomberg," he tried again. "I want to wake up every morning and see the light reflected in your eyes. And in the evenings, I want to sit on the couch with you and watch mindless TV and argue over the volume. And just . . . be. You know. Together. For good. Because I never thought I would meet a person who would make me feel . . . so much . . ." His eyes misted, and he lifted a finger in the air. "One sec."

Meg waited, feeling a tightness in her own throat that mirrored his emotions.

"Okay. I got this." He started again. "Do you remember that kiss? That kiss in the hammock?"

Nodding, she pictured it. The yearning. The feeling of completion.

"We had been talking about my dad, and I remember thinking: I am going to be the opposite of that guy. A one-person person. And then . . . that kiss. That kiss sealed you into my soul and my mind. And I knew then like I know now that I want to be with only you."

Beaming, she felt the warmth spread through her chest.

"I want to make love to you in our own home with the sound of the waves out our window. Or in a mountain hammock where we can try out the Cheeky Chipmunk. Without my mom coming by, preferably."

She laughed.

His features shifted. Concentration marked his brow like he was solving a difficult math problem while reading nostalgic poetry.

He said, "I make a mean clam chowder, Meg, and if you don't like it, we can go to Pike Place and get the one they serve in the sourdough bowl, because actually, that one is a little better than mine.

"But mostly," he exhaled, "I just want to spend my life with you. For good. Because you bring out my best self. And I promise to make you smile when I can, and I promise to try to be patient and supportive when things get hard, too, and . . . I don't know what else I was gonna say." He clasped both of her hands. "I love you, Meg. Will you marry me?"

A droplet spilled over her lower lid. "That was a pretty good speech," she whispered, smiling through the tears.

"So . . . ?"

"Yes," she mouthed, and delight flooded her system as he slid the ring onto her finger. "Yes," she said, repeating the word between the gentle kisses Ethan pressed on her lips until no more words were capable of escaping.

"Yes?" Annie asked.

They startled apart. Ethan and Meg turned to find their hostess eavesdropping from several feet away. "Michael," she called toward the house. "It's a yes!"

"For god's sake, Annie." Ethan regarded her incredulously. "Can we have a minute?"

"Right. Sorry," she said. "But can I just"—Annie mock tiptoed toward them—"I figure since I already interrupted. Can I see the ring?"

Laughing, Meg held out her hand, and Annie grasped it greedily. She gasped. "So, so beautiful."

"So . . . that whole consulting-with-a-patient thing was a ruse?" Meg teased.

"It's nine at night. What did you think?"

"And Michael cleaning the barbecue?"

"Clean that thing? Never. He thinks the buildup adds flavor."

Ethan said, "Annie . . ."

"Oh!" she remembered herself. "I'll just"—she pointed a thumb toward the house—"check to see if Michael needs any help . . . not cleaning the grill."

Relish slobbered on the busted pickleball and snorted with exertion, pausing for only a moment to see who might be impressed with the hole he was digging in the dirt.

"Relish!" Annie scolded. "Come." She patted her thigh for the dog, who trailed after her, chewing happily on the busted ball.

Then it was just the two of them once again. In the golden hour before sunset, their faces glowed in the gilded light. He reached to brush the blonde wisps off her cheek and slipped his fingers beneath the hair at the nape of her neck, sending a shimmery shock wave through her veins.

"Mmm." She whispered, "We should go inside." She yanked him along and led him toward the house. "Let's celebrate."

"You know Annie's not going to let us off the pickleball hook."

Meg huffed. "Fine. One game." She walked her fingers up his chest. "And then—"

He caught her fingers in his. Annie had appeared beside them, paddle in hand. "I turned on the court lights."

"One game," Ethan promised.

· · · · ·

Meg's smile lingered even while she warmed up, dinking diagonally with Ethan and returning Annie's low, arcing hits. Michael appeared, bringing out his company's latest product: a quieter ball made of durable plastic. As they tested and admired it, he explained the ball was 2Win's solution to two of the sport's trickiest pickles:

how to cut down on noise and breakage. And bonus: the ball glowed in the dark.

"Enough with the friendly chatter," Annie said, fire in her eyes. "1 serve first."

As the evening darkened, the court lights brightened, illuminating the glowing sphere as it soared through the air. Back and forth, they batted the ball: serving, lobbing, spinning, dinking. They passed the winning score of 11–8, but still, the dim tick-tock of the ball continued.

"12–14," Annie called. She paused before serving. Her cheery voice warned, "You better let us have this point, or we're never going to get to bed tonight."

"If you have to forfeit, you can forfeit," Meg goaded.

There would be no ceasefire and they all knew it. The minutes ticked on, and the volleys continued. "16–17," Annie called, harnessing the excitement that hovered in the air. Together, the players focused, open to the opportunity before them.

Annie served. The ball whirred, whizzed through the cooling air, skimmed past Meg's paddle, and struck the court beyond Ethan's reach. All four players whooped.

"Game over!" Meg leapt to Ethan for a high five. Their voices overlapped as a dance of champions ensued on all quarters of the court. "17 to 17!" and "Finally," and "We did it!" they all chimed, gathering at the net to tap paddles.

In the wash of the moonlight, they reviewed the highlights and ribbed one another about shot choices. Michael jibed, "1 was worried you would never catch us. We had you at 5–love for the longest time."

"You mean 5–0, honey." Annie explained, "Not 5–love. That's only in tennis that love means nothing."

"That's right," Ethan added, holding Meg's gaze. "In pickleball, love is everything."

Clutching at her chest, Annie cooed, "Awww," and Michael clapped Ethan on the shoulder. "Buddy, you are in deep."

They joked and reminisced until the conversation circled back to Meg and Ethan and well-wishes for their bright future. Their laughter floated above the courts and drifted on the wind out to sea. Michael yawned and apologized, and Annie went to hit the lights. They flickered out like fireflies. Cheerfully wiped out from the events of the day, Annie and Michael retired to the house.

"That was fun," Meg said, smiling up at Ethan. "I love playing until we're even instead of trying to win. Takes all the pressure off. You know, that might have been our longest match yet."

Ethan's lovely fingernails bunched a handful of her hair against her scalp. "Kiss me."

"Seventeen . . ." she said, teasing him with a saucy smooch, "to seventeen."

"Stop talking," he whispered.

Meg wasn't certain which made her shiver more—the cool of the salt breeze or the freckled thumb brushing her hip bone. She sank into the sensation, swaddled in a cocoon of contentedness.

Yes, she reasoned, there was great satisfaction in ending when everything was neatly tied up.

END OF GAME

ACKNOWLEDGMENTS

First off, I am crazy grateful for the abundance of friendships, pickle-ball, and love that inspired this story, and to all the people who brought their A game to help bring this book to fruition.

Thanks to my agent, Elizabeth Rudnick, for her unwavering faith, and for continuing to be a sounding board, a support, an idea flint, and a friend. Our conversations feel like finally turning on the windshield wipers. Also, to Rachel Crawford, the agent who first saw promise in my writing and helped to shape it.

With gratitude to Sarah Blumenstock, editorial maven, for her vision in guiding me to find the true heart of the story. Her spot-on feedback helped me see the big picture, and her encouragement amplified this book's romance, descriptive language, and humor. To Liz Sellers for her speedy, easygoing support. For Jessine Hein's artistic pizzazz in designing the rockin' cover art that fulfilled my wildest pop-art dreams. With appreciation to the copy editor, the interior designer, the marketing and publicity crews, and the whole team at Berkley for their creativity, savvy, responsiveness, attention to detail, and dedication.

Without my pickleballers, where would I be? Here's to my regu-lar play pals in Bellevue, WA; in Costa Rica; and in Puerto Vallarta, MX. Special thanks to those patient and positive players on my home court who hung in there with me when I was new to the sport. And shout-out to my fellow pickleball peeps on the courts worldwide, for keeping the sport vibrant and for being equally obsessed.

To my students and my teaching colleagues: you lit a fire under me with your own passions for writing, reading, and innovating for a better world. And here's to my beta readers, especially writer Melissa Macomber for sharing feedback and bug spray on her jungly Costa Rican porch.

With appreciation to my incredible group of supportive friends, for whom laughter could be an Olympic-level sport. Thanks to each of you for your generous hearts and your particular brands of wonderful. Special thanks to Sara Fenstermacher, whose medical know-how, wacky humor, and boundless friendship are evidenced in this story.

And a big, oppressively long hug to my family. Thanks, Marina, for your encouragement—my daughter, whose compassion and effervescent spirit add a pinch of fabulous to my days. To my son, Benji, for his insightful conversations and quirky humor, for his contagious love of the Pacific Northwest, and for inventing all Sasquatch references. Thanks to my niece, author Danya Kukafka, for setting a high bar and for her sage advice along the way. To my parents, who assured me I could do anything I set my mind to and always told me I was the best at it!

And for his love, adventurousness, passion, and support, thanks to my husband, Steve Blatt, who will tell you he wrote all the funny parts in this book. And, okay, I'll admit it here, only this once, and you'll never hear it from me again. He did write some of them.

Don't miss

PICKLE PERFECT

Ilana Long's next novel from Berkley Romance!

Lulu stared at her laptop, willing away the distractions. Behind her, Aunt Laverne muttered while she sorted the greener tomatoes into a cardboard box marked *Neighbors*. Below the table, Lulu's three-year-old daughter, Zoe, tested out a variety of animal growls while slamming a plastic dinosaur into the underside of the wooden table. And while her uncle Rooster's footsteps clunked as he rounded up sports glasses and sunscreen for their Costa Rican pickleball vacation, Lulu knocked her knuckles against her forehead to keep her head in the game.

Yet there was hope on the horizon. If she powered through, she could finish grading this batch of assignments by three o'clock and put Zoe down for her nap. Then, she could stand in the shower for at least five blissfully undisturbed minutes. Lulu's attention drifted as she indulged in a daydream involving a closed door and nothing but quiet. Since her daughter's birth, her fantasies had shifted from hot and steamy sex to hot and steamy showers.

Aunt Laverne brushed aside Lulu's dark, springy curls and placed a hand on her niece's shoulder. "How 'bout a break."

"I will. In a bit."

Her aunt tsked softly. "You've been at it for hours. Tell me. How are the young entrepreneurs doing this year?"

"What they lack in academic integrity, they make up for in technology skills. Listen to this." Tilting the screen, Lulu read from her laptop. "'In this plan, I will endeavor to machinate my revenue projections by estimating income based on indexed market research and recumbent pricing strategies.'"

Rooster appeared in the kitchen. "What kind of gibberish is that?"

"My Intro to Business class. They have to build a marketing plan and tell me the best way to pull an audience to their brand. But I'm going to go out on a limb here and guess that this one was not written by a ninth grader."

"Probably the kid's parents wrote it," Rooster pitched in as he opened the cereal cupboard. "Or they copied the paper from a webline."

"More likely, the kid's AI generator wrote it. And it's *on*line. Or web*site*. There's no webline."

"Ought to be." Rooster sighed. "I give up. Has anyone seen my spare pickleball paddle?"

"Did you check the car?" Laverne asked. "I think I saw your pickleball bag in the trunk."

"The car?!" Rooster asked, incredulous. "Why would I put my pickleball paddle in the car?" A hand injury had stymied Rooster's hopes to play with his partner, Meg, in the high-stakes Picklesmash tournament three years ago, but since then, he had been making up for lost time. And now, with an all-inclusive pickleball vacation less than three days away, he was downright exuberant. Lulu hadn't seen Rooster this excited about something since Zoe's birth.

As Rooster lumbered off to the garage in search of his paddle, Lulu clicked open her grading rubric—the instructions she had given to her business students on this recent marketing assignment. She let out a whispered "Dammit!" when she reread the bolded information she had posted. Instead of writing "Servicing the public sector," she had written "Servicing the pubic sector."

"Dammit!" Zoe whispered to herself.

Lulu massaged her scalp and consoled herself with the fact that she was, likely, the only one who actually read the instructions. She wondered, not for the first time, how she had ended up teaching business to kids who wanted her out of their business.

But she knew why. Lulu loved the perfect balance of business, of noticing a need and bringing the solution into the world. The click of the key shifting perfectly into the groove. Sharing that excitement with her students felt like a way to reclaim the surge of energy that sometimes waned in the wake of single parenting.

In fact, Rooster's pickleball enthusiasm reminded her of her own fire, that vibrant readiness she had once felt with a racket in her hand. Once in a while, she still sensed that longing around the fringes of tangible memory, like it was only last week and not fifteen years ago—when the pleasure of discovering the right tennis shot was a win in itself, back when she had every intention of playing professionally. In fact, until her parents' death in a car accident at the end of her senior year, Lulu had designed a precise trajectory to guarantee her own success.

Now Lulu was struck with the irony. She taught her students to build business plans but had put her own future on the back burner. At this stage in her life, building a start-up where she could flex her business muscles and be her own boss, or indulging in a pickleball vacation to Costa Rica—those were luxuries as out of reach as the moon.

"What do you think?" Waving a head of broccoli, Laverne swooped into Lulu's line of vision. "Does it last ten days? Or should I put it in the box for the neighbors?"

"Please. Just leave it in the fridge," Lulu said, pulling some patience in through her nose. "Zoe and I will eat it," she assured her aunt. "That's all I will do, I promise. I will sit in this chair, and I will eat the broccoli until it is gone. I will eat the spinach, and the apples, and the lettuce, and the asparagus. All of it. And then some."

"But what about the kale?"

Fuck the kale, Lulu wanted to say, but instead she blew a curl off her forehead.

"Found it!" Rooster said, coming back into the kitchen as he smacked the paddle at an invisible ball. "My paddle was in the car! Can you believe it?"

Beneath the table, Zoe tugged on Lulu's shirttail. "Lookit, Mommy. Mr. T likes jelly. Just like me and Pop-Pop." She offered her mom the plastic Tyrannosaurus, coated with purple goop.

"Jelly?" Lulu plucked the sticky dinosaur from her daughter's fingers and bit back a groan. Clearly, Rooster did not understand that sugar was akin to toddler jet-engine fuel. "Zoe? Are you ready for your nap?" she asked, knowing the answer.

"Nope." The three-year-old sighed sadly, like a fifty-year-old boss who was going to have to let go of a longtime employee. "No nap."

Lulu shut her eyes a moment. "No nap," she reminded herself, was not a global crisis. "Could we all try," she said, tipping her head toward Rooster, "to be on the same page with Zoe's nap schedule? And snack choices?"

"Of course." Laverne rubbed comforting circles on Lulu's back. She nodded to the business plans on Lulu's laptop. "How 'bout I help you with some of that grading?"

Lulu paused, tempted. Her aunt *did* have a keen eye for language. "I could preread them for you," Laverne suggested. "Then you can slap on a grade after I'm done."

Lulu fairly shielded her laptop with her body. There would be no grade-slapping. "No thanks. I got this."

Rooster threw his hands in the air. "Ach! I think I left my keys in the trunk. Or in the medicine cabinet when I was . . ." His voice trailed off as he trundled away.

Laverne pulled up a chair and hunched into Lulu's personal-space bubble. "Let me try. Just show me one."

"Fine." Scooting her chair out of the mix to make way for the hostile takeover of her laptop, Lulu offered, "Skim it, then read it, then click on the student's name, then you can write a comment. Or you can push this button here to record a comment, and I'll score it later. The essential question is, 'What techniques attract a consumer to a product?'"

Laverne's eyes glazed over. "You lost me at skim it. But I'll figure it out." Peering at the screen, the older woman mumbled as she scanned the writing, until finally, she barked out a laugh. In her theatrical voice, she read, "'I would market my car wash business by writing "Wash Me" on the teachers' cars with my finger.'" Laverne shot Lulu a look of wry surprise. "'And if I'm still not earning enough money, I bet I can make the cars dirtier.'"

Lulu shrugged. "Welcome to my world." But the grading had to be done, and it was kind of nice that someone else could commiserate for once.

"If you want to give it a try, you can make a comment," Lulu offered. "Type it into this comments box. Or just record with the microphone. What advice do you have for"—she read the header—"Carson Manning?"

"Well." Pursing her lips, Laverne turned back to the screen. "It's not very good."

"You can't say that. These are fourteen-year-olds. You have to say something encouraging."

Laverne bent over the laptop, clicked on the microphone, and said, "Good work. A+."

Carson Manning's name turned green. A little "read" check-mark appeared with a ping.

"O-kay." Lulu pinched the bridge of her nose. "You just sent that." Carson Manning was probably jumping up and down on his bed or texting his classmates about his first A ever. "I better take back the wheel."

"One more. Let me try one more." Laverne fiddled with the mouse, scrolling through the student names, and checking and un-checking boxes.

"You don't have to do all that. Just click on another student. Here." Lulu reached over and pointed the cursor on Kavya Bhatt's responses. "Try Kavya."

From under the table, Zoe sang, "I need to go potty."

"One sec, sweetie."

"Oh, this student's answer is much better than the other one," Laverne murmured, invested in Kavya's business plan. "Listen to this." She read, "'There are many ways to attract consumers to products, but traditional advertising is not always the solution. Sometimes, stirring up bad press is a great way to get attention from your target audience. Like how "The Rocket" got himself kicked off the pickle-ball pro tour. On purpose, if you ask me. And now, everybody's talk-ing about his brand.'" Laverne squinted. "The Rocket?"

"The Rocket?" Rooster, who had appeared from who knows where, repeated. "Whoo, boy. She's got that right. *Everybody's* talk-ing about Tyler 'The Rocket' Demming."

At the mention of Tyler's name, Lulu's head snapped up. She shot her uncle a startled look. Rooster guffawed. "You didn't hear about that? Tyler Demming. Your old tennis team friend, right? Hold on. Let me find it."

"Rooster . . ." Laverne warned. "I don't think Lulu wants to see that."

But Rooster had already pulled up the video and pressed the phone into Lulu's palm. Her heart jackhammering, Lulu watched the action on the little screen.

There was Tyler Demming in all his long-haired, tatted-up glory, just as handsome as when she'd last seen him in the flesh fifteen years ago. Just as dreamy as that night on Bainbridge Island, back when they were dizzy and drowning in young love; when they'd lain on the cool pavement of the moonlit courts and he had promised to never break her heart—and then instead gone and crushed it to smithereens.

A familiar pang pinched at Lulu's gut. Sure, she had caught glimpses of him in the media over the years. During the hype over his switch from tennis to pickleball and his subsequent rise to glory on the small court, it seemed Tyler Demming was everywhere. Lulu would be going about her day when his famous physique would pop up online, advertising men's cologne and boxer briefs and tooth whitener. Or gracing the cover of the sports section of the *Seattle Times* when he took gold at pickleball nationals. Or in the tabloids while she waited in line at the supermarket, bravely hanging on through his divorce. But those were just static images, easy to shake her head over and dismiss.

But now, this. As Tyler "The Rocket" Demming grinned at the camera in living, moving color, her nerves began to whistle. Time had not dampened her dichotomous reaction to him, a twin push-pull that felt like it was breaking her apart.

His muscles glistened with a sexy sheen of recent exercise, and he was grinning his annoyingly charismatic grin. "Winner, winner!" Tyler crowed as he pulled several paddles from his bag. Laying the paddles on the pavement, he took his time swaddling the handles in cotton bandages. The video caption scrolled. *Wild-man Tyler "The Rocket" Demming takes gold but gets tossed off tour.*

"Unbelievable." Lulu shook her head in disgust. Of course he would go ahead and throw away a golden opportunity. Talk about on brand.

"Just watch," Rooster crowed, still absorbed in the video. "It's a doozy."

Lulu glared at the screen in disbelief as Tyler, a mischievous gleam in his eye, held the paddle heads and took a lighter to the wrapped handles. Whooping with glee, the pro player began juggling the flaming pickle paddles. Midtoss, he called out, "This is for you, Olivia." He beamed and shouted, "And now, the spin maneuver!"

Lulu scolded the part of her brain that wanted to stare at his bicep. His skin had been untouched when they were together. Now tattoos moved with each flex of his perfectly conditioned muscles. She swallowed. "Idiot," Lulu mumbled.

"Idiot," Zoe parroted from somewhere near the refrigerator, and then added, "Look! I pottied all by myself."

"Code yellow. Code yellow," Rooster called.

But Lulu could not take her eyes off the miniature screen. Paddles a-flyin', Tyler executed a three-sixty. Midtwirl, he glanced up at the windmilling flames, shrieked, and jumped backward without catching a single one. Noisily, the paddles scattered across the pavement, where they sparked and smoldered—all except one, which flew onto the straw-colored grass of the empty spectator area. The spark caught, and in seconds the flame rolled across the dry grasses.

Another caption scrolled. *Demming charged with reckless endangerment and destruction of property.* Whoever was holding the camera yelped, and when the video righted itself, Tyler was aiming the lens at himself. "I promised that if I won gold, I'd juggle fire. And I keep my promises."

Rooster chuckled, and the reel started again. Lulu felt her hands curl into fists. Tyler Demming. Lighting the paddles. Juggling them.

Setting the field on fire. Again with his swagger, his smugness, those damned taut buttocks.

Her head swam with the fury and disappointment that she had managed to keep at bay for fifteen years. But now, here was Tyler Demming butting into her life again when she was simply minding her own business. Lulu watched, her attention trapped in the looping video, finding the whole spectacle seriously triggering. Because there was no deeper betrayal, Lulu thought, than to draw in your rival, seduce her, then disappear in her moment of need without looking back.

Beneath the video, she caught a glimpse of the final caption. *The Rocket keeps his promises.*

Lulu's eyes narrowed to slits and her back teeth clamped together. Forget about him, she told herself. Take ten calming breaths. One. Two . . . Okay. Screw that.

"Keeps his promises! Ha!" Her voice erupted like years of contained lava.

Wrath lifted her to her feet, but a rush of dizziness threw off her footing. Still, her tirade continued, even as she threw out her hands to steady herself. Even as she fell toward the keyboard that would seal her fate.

Even as the heel of her palm landed on the record button.

Her voice had reached a venomous peak. "What an asshole!" Lulu raged. "That is the biggest load of bullshit I have read in my *life*."

Ping, went her laptop. On her screen, 153 check marks rippled down the line.

Message sent to all students.

Ilana Long first heard about pickleball when her sporty friend confessed that she was addicted to a game that was "like Ping-Pong but standing on the table." Shortly after, Long joined the pickleball craze despite her utter lack of hand-eye coordination. A stand-up and sketch comedy writer and actor, Long studied improv and performed at the Second City in Chicago. She is the author of the picture book *Ziggy's Big Idea*, and her essays appear in multiple books in the Chicken Soup for the Soul series.

VISIT ILANA LONG ONLINE
———————————————

IlanaLong.com

🅞 IlanaLongWrites

Ready to find
your next great read?

Let us help.

Visit prh.com/nextread